THE
PARTNER

John Grisham is the author of forty works of fiction and one of non-fiction. His works have been translated into forty-two languages. He lives in Virginia.

Find out more at jgrisham.com and stay in touch via Facebook at John Grisham Books.

Praise for John Grisham

'The best thriller writer alive.'
Evening Standard

'The suspense does not let up for a minute.'
Daily Telegraph

'He keeps us turning the pages until well after bedtime . . . as exciting as a car chase with a load of dynamite thrown in.'
Daily Mail

'The book stays in the hands as if superglued . . . compelling.'
Sunday Express

D0994728

John Grisham

THE PARTNER

PENGUIN BOOKS

PENGUIN BOOKS

UK | USA | Canada | Ireland | Australia
India | New Zealand | South Africa

Penguin Books is part of the Penguin Random House group of companies
whose addresses can be found at global.penguinrandomhouse.com

First published in the UK by Century in 1997
First published in paperback by Arrow Books in 1998
This reissue published in Penguin Books 2022
015

Typeset by Jouve (UK), Milton Keynes

Printed and bound in Great Britain by Clays Ltd, Elcograf S.p.A.

The authorised representative in the EEA is Penguin Random House
Ireland, Morrison Chambers, 32 Nassau Street, Dublin D02 YH68

A CIP catalogue record for this book is available from the British Library

ISBN: 978–0–099–53715–1

www.greenpenguin.co.uk

*For David Gernert
friend, editor, agent*

ONE

They found him in Ponta Porã, a pleasant little town in Brazil, on the border of Paraguay, in a land still known as the Frontier.

They found him living in a shaded brick house on Rua Tiradentes, a wide avenue with trees down the center and barefoot boys dribbling soccer balls along the hot pavement.

They found him alone, as best they could tell, though a maid came and went at odd hours during the eight days they hid and watched.

They found him living a comfortable life but certainly not one of luxury. The house was modest and could've been owned by any local merchant. The car was a 1983 Volkswagen Beetle, manufactured in São Paulo with a million others. It was red and clean, polished to a shine. Their first photo of him was snapped as he waxed it just inside the gate to his short driveway.

They found him much thinner, down considerably from the two hundred and thirty pounds he'd been carrying when last seen. His hair and skin were darker, his chin had been squared, and his nose had been slightly pointed. Subtle changes to the face. They'd paid a steep bribe to the surgeon in Rio who'd performed the alterations two and a half years earlier.

They found him after four years of tedious but

diligent searching, four years of dead ends and lost trails and false tips, four years of pouring good money down the drain, good money chasing bad, it seemed.

But they found him. And they waited. There was at first the desire to snatch him immediately, to drug him and smuggle him to a safe house in Paraguay, to seize him before he saw them or before a neighbor became suspicious. The initial excitement of the finding made them consider a quick strike, but after two days they settled down and waited. They loitered at various points along Rua Tiradentes, dressed like the locals, drinking tea in the shade, avoiding the sun, eating ice cream, talking to the children, watching his house. They tracked him as he drove downtown to shop, and they photographed him from across the street as he left the pharmacy. They eased very near him in a fruit market and listened as he spoke to the clerk. Excellent Portuguese, with the very slight accent of an American or a German who'd studied hard. He moved quickly downtown, gathering his goods and returning home, where he locked the gate behind him. His brief shopping trip yielded a dozen fine photos.

He had jogged in a prior life, though in the months before he disappeared his mileage shrunk as his weight ballooned. Now that he teetered on the brink of emaciation, they were not surprised to see him running again. He left his house, locking the gate behind him, and began a slow trot down the sidewalk along Rua Tiradentes. Nine minutes for the first mile, as the street went perfectly straight and the houses grew farther apart. The pavement turned to gravel on the edge of town, and halfway into the second mile his pace was down to eight minutes a mile and Danilo had himself a nice sweat. It was midday in October, the temperature near eighty, and he gained speed as he left town, past a small clinic packed with young mothers, past a small church the Baptists had built.

2

The roads became dustier as he headed for the countryside at seven minutes a mile.

The running was serious business, and it pleased them mightily. Danilo would simply run into their arms.

The day after the first sighting, a small unclean cottage on the edge of Ponta Porã was rented by a Brazilian named Osmar, and before long the rest of the pursuit team poured in. It was an equal mix of Americans and Brazilians, with Osmar giving the orders in Portuguese and Guy barking in English. Osmar could handle both languages, and had become the official interpreter for the team.

Guy was from Washington, an ex-government type who'd been hired to find Danny Boy, as he'd been nicknamed. Guy was considered a genius at some levels and immensely talented at others, and his past was a black hole. He was well into his fifth one-year contract to find Danny Boy, and there was a nice bonus for snagging the prey. Though he hid it well, Guy had been slowly cracking under the pressure of not finding Danny Boy.

Four years and three and a half million dollars, with nothing to show for it.

But now they'd found him.

Osmar and his band of Brazilians had not the slightest hint of Danny Boy's sins, but a fool could see that he'd disappeared and taken a trainload of money. And, although he was very curious about Danny Boy, Osmar had learned quickly not to ask questions. Guy and the Americans had nothing to say on the subject.

The pictures of Danny Boy were enlarged to eight by tens, and tacked along a wall in the kitchen of the dirty little cottage where they were studied by grim men with hard eyes, men who chain-smoked strong cigarettes and shook their heads at the photos. They whispered among themselves and compared the new photos to the old ones, the ones from his previous life. Smaller man, odd chin, different nose. His hair was shorter and his skin darker. Was it really him?

They had been through this before, in Recife, on the northeastern coast, nineteen months earlier when they'd rented an apartment and looked at photos on the wall until the decision was made to grab the American and check his fingerprints. Wrong prints. Wrong American. They pumped some more drugs in him and left him in a ditch.

They were afraid to dig too deeply into the current life of Danilo Silva. If he was in fact their man, then he had plenty of money. And cash always worked wonders with the local authorities. For decades, cash had bought protection for Nazis and other Germans who'd smuggled themselves into Ponta Porã.

Osmar wanted to grab him. Guy said they'd wait. He vanished on the fourth day, and the dirty little cottage was in chaos for thirty-six hours.

They saw him leave home in the red Beetle. He was in a hurry, came the report. He raced across town to the airport, jumped on a small commuter at the last moment, and was gone. His car was parked in the only lot, and they watched it every second of every hour. The plane was headed in the general direction of São Paulo, with four stops in between.

There was instantly a plan to enter his home and catalog everything. There had to be records. The money had to be tended to. Guy dreamed of finding bank statements, wire transfer reports, account summaries; all sorts of documents arranged in a neat portfolio which would lead him directly to the money.

But he knew better. If Danny Boy ran because of them, then he would never leave behind the evidence. And if he was in fact their man, then his home would be carefully secured. Danny Boy, wherever he was,

4

would probably know the instant they opened his door or window.

They waited. They cursed and argued and strained even more under the pressure. Guy made his daily call to Washington, a nasty one. They watched the red Beetle. Each arrival brought out the binoculars and cell phones. Six flights the first day. Five the second. The dirty little cottage grew hot and the men settled outdoors – the Americans napping under a scrawny shade tree in the backyard and the Brazilians playing cards along the fence in the front.

Guy and Osmar took a long drive and vowed to grab him if he ever returned. Osmar was confident he would be back. Probably just out of town on business, whatever his business was. They'd snatch him, identify him, and if he happened to be the wrong man they'd simply throw him in a ditch and run. It had happened before.

He returned on the fifth day. They trailed him back to Rua Tiradentes, and everybody was happy.

On the eighth day, the dirty cottage emptied as all the Brazilians and all the Americans took their positions.

The course was a six-miler. He had covered it each day he'd been home, leaving at almost the same time, wearing the same blue and orange runner's shorts, well-worn Nikes, ankle socks, no shirt.

The perfect spot was two and a half miles from his house, over a small hill on a gravel road, not far from his turning-around point. Danilo topped the hill twenty minutes into his run, a few seconds ahead of schedule. He ran harder, for some reason. Probably the clouds.

A small car with a flat tire was just over the hill, blocking the road, trunk opened, its rear jacked up. Its driver was a burly young man who pretended to be startled at the sight of the skinny racer sweating and panting as he topped the hill. Danilo slowed for a second. There was more room to the right.

'*Bom dia*,' the burly young man said as he took a step toward Danilo.

'*Bom dia*,' Danilo said, approaching the car.

The driver suddenly pulled a large shiny pistol from the trunk and shoved it into Danilo's face. He froze, his eyes locked onto the gun, his mouth open with heavy breathing. The driver had thick hands and long, stout arms. He grabbed Danilo by the neck and yanked him roughly toward the car, then down to the bumper. He stuck the pistol in a pocket and with both hands folded Danilo into the trunk. Danny Boy struggled and kicked, but was no match.

The driver slammed the trunk shut, lowered the car, tossed the jack into the ditch, and drove off. A mile away, he turned on to a narrow dirt path where his pals were anxiously waiting.

They tied nylon ropes around Danny Boy's wrists and a black cloth over his eyes, then shoved him into the back of a van. Osmar sat to his right, another Brazilian to his left. Someone removed his keys from the Velcro runner's pouch stuck to his waist. Danilo said nothing as the van started and began moving. He was still sweating and breathing even harder.

When the van stopped on a dusty road near a farm field, Danilo uttered his first words. 'What do you want?' he asked, in Portuguese.

'Don't speak,' came the reply from Osmar, in English. The Brazilian to Danilo's left removed a syringe from a small metal box and deftly filled it with a potent liquid. Osmar pulled Danilo's wrists tightly toward him while the other man jabbed the needle into his upper arm. He stiffened and jerked, then realized it was hopeless. He actually relaxed as the last of the drug entered his body. His breathing slowed; his head began to wobble. When his chin hit his chest,

Osmar gently, with his right index finger, raised the shorts on Danilo's right leg, and found exactly what he expected to find. Pale skin.

The running kept him thin, and it also kept him brown.

Kidnappings were all too common in the Frontier. Americans were easy targets. But why him? Danilo asked himself this as his head wobbled and his eyes closed. He smiled as he fell through space, dodging comets and meteors, grabbing at moons and grinning through entire galaxies.

They stuffed him under some cardboard boxes filled with melons and berries. The border guards nodded without leaving their chairs, and Danny Boy was now in Paraguay, though he couldn't have cared less at the moment. He bounced happily along on the floor of the van as the roads grew worse and the terrain steeper. Osmar chain-smoked and occasionally pointed this way and that. An hour after they grabbed him, they found the last turn. The cabin was in a crevice between two pointed hills, barely visible from the narrow dirt road. They carried him like a sack of meal and poured him onto a table in the den where Guy and the fingerprint man went to work.

Danny Boy snored heavily as prints were made of all eight fingers and both thumbs. The Americans and the Brazilians crowded around, watching every move. There was unopened whiskey in a box by the door, just in case this was the real Danny Boy.

The print man left abruptly and went to a room in the back where he locked the door and spread the fresh prints before him. He adjusted his lighting. He removed the master set, those freely given by Danny Boy when he was much younger, back when he was Patrick and seeking admission to the State Bar of Louisiana. Odd, this fingerprinting of lawyers.

Both sets were in fine shape, and it was immediately obvious they were a perfect match. But he meticulously checked all ten. There was no hurry. Let them wait out there. He rather enjoyed the moment. He finally opened the door and frowned hard at the dozen faces searching his. Then he smiled. 'It's him,' he said, in English, and they actually clapped.

Guy approved the whiskey, but only in moderation. There was more work to do. Danny Boy, still comatose, was given another shot and carried to a small bedroom with no window and a heavy door which locked from the outside. It was here that he would be interrogated, and tortured, if necessary.

The barefoot boys playing soccer in the street were too involved in their game to look up. Danny Boy's key ring had only four keys on it, and so the small front gate was unlocked quickly, and left open. An accomplice in a rented car came to a stop near a large tree four houses down. Another, on a motorbike, parked himself at the other end of the street and began tinkering with his brakes.

If a security system started howling upon entry, the intruder would simply run and never be seen again. If not, then he would lock himself in and take inventory.

The door opened without sirens. The security panel on the wall informed whoever might be looking that the system was disarmed. He breathed lightly and stood perfectly still for a full minute, then began to move around. He removed the hard drive from Danny Boy's PC, and collected all the disks. He rummaged through files on his desk, but found nothing but routine bills, some paid, others waiting. The fax was cheap and featureless, and declared itself to be out of order. He took photos of clothing, food, furniture, bookshelves, magazine racks.

Five minutes after the door opened, a silent signal

was activated in Danilo's attic and a phone call was placed to a private security firm eleven blocks away, in downtown Ponta Porã. The call went unanswered because the security consultant on duty was swaying gently in a hammock out back. A recorded message from Danilo's house informed whoever was supposed to be listening that there was a break-in. Fifteen minutes passed before human ears heard the message. By the time the consultant raced to Danilo's house, the intruder was gone. So was Mr Silva. Everything appeared to be in order, including the Beetle under the carport. The house and gate were locked.

The directions in the file were specific. On such alarms, do not call the police. Try first to locate Mr Silva, and in the event he cannot be found at once, then call a number in Rio. Ask for Eva Miranda.

With barely suppressed excitement, Guy made his daily call to Washington. He actually closed his eyes and smiled when he uttered the words, 'It's him.' His voice was an octave higher.

There was a pause on the other end. Then, 'You're certain?'

'Yes. Prints are a perfect match.'

Another pause while Stephano arranged his thoughts, a process that usually took milliseconds. 'The money?'

'We haven't started yet. He's still drugged.'

'When?'

'Tonight.'

'I'm by the phone.' Stephano hung up, though he could've talked for hours.

Guy found a perch on a stump behind the cabin. The vegetation was dense, the air thin and cool. The soft voices of happy men drifted up to him. The ordeal was over, for the most part.

He had just earned an extra fifty thousand dollars. Finding the money would mean another bonus, and he was certain he'd find the money.

TWO

Downtown Rio. In a small neat office on the tenth floor of a high-rise, Eva Miranda squeezed the phone with both hands and slowly repeated the words she had just heard. The silent alarm had summoned the security guard. Mr Silva wasn't at home, but his car was parked in the drive and the house was locked.

Someone had entered, tripped the alarm, and it couldn't be a false one because it was still activated when the security guard arrived.

Danilo was missing.

Maybe he'd gone jogging and neglected the routine. According to the guard's account, the silent alarm had been activated an hour and ten minutes ago. But Danilo jogged for less than an hour – six miles at seven to eight minutes per, total of fifty minutes max. No exceptions. She knew his movements.

She called his home on Rua Tiradentes, and no one answered. She called the number to a cell phone he sometimes kept nearby, and no one answered.

He had accidentally tripped the alarm three months ago, and scared them both badly. But a quick phone call from her had cleared up the matter.

He was much too careful about the security system to get careless. It meant too much.

She made the calls again, with the same results. There is an explanation for this, she told herself.

She dialed the number to an apartment in Curitiba, a city of a million and a half, and the capital of the state of Paraná. To their knowledge, no one knew of the apartment. It was leased under another name and used for storage and infrequent meetings. They spent short weekends there occasionally; not often enough to suit Eva.

She expected no answer at the apartment, and got none. Danilo would not go there without first calling her.

When the phone calls were finished, she locked her office door and leaned against it with her eyes closed. Associates and secretaries could be heard in the hallway. The firm had thirty-three lawyers at the moment, second largest in Rio with a branch in São Paulo and another in New York. Telephones and faxes and copiers blended together in a busy distant chorus.

At thirty-one, she was a seasoned five-year associate with the firm; seasoned to the point of working the long hours and coming in on Saturdays. Fourteen partners ran the firm, but only two were women. She had plans to change that ratio. Ten of the nineteen associates were female, evidence that in Brazil, as in the United States, women were rapidly entering the profession. She studied law at the Catholic University in Rio, one of the finer schools, in her opinion. Her father still taught philosophy there.

He had insisted she study law at Georgetown after studying law in Rio. Georgetown was his alma mater. His influence, along with her impressive résumé, striking looks, and fluent English made finding a top job with a top firm a quick chore.

She paused at her window and told herself to relax. Time was suddenly crucial. The next series of moves required steady nerves. Then she would have to disappear. There was a meeting in thirty minutes, but it would have to be postponed.

The file was locked in a small fireproof drawer. She removed it and read again the sheet of instructions; directions she and Danilo had covered many times.

He knew they would find him.

Eva had preferred to ignore the possibility.

Her mind drifted as she worried about his safety. The phone rang and startled her. It was not Danilo. A client was waiting, her secretary said. The client was early. Apologize to the client, she instructed, and politely reschedule the appointment. Do not disturb again.

The money was currently parked in two places: a bank in Panama, and an offshore holding trust in Bermuda. Her first fax authorized the immediate wire transfer of the money out of Panama and into a bank in Antigua. Her second fax scattered it among three banks on Grand Cayman. The third yanked it out of Bermuda and parked it in the Bahamas.

It was almost two in Rio. The European banks were closed, so she would be forced to skip the money around the Caribbean for a few hours until the rest of the world opened.

Danilo's instructions were clear but general. The details were left to her discretion. The initial wires were determined by Eva. She decided which banks got how much money. She had made the list of the fictitious corporate names under which the money was hidden; a list Danilo had never seen. She divided, dispersed, routed, and rerouted. It was a drill they had rehearsed many times, but without the specifics.

Danilo couldn't know where the money went. Only Eva. She had the unbridled discretion, at this moment and under these extreme circumstances, to move it as she saw fit. Her specialty was trade law. Most of her clients were Brazilian businessmen who wanted to develop exports to the United States and Canada. She understood foreign markets, currencies, banking.

13

What she hadn't known about zipping money around the world, Danilo had taught her.

She glanced repeatedly at her watch. More than an hour had passed since the phone call from Ponta Porã.

As another fax rolled through the machine, the phone rang again. Certainly it was Danilo, finally, with a wild story and all of this was for nothing. Perhaps just a dry run, a rehearsal to test her mettle under pressure. But he was not one to play games.

It was a partner, quite perturbed that she was late for yet another meeting. She apologized with short words and returned to her fax.

The pressure mounted with each passing minute. Still no word from Danilo. No answers to her repeated calls. If they had in fact found him, then they wouldn't wait long before they tried to make him talk. That was what he feared the most. That was why she had to run.

An hour and a half. Reality was settling hard on her shoulders. Danilo was missing, and he would never disappear without first telling her. He planned his movements too carefully, always fearful of the shadows behind him. Their worst nightmare was unfolding, and quickly.

At a pay phone in the lobby of her office building, Eva made two calls. The first was to her apartment manager, to see if anyone had been to her apartment in Leblon, in Rio's South Zone, where the wealthy lived and the beautiful played. The answer was no, but the manager promised to watch things. The second call was to the office of the FBI in Biloxi, Mississippi. It was an emergency, she explained as calmly as possible with her best effort at accentless American English. She waited, knowing that from this moment forward there was no turning back.

Someone had taken Danilo. His past had finally caught him.

'Hello,' came the voice, as if it were only a block away.

'Agent Joshua Cutter?'

'Yes.'

She paused slightly. 'Are you in charge of the Patrick Lanigan investigation?' She knew perfectly well that he was.

A pause on his end. 'Yes. Who is this?'

They would trace the call to Rio, and that would take about three minutes. Then their tracking would drown in a city of ten million. But she looked around nervously anyway.

'I'm calling from Brazil,' she said, according to script. 'They've captured Patrick.'

'Who?' Cutter asked.

'I'll give you a name.'

'I'm listening,' Cutter said, his voice suddenly edgy.

'Jack Stephano. Do you know him?'

A pause as Cutter tried to place the name. 'No. Who is he?'

'A private agent in Washington. He's been searching for Patrick for the past four years.'

'And you say he's found him, right?'

'Yes. His men found him.'

'Where?'

'Here. In Brazil.'

'When?'

'Today. And I think they might kill him.'

Cutter pondered this for a second, then asked, 'What else can you tell me?'

She gave him Stephano's phone number in D.C., then hung up and wandered out of the building.

Guy carefully flipped through the assorted papers taken from Danny Boy's house, and marveled at the invisible trail. A monthly statement from a local bank listed a balance of three thousand dollars, not exactly

15

what they had in mind. The only deposit was for eighteen hundred, debits for the month of less than a thousand. Danny Boy lived quite frugally. His electric and phone bills were unpaid but not past due. A dozen other small bills were marked paid.

One of Guy's men checked all the phone numbers on Danny Boy's bill, but turned up nothing interesting. Another scoured the hard drive from his little computer and quickly learned that Danny Boy was not much of a hacker. There was a lengthy journal about his adventures in the Brazilian outback. The last entry was almost a year old.

The scarcity of paperwork was in itself very suspicious. Only one bank statement? Who on the face of the earth keeps only last month's bank statement in the house? What about the month before? Danny Boy had a storage place somewhere, away from his home. It all fit nicely with a man on the run.

At dusk, Danny Boy, still unconscious, was stripped to his underwear, tight cotton briefs. His dirty running shoes and sweaty running socks were pulled off, revealing feet that nearly glowed in their whiteness. His new dark skin was counterfeit. He was placed on a one-inch-thick sheet of plywood next to his bed. Holes had been cut in the board and nylon ropes were used to tightly secure his ankles, knees, waist, chest, and wrists. A wide black plastic belt was strapped tightly across his forehead. An IV drip bag hung directly above his face. The tube ran to a vein above his left wrist.

He was poked with another needle; a shot in his left arm to wake him up. His labored breathing grew more rapid, and when his eyes opened they were red and glazed and took a while to study the drip bag. The Brazilian doctor stepped into the picture, and without saying a word stuck a needle into Danny Boy's left

16

arm. It was sodium thiopental, a crude drug some-times used to make people talk. Truth serum. It worked best if the captive had things he wanted to confess. A perfect tell-all drug had yet to be developed.

Ten minutes passed. He tried to move his head, without success. He could see a few feet on either side. The room was dark except for a small light somewhere in a corner behind him.

The door opened, then closed. Guy entered alone. He walked straight to Danny Boy, placed his fingers on the edge of the plywood, and said, 'Hello, Patrick.'

Patrick closed his eyes. Danilo Silva was behind him now, gone forever. An old trusted friend vanished, just like that. The simple life on Rua Tiradentes faded away with Danilo; his precious anonymity ripped away from him with the pleasant words, 'Hello, Patrick.'

For four years, he had often wondered how it would feel if they caught him. Would there be a sense of relief? Of justice? Any excitement at the prospect of going home to face the music?

Absolutely not! At the moment, Patrick was terror-stricken. Practically naked and strapped down like an animal, he knew the next few hours would be insufferable.

'Can you hear me, Patrick?' Guy asked, peering downward, and Patrick smiled, not because he wanted to but because an urge he couldn't control found something amusing.

The drug was taking effect, Guy noted. Sodium thiopental is a short-acting barbiturate that must be administered in very controlled doses. It was extremely difficult to find the proper level of con-sciousness where one would be susceptible to interrog-ation. Too small a dose, and the resistance is not broken. A bit too much, and the subject is simply knocked out.

The door opened and closed. Another American slipped into the room to listen, but Patrick could not see him.

'You've been sleeping for three days, Patrick,' Guy said. It was closer to five hours, but how could Patrick know? 'Are you hungry or thirsty?'

'Thirsty,' Patrick said.

Guy unscrewed the top from a small bottle of mineral water, and carefully poured it between Patrick's lips.

'Thanks,' he said, then smiled.

'Are you hungry?' Guy asked again.

'No. What do you want?'

Guy slowly sat the mineral water on a table and leaned closer to Patrick's face. 'Let's settle something first, Patrick. While you were sleeping, we took your fingerprints. We know precisely who you are, so can we please forgo the initial denials?'

'Who am I?' Patrick asked with another grin.

'Patrick Lanigan.'

'From where?'

'Biloxi, Mississippi. Born in New Orleans. Law school at Tulane. Wife, one daughter, age six. Missing now for over four years.'

'Bingo. That's me.'

'Tell me, Patrick, did you watch your own burial service?'

'Is that a crime?'

'No. Just a rumor.'

'Yes. I watched it. I was touched by it. Didn't know I had so many friends.'

'How nice. Where did you hide after your burial?'

'Here and there.'

A shadow emerged from the left and a hand adjusted the valve at the bottom of the drip bag. 'What's that?' Patrick asked.

'A cocktail,' Guy answered, nodding at the other man, who retreated to the corner.

'Where's the money, Patrick?' Guy asked with a smile.

'What money?'

'The money you took with you.'

'Oh, that money,' Patrick said, and breathed deeply. His eyelids closed suddenly and his body relaxed. Seconds passed and his chest moved slower, up and down.

'Patrick,' Guy said, gently shaking his arm. No response, just the sounds of a deep sleep.

The dosage was immediately reduced, and they waited.

The FBI file on Jack Stephano was a quick study; former Chicago detective with two degrees in criminology, former highpriced bounty hunter, expert marksman, self-taught master of search and espionage, and now the owner of a shady D.C. firm which apparently charged huge fees to locate missing people and conduct expensive surveillance.

The FBI file on Patrick Lanigan filled eight boxes. It made sense that one file would attract the other. There was no shortage of people who wanted Patrick found and brought home. Stephano's group had been hired to do it.

Stephano's firm, Edmund Associates, occupied the top floor of a nondescript building on K Street, six blocks from the White House. Two agents waited in the lobby by the elevator as two others stormed Stephano's office. They almost scuffled with a heavy secretary who insisted Mr Stephano was too busy at the moment. They found him at his desk, alone, chatting happily on the phone. His smile vanished when they barged in with badges flashing.

'What the hell is this!' Stephano demanded. The

wall behind his desk was a richly detailed map of the world, complete with little red blinking lights stuck on green continents. Which one was Patrick?

'Who hired you to find Patrick Lanigan?' asked Agent One.

'That's confidential,' Stephano sneered. He'd been a cop for years, and was not easy to intimidate.

'We got a call from Brazil this afternoon,' said Agent Two.

So did I, thought Stephano, stunned by this but desperately trying to appear unfazed. His jaw dropped an inch and his shoulders sagged as his mind raced wildly through all the possible theories that would bring these two thugs here. He'd talked to Guy and no one else. Guy was utterly dependable. Guy would never talk to anyone, especially the FBI. It couldn't be Guy.

Guy used a cell phone from the mountains of eastern Paraguay. There was no way the call could have been intercepted.

'Are you there?' asked Two smartly.

'Yeah,' he said, hearing but not hearing.

'Where's Patrick?' asked One.

'Maybe he's in Brazil.'

'Where in Brazil?'

Stephano managed a shrug, a stiff one. 'I dunno. It's a big country.'

'We have an outstanding warrant for him,' One said. 'He belongs to us.'

Stephano shrugged again, this time a more casual one as if to say, 'Big deal.'

'We want him,' demanded Two. 'And now.'

'I can't help you.'

'You're lying,' snarled One, and with that both of them joined together in front of Stephano's desk and glared down. Agent Two did the talking. 'We have men downstairs, outside, around the corner, and

20

outside your home in Falls Church. We'll watch every move you make from now until we get Lanigan.'

'Fine. You can leave now.'

'And don't hurt him, okay? We'll be happy to nail your ass if anything happens to our boy.'

They left in step and Stephano locked the door behind them. His office had no windows. He stood before his map of the world. Brazil had three red lights, which meant little. His head shook slowly, in complete bewilderment.

He spent so much time and money covering his tracks.

His firm was known in certain circles as the best at taking the money and disappearing into the shadows. He'd never been caught before. No one ever knew who Stephano was stalking.

THREE

Another shot to rouse him. Then a shot to sensitize the nerves.

The door opened loudly and the room was suddenly lit. It filled with the voices of many men, busy men, all with a purpose, all with heavy feet, it seemed. Guy gave orders, and someone growled in Portuguese.

Patrick opened and closed his eyes. Then he opened them for good as the drugs found their mark. They hovered over him, busy hands everywhere. His underwear was cut off, without much finesse, and he lay bare and exposed. An electric razor began buzzing, hitting his skin sharply at points on the chest, groin, thighs, and calves. He bit his lip and grimaced, his heart hammered away, though the pain had yet to start.

Guy hovered above him, his hands still but his eyes watching everything.

Patrick made no effort to speak, but just to be safe, more hands appeared from above and slapped a thick strip of silver duct tape over his mouth. Cold electrodes were stuck to the shaved points with alligator clips, and he heard a loud voice ask something about 'current.' Tape was then applied over the electrodes. He thought he counted eight sharp spots on his flesh. Maybe nine. His nerves were jumping. In his darkness, he could feel the hands moving above him. The tape stuck hard to skin.

Two or three men were busy in a corner, adjusting a device Patrick could not see. Wires were strung like Christmas lights across his body.

They were not going to kill him, he kept telling himself, though death might be welcome at some point in the next few hours. He had imagined this nightmare a thousand times in four years. He had prayed it would never happen, but he always knew it would. He always knew they were back there, somewhere in the shadows, tracking and bribing and looking under rocks.

Patrick always knew. Eva was too naive.

He closed his eyes, tried to breathe steadily and tried to control his thoughts as they scurried above him, preparing his body for whatever lay ahead. The drugs made his pulse race and his skin itch.

I don't know where the money is. I don't know where the money is. He almost chanted this aloud. Thank God for the tape across his mouth. I don't know where the money is.

He called Eva *every* day between 4 P.M. and 6 P.M. Every day. Seven days of the week. No exceptions unless one was planned. He knew in his pounding heart that she had moved the money by now, that it was safely hidden in two dozen places around the world. And he didn't know where it was.

But would they believe him?

The door opened again, and two or three figures left the room. The activity around his plywood cot was slowing. Then it was quiet. He opened his eyes and the IV drip bag was gone.

Guy was looking down at him. He gently took one corner of the silver duct tape and pulled it free so Patrick could talk, if he so chose.

'Thanks,' Patrick said.

The Brazilian doctor appeared again from the left

and stuck a needle in Patrick's arm. The syringe was long and filled with nothing but colored water, but how could Patrick know?

'Where is the money, Patrick?' Guy asked.

'I don't have any money,' Patrick replied. His head ached from being pressed into the plywood. The tight plastic band across his forehead was hot. He hadn't moved in hours.

'You will tell me, Patrick. I promise you'll tell me. You can do it now, or you can do it ten hours from now when you're half-dead. Make it easy on yourself.'

'I don't want to die, okay?' Patrick said, his eyes filled with fear. They will not kill me, he told himself.

Guy lifted a small, simple, nasty device from beside Patrick and displayed it close to his face. It was a chrome lever with a black rubber tip, mounted on a small square block with two wires running from it. 'See this,' Guy said, as if Patrick had a choice. 'When the lever is up, the circuit is broken.' Guy delicately gripped the rubber tip with his thumb and index finger, and slowly lowered it. 'But when it moves down to this little contact point here, the circuit is closed and the current moves through the wires to the electrodes attached to your skin.' He stopped the lever just centimeters from the contact point. Patrick held his breath. The room was still.

'Would you like to see what happens when the shock is delivered?' Guy asked.

'No.'

'Then where's the money?'

'I don't know. I swear.'

Twelve inches in front of Patrick's nose, Guy pushed the lever down to the contact point. The shock was instant and horrific – hot bolts of current ripped into his flesh. Patrick jerked and the nylon ropes stretched. He closed his eyes fiercely and clamped his teeth together in a determined effort not to scream, but gave up after a split second and let out a piercing shriek that was heard throughout the cabin.

Guy lifted the lever, waited a few seconds for Patrick to catch his breath and open his eyes, then said, 'That's level one, the lowest current. I have five levels, and I'll use them all if necessary. Eight seconds of level five will kill you, and I'm perfectly willing to do that as a last resort. Are you listening, Patrick?'

His flesh still burned from his chest to his ankles. His heart pumped furiously and he exhaled quickly.

'Are you listening?' Guy repeated.

'Yes.'

'Your situation is really quite simple. Tell me where the money is, and you leave this room alive. Eventually, we'll take you back to Ponta Porã, and you can carry on as you see fit. We have no interest in notifying the FBI.' Guy paused for drama and toyed with the chrome lever. 'If, however, you refuse to tell me where the money is, then you'll never leave this room alive. Do you understand, Patrick?'

'Yes.'

'Good. Where's the money?'

'I swear I don't know. If I knew, I'd tell you.'

Guy snapped the lever down without a word, and the currents hit like boiling acid. 'I don't know!' Patrick screamed in anguish. 'I swear I don't know.'

Guy raised the lever, and waited a few seconds for Patrick to recover. Then, 'Where's the money?' he asked calmly.

'I swear I don't know.'

Another scream filled the cabin, and escaped through the open windows, into the crevice between the mountains where it echoed lightly before losing itself in the jungle.

The apartment in Curitiba was near the airport. Eva told the cabdriver to wait in the street. She left her overnight bag in the trunk, but carried her thick briefcase with her.

She took the elevator to the ninth floor where the hallway was dark and quiet. It was almost 11 P.M. She moved slowly, eyes looking in all directions. She unlocked the door to the apartment, then quickly disarmed the security system with another key.

Danilo was not in the apartment, and though this was not a surprise it was still a disappointment. No message on the phone recorder. No sign of him whatsoever. Her anxiety reached another level.

She could not stay long, because the men who had Danilo might be coming there. Though she knew exactly what to do, her movements were forced and slow. The apartment had only three rooms, and she searched them quickly.

The papers she wanted were in a locked file cabinet in the den. She opened the three heavy drawers and neatly placed the paperwork in a handsome leather suitcase he kept in a nearby closet. The bulk of the files contained financial records, though not much for such a large fortune. His paper trail was as narrow as possible. He came here once a month to hide records from his home, and at least once a month he shredded the old stuff.

And for the moment, Danilo couldn't know where his papers were.

She rearmed the security system and made a hasty exit. No one in the cramped building had noticed her. She found a room in a small hotel downtown, near the Museum of Contemporary Arts. The Asian banks were open, and it was almost four in Zurich. She unpacked a compact fax and rigged it to the phone jack in her room. The small bed was soon covered with sheets of instructions and wire authorizations.

She was tired, but sleep was out of the question. Danilo said they'd come looking for her. She could not go home. Her thoughts were not on money, but on him. Was he alive? If so, how much was he suffering? How much had he told them, and at what price?

She wiped her eyes and began to arrange the papers. There was no time for tears.

With torture, the best results come after three days of episodic abuse. The more obstinate wills are slowly broken. The pain is dreamed of, and looms larger as the victim waits for the next session. Three days, and most people break and crumble into small pieces.

Guy didn't have three days. His prisoner was not one taken in war, but a U.S. citizen wanted by the FBI.

Around midnight, they left Patrick alone for a few minutes to suffer and think about the next round. His body was drenched with sweat; his skin red from the voltage and the heat. Blood trickled from under the tape on his chest where the electrodes had been stuck too tightly and were burning into his flesh. He gasped for breath and licked his dry shriveled lips. The nylon ropes on his wrists and ankles had rubbed the skin raw.

Guy returned alone, and sat on a stool next to the sheet of plywood. For a minute the room was quiet, the only sound was Patrick breathing and trying to control himself. He kept his eyes closed tightly.

'You're a very stubborn man,' Guy said, finally.

No response.

The first two hours had yielded nothing. Every question had been about the money. He didn't know where it was, he'd said a hundred times. Did it exist? No, he had said repeatedly. What happened to it? He didn't know.

Guy's experience with torture was extremely limited. He'd consulted an expert, a really twisted freak who seemed to actually enjoy it. He'd read a crude how-to manual, but finding practice time was difficult.

Now that Patrick knew how horrible things could get, it was important to chat him up.

'Where were you when your funeral took place?' Guy asked.

There was a slight relaxing of Patrick's muscles. Finally, a question not about the money. He hesitated and thought about it. What was the harm? He was caught. His story was about to be told. Maybe if he cooperated they'd lay off the voltage.

'In Biloxi,' he said.

'Hiding?'

'Yes, of course.'

'And you watched your graveside service?'

'Yes.'

'From where?'

'I was in a tree, with binoculars.' He kept his eyes closed and his fists clenched.

'Where did you go after that?'

'Mobile.'

'Was that your hiding place?'

'Yes, one of them.'

'How long did you stay there?'

'Off and on, coupla months.'

'That long, huh? Where did you live in Mobile?'

'Cheap motels. I moved around a lot. Moved up and down the Gulf. Destin. Panama City Beach. Back to Mobile.'

'You changed your appearance.'

'Yeah. I shaved, colored my hair, dropped fifty pounds.'

'Did you study a language?'

'Portuguese.'

'So you knew you were headed here?'

'Where's here?'

'Let's say it's Brazil.'

'Okay. Yeah, I figured this was a good place to hide.'

'After Mobile, where did you go?'

'Toronto.'

'Why Toronto?'

'I had to go somewhere. It's a nice place.'

'Did you get new papers in Toronto?'

'Yeah.'

'You became Danilo Silva in Toronto?'

'Yeah.'

'Did you take another language course?'

'Yeah.'

'Dropped some more weight?'

'Yeah. Another thirty pounds.' He kept his eyes closed and tried to ignore the pain, or at least live with it for the moment. The electrodes on his chest were smoldering and cutting deeper into his skin.

'How long did you stay there?'

'Three months.'

'So you left there around July of '92?'

'Something like that.'

'And where did you go next?'

'Portugal.'

'Why Portugal?'

'Had to go somewhere. It's a nice place. Never been there.'

'How long were you there?'

'Coupla months.'

'Then where?'

'São Paulo.'

'Why São Paulo?'

'Twenty million people. A wonderful place to hide.'

'How long did you stay there?'

'A year.'

'Tell me what you did there.'

Patrick took a deep breath, then grimaced when he moved his ankles. He relaxed. 'I got lost in the city. I hired a tutor and mastered the language. Lost a few more pounds. Moved from one small apartment to another.'

'What did you do with the money?'

A pause. A flinch of the muscles. Where was the wretched little chrome lever? Why couldn't they continue chatting about the chase and lay off the money?

'What money?' he asked, with a passable effort at desperation.

'Come on, Patrick. The ninety million dollars you stole from your law firm and its client.'

'I told you. You got the wrong guy.'

Guy suddenly yelled at the door. It opened instantly and the rest of the Americans rushed in. The Brazilian doctor emptied two more syringes into Patrick's veins, then left. Two men huddled over the device in the corner. The tape recorder was turned on. Guy hovered over Patrick with the chrome lever in an upright position, scowling and angry and even more determined to kill him if he didn't talk.

'The money arrived by wire to your law firm's account offshore in Nassau. The time was exactly ten-fifteen, Eastern Standard. The date was March 26, 1992, forty-five days after your death. You were there, Patrick, looking fit and tanned and posing as someone else. We have photos taken from the bank's security camera. You had perfect forged papers. Shortly after the money arrived it was gone, sent by wire to a bank in Malta. You stole it, Patrick. Now, where is it? Tell me, and you'll live.'

Patrick took a last look at Guy, and a last glance at the lever, then he closed his eyes tightly, braced himself, and said, 'I swear I don't know what you're talking about.'

'Patrick, Patrick –'

'Please don't do it!' he begged. 'Please!'

'This is only level three, Patrick. You're halfway there.' Guy pushed the lever down, and watched the body bolt and straighten.

Patrick screamed with no restraint, a scream so fierce and horrible that Osmar and the Brazilians froze for a second on the front porch. Their conversation stopped in the darkness. One of them offered a silent prayer.

Down the road, a hundred yards away, a Brazilian with a gun sat by the dirt trail and watched for approaching cars. None were expected. The nearest dwelling was miles away. He too offered a small prayer when the screaming started again.

FOUR

It was either the fourth or fifth call from the neighbors that sent Mrs Stephano over the edge, and it also forced Jack to tell his wife the truth. The three men in dark suits loitering outside the car parked in the street directly in front of their house were FBI agents. He explained why they were there. He told her most of the Patrick story, a serious breach of professional etiquette. Mrs Stephano never asked questions.

She didn't care what her husband did at the office. She did, however, hold some rather strong feelings about what the neighbors might think. This was, after all, Falls Church, and, well, people would talk.

She went to bed at midnight. Jack napped on the sofa in the den, rising every half-hour to peek through the blinds and see what they were doing out there. He happened to be asleep at 3 A.M. when the doorbell rang.

He answered it in his sweatsuit. Four of them were at the door, one of whom he immediately recognized as Hamilton Jaynes, Deputy Director, FBI. The number-two man at the Bureau, who just happened to live four blocks over and belong to the same golf club, though the two had never met.

He allowed them into his spacious den. Stiff introductions were made. They sat while Mrs Stephano wandered down in her bathrobe, then scurried back up at the sight of a room full of men in dark suits.

Jaynes did all the talking for the FBI. 'We're working nonstop on this Lanigan discovery. Our intelligence informs us that he's in your custody. Can you confirm or deny?'

'No.' Stephano was as cool as ice.

'I'm holding a warrant for your arrest.'

The ice melted a bit. Stephano glanced at another stone-faced agent. 'On what charges?'

'Harboring a federal fugitive. Interference. You name it, we'll include it. What difference does it make? I'm not interested in convicting you. All I want is to haul your ass off to jail, then later we'll get the rest of your firm, then we'll lock up your clients. Take about twenty-four hours to round up everybody. We'll get the indictments later, depending on whether or not we get Lanigan. You get the picture?'

'Yeah. I think so.'

'Where's Lanigan?'

'Brazil.'

'I want him. And now.'

Stephano blinked a couple of times, and things fell into place. Under the circumstances, handing over Lanigan was not a bad move. The feds had ways of making him talk. Faced with life in prison, Patrick just might snap his fingers and make the money appear. There would be enormous pressure from all angles to produce it.

Later, Stephano would again ponder the incredible question of how anyone in the world knew he had captured Lanigan.

'All right, here's the deal,' Stephano said. 'Give me forty-eight hours, I'll give you Lanigan. And you burn my warrant and drop the threats of future prosecution.'

'It's a deal.'

There was a moment of silence as both sides

savored the victory. Jaynes said, 'I need to know where to pick him up.'

'Send a plane to Asunción.'

'Paraguay? What happened to Brazil?'

'He has friends in Brazil.'

'Whatever.' Jaynes whispered to an associate, who then left the house. 'Is he in one piece?' he asked Stephano.

'Yeah.'

'He'd better be. One bruise on his body, and I'll hound you to hell.'

'I need to make a phone call.'

Jaynes actually managed a grin. He scanned the walls and said, 'It's your house.'

'Are my lines tapped?'

'No.'

'You swear?'

'I said no.'

'Excuse me.' Stephano stepped into the kitchen, then to a utility room where he kept a hidden cell phone. He walked onto the rear patio where he stood in the wet grass by a gaslight. He called Guy.

The screaming had stopped for the moment when the Brazilian guarding the van heard the phone ringing. It rested on its power unit in the front seat of the van, its antenna shooting fifteen feet beyond the roof. He answered it in English, then ran to get an American.

Guy rushed from the cabin and grabbed it.

'Is he talking?' Stephano asked.

'A little. He broke about an hour ago.'

'What do you know?'

'The money still exists. He doesn't know where. It's controlled by a woman in Rio, a lawyer.'

'Do you have her name?'

'Yes. We're making calls now. Osmar has people in Rio.'

34

'Can you get any more out of him?'

'I don't think so. He's half-dead, Jack.'

'Stop whatever you're doing. Is the doctor there?'

'Sure.'

'Get the boy treated and spruced up. Drive him toward Asunción as soon as possible.'

'But why –'

'Don't ask questions. There's no time for it. The feds are all over us. Just do as I say, and make sure he's not hurt.'

'Not hurt? I've been trying to kill him for five hours.'

'Just do as I say. Put him back together. Drug him. Start toward Asunción. Call me every hour, on the hour.'

'Whatever.'

'And find the woman.'

Patrick's head was lifted gently and cool water was poured on his lips. The ropes were cut from his wrists and ankles, and they very slowly removed the tape and the wires and the electrodes. He jerked and twitched, moaning words no one could understand. A shot of morphine was pumped into his well-worn veins, then a light depressant, and Patrick floated away again.

At dawn, Osmar was in the airport at Ponta Porã waiting for a flight that would eventually get him to Rio by the end of the day. He had made contact with people in Rio. He had pulled them out of bed with promises of big bucks. They were supposed to be on the streets.

She called her father first, just after sunrise, a time of the day he always enjoyed on his small terrace with his newspaper and his coffee. He lived in a small apartment in Ipanema, three blocks from the shore, not far from his beloved Eva. His apartment building was over thirty years old, making it one of the oldest in the poshest section of Rio. He lived alone.

He knew from her voice something was wrong. She assured him she was safe and would remain so, that a client in Europe suddenly needed her for two weeks, and that she would call every day. She went on to explain that this particular client was perhaps a bit shady and very secretive, and therefore he might send representatives to poke around in her past. Don't be alarmed. It was not unusual in international trade.

He had several questions, but he knew there would be no answers.

The call to her supervising partner was much more difficult. The story she had rehearsed delivered well, but there were huge gaps in it. A new client had called late yesterday, a referral from an American lawyer she went to school with, and she was needed immediately in Hamburg. She was taking an early flight. The client was in telecommunications, with plans for a large expansion in Brazil.

The partner was half-asleep. He asked her to call later with more details.

She called her secretary with the same story, and asked her to postpone all appointments and meetings until she returned.

From Curitiba, she flew to São Paulo, where she boarded an Aerolineas Argentinas flight to Buenos Aires, nonstop. For the first time, she used her new passport, one Danilo had helped her acquire a year earlier. She had kept it hidden in the apartment, along with two new credit cards and eight thousand dollars in U.S. cash.

She was Leah Pires now, same age but different birthday. Danilo didn't know these details; he couldn't know.

She certainly felt like someone else.

There were many scenarios. He could've been shot by bandits making a routine heist along a rural road. Happened occasionally along the Frontier. He could've been grabbed by the shadows from his past, tortured, killed, buried in the jungle. Maybe he talked, and if he did maybe her name got mentioned. She could spend the rest of her life on the run. At least he had warned her of this in the beginning. Maybe he didn't talk, and she could remain Eva.

Perhaps Danilo was still alive somewhere. He had promised her they wouldn't kill him. They might make him beg for death, but they couldn't afford to kill him. If the American authorities found him first, it would be a matter of extradition. He'd picked Latin America because of its historical reluctance to extradite.

If the shadows found him first, they would beat him until he told them where the money was. That's what he feared most – the coercion.

She tried to nap in the Buenos Aires airport, but sleep was impossible. She called his home again in Ponta Porã, then the cell phone and the apartment in Curitiba.

In Buenos Aires, she boarded a flight to New York, where she waited three hours then caught another one to Zurich on SwissAir.

They laid him across the rear seat of the Volkswagen van, and wrapped a seat belt around his waist so he wouldn't bounce off. The roads ahead were rough. He was dressed in his running shorts only. The doctor checked the heavy gauze bandages – eight of them in all. He had covered the burns with ointments and shot antibiotics into Patrick's blood. The doctor took the seat in front of his patient, and tucked his little black bag between his feet. Patrick had suffered enough. He would protect him now.

A day or two of rest and more painkillers, and Patrick would be on his way to recovery. The burns would leave small scars, which would probably fade with time.

The doctor turned around and patted him on the shoulder. He was so pleased they hadn't killed him. 'He's ready,' he said to Guy in the front seat. A Brazilian driver started the van and backed away from the cabin.

They stopped every hour, precisely every sixty minutes, so the antenna could be raised and the cell phone could work around the mountains. Guy called Stephano, who was in his D.C. office with Hamilton Jaynes and a top official with the State Department. The Pentagon was being consulted.

What the hell was going on, Guy wanted to ask. Where did the feds come from?

In the first six hours they traveled a hundred miles. At times, the roads were almost impassable. They often fought with the phone trying to get Washington. At two in the afternoon, the roads improved as they left the mountains.

The extradition issue was sticky, and Hamilton Jaynes wanted no part of it. Important diplomatic strings were pulled. The Director of the FBI called the President's Chief of Staff. The American Ambassador to Paraguay got involved. Promises and threats were made.

A suspect with cash and resolve can stifle extradition from Paraguay for years, if not forever. This suspect had no money on him, and didn't even know what country he was in.

The Paraguayans reluctantly agreed to ignore extradition.

At four, Stephano instructed Guy to find the airport at Concepción, a small city three hours by car from Asunción. The Brazilian driver cursed, in Portuguese, when told to turn around and head north.

★

It was dusk when they entered Concepción, and it was dark when they finally found the airport, a small brick building next to a narrow asphalt strip. Guy called Stephano, who instructed him to leave Patrick in the van, with the keys in the ignition, and walk away from it. Guy, the doctor, the driver, and another American eased away slowly while looking over their shoulders at the van. They found a spot a hundred yards away, under a large tree where they couldn't be seen. An hour passed.

Finally, a King Air with American registration landed and taxied to the small terminal. Two pilots emerged, and went inside the terminal. A moment later, they walked to the van, opened the doors, got inside, and drove it to a spot near their airplane.

Patrick was gently removed from the back of the van and loaded onto the turboprop. An Air Force medic was on board, and he immediately took possession of the prisoner. The two pilots returned the van to its original spot in the parking lot. Minutes later, the plane took off.

The King Air refueled in Asunción, and while it was on the ground there Patrick began to move. He was too weak and sore and groggy to sit up. The medic gave him cold water and crackers.

They refueled again in La Paz and Lima. In Bogotá, they transferred him to a small Lear, which flew at twice the speed of the King Air. It refueled on Aruba, off the coast of Venezuela, then flew nonstop to a U.S. Navy base outside San Juan, Puerto Rico. An ambulance took him to the base hospital.

After almost four and a half years, Patrick was back on American soil.

FIVE

The law firm Patrick worked for before he died filed for bankruptcy protection a year after his funeral. After his death, the firm's letterhead properly included him: Patrick S. Lanigan, 1954–1992. He was listed up in the right-hand corner, just above the paralegals. Then the rumors got started and wouldn't stop. Before long, everyone believed he had taken the money and disappeared. After three months, no one on the Gulf Coast believed he was dead. His name came off the letterhead as the debts piled up.

The four remaining partners were still together, attached unwillingly at the hip by the bondage of bankruptcy. Their names had been joined on the mortgages and the bank notes, back when they were rolling and on the verge of serious wealth. They had been joint defendants in several unwinnable lawsuits; thus the bankruptcy. Since Patrick's departure, they had tried every possible way to divorce one another, but nothing would work. Two were raging alcoholics who drank at the office behind locked doors, but never together. The other two were in recovery, still teetering on the brink of sobriety.

He took their money. Their millions. Money they had already spent long before it arrived, as only lawyers can do. Money for their richly renovated office building in downtown Biloxi. Money for new homes,

40

yachts, condos in the Caribbean. The money was on the way, approved, the papers signed, orders entered; they could see it, smell it, almost touch it when their dead partner snatched it at the last possible second.

He was dead. They buried him on February 11, 1992. They had consoled the widow and put his rotten name on their handsome letterhead. Yet six weeks later, he somehow stole their money.

They had brawled over who was to blame. Charles Bogan, the firm's senior partner and its iron hand, had insisted the money be wired from its source into a new account offshore, and this made sense after some discussion. It was ninety million bucks, a third of which the firm would keep, and it would be impossible to hide that kind of money in Biloxi, population fifty thousand. Someone at the bank would talk. Soon everyone would know. All four vowed secrecy, even as they made plans to display as much of their new wealth as possible. There had even been talk of a firm jet, a six-seater.

So Bogan took his share of the blame. At forty-nine, he was the oldest of the four, and, at the moment, the most stable. He was also responsible for hiring Patrick nine years earlier, and for this he had received no small amount of grief.

Doug Vitrano, the litigator, had made the fateful decision to recommend Patrick as the fifth partner. The other three had agreed, and when Lanigan was added to the firm name, he had access to virtually every file in the office. Bogan, Rapley, Vitrano, Havarac, and Lanigan, Attorneys and Counselors-at-Law. A large ad in the yellow pages claimed 'Specialists in Offshore Injuries.' Specialists or not, like most firms they would take almost anything if the fees were lucrative. Lots of secretaries and paralegals. Big overhead, and the strongest political connections on the Coast.

They were all in their mid- to late forties. Havarac had been raised by his father on a shrimp boat. His hands were still proudly calloused, and he dreamed of choking Patrick until his neck snapped. Rapley was severely depressed and seldom left his home, where he wrote briefs in a dark office in the attic.

Bogan and Vitrano were at their desks just after nine when Agent Cutter entered the building on Vieux Marche, in the old section of Biloxi. He smiled at the receptionist and asked if any of the lawyers were in. It was a fair question. They were known as a bunch of drunks who occasionally showed up for work.

She led him to a small conference room and gave him coffee. Vitrano came first, looking remarkably starched and clear-eyed. Bogan was just seconds behind. They mixed sugar in the coffee and talked about the weather.

In the months immediately following the disappearance of both Patrick and the money, Cutter would drop in periodically and deliver the latest update on the FBI's investigation. They became pleasant acquaintances, though the meetings were always disheartening. As the months became years, the updates grew further apart. And the updates had the same endings: no trace of Patrick. It had been almost a year since Cutter had spoken to any of them.

And so they figured he was simply being nice, happened to be downtown for something, probably wanted a cup of coffee, and this would be routine and quick.

Cutter said, 'We have Patrick in custody.'

Charlie Bogan closed his eyes and displayed every one of his teeth. 'Oh my God!' he exclaimed, then buried his face in his palms. 'Oh my God.'

Vitrano's head fell back, his mouth too fell open. He

gazed in utter disbelief at the ceiling. 'Where?' he managed to ask.

'He's at a military base in Puerto Rico. He was captured in Brazil.'

Bogan stood and walked to a corner, next to some bookcases, where he hid his face and tried to hold back the tears. 'Oh my God,' he kept repeating.

'Are you sure it's him?' Vitrano asked in disbelief.

'Positive.'

'Tell me more,' Vitrano said.

'Like what?'

'Like how did you find him? And where? And what was he doing? What does he look like?'

'We didn't find him. He was given to us.'

Bogan sat down at the table, a handkerchief over his nose. 'I'm sorry,' he said, embarrassed.

'Do you know a man named Jack Stephano?' Cutter asked.

They both nodded with some reluctance.

'Are you part of his little consortium?'

They both shook their heads in the negative.

'You're lucky. Stephano found him, tortured him, damned near killed him, then gave him to us.'

'I like the part about the torture,' Vitrano said. 'Tell us about that.'

'Skip it. We picked him up last night in Paraguay, flew him to Puerto Rico. He's in the hospital there. He'll be released and sent here in a few days.'

'What about the money?' Bogan managed to ask, his voice scratchy and dry.

'No sign of it. But then, we don't know what Stephano knows.'

Vitrano stared at the table, his eyes dancing. Patrick had stolen ninety million dollars when he disappeared four years earlier. It would be impossible to spend all of it. He could have bought mansions and helicopters

43

and lots of women and still have tens of millions left. Surely they could find it. The firm's fee was a third.

Maybe, just maybe.

Bogan worked on his moist eyes and thought of his ex-wife, a congenial woman who'd turned vicious when the sky fell. She had felt disgraced after the bankruptcy, and so she took their youngest child and moved to Pensacola where she filed for divorce and made ugly accusations. Bogan was drinking and using coke. She knew it and beat him over the head with it. He couldn't offer much resistance. He eventually cleaned himself up, but was still denied access to the child.

Oddly enough, he still loved his ex-wife; still dreamed of getting her back. Maybe the money would get her attention. Maybe there was hope. Surely they could find it.

Cutter broke the silence. 'Stephano's in all sorts of trouble. There were burns all over Patrick's body where they tortured him.'

'Good,' Vitrano said with a smile.

'You expect sympathy from us?' Bogan asked.

'Anyway, Stephano is a side issue. We'll watch him, maybe he'll lead us to the money.'

'The money will be easy to find,' Vitrano said. 'There was a dead body. Somebody got killed by our boy Patrick. It's a death penalty case, open and shut. Murder for the sake of money. Patrick will sing when the pressure is applied.'

'Better yet, give him to us,' Bogan said, without a smile. 'Ten minutes, and we'll know everything.'

Cutter glanced at his watch. 'I gotta go. I have to go to Point Clear and break the news to Trudy.'

Bogan and Vitrano snorted in perfect unison, then laughed. 'Oh, she doesn't know?' Bogan said.

'Not yet.'

'Please video it,' Vitrano said, still laughing quietly. 'I'd love to see her face.'

44

'I'm actually looking forward to it,' Cutter said.

'The bitch,' Bogan said.

Cutter stood and said, 'Tell the other partners, but sit on it until noon. We've scheduled a press conference then. I'll be in touch.'

They didn't say a word for a long time after he left. There were so many questions, so much to say. The room spun with possibilities and scenarios.

The victim of a fiery one-car collision, on a rural road with no witnesses, Patrick was laid to rest by his lovely wife Trudy on February 11, 1992. She was a striking widow, dressed in black Armani, and as they shoveled dirt onto his casket she was already spending the money.

His will left everything to her. It was simple and had been recently updated. Hours before the funeral mass, Trudy and Doug Vitrano had carefully opened the lockbox in Patrick's office and inventoried the contents. They found the will, two car titles, the deed to the Lanigan home, a life insurance policy in the amount of half a million dollars that Trudy knew about, and another policy for two million that she'd never heard of.

Vitrano had quickly scanned the unexpected policy. It had been purchased by Patrick eight months earlier. Trudy was the sole beneficiary. The same company had sold both policies, and it was huge and solvent.

She swore she knew nothing about it, and the smile on her face convinced Vitrano she was genuinely shocked. Funeral or no funeral, Trudy was quite thrilled about her good fortune. With her pain eased considerably, she somehow managed to suffer through the funeral service and burial without a serious breakdown.

The life insurance company balked, as they all do initially, but Vitrano made sufficient threats to force

45

payment. Four weeks after the burial, Trudy got her two and a half million.

A week later, she was driving a red Rolls-Royce around Biloxi, and people began to hate her. Then the ninety million vanished into thin air, and the rumors got started.

Perhaps she wasn't a widow.

Patrick was the first suspect, and eventually the only one. The gossip grew vicious, so Trudy loaded her small daughter and her boyfriend, Lance, a holdover from high school, into the red Rolls and fled to Mobile, an hour east of Biloxi. She found a slick lawyer who gave her lots of advice on how to protect the money. She bought a beautiful old home in Point Clear, overlooking Mobile Bay, and put it in Lance's name.

Lance was a strong, handsome loser she'd first slept with at the age of fourteen. He'd been convicted of smuggling pot at nineteen, and spent three years in prison while she was having a wonderful time at college, playing cheerleader and seducing football players, a legendary party girl who also managed to graduate with honors. She married a wealthy fraternity boy, and divorced him after two years. Then she enjoyed the single life for a few years until she met and married Patrick, a promising young lawyer who was new to the Coast. Their courtship had been long on passion and short on planning.

Through college, both marriages, and various short careers, Trudy had always kept Lance nearby. He was an addiction, a strapping, lusty boy she could never get enough of. She knew when she was fourteen that she would never be without Lance.

Lance opened the door, bare-chested, black hair pulled back tightly into the obligatory ponytail, a large diamond earring in the left lobe. He sneered at Cutter as he sneered at the world, and didn't say a word.

'Is Trudy in?' Cutter asked.

'Maybe.'

The badge flashed, and for a second the sneer vanished. 'Agent Cutter, FBI. I've talked to her before.'

Lance imported marijuana from Mexico with a large, fast boat Trudy had purchased for him. He sold the pot to a gang in Mobile. Business was slow because the DEA was asking questions.

'She's in the gym,' Lance said, nodding past Cutter. 'What do you want?'

Cutter ignored him and walked across the drive to a converted garage where the music was booming. Lance followed.

Trudy was in the midst of a high-level aerobics challenge being dictated to her by a supermodel on a large-screen TV at one end of the room. She bounced and gyrated and mouthed the words to a nameless song, and looked damned good doing it. Tight yellow spandex. Tight blond ponytail. Not an ounce of fat anywhere. Cutter could've watched for hours. Even her sweat was cute.

She did this two hours a day. At thirty-five, Trudy still looked like everybody's high school sweetheart.

Lance hit a switch and the video stopped. She twirled, saw Cutter, and gave him a look that would melt cheese. 'Do you mind?' she snapped at Lance. Evidently, this workout was not to be disturbed.

'I'm Special Agent Cutter, FBI,' he said, whipping out his badge and walking to her. 'We met once before, a few years back.'

She dabbed her face with a towel, a yellow one that matched the spandex. She was hardly breathing.

She flashed perfect teeth, and everything was okay. 'What can I do for you?' Lance stood beside her. Matching ponytails.

47

'I have some wonderful news for you,' Cutter said with a broad smile.

'What?'

'We've found your husband, Mrs Lanigan, and he's alive.'

A slight pause as it registered. 'Patrick?' she said.

'He would be the one.'

'You're lying,' Lance sneered.

'Afraid not. He's in custody in Puerto Rico. Should make it back here in a week or so. Just thought you should hear the good news before we release it to the press.'

Stunned and staggering, she backed away and sat on a workout bench next to a weight machine. Her glistening bronze flesh was growing pale. Her pliant body was crumbling. Lance scurried to help her. 'Oh my God,' she kept mumbling.

Cutter threw a card in front of them. 'Call me if I can be of any help.' They said nothing as he left.

It was obvious to him that she held no anger at having been duped by a man who faked his death. Nor was there the smallest hint of joy at his return. No relief whatsoever at the end of an ordeal.

There was nothing but fear; the horror of losing the money. The life insurance company would sue immediately.

While Cutter was in Mobile, another agent from the Biloxi office went to the home of Patrick's mother in New Orleans, and delivered the same news. Mrs Lanigan was overcome with emotion, and begged the agent to sit for a while and answer questions. He stayed for an hour, but had few answers for her. She cried for joy, and after he left she spent the rest of the day calling friends with the wonderful news that her only child was alive after all.

SIX

Jack Stephano was arrested by the FBI in his D.C. office. He spent thirty minutes in jail, then was rushed to a small courtroom in the federal courthouse where he faced a U.S. Magistrate in a closed hearing. He was informed that he would be released immediately on his own recognizance, that he couldn't leave the area, and that he would be watched by the FBI around the clock. While he was in court, a small army of agents entered his office, seized virtually every file, and sent the employees home.

After being dismissed by the Magistrate, Stephano was driven to the Hoover Building on Pennsylvania Avenue where Hamilton Jaynes was waiting. When the two were alone in Jaynes' office, the Deputy Director offered a lukewarm apology for the arrest. But he had no choice. You can't snatch a federal fugitive, drug him, torture him, and damned near kill him without being charged with something.

The issue was the money. The arrest was the leverage. Stephano swore Patrick had told them nothing.

As they spoke, the doors to Stephano's office were being chained shut and ominous federal bulletins were being taped to the windows. His home phones were being bugged while Mrs Stephano played bridge.

After the brief and fruitless meeting with Jaynes, he

49

was dropped off near the Supreme Court. Since he'd been ordered to stay away from his office, he flagged a cab and told the driver to go to the Hay-Adams Hotel, corner of H and Sixteenth. He sat in traffic, calmly reading a newspaper, occasionally rubbing the tracking device they'd sewn in the hem of his jacket when they booked him. It was called a tracing cone, a tiny but powerful transmitter used to monitor movements of people, packages, even automobiles. He'd frisked himself while chatting with Jaynes, and had been tempted to rip out the cone and toss it on his desk.

He was an expert at surveillance. He stuffed his jacket under the seat of the cab, and walked quickly into the Hay-Adams Hotel, across from Lafayette Park. There were no rooms, he was told. He asked to see the manager, a former client, and within minutes Mr Stephano was escorted to a suite on the fourth floor, with a splendid view of the White House. He stripped to his socks and shorts and carefully placed each item of clothing on the bed where he examined and even caressed every inch of fabric. He ordered lunch. He called his wife, but there was no answer.

Then he called Benny Aricia, his client, the man whose ninety million got diverted just minutes after it had arrived at the bank in Nassau. Aricia's take was to have been sixty million, with thirty going to his lawyers, Bogan and Vitrano and the rest of those filthy crooks in Biloxi. But it had vanished, just before it reached Benny.

He was at the Willard Hotel, also near the White House, hiding and waiting to hear from Stephano.

They met an hour later at the Four Seasons Hotel in Georgetown, in a suite Aricia had just reserved for a week.

Benny was almost sixty, but looked ten years younger. He was lean and bronze, with the perpetual tan of an affluent South Florida retiree who played

50

golf every day. He lived in a condo on a canal with a Swedish woman who was young enough to be his daughter.

When the money was stolen, the law firm owned an insurance policy covering fraud and theft by its partners and employees. Embezzlement is common in law firms. The policy, sold by Monarch-Sierra Insurance Company, had a limit of four million dollars, payable to the firm. Aricia sued the law firm with a vengeance. His lawsuit demanded sixty million; all that he was entitled to.

Because there was little else to collect, and because the firm was about to run to bankruptcy court, Benny had settled for the four million paid by Monarch-Sierra. He'd spent almost half of that searching for Patrick. The fancy condo in Boca had cost a half a million. Other expenditures here and there, and Benny was down to his last million.

He stood in the window and sipped decaffeinated coffee. 'Am I going to be arrested?' he asked.

'Probably not. But I'd keep low anyway.'

Benny placed his coffee on the table and sat across from Stephano. 'Have you talked to the insurance companies?' he asked.

'Not yet. I'll call later. You guys are safe.'

Northern Case Mutual, the life insurance company which had made Trudy rich, had secretly set aside half a million for the search. Monarch-Sierra had put up a million. In all, Stephano's little consortium had pledged and spent over three million dollars in the hunt for Patrick.

'Any luck with the girl?' Aricia asked.

'Not yet. Our people are in Rio. They found her father, but he wouldn't talk. Same at her law firm. She's out of town on business, they say.'

Aricia folded his hands and calmly said, 'Now tell me, what exactly did he say?'

51

'I haven't heard the tape yet. It was supposed to be delivered to my office this afternoon, but now things are complicated. Plus, it was sent from the jungles of Paraguay.'

'I know that.'

'According to Guy, he broke after five hours of shock. He said the money was still intact, hidden in various banks, none of which he could name. Guy damned near killed him when he couldn't, or wouldn't, name the banks. By then, Guy figured, correctly, that someone else had control of the money. A few more jolts, and the girl's name came out. Guy's men immediately called Rio, and confirmed her identity. She had already vanished.'

'I want to hear that tape.'

'It's brutal, Benny. The man's skin is burning and he's screaming for mercy.'

Benny couldn't stop the smile. 'I know. That's what I want to hear.'

They put Patrick at the end of a wing on the base hospital. His was the only room with doors which could be locked from the outside and windows that wouldn't open. The blinds were closed. Two military guards sat outside the hallway, for whatever reason.

Patrick wasn't going anywhere. The voltage had severely bruised the muscles and tissue in his legs and chest. Even his joints and bones were tender. The burns had laid open his flesh in four places, two on his chest, one on his thigh, one on his calf. Four other spots were being treated as second-degree burns.

The pain was intense, and so his doctors, all four of them, had made the simple decision to keep him sedated for the time being. There was no rush to move him. He was a wanted man, but it would take a few days to determine who got him first.

They kept the room dark, the music low, the IV full

of delightful narcotics, and poor Patrick snored away the hours dreaming of nothing and oblivious to the storm brewing back home.

In August of 1992, five months after the money vanished, a federal grand jury in Biloxi indicted Patrick for the theft. There was sufficient evidence that he had pulled the heist, and there was not the slightest hint that anyone else might be a suspect. It occurred internationally, thus the feds had jurisdiction.

The Harrison County Sheriff's Department and the local District Attorney had started a joint investigation into the murder, but had long since moved on to other, more pressing matters. Suddenly they were back in business.

The noon press conference was delayed while the authorities met in Cutter's office in downtown Biloxi to sort things out. It was a tense meeting, attended by people with competing interests. On one side of the table sat Cutter and the FBI, who took their orders from Maurice Mast, the U.S. Attorney for the Western District of Mississippi, who had driven in from Jackson. On the other side sat Raymond Sweeney, the Sheriff of Harrison County, and his right-hand man, Grimshaw, both of whom despised the FBI. Their spokesman was T.L. Parish, the District Attorney for Harrison and surrounding counties.

It was federal versus state, big budgets versus low, with serious egos around the room and everyone wanting most of the Patrick show.

'The death penalty is crucial here,' D.A. Parrish said.

'We can use the federal death penalty,' U.S. Attorney Mast said, a little timid, if that was possible.

Parrish smiled and cast his eyes down. The federal death penalty had just recently been passed by a

Congress with little clue of how to implement it. It certainly sounded good when the President signed it into law, but the kinks were enormous.

The state, on the other hand, had a rich and proven history of legal executions. 'Ours is better,' Parrish said. 'And we all know it.' Parrish had sent eight men to death row. Mast had yet to indict one for capital murder.

'And then there is the issue of prison,' Parrish continued. 'We send him to Parchman, where he's locked down twenty-three hours a day in a steam room with bad food served twice a day, two showers a week, lots of roaches and rapists. If you get him, he gets a country club for the rest of his life while the federal courts pamper him and find a thousand ways to keep him alive.'

'It won't be a picnic,' Mast said, on the ropes and covering badly.

'A day at the beach maybe. Come on, Maurice. The issue is leverage. We have two big mysteries, two questions that must be answered before Lanigan is put to rest. The big one is money. Where is it? What did he do with it? Can it be recovered and given to its owners? The second is just exactly who is buried out there. I gotta hunch that only Lanigan can tell us, and he won't unless he's forced to. He's gotta be scared, Maurice. Parchman is terrifying. I promise you, he's praying for a federal indictment.'

Mast was convinced but he couldn't agree. The case was simply too big to hand over to the locals. Cameras were arriving at the moment.

'There are other charges, you know,' he said. 'The theft happened offshore, a long way from here.'

'Yeah, but the victim was a resident of this county at the time,' Parrish said.

'It's not a simple case.'

'What are you proposing?'

'Perhaps we should do it jointly,' Mast said, and the ice melted considerably. The feds could preempt at any time, and the fact that the U.S. Attorney was offering to share was the best Parrish could hope for.

Parchman was the key, and everyone in the room knew it. Lanigan the lawyer had to know what awaited him there, and the prospect of ten years in hell prior to death could loosen his tongue.

A plan was devised to divide the pie, with both men, Parrish and Mast, tacitly agreeing to share the spotlight. The FBI would continue its search for the money. The locals would concentrate on the murder. Parrish would hastily summon his grand jury. A united front would be presented to the public. Such sticky matters as the trial and its subsequent appeals were glossed over with a hasty promise to address them later. It was important now to reach a truce so that one side wouldn't be worrying about the other.

Because a trial was in progress in the federal building, the press was herded directly across the street into the Biloxi courthouse, where the main courtroom on the second floor was available. There were dozens of reporters. Most were wild-eyed locals, but others were from Jackson, New Orleans, and Mobile. They pressed forward and bunched together like children at a parade.

Mast and Parrish walked grim-faced to a podium laden with microphones and wires. Cutter and the rest of the cops made a wall behind them. Lights came on and cameras flashed.

Mast cleared his throat, and said, 'We are pleased to announce the capture of Mr Patrick S. Lanigan, formerly of Biloxi. He is indeed alive and well, and now in our custody.' He paused for dramatic effect, savoring his moment in the sun, listening as a ripple of excitement played through the throng of vultures. He then gave a few details of the capture – Brazil, two days ago, assumed identity – without giving the slightest hint that neither he nor the FBI had had anything to do with the actual locating of Patrick. Next, some useless details about the arrival of the prisoner, the pending charges, the swift and sure hand of federal justice.

Parrish was not as dramatic. He promised a quick indictment for capital murder, and for any other charge he might think of.

The questions came in torrents. Mast and Parrish declined comment on just about everything, and managed to do so for an hour and a half.

She insisted that Lance be allowed to sit through the appointment with her. She needed him, she said. He was quite cute in his tight denim shorts. His muscular legs were hairy and brown. The lawyer was scornful, but then, he'd seen everything.

Trudy was dressed to the nines – tight short skirt, tasteful red blouse, full complement of makeup and jewelry. She crossed her shapely legs to get the lawyer's attention. She patted Lance on the arm as he massaged her knee.

The lawyer ignored her legs as he ignored their groping.

She had to file for divorce, she declared, though she had already given the short version on the phone. She was mad and bitter. How could he do this to her? And to Ashley Nicole, their precious daughter? She had loved him dearly. Their lives together had been good. Now this.

'The divorce is no problem,' the lawyer said, more than once. His name was J. Murray Riddleton, an accomplished divorce practitioner with many clients. 'It's an easy case of abandonment. Under Alabama law, you'll get the divorce, full custody, all assets, everything.'

'I want to file as fast as possible,' she said, looking at the Ego Wall behind the lawyer.

'I'll do it first thing in the morning.'

'How long will it take?'

'Ninety days. Piece of cake.'

This did nothing to relieve her anxiety. 'I just don't see how a person could do this to someone he loved. I feel like a fool.' Lance's hand moved slightly upward, still massaging.

The divorce was the least of her worries. The lawyer knew it. She could try to fake a broken heart, but it wasn't working.

'How much did you get in life insurance?' he asked, flipping through the file.

She looked absolutely shocked at the mention of her life insurance. 'Why is that relevant?' she snapped.

'Because they're gonna sue you to get it back. He isn't dead, Trudy. No death, no life insurance.'

'You must be kidding.'

'Nope.'

'They can't do that. Can they? Surely not.'

'Oh yes. In fact, they'll do it quickly.'

Lance withdrew his hand and slumped in his chair. Trudy's mouth opened and her eyes watered. 'They just can't.'

He took a fresh legal pad and uncapped his pen. 'Let's make a list,' he said.

She paid a hundred and thirty thousand dollars for the Rolls, and still owned it. Lance drove a Porsche, which she'd bought for eighty-five thousand. The house had been purchased for nine hundred thousand, cash, no mortgage, and it was in Lance's name. Sixty thousand for his dope boat. A hundred thousand for her jewelry. They figured and pondered and pulled numbers from the air. The list stopped at about a million and a half. The lawyer didn't have the heart to tell them that these precious assets would be the first to go.

Like pulling teeth without Novocain, he made Trudy estimate their monthly living expenses. She reckoned it was around ten grand a month, for the past four years. They had taken some fabulous trips, money spilled down the drain that no life insurance company could ever recover.

She was unemployed, or retired, as she preferred to call it. Lance was not about to mention his narcotics business. Nor did they dare reveal, even to their own lawyer, that they had hidden three hundred thousand in a bank in Florida.

'When do you think they'll sue?' she asked.

'Before the week is out,' said the lawyer.

It was, in fact, much faster. In the middle of the press conference, when the news of Patrick's resurrection was being made, attorneys for Northern Case Mutual quietly entered the clerk's office downstairs and sued Trudy Lanigan for the full two and a half million dollars, plus interest and attorneys' fees. The lawsuit also included a petition for a temporary restraining order to prevent Trudy from moving assets now that she was no longer a widow.

The attorneys carried their petition down the hall to the chambers of an accommodating judge, one they had spoken to hours earlier, and in an emergency and perfectly proper closed hearing, the judge granted the restraining order. As an established member of the legal community, the judge was very familiar with the saga of Patrick Lanigan. His wife had been snubbed by Trudy shortly after she took delivery of the red Rolls.

As Trudy and Lance pawed each other and schemed with their lawyer, a copy of the restraining order was driven to Mobile and enrolled with the county clerk. Two hours later, as they sipped their first drink on their patio and gazed forlornly across Mobile Bay, a process server intruded long enough to hand Trudy a copy of the lawsuit filed by Northern Case Mutual, a summons to appear in court in Biloxi, and a certified copy of the restraining order. Among its list of prohibitions was an order for her not to write another check until the judge said so.

SEVEN

Attorney Ethan Rapley left his dark attic, showered
and shaved and poured eye drops into his bloodshot
retinas, and sipped strong coffee as he found a
semiclean navy blazer to wear downtown. He hadn't
been to the office in sixteen days. Not that he was
missed, and he certainly didn't miss anyone there.
They faxed him when they needed him, and he faxed
them back. He wrote the briefs and memos and
motions the firm needed to survive, and he did the
research for people he despised. He was occasionally
forced to put on a tie and meet a client or attend some
hideous conference with his fellow partners. He hated
his office; he hated the people, even the ones he barely
knew; he hated every book on every shelf and every file
on every desk. He hated the photos on his wall, and
the smell of everything – the stale coffee in the hall, the
chemicals near the copier, the perfume of the secretaries. Everything.

Yet, he caught himself almost smiling as he eased
through the late afternoon traffic along the Coast. He
nodded at an old acquaintance as he walked rather
briskly down the Vieux Marche. He actually spoke to
the receptionist, a woman he helped pay but whose
last name he couldn't recall.

In the conference room, a crowd mingled; mostly
lawyers from nearby offices, a judge or two, some

courthouse types. It was after five, and the mood was loud and festive. Cigar smoke filled the air.

Rapley found the liquor on a table at one end of the room, and spoke to Vitrano as he poured a Scotch and tried to appear pleased. At the other end, a variety of bottled waters and soft drinks was being ignored.

'It's been like this all afternoon,' Vitrano said as they looked at the crowd and listened to the happy talk. 'Soon as word got out, this place started hopping.'

The Patrick news raced through the legal community along the Coast in a matter of minutes. Lawyers thrive on gossip, tend even to embellish it, and repeat it with amazing rapidity. Rumors were heard, collected, invented. He weighs a hundred and thirty pounds and speaks five languages. The money was found. The money is gone forever. He lived in near poverty. Or was it a mansion? He lived alone. He has a new wife and three kids. They know where the money is. They haven't a clue.

All rumors eventually got back to the money. As the friends and the curious gathered in the conference room and chatted about this and that, everything drifted back to the money. Secrets were scarce among this crowd. For years now everyone knew the firm lost one third of ninety million. And the remotest chance of collecting that money brought in the friends and the curious for a drink or two and a story or a rumor and an update and the inevitable, 'Damn, I hope they find the money.'

Rapley disappeared into the crowd with his second drink. Bogan slugged down sparkling water and chatted with a judge. Vitrano worked the crowd and confirmed or denied as much as possible. Havarac huddled in a corner with an aging court reporter who suddenly found him cute.

The liquor flowed as night fell. Hopes were raised and raised as the gossip got recycled.

Patrick essentially *was* the evening news on the Coast station. It reported little else. There were Mast and Parrish staring grimly at the bank of microphones as if they'd been whipped and dragged there against their wills. There was a close-up of the front door of the law office, with no comments from anyone inside. There was a drippy little chronicle from Patrick's gravesite, complete with brooding possibilities of what may have happened to the poor soul whose ashes were buried down there. There was a flashback to the fiery crash four years earlier, with shots of the site and the burned hulk of Mr Patrick Lanigan's Chevy Blazer. No comments from the wife, the FBI, the Sheriff. No comments from the players, but lots of wild speculation from the reporters.

The news also played well in New Orleans, Mobile, Jackson, and even Memphis. CNN picked it up mid-evening, and ran it nationally for an hour before sending it abroad. It was such an irresistible story.

It was almost 7 A.M., Swiss time, when Eva saw it in her hotel room. She had fallen asleep with the TV on sometime after midnight, and had slept on and off throughout the night, waiting as long as possible for news of Patrick before drifting away. She was tired and scared. She wanted to go home but knew she couldn't.

Patrick was alive. He had promised her a hundred times they would never kill him if and when they found him. For the first time, she believed him.

How much had he told them? That was the question.

How badly was he hurt? How much did they get from him?

She whispered a short prayer and thanked God that Patrick was still alive.

Then she made a checklist.

Under the indifferent gaze of two uniformed guards, and with the feeble assistance of Luis, his ancient Puerto Rican orderly, Patrick shuffled down the hallway in his bare feet and baggy white military boxer shorts. His wounds needed air – no clothing or bandages now. Just ointments and oxygen. His calves and thighs were painfully tender, and his knees and ankles quivered with each step.

He wanted to clear his head, dammit. He welcomed the pain from the open burns because it sharpened his brain. Only God knew what vile blend of chemicals had been pumped into his blood during the past three days.

The torture was a dense, horrible fog, but it was lifting now. As the chemicals broke down and dissolved and were flushed out, he began to hear his anguished screams. How much had he told them about the money?

He leaned on the windowsill in the empty canteen while the orderly fetched a soft drink. The ocean was a mile away, with rows of barracks in between. He was on some type of military base.

Yes, he'd admitted the money still existed, he remembered that because the shocks had ceased for a moment when this came out. Then he'd passed out, it seemed now, because there was a long break before he was awakened with cold water splashed in his face. He remembered how soothing the water felt, but they wouldn't allow him a drink. They had kept poking him with needles.

Banks. He'd almost given his life for the names of some lousy banks. With hot current running through his body, he had tracked the money for them from the moment he stole it from the United Bank of Wales in the Bahamas, onward to a bank in Malta, then to Panama, where no one could find it.

He didn't know where the money was once they'd snatched him. It still existed, all of it plus interest and earnings, he had most certainly told them that, he remembered now, remembered quite clearly because he had figured what the hell – they know I stole it, know I've got it, know it would be impossible to blow ninety million in four years – but he honestly didn't know precisely where the money was as his flesh melted.

The orderly handed him a soda and he said, '*Obrigado.*' Thanks in Portuguese. Why was he speaking Portuguese?

There had been a blackout then, after the money trail stopped. 'Stop!' someone had yelled from the corner of the room, someone he never saw. They thought they'd killed him with the current.

He had no idea how long he was unconscious. At one point he woke up blind; the sweat and drugs and the horrific screaming had blinded him. Or was it a blindfold? He remembered that now – thinking that maybe it was a blindfold because maybe they were about to implement some new, even more hideous means of torture. Amputation of body parts, maybe. And he lay there naked.

Another shot in the arm, and suddenly his heart raced away and his skin jumped. His buddy was back with his little play toy. Patrick could see again. So who's got the money? he asked.

Patrick sipped his soda. The orderly loitered nearby, smiling pleasantly, the way he did for every patient. Patrick was suddenly nauseous, though he'd eaten little. He was light-headed and dizzy, but determined to remain on his feet so the blood would move and maybe he could think. He focused on a fishing boat, far on the horizon.

They'd blasted him a few times, wanting names. He had screamed his denials. They taped an electrode to his testicles, and the pain soared to a different level. Then there were blackouts.

Patrick couldn't remember. He simply couldn't remember the last stage of his torture. His body was on fire. He was near death. He had called her name, but was it to himself? Where was she now?

He dropped the soda and reached for the orderly.

Stephano waited until one in the morning before leaving the house. He drove down his dark street in his wife's car. He waved at the two agents sitting in a van at the intersection. He drove slowly so they could turn around and follow him. By the time he crossed the Arlington Memorial Bridge, there were at least two cars trailing.

The little convoy slid through empty streets until it reached Georgetown. Stephano held the advantage of knowing where he was going. He took a sudden right off K Street on to Wisconsin, then another on M. He parked illegally, and quickly, and walked half a block to a Holiday Inn.

He took the elevator to the third floor, where Guy was waiting in a suite. Back in the United States for the first time in months, he'd slept little in three days. Stephano couldn't have cared less.

There were six tapes, all labeled and neatly arranged, sitting on a table next to a battery-operated player. 'The rooms next door are empty,' Guy said, pointing in both directions. 'So you can listen at full volume.'

'It's nasty, I take it,' Stephano said, staring at the tapes.

'Pretty sick. I'll never do it again.'

'You can leave now.'

'Good. I'm down the hall if you need me.'

Guy left the room. Stephano made a call, and a minute later Benny Aricia knocked on the door. They ordered black coffee, and spent the rest of the night listening to Patrick scream in the jungles of Paraguay. It was Benny's finest hour.

EIGHT

To say it was Patrick's day in the papers would be an understatement. The Coast morning daily ran *nothing* on the front page but Patrick.

LANIGAN BACK FROM THE DEAD

shouted the headline in thick block letters. Four stories with no less than six photos covered the front page and continued inside. He also played well on the front page in New Orleans, his hometown, as well as in Jackson and Mobile. Memphis, Birmingham, Baton Rouge, and Atlanta also ran photos of the old Patrick with small front-page stories.

Throughout the morning, two television vans kept a vigil outside his mother's home in Gretna, a New Orleans suburb. She had nothing to say, and was protected by two vigorous ladies from down the street who took turns walking to the front door and glaring at the vultures.

The press also congregated near the front of Trudy's home on Point Clear, but were kept at bay by Lance, who sat under a shade tree with a shotgun. He wore a tight black tee shirt, black boots and trousers, and looked very much the part of a successful mercenary. They yelled banal questions at him. He only scowled. Trudy hid inside with Ashley Nicole, the six-year-old, who'd been kept home from school.

They flocked to the law office downtown and waited on the sidewalk. They were denied entrance by two beefy security guards who'd been hurriedly pressed into action.

They loitered around the Sheriff's office, and Cutter's office, and anywhere else they might pick up a scent. Someone got a tip, and they gathered at the Circuit Clerk's office just in time to see Vitrano, in his finest gray suit, hand the clerk a document which he described as a lawsuit the firm was filing against Patrick S. Lanigan. The firm wanted its money back, plain and simple, and Vitrano was perfectly willing to discuss this with the press for as long as he could hold an audience.

It would prove to be a litigious morning. Trudy's lawyer leaked the earth-shattering news that at 10 A.M. he would stride over to the clerk's office in Mobile and file a petition for divorce. He performed this task admirably. Though he'd filed a thousand divorces, this was the first time he'd done it in front of a TV news crew. He reluctantly agreed to be interviewed, at length. The grounds were abandonment, and the petition alleged all sorts of heinous sins. He posed for some pictures in the hallway outside the clerk's office.

Word spread quickly about yesterday's lawsuit, the one in which Northern Case Mutual sued Trudy Lanigan for the return of the two-point-five million. The court file was ransacked for details. The attorneys involved were contacted. A leak here, a casual word there, and before long a dozen reporters knew Trudy couldn't write a check for groceries without court approval.

Monarch-Sierra Insurance wanted its four million dollars back, plus interest and attorney's fees, of course. Its Biloxi lawyers hurriedly threw together a suit against the law firm for receiving the policy limit and against poor Patrick for defrauding everyone. As was becoming customary, the press got tipped off, and copies of the lawsuit were in hand only minutes after its filing.

Not surprisingly, Benny Aricia wanted his ninety million from Patrick. His new lawyer, a flamboyant mouthpiece, had a different approach in dealing with the media. He called a press conference for 10 A.M., and invited everyone into his spacious conference room to discuss every insignificant aspect of his client's claim *before* he filed suit. Then he invited his new pals in the press corps to stroll with him down the sidewalk as he went to file it. He talked every step of the way.

The capture of Patrick Lanigan did more to create legal work on the Coast than any single event in recent history.

With the Harrison County Courthouse bustling to a near frenzy, seventeen members of the grand jury quietly entered an unmarked room on the second floor. They had received urgent phone calls during the night from the District Attorney himself, T.L. Parrish. They knew the nature of this meeting. They got coffee and took their designated seats around the long table. They were anxious, even excited to be in the middle of the storm.

Parrish said hello, apologized for the emergency session, then welcomed Sheriff Sweeney and his chief investigator, Ted Grimshaw, and Special Agent Joshua Cutter. 'Seems we suddenly have a fresh murder on our hands,' he said, unfolding a copy of the morning paper. 'I'm sure most of you have seen this.' Everyone nodded.

Pacing slowly along one wall with a legal pad in hand, Parrish recited the particulars: background on

Patrick; his firm's representation of Benny Aricia; Patrick's death, faked now, of course; his burial; most of the details they'd read in the morning paper Parrish had just laid on the table.

He passed around photos of Patrick's burned-out Blazer at the site; photos of the site the next morning without the Blazer; photos of the charred brush, soil, the burned weeds and trunk of a tree. And, quite dramatically and with a warning, Parrish passed around color eight by tens of the remains of the only person in the Blazer.

'We, of course, thought it was Patrick Lanigan,' he said with a smile. 'We now know we were wrong.'

There was nothing about the blackened hulk to suggest it was human remains. No distinguishable body parts, except for a protruding pale bone which Parrish gravely explained came from the pelvis. 'A human pelvis,' he added, just in case his grand jurors got confused and thought that perhaps Patrick had murdered a hog or some other beast.

The grand jurors took it well, mainly because there was little to see. No blood, tissue, or gore. Nothing to get sick over. He, or she, or whatever it was, had come to rest in the right front passenger seat, which had been burned to the frame, like everything else.

'Of course it was a gasoline fire,' Parrish explained. 'We know that Patrick had filled his tank eight miles up the road, so twenty gallons exploded. Our investigator did, however, make a note that the fire seemed unusually hot and intense.'

'Did you find the remains of any containers in the vehicle?' asked one grand juror.

'No. Plastic containers are typically used in fires such as this. Gallon milk jugs and antifreeze containers seem to be the favorite of arsonists. They don't leave a trace. We see it all the time, though rarely in a car fire.'

'Are the bodies always this bad?' asked another.

Parrish answered quickly, 'No, as a matter of fact they are not. I've never seen a corpse burned this badly, frankly. We would try to exhume it, but, as you probably know, it was cremated.'

'Any idea who it is?' asked Ronny Burkes, a dockworker.

'We have one person in mind, but it's only speculation.'

There were other questions about this and that, nothing of significance, just little inquiries served up in hopes of taking something from the meeting that the papers had left out. They voted unanimously to indict Patrick on one count of capital murder – murder committed in the perpetration of another crime, to wit, grand larceny. Punishable by death, by lethal injection up at the state penitentiary at Parchman.

In less than twenty-four hours, Patrick managed to get himself indicted for capital murder, sued for divorce, sued for ninety million by Aricia, plus punitive damages, sued for thirty million by his old law firm buddies, plus punitive, and sued for four million by Monarch-Sierra Insurance, plus another ten million in punitive, for good measure.

He watched it all, compliments of CNN.

The prosecutors, T.L. Parrish and Maurice Mast, once again stood glumly before the cameras and announced, jointly, though the feds had nothing to do with this indictment, that the good people of Harrison County, acting by and through the office of its grand jury, had now moved swiftly to lay charges against Patrick Lanigan, a murderer. They deflected the questions they could not answer, evaded the ones they could, and hinted strongly that more charges would follow.

When the cameras left, the two men met quietly with the Honorable Karl Huskey, one of the three circuit judges for Harrison County, and a close friend of Patrick's, before the funeral. Cases were supposedly assigned at random, but Huskey, as well as the other judges, knew how to manipulate the filing clerk so that he could receive, or not receive, any particular case. Huskey wanted Patrick's case, for now.

While eating a tomato sandwich in the kitchen, alone, Lance saw something move in the rear yard, near the pool. He grabbed his shotgun, eased from the house, around some shrubs on the patio, and spotted a chubby photographer squatting by the pool house, three bulking cameras dangling from his neck. Lance tiptoed barefoot around the pool house, gun at the ready, and crouched to within two feet of the man's back. He leaned forward, placed the gun near the man's head with the barrel pointed upward, and pulled the trigger.

The photographer lurched forward and fell on his face, screaming frightfully and floundering on top of his cameras. Lance kicked him between the legs, then again as he rolled over and finally got a glimpse of his assailant.

Lance ripped off the three cameras and threw them into the pool. Trudy was on the patio, horrified. Lance yelled at her to call the police.

NINE

'I'm going to scrape the dead skin away now,' the doctor said, gently probing a chest wound with a pointed instrument. 'I really think you should consider some pain medication.'

'No thanks,' Patrick said. He was sitting on his bed, naked, with the doctor, two nurses, and the Puerto Rican orderly, Luis, huddled around him.

'It's gonna hurt, Patrick,' said the doctor.

'I've been through worse. Besides, where would you stick me?' he asked, lifting his left arm. It was covered with purple and dark blue bruises where the Brazilian doctor had relentlessly poked him during his ordeal. His entire body was a rainbow of bruises and scar tissue. 'No more drugs,' he said.

'Okay. As you wish.'

Patrick reclined and gripped the side rails to his bed. The nurses and Luis held his ankles as the doctor began scraping the raw, third-degree burns on his chest. With surgical scalpels, he pulled the dead skin off the wound, then cut it free.

Patrick flinched and closed his eyes.

'How about a shot, Patrick?' asked the doctor.

'No,' he grunted.

More scalpels. More dead skin.

'These are healing nicely, Patrick. I tend to think you might not need skin grafts after all.'

'Good,' he said, then flinched again.

Four of the nine burns were severe enough to be considered third degree; two on the chest, one on the left thigh, and one on the right calf. The rope burns on his wrists, elbows, and ankles were raw and covered with ointments.

The doctor finished in half an hour, and explained that it would be best to remain still, unclothed and unbandaged, at least for now. He applied a cool antibacterial salve, and again offered pills for the pain. Patrick again declined.

The doctor and the nurses left, and Luis loitered long enough to see them off. He closed the door behind them, and pulled down the blinds. From a pocket under his white orderly's jacket, he produced a disposable Kodak camera, with a flash.

'Start there,' Patrick said, pointing to the foot of the bed. 'Get the entire body, including my face.' Luis stuck the camera to his head, fiddled with it, backed to the wall, then pushed the button. The camera flashed.

'Again, from there,' Patrick directed.

Luis did as he was told. At first, he'd been reluctant to agree to this venture, said his boss might need to approve it. Living on the border of Paraguay, Patrick not only had perfected his Portuguese but he'd also learned to handle Spanish. He could understand almost everything Luis said. Luis had more trouble understanding Patrick.

The language of money prevailed, with Luis eventually comprehending the offer of five hundred U.S. dollars in return for his services as a photographer. He agreed to purchase three disposable cameras, take almost a hundred shots, get them developed overnight, and to hide them far from the hospital until further orders.

Patrick didn't have five hundred dollars on him, but he persuaded Luis that he was an honest man, regardless of what he might have heard, and that he would send the money as soon as he got home.

Luis wasn't much of a photographer, but then he didn't have much of a camera. Patrick coordinated every shot. There were close-ups of the serious burns on his chest and thigh, close-ups of his badly bruised limbs, full-length shots from every angle. They worked fast so they wouldn't get caught. It was almost time for lunch and another round of busy nurses with charts and incessant chatter.

Luis left the hospital on his lunch break and dropped the film off at a camera shop.

In Rio, Osmar convinced a low-paid secretary at Eva's law firm to accept a thousand dollars in cash in exchange for all the current in-house gossip. There wasn't much. Things were very quiet among the partners. But the phone records revealed two calls to the firm from a number in Zurich. It was a hotel, Guy determined from Washington, but no other information was available. The Swiss were so discreet.

Her partners had no patience with her disappearance. Their quiet gossip about her soon changed to daily meetings about what to do. She'd called once the first day, once the second, then no word. The mysterious client she had flown off to see could not be verified. Meanwhile, her legitimate clients were making demands and threats. She missed appointments, meetings, deadlines.

Finally, they decided to temporarily remove her from the firm, and deal with her later when she returned.

Osmar and his men stalked Eva's father until the poor man was unable to sleep. They watched his apartment lobby and followed him in traffic and along the busy sidewalks of Ipanema. There was talk of snatching him and roughing him up a bit, forcing him to talk, but he was careful and never allowed himself to be isolated.

On his third trip to her bedroom, Lance finally found the door unlocked. He entered quietly with another Valium and her favorite bottled sparkling water, from Ireland, four bucks a bottle, and he sat next to her on the bed without a word and held out the pill. She took it, her second in an hour, and she sipped the water.

The police car carrying the chubby photographer had left an hour ago. Two cops hung around for twenty minutes, asking their questions, apparently not anxious to press charges since it was private property, and the press had been told to stay away, the publication was a sleazy magazine from up North anyway. The cops seemed quite sympathetic, even respectful of the way Lance handled the situation. They were given the name of Trudy's attorney downtown in case charges were to be pressed. Lance threatened to press charges of his own if hauled into court.

Trudy snapped after the cops left. She threw cushions from a sofa into the fireplace as the nanny raced off with the child. She yelled obscenities at Lance because he was the nearest target. It was just too much – the news about Patrick, the lawsuit by the insurance company, the restraining order, the horde of vultures out front, and then Lance had caught a photographer by the pool.

But she was quiet now. He'd had a Valium too, and he sighed relief that she was under control. He wanted to touch her, to pat her on the knee and say something nice, but such gestures never worked on her in these situations. A wrong move and she would snap again. Trudy would cool down, but only on her own terms.

Trudy reclined on the bed, closed her eyes, placed the back of her wrist on her forehead. The room was dark, like the rest of the house – blinds and shades pulled tight, lights off or dimmed. There were a hundred people loitering out by the road taking pictures and shooting film to be used with all those wretched Patrick stories. At noon, she'd seen her house on the local news, in the background as some silly orange-faced woman with large teeth gushed on about Patrick this and Patrick that, and the divorce filed by Patrick's wife that very morning.

Patrick's wife! The thought made her numb with disbelief. She hadn't been Patrick's wife for almost four and a half years. She'd buried him right properly, then tried to forget about him as she waited for the money. By the time she received it, he was a fading memory.

The only painful moment had come when she sat down with Ashley Nicole to inform the child, then barely two, that her father would no longer be around, that he had gone on to heaven where he would certainly be happier. The child was puzzled for a while, then shook it off as only a toddler can. No one was allowed to mention Patrick's name in the presence of the child. This was to protect her, Trudy had explained. She doesn't remember her father, so please don't try and make her.

Other than that one brief episode, she had shouldered the weight of widowhood with remarkable resiliency. She shopped in New Orleans, ordered health foods from California, sweated two hours a day in designer spandex, and treated herself to expensive facials and treatments. She had a nanny to keep the kid so she and Lance could travel. They loved the Caribbean, especially St Barts with its nude beaches. They stripped and strutted with the French.

Christmas was in New York at the Plaza. January was in Vail with the rich and beautiful. May meant Paris and Vienna. They longed for a private jet like some of the wonderful people they'd met in the fast lane. A small, used Lear could be bought for a million, but for now was out of the question.

Lance claimed to be working on this idea, and she worried anytime he grew serious about business matters. She knew he smuggled dope, but it was just pot and hash from Mexico and there was little risk. They needed the income, and she liked him out of the house occasionally.

She didn't hate Patrick, not the dead one anyway. She just hated the fact that he wasn't dead, that he had been resurrected and was back to complicate things. She'd first met him at a party in New Orleans, during a period of time when she was pouting with Lance and looking for another husband, preferably one with money and promise. She was twenty-seven, four years out of a bad marriage and restless for stability. He was thirty-three, still single and ready to settle down. He had just accepted a job with a nice firm in Biloxi, which was where she happened to be living at the time. After four months of nonstop passion, they were married in Jamaica. Three weeks after the honeymoon, Lance sneaked into their new apartment and spent the night while Patrick was away on business.

She couldn't lose the money, that was for certain. Her lawyer would simply have to do something, find some loophole which would allow her to keep it. That's what he got paid to do. Surely the insurance company couldn't get the house, the furniture and cars and clothes, the bank accounts, the boat, the fabulous things she'd bought with the money. It just didn't seem fair. Patrick had died. She'd buried him. She'd been a widow now for over four years. That must count for something.

It wasn't her fault he was alive.

'We'll have to kill him, you know,' Lance said in the semidarkness. He had moved to a cushioned chair between the bed and the window, his bare feet draped over an ottoman.

She didn't move, didn't flinch in the smallest way, but thought about it for a second before saying, 'Don't be stupid.' This she offered with little conviction.

'There is no alternative, you know that.'

'We're in enough trouble.'

She only breathed, her wrist still stuck to her forehead, eyes closed, perfectly still, and actually quite happy that Lance had broached the subject. She, of course, had thought about this within minutes of being told that Patrick was headed home. She had walked through various scenarios, each leading to the same inescapable conclusion: to keep the money, Patrick must be dead. It was, after all, an insurance policy on his life.

She couldn't kill him; that was a ridiculous notion. Lance, on the other hand, had lots of shadowy friends in dark places.

'You wanna keep the money, don't you?' he asked.

'I can't think about it now, Lance. Maybe later.' Perhaps real soon. She couldn't seem eager or Lance would get too excited. As usual, she would manipulate him, string him along into some devilish plot until it was too late for *him* to back out.

'We can't wait too long, baby. Hell, the life insurance company's already got us choked.'

'Please, Lance.'

'There ain't no way around it. You wanna keep this house, the money, everything we've got, then he's gotta die.'

She didn't speak or move for a long time, but his words delighted her soul. In spite of half a brain and many other flaws, Lance was the only man she'd ever loved. He was nasty enough to take care of Patrick, but was he smart enough not to get caught?

★

79

The agent's name was Brent Myers, from the office in Biloxi, sent by Cutter to make contact with their prize. He introduced himself and flashed a badge at Patrick, who hardly acknowledged it while reaching for the remote. 'A pleasure,' he said as he pulled the sheets over his boxer shorts.

'I'm from the office in Biloxi,' Myers said, genuinely trying to be nice.

'Where's that?' Patrick asked, poker-faced.

'Yes, well, I thought we should meet and get to know each other. We'll be spending some time together during the next few months.'

'Don't be so sure of that.'

'Do you have a lawyer?'

'Not yet.'

'Do you plan to hire one?'

'Absolutely none of your business.'

Myers was obviously no match for a seasoned lawyer like Lanigan. He placed his hands on the railing across the foot of the bed, and stared at Patrick with his best effort at intimidation. 'Doc says you might be ready to transport in two days,' he said.

'So. I'm ready now.'

'There's quite a party waiting on you in Biloxi.'

'I've been watching,' Patrick said, nodding at the television.

'Don't suppose you'd want to answer some questions.'

Patrick snorted his contempt at this ludicrous suggestion.

'Didn't think so,' Myers said, and took a step for the door. 'Anyway, I'll be escorting you home.' He tossed a card on the sheets. 'Here's my hotel number, in case you want to talk.'

'Don't sit by the phone.'

TEN

Sandy McDermott had read with great interest the news accounts of the amazing discovery of his old pal from law school. He and Patrick had studied and partied together for three years at Tulane. They had clerked for the same Judge after they passed the bar exam, and they had spent many hours in their favorite pub on St Charles plotting their assault upon the legal world. They would build a firm together – a small but powerful firm of hard-charging trial lawyers with impeccable ethics. They would get rich in the process, and they would donate ten hours a month to clients who couldn't afford to pay. It was all planned.

Life intervened. Sandy took a job as an assistant federal prosecutor, primarily because the pay was good and he was a newlywed. Patrick got lost in a firm with two hundred lawyers in downtown New Orleans. Marriage eluded him because he worked eighty hours a week.

Their plans for their perfect little firm lasted until they were about thirty. They tried to meet for a quick lunch or a drink whenever possible, though the meetings and the phone calls happened less frequently as the years passed. Then Patrick escaped to a calmer life in Biloxi, and they hardly spoke once a year.

Sandy's big break in the suing game came when the friend of a cousin was maimed on an offshore oil rig in the Gulf. He borrowed ten thousand dollars, opened his own shop, sued Exxon and collected close to three million dollars, one third of which he kept. He was in business. Without Patrick, he built a nice little firm of three lawyers whose specialty was offshore injuries and deaths.

When Patrick died, Sandy actually sat down with his calendar and determined that it had been nine months since he'd talked to his buddy. Of course he felt lousy about this, but he was also realistic. Like most college friends, they had simply gone their separate ways.

He sat with Trudy through the ordeal, and he helped carry the casket to the grave.

When the money disappeared six weeks later, and the gossip started, Sandy had laughed to himself and wished his buddy well. Run Patrick run, he'd thought many times over the past four years, and always with a smile.

Sandy's office was off Poydras Street, nine blocks from the Superdome, near the intersection of Magazine, in a beautiful nineteenth-century building he'd bought with an offshore settlement. He leased the second and third floors, and kept the bottom one for himself, his two partners, three paralegals, and half a dozen secretaries.

He was very busy when his secretary entered his office with a grim face and said, 'There's a lady here to see you.'

'Does she have an appointment?' he asked, glancing at one of three daily-weekly-monthly planners on the edge of his desk.

'No. She says it's urgent. She's not leaving. It's about Patrick Lanigan.'

He looked at her curiously. 'She says she's a lawyer,' the secretary said.

'Where's she from?'

'Brazil.'

'Brazil?'

'Yes.'

'Does she look, you know, Brazilian?'

'I guess.'

'Show her in.'

Sandy met her at the door and greeted her warmly. Eva gave her name as Leah, with nothing behind it.

'I didn't catch your last name,' Sandy said, all smiles.

'I don't use one,' she said. 'Not yet, anyway.'

Must be a Brazilian thing, Sandy thought. Like Pelé, the soccer player. Just a first name with no last.

He escorted her to a chair in the corner and sent for coffee. She declined and sat slowly. He glanced at her legs. She was dressed casually, nothing flashy. He sat across the coffee table from her and noticed her eyes – beautiful eyes, light brown, but very tired. Her long dark hair fell past her shoulders.

Patrick always had a good eye. Trudy was a mismatch, but she could certainly stop traffic.

'I'm here on behalf of Patrick,' she said, haltingly.

'Did he send you?' Sandy asked.

'Yes, he did.'

She spoke slowly, her words soft and low. The accent was very slight.

'Did you study in the States?' he asked.

'Yes. I have a degree in law from Georgetown.'

That would explain the near perfect American-English.

'And you practice where?'

'In a firm in Rio. My work is in international trade.'

She had yet to smile, and this bothered Sandy. A visitor from afar. A beautiful one at that; one with a brain and nice legs. He wanted her to relax in the warmth of his office. This was, after all, New Orleans.

83

'Is that where you met Patrick?' he asked.

'Yes. In Rio.'

'Have you spoken to him since –'

'No. Not since he was taken.' She almost added that she was desperately worried about him, but that would seem unprofessional. She was not to divulge much here; nothing about her relationship with Patrick. Sandy McDermott could be trusted, but he was to be fed information in small doses.

There was a pause as they both looked away, and Sandy instinctively knew that there were many chapters to this story he would never know. But, oh, the questions! How did he steal the money? How did he get to Brazil? How did he pick her up along the way? And the big one: Where's the money?

'So what am I supposed to do?' he asked.

'I want to retain you, for Patrick.'

'I'm available.'

'Confidentiality is crucial.'

'It always is.'

'This is different.'

Got that right. Different to the tune of ninety million bucks.

'I assure you that anything you and Patrick tell me will be held in the strictest of confidence,' he said with a reassuring smile, and she managed a very slight one in return.

'You might be pressured to divulge client secrets,' she said.

'I'm not worried about that. I can take care of myself.'

'You might be threatened.'

'I've been threatened before.'

'You might be followed.'

'By whom?'

'Some very nasty people.'

'Who?'

'The people chasing Patrick.'

'I think they've caught him.'

'Yes, but not the money.'

'I see.' So the money was still around; that was not surprising. Sandy, and everyone else for that matter, knew Patrick couldn't go through such a fortune in four years. But how much was left?

'Where is the money?' he asked, somewhat tentatively, not for a moment expecting an answer.

'You can't ask that question.'

'I just did.'

Leah smiled, and quickly moved on. 'Let's settle some details. How much is your retainer?'

'For what am I being retained?'

'To represent Patrick.'

'For which batch of sins? According to the newspapers, it'll take an entire army of lawyers to cover his flanks.'

'A hundred thousand dollars?'

'That'll do for starters. Am I doing the civil as well as the criminal?'

'Everything.'

'Just me?'

'Yes. He wants no other lawyer.'

'I'm touched,' Sandy said, and he meant it. There were dozens of lawyers Patrick could turn to now, bigger lawyers with more death penalty experience, connected lawyers on the Coast with local clout, lawyers in bigger firms with more resources, and, undoubtedly, lawyers who'd been closer friends than Sandy had been for the past eight years.

'Then I'm hired,' he said. 'Patrick's an old friend, you know.'

'I know.'

How much did she really know? he wondered. Was she more than a lawyer?

85

'I'd like to wire the money today,' she said. 'If you could give me wiring instructions.'

'Of course. I'll prepare a contract for legal services.'

'There are some other things Patrick is concerned about. One is publicity. He wants you to say nothing to the press. Never. Not a word. No press conferences unless approved by him. Not even a casual "no comment."'

'No problem.'

'You can't write a book about it when it's over.'

Sandy actually laughed, but she missed the humor. 'I wouldn't think of it,' he said.

'He wants it in the contract.'

He stopped laughing, and scribbled something to that effect on the legal pad. 'Anything else?'

'Yes, you can expect your office and home to get wired. You should hire a surveillance expert to protect you. Patrick is willing to pay for this.'

'Done.'

'And it will be best if we don't meet here again. There are people trying to find me, because they think I can lead them to the money. So we'll meet in other places.'

There was nothing Sandy could say to this. He wanted to help, to offer protection, to question her about where she would go and how she would hide, but Leah seemed to have things very much under control.

She glanced at her watch. 'There's a flight to Miami in three hours. I have two first-class tickets. We can talk on the plane.'

'Uh, where might I be going?'

'You'll fly on to San Juan, to see Patrick. I've made arrangements.'

'And you?'

'I'll go another direction.'

*

86

Sandy ordered more coffee and muffins while they waited for the wiring instructions to be finalized. His secretary canceled his appointments and court appearances for the next three days. His wife brought an overnight bag to the office.

A paralegal drove them to the airport, and at some point along the way Sandy noticed she had no luggage, nothing but a small brown leather satchel, well used and quite handsome.

'Where are you staying?' he asked as they sipped a cola in an airport deli.

'Here and there,' she said, looking out the window.

'How do I contact you?' he asked.

'We'll work that out later.'

They sat next to each other in the third row in first class, and for twenty minutes after takeoff she said nothing as she skimmed a fashion magazine and he tried to read a thick deposition. Sandy didn't want to read the deposition – it could wait. He wanted to talk, to fire away the endless questions, the same questions everyone else wanted to ask.

But there was a wall between them, a rather thick one that went far beyond gender and familiarity. She had the answers, but she was perfectly willing to keep them to herself. He tried his best to match her coolness.

Salted peanuts and pretzels were distributed. They declined the complimentary champagne. Bottled water was poured. 'So how long have you known Patrick?' he asked, cautiously.

'Why do you ask?'

'Sorry. Look, is there anything you can tell me about what's happened to Patrick in the past four years? I am, after all, old friend. And now I'm his lawyer. You can't blame me for being curious.'

'You'll have to ask him,' she said, with a trace of

sweetness, then returned to her magazine. He ate her peanuts.

She waited until they started their descent into Miami before speaking again. It came fast, clearly well rehearsed. 'I won't see you again for a few days. I have to keep moving because of the people after me. Patrick will give you instructions, and for the time being he and I will communicate through you. Watch for the unusual. A stranger on the phone. A car behind you. Someone hanging around your office. Once you're identified as his lawyer, you will attract the people who are looking for me.'

'Who are they?'

'Patrick will tell you.'

'You have the money, don't you?'

'I can't answer that question.'

He watched the clouds get closer below the wing. Of course the money had grown. Patrick wasn't an idiot. He'd stashed it away in a foreign bank where pros handled it. Probably earned at least twelve percent a year.

There was no more conversation until they landed. They hurried through the terminal to catch his flight to San Juan. She shook his hand firmly, and said, 'Tell Patrick I'm fine.'

'He'll ask where you are.'

'Europe.'

He watched her disappear into the mass of hustling travelers, and as he did he envied his old friend. All that money. A gorgeous lady with exotic charm and class.

A boarding call woke him up. He shook his head and asked himself how he could envy a man who now faced the possibility of spending the next ten years on death row waiting to be executed. And a hundred hungry lawyers anxious to peel away his skin in search of the money.

Envy! He took his seat, first class again, and began to feel the magnitude of representing Patrick.

Eva took a cab back to the trendy hotel on South Beach where she had spent the night. She would be there for a few days, depending on what happened in Biloxi. Patrick had told her to move around, and not to stay in one place more than four days. She was registered under the name of Leah Pires, and now had a gold credit card issued to her in that name. Her address was in São Paulo.

She quickly changed and went to the beach. It was mid-afternoon, the beach was crowded, and that suited her fine. Her beaches in Rio were crowded, but there were always friends around. Now she was a stranger, another nameless beauty in a small bikini baking in the sun. She wanted to go home.

ELEVEN

It took Sandy an hour to bully his way through the outer walls of the Navy base. His new client had not made things easy. No one seemed to know he was expected. He was forced to rely upon the attorney's usual repertoire: threats of instantaneous lawsuits, threats of ominous phone calls to senators and others in high places, and loud and angry complaints of all sorts of rights violations. He made it to the hospital office at dark, and hit another line of defense. But this time a nurse simply called Patrick.

His room was dark, lit only by the bluish light of the muted television hanging high in a corner – a soccer game from Brazil. The two old pals shook hands gently. They had not seen each other in six years. Patrick kept a sheet pulled to his chin, hiding his wounds. For the moment, the soccer game seemed more important than serious conversation.

If Sandy was hoping for a warm reunion, he quickly adjusted to a subdued one. While trying not to stare, he studied Patrick's face. It was thin, almost gaunt, with a newly squared chin and a sharper nose. He could pass for someone else, but for the eyes. And the voice was unmistakable.

'Thanks for coming,' Patrick said. All of his words were very soft, as if the act of speaking required great effort and thought.

90

'Sure. Didn't have much of a choice, you know. Your friend is very persuasive.'

Patrick closed his eyes and bit his tongue. He said a quick prayer of thanks. She was out there and she was fine.

'How much did she pay you?' he asked.

'A hundred thousand.'

'Good,' Patrick said, and then said no more. A long pause, and Sandy slowly realized that their conversations would be built around long silent intervals.

'She's fine,' he said. 'She's a beautiful woman. She's smart as hell and fully in control of whatever she's supposed to be in control of. In case you're wondering.'

'That's nice.'

'When was the last time you saw her?'

'Couple of weeks. I've lost track of time.'

'Is she the wife, girlfriend, mistress, hooker –'

'Lawyer.'

'Lawyer?'

'Yes, lawyer.' Sandy was amused by this. Patrick shut down again, no words, no movement anywhere under the sheet. Minutes passed. Sandy took a seat in the only chair, content to wait for his friend. Patrick was reentering an ugly world where the wolves were waiting, and if he wanted to lie there and stare at the ceiling then that was fine with Sandy. They would have lots of time to talk. And no shortage of topics.

He was alive, and right now nothing else mattered. Sandy amused himself by recalling images of the funeral and burial, of the casket being lowered on a cold and cloudy day, of the priest's last words and Trudy's controlled sobs. It was downright funny, to think that old Patrick had been hiding in a tree not far away watching them grieve, as had been reported for three days now.

He laid low somehow, then snatched the money.

91

Some men crack up when they near forty. The midlife crisis drives them to a new wife, or back to college. Not old Patrick. He celebrated his angst by killing himself, stealing ninety million dollars, and disappearing.

The real dead body in the car suddenly erased the humor, and Sandy wanted to talk. 'There's quite a welcome committee back home, Patrick,' he said.

'Who's the chairman?'

'Hard to say. Trudy filed for divorce two days ago, but that's the least of your problems.'

'You're right about that. Let me guess, she wants half of the money.'

'She wants many things. The grand jury has indicted you for capital murder. State not federal.'

'I've watched it on television.'

'Good. So you know about all the lawsuits.'

'Yeah. CNN has been quite diligent in keeping me up to date.'

'You can't blame them, Patrick. It's such a wonderful story.'

'Thanks.'

'When do you want to talk?'

Patrick rolled to his side and gazed past Sandy. There was nothing to look at but the wall, painted antiseptic white, but he wasn't looking at it. 'They tortured me, Sandy,' he said, his voice even quieter, and breaking.

'Who?'

'They taped wires to my body and shot current through me until I talked.'

Sandy stood and walked to the edge of the bed. He placed his hand on Patrick's shoulder. 'What did you tell them?'

'I don't know. I can't remember everything. They were shooting drugs in me. Here, look.' He lifted his left arm so Sandy could inspect the bruises.

Sandy found a switch and flipped on the table lamp so he could see. 'Good Lord,' he said.

'They kept on about the money,' Patrick said. 'I blacked out, then I came to and they shocked me some more. I'm afraid I told them about the girl, Sandy.'

'The lawyer?'

'Yeah, the lawyer. What name did she give you?'

'Leah.'

'Okay, good. Her name is Leah then. I might have told them about Leah. In fact, I'm almost certain I did.'

'Told who, Patrick?'

He closed his eyes and grimaced as the pain returned to his legs. The muscles were still raw and the cramping had begun. He gently rolled again and rested on his back. He pulled the sheet down to his waist. 'Look, Sandy,' he said, waving his hand across the two nasty burns on his chest. 'Here's the proof.'

Sandy leaned a bit closer and inspected the evidence – the red sores surrounded by shaved skin. 'Who did this?' he asked again.

'I don't know. A bunch of people. There was a whole room full of them.'

'Where?'

Patrick felt sorry for his friend. He was so eager to know what had happened, and not just about the torture. Sandy, as well as the rest of the world, wanted the irresistible details. It was indeed a wonderful story, but he wasn't sure how much he could tell. No one knew the details of the car crash that burned John Doe. But he could tell his lawyer and friend about his seizure and torture. He shifted his weight again and pulled the sheet up to his neck. Drug free for two days now, he was coping with the pain and trying mightily to avoid more injections. 'Pull that chair closer and take a seat, Sandy. And turn off that switch. The light bothers me.'

Sandy hurriedly followed orders. He sat as close to the bed as possible. 'This is what they did to me, Sandy,' Patrick said, in the semidarkness. He started in Ponta Porã, with the jogging and the small car with a flat tire, and told the entire story of how they grabbed him.

Ashley Nicole was twenty-five months old when her father was buried. She was too young to remember Patrick. Lance was the only man who lived in the house, the only man she'd ever seen with her mom. He took her to school occasionally. They sometimes ate dinner as a family.

After the funeral, Trudy hid all photos and other evidence of her life with Patrick. Ashley Nicole had never heard his name mentioned.

But after three days of reporters camping on their street, the child naturally was asking questions. Her mother was acting strange. There was so much tension around the house that even a six-year-old could feel it. Trudy waited until Lance left for a visit with the lawyer, then she sat her daughter on her bed for a little chat.

She began by admitting that she had been married before. Actually, she had been married twice before, but she figured Ashley Nicole wouldn't need to know about the first husband until she was much older. The second husband was the issue for the moment.

'Patrick and I were married for four years, and then he did a very bad thing.'

'What?' Ashley Nicole asked, wide-eyed and absorbing more than Trudy wanted.

'He killed a man, and he made it look like, well, there was a big car wreck, you see, a big fire, and it was Patrick's car, and the police found a body inside the

94

car, once the fire was out, and the police figured it was Patrick. Everybody did. Patrick was gone, burned up in his car, and I was very sad. He was my husband. I loved him dearly, and he was suddenly gone. We buried him in the cemetery. Now, four years later, they found Patrick off hiding on the other side of the world. He ran away and hid.'

'Why?'

'Because he stole a bunch of money from his friends, and since he's a very bad man he wanted to keep all of this money for himself.'

'He killed a man and he stole money.'

'That's right, honey. Patrick is not a nice person.'

'I'm sorry you were married to him, Mommy.'

'Yes. But look, honey, there's something you need to understand. You were born when Patrick and I were married.' She let the words drift through the air, and watched the little eyes to see if she caught the message. Evidently not. She squeezed Ashley Nicole's hand, and said, 'Patrick is your father.'

She looked blankly at her mother, the wheels turning rapidly in her head. 'But I don't want him to be —'

'I'm sorry, honey. I was gonna tell you when you were much older, but Patrick is about to come back now, and it's important for you to know.'

'What about Lance? Isn't he my father?'

'No. Lance and I are just together, that's all.' Trudy had never allowed her to refer to Lance as her father. And Lance, for his part, had never shown the slightest interest in approaching the arena of fatherhood. Trudy was a single mom. Ashley Nicole had no father. This was perfectly common and acceptable.

'Lance and I have been friends for a long time,' Trudy said, keeping the initiative and trying to prevent a thousand questions. 'Very close friends. He loves you very much, but he is not your father. Not your real father anyway. Patrick, I'm afraid, is your real father, but I don't want you to worry about him.'

'Does he want to see me?'

'I don't know, but I'll fight forever to keep him away from you. He is a very bad person, honey. He left you when you were two years old. He left me. He stole a bunch of money and disappeared. He didn't care about us then, and he doesn't care about us now. He wouldn't be coming back if they hadn't caught him. We would never have seen him again. So don't worry about Patrick and what he might do.'

Ashley Nicole crawled across the end of the bed and cuddled in her mother's lap. Trudy squeezed and patted her. 'It's going to be all right, honey. I promise. I hated to tell you this, but with all those reporters out there and all the stuff on television, well, I just thought it best.'

'Why are those people out there?' she asked, clutching her mother's arms.

'I don't know. I wish they would leave.'

'What do they want?'

'Pictures of you. Pictures of me. Pictures they can put in the newspapers when they talk about Patrick and all the bad things he's done.'

'So they're out there because of Patrick?'

'Yes, honey.'

She turned and looked at Trudy square in the eyes, and said, 'I hate Patrick.'

Trudy shook her head as if the child were naughty, then she clutched her tightly, and smiled.

Lance was born and raised on Point Cadet, an old fishing community on a small peninsula jutting into the Bay of Biloxi. The Point was a working neighborhood where the immigrants landed and the shrimpers lived. He grew up in the streets on the Point, and still had many friends there, one of whom was Cap. It was

Cap who had been behind the wheel of the van loaded with marijuana when the narcs stopped them. They had awakened Lance, who'd been asleep with his shotgun amid the thick blocks of cannabis. Cap and Lance had used the same lawyer, received the same sentence, and at nineteen been sent away together.

Cap ran a pub and loan-sharked money to cannery workers. Lance met him for a drink in the rear of the pub, something they tried to do at least once a month, though Cap saw less and less of Lance now that Trudy had become wealthy and they had moved to Mobile. His friend was troubled. Cap had read the papers, had in fact been waiting for Lance to appear with a long face, looking for a sympathetic ear.

They caught up on the gossip over beer – who had won how much at the casinos, where the newest crack source was, who was being shadowed by the DEA – the usual idle chitchat of small-time Coast crooks still dreaming of riches.

Cap despised Trudy, and in the past he had often laughed at Lance for trailing behind her wherever she might go. 'So how's the whore?' he asked.

'She's fine. Worried, you know, since they've caught him.'

'She oughta be worried. How much life insurance did she collect?'

'Coupla mill.'

'Paper said two point five. Way that bitch spends it, though, I'm sure there ain't much left.'

'It's safe.'

'Safe my ass. Paper said she's already been sued by the life insurance company.'

'We got lawyers too.'

'Yeah, but you ain't here 'cause you got lawyers, Lance, are you? You're here 'cause you need help. Lawyers can't do what she needs.'

Lance smiled and sipped his beer. He lit a cigarette,

something he could never do around Trudy. 'Where's Zeke?'

'That's exactly what I figured,' Cap said angrily. 'She gets in trouble, her money is threatened, and so she sends you down here looking for Zeke or some other klutz you can grease to do something stupid. He gets caught. You get caught. You take the fall and she forgets your name. You're a dumbass, Lance, you know that.'

'Yeah, I know. Where's Zeke?'

'In jail.'

'Where?'

'Texas. Feds got him running guns. You're stupid, you know that. Don't do this. When they bring your guy back, there'll be cops crawling all around him. They'll lock him away some place, his mother can't even get near him. There's serious money at stake here, Lance. They gotta protect this guy until he breaks and tells where he's buried it, you know. You try to hit him, and you'll kill half a dozen cops. And die tryin'.'

'Not if it's done right.'

'And I suppose you know how to do it. Could that be because you ain't ever done it before? When did you get so damned smart?'

'I can find the right people.'

'For how much?'

'Whatever it takes.'

'You got fifty grand?'

'Yeah.'

Cap took a deep breath and glanced around his pub. Then he leaned forward on his elbows and glared at his friend. 'Lemme tell you why it's a bad idea, Lance. You never were too bright, you know. Girls always liked you because they think you're cute, but thinking was never your strong suit.'

'Thanks, pal.'

'Everybody wants this guy alive. Think about it. Everybody. Feds. The lawyers. The cops. The guy whose money got stolen. Everybody. Except, of course, that fleabag who lets you live in her house. She needs him dead. If you pull this, and somehow knock him off, the cops go straight to her. She, of course, will be completely innocent because you'll be there to take the fall. That's what little stud puppies are for. He's dead. She keeps the money, which you and I know is the only thing that matters to her, and you go back to Parchman because you've got a record, remember? For the rest of your life. She won't even write you.'

'Can we get it done for fifty?'

'We?'

'Yeah. Me and you.'

'I can give you a name, that's all. I'm not touching this. It won't work, and there's nothing in it for me.'

'Who is it?'

'A guy from New Orleans. He hangs around here some.'

'Can you make the call?'

'Yeah, but that's it. And remember, I told you not to mess with this.'

TWELVE

Eva left Miami on a flight to New York where she
boarded the Concorde and flew to Paris. The Concorde was an extravagance, but she now considered
herself to be a wealthy woman. From Paris to Nice,
and from there across the countryside by car to Aix-
en-Provence, a journey she and Patrick had made
almost one year earlier. It was the only time he'd left
Brazil since he'd arrived. He was terrified of crossing
borders, even with a perfect new phony passport.

Brazilians love all things French, and virtually all
with education know the language and culture. They
had taken a suite at the Villa Gallici, a beautiful inn on
the edge of town, and spent a week strolling the
streets, shopping, eating, and occasionally venturing
into the villages between Aix and Avignon. They also
spent a lot of time in their room, like newlyweds.
Once, after too much wine, Patrick referred to it as
their honeymoon.

She found a smaller room at the same hotel, and after
a nap had tea on the patio in her bathrobe. Later, she
dressed in jeans and took a casual walk into town, to
the Cours Mirabeau, the main avenue of Aix. She
sipped a glass of red wine at a crowded sidewalk café
and watched the college kids parade back and forth.
She envied the young lovers strolling aimlessly hand in

hand, nothing to worry about. She and Patrick had made these walks, arm in arm, whispering and laughing as if the shadows behind him had vanished.

It was in Aix, during the only week they had ever spent together without interruption, that she first realized how little he slept. Regardless of when she awoke, he was already awake, lying still and quiet and staring at her as if she were in danger. A table lamp was on. The room would be dark when she fell asleep, but a light would be on when she awoke. He would turn it off, rub her gently until she fell asleep, then sleep himself for half an hour before turning the light on again. He was up well before dawn, and usually had read the newspapers and several chapters of a mystery by the time she ambled forth and found him on the patio.

'Never more than two hours,' he answered when she asked how long he could sleep. He seldom napped and never went to bed early.

He didn't carry a weapon or peek around corners. He wasn't overly suspicious of strangers. And he seldom talked about life on the run. Except for his sleeping habits, he seemed so perfectly normal that she often forgot he was one of the most wanted men in the world.

Though he preferred not to talk about his past, there were times in their conversations when it became unavoidable. They were together, after all, only because he had fled and re-created himself. His favorite topic was his boyhood in New Orleans; not the adult life he was running from. He almost never mentioned his wife, but Eva knew she was a person Patrick deeply despised. It had become a miserable marriage, and as it deteriorated he became determined to flee it.

He had tried to talk about Ashley Nicole, but the thought of the child brought tears to his eyes. His voice quit him, and he said he was sorry. It was too painful.

Because the past was not yet complete, the future was difficult to contemplate. Plans were impossible as long as shadows were moving back there somewhere. He would not allow himself to speculate on the future until the past was settled.

The shadows kept him awake, she knew that. Shadows he couldn't see. Shadows only he could feel.

They had met in her office, in Rio, two years earlier, when he presented himself as a Canadian businessman who now lived in Brazil. He said he needed a good lawyer to advise him on import and taxation matters. He was dressed for the part in a handsome linen suit with a white starched shirt. He was lean and tanned and friendly. His Portuguese was very good, though not as good as her English. He wanted to speak in her language; she insisted on his. They had a business lunch that lasted three hours, with the languages switching back and forth, and both realized there would be others. Then there was a long dinner, and a barefoot walk on the beach at Ipanema.

Her husband was an older man who'd been killed in a plane crash in Chile. No children. Patrick, or Danilo, as he was at first called, claimed to be happily divorced from his first wife, who still lived in Toronto, their home.

Eva and Danilo saw each other several times a week during the first two months, as the romance flourished. Finally, he told the truth. All of it.

After a late dinner in her apartment, and a bottle of good French wine, Danilo confronted his past and bared his soul. He talked nonstop until the early hours of the morning, and went from a confident businessman to a frightened man on the run. Frightened and anxious, but extremely wealthy.

102

The relief was so forceful he almost cried, but caught himself. This was, after all, Brazil, and men simply did not cry. Especially in front of beautiful women.

She loved him for it. She embraced him and kissed him and cried when he couldn't, and promised to do everything in her power to hide him. He had given her his darkest, deadliest secret, and she promised to always protect it.

During the next weeks, he told her where the money was and taught her how to move it quickly around the world. Together, they studied offshore tax havens and found safe investments.

He had been in Brazil for two years by the time they met. He had lived in São Paulo, his first home there, and Recife and Minas Gerais and half a dozen other places. He had spent two months working on the Amazon, sleeping on a floating barge under a thick mosquito net, the insects so thick he couldn't see the moon. He had cleaned wild game killed by rich Argentines in the Pantanal, a mammoth preserve the size of Great Britain in the states of Mato Grosso and Mato Grosso do Sul. He had seen more of her country than she; he'd been to places she'd never heard of. He had carefully selected Ponta Porã as his home. It was small and remote, and in a land of a million perfect hiding places, Danilo decided Ponta Porã was the safest. Plus, it had the tactical advantage of being on the Paraguayan border – an easy place to run to if a threat occurred.

She didn't argue with this. She preferred that he stay in Rio, close to her, but she knew nothing about life on the run, and she reluctantly deferred to his judgment. He promised many times that they would be together someday. They occasionally met at the apartment in Curitiba; brief little honeymoons that never lasted much more than a few days. She longed for more, but he was unwilling to make plans.

As the months passed, Danilo – she never called him Patrick – became more convinced that he would be found. She refused to believe this, especially given the meticulous steps he took to avoid his past. He worried more; slept even less; talked more about what she should do in this scenario, or that one. He stopped talking about the money. His premonitions were haunting him.

She would stay in Aix for a few days, watching CNN International and reading what she could find in American newspapers. They would move Patrick shortly, take him home and put him in jail and file all sorts of hideous charges against him. He knew he would be locked up, but he'd assured her he would be fine. He would cope; he could handle anything as long as she promised to wait for him.

She'd probably return to Zurich and tidy up her affairs. Beyond that, she wasn't certain. Home was out of the question, and this weighed heavy on her mind. She had talked to her father three times, always calling from airport pay phones, always reassuring him she was okay. She just couldn't come home now, she explained.

She and Patrick would communicate through Sandy, but weeks would pass before she would actually see him.

He called for the first pill just before 2 A.M., after waking with a sharp pain. It felt like the voltage returning to his legs. And the cruel voices of his captors were taunting him. 'Where's the money, Patrick?' they chanted like a demonic chorus. 'Where's the money?'

The pill arrived on a tray carried by a lethargic night

104

orderly who forgot to bring cold water. He demanded a glass, then swallowed the pill and washed it away with warm soda from a leftover can.

Ten minutes, and nothing happened. His body was covered with sweat. The sheets were drenched. The sores burned from the salt in the sweat. Another ten minutes. He turned on the television.

The men who had tied him down and burned him were still out there, looking for the money, no doubt fully aware of where he was at this moment. He felt safer in daylight. Darkness and dreams brought them back. Thirty minutes. He called the nurses' station, but no one answered.

He drifted away.

At six, he was awake when his doctor entered, smileless today, all business as he poked the wounds quickly, then declared, 'You're ready to go. They have good doctors waiting for you where you're going.' He scribbled in his chart and left without another word.

Thirty minutes later, Agent Brent Myers sauntered into the room with a nasty smile and a flash of the badge, as if he needed to practice its delivery. 'Good morning,' he said. Patrick didn't look at him, but said, 'Couldn't you knock first?'

'Sure, sorry. Look, Patrick, I just talked to your doc. Great news, man, you're going home. You'll be released tomorrow. I've got orders to bring you back. We'll leave in the morning. Your government is giving you a special flight back to Biloxi on a military plane. Isn't that exciting? And I'll be with you.'

'Could you leave now?'

'Sure. See you early in the morning.'

'Just leave.'

He bounced from the room and closed the door. Luis was next, arriving quietly with a tray of coffee and juice and sliced mangoes. He slid a package under

105

Patrick's mattress, and asked if he needed anything else. No, Patrick said, thanking him softly.

An hour later, Sandy arrived for what he thought would be a long day of digging through the past four years and finding answers to his countless questions. The television went off, the shades opened, the room brightened up as the day began.

'I want you to go home, immediately,' Patrick said. 'And take these with you.' He handed over the package. Sandy sat in the only chair, flipping through the photos of his naked friend, taking his time.

'When were these taken?' he asked.

'Yesterday.' Sandy made a note of this on a yellow legal pad.

'By whom?'

'Luis, the orderly.'

'Who did this to you?'

'Who has custody of me, Sandy?'

'The FBI.'

'So, I think the FBI did it to me. My own government tracked me down, caught me, tortured me, and is now hauling me back. The government Sandy. The FBI, Justice Department, and the locals – the D.A. and the rest of my welcoming party. Just look at what they've done to me.'

'They should be sued for this,' Sandy said.

'For millions. And quickly. Here's the plan: I'm leaving in the morning on some type of military flight to Biloxi. You can imagine the reception I'll get. We should take advantage of it.'

'Take advantage?'

'Exactly. We should file our lawsuit late this afternoon so it'll be in the paper tomorrow. Leak it to the press. Show them two of the photos, the two I've got marked there on the back.'

Sandy shuffled until he picked out the photos. One was a close-up of the burns on Patrick's chest, with his

106

face visible. The other showed the third-degree burn on his left thigh. 'You want me to give these to the press?'

'Only to the Coast paper. That's the only one I'm worried about. It's read by eighty percent of Harrison County, where I'm sure our jury will come from.'

Sandy smiled, then chuckled. 'You didn't sleep much last night, did you?'

'I haven't slept in four years.'

'This is brilliant.'

'No, but it's one of the few tactical advantages we can spring on those hyenas circling my carcass. We broadside them with this, and we soften up the sentiment a bit. Think of it, Sandy. The FBI torturing a suspect, an American citizen.'

'Brilliant, just brilliant. We sue only the FBI?'

'Yes, keep it simple. Me versus the FBI, the government – for permanent physical and psychological injuries sustained during a brutal torture and interrogation session somewhere in the jungles of Brazil.'

'Sounds wonderful to me.'

'It'll sound even better when the press gets finished with it.'

'How much?'

'I don't care. Ten million in actual damages, a hundred million in punitive.'

Sandy scrawled notes and flipped to the next page. Then he stopped and studied Patrick's face. 'It wasn't really the FBI, was it.'

'No,' Patrick said, 'it wasn't. I was delivered to the FBI by some faceless thugs who've been chasing me for a long time. And they're still lurking out there somewhere.'

'Does the FBI know about them?'

'Yes.'

The room went silent, as Sandy waited for more and

Patrick became tight-lipped. Nurses could be heard prattling in the hallway.

Patrick shifted his weight. Three days on his back, and he was ready for a change of scenery. 'You need to hurry home, Sandy. We'll have plenty of time to talk later. I know you have questions, just give me some time.'

'Okay, pal.'

'File the lawsuit with as much noise as possible. We can always amend it later to bring in the real defendants.'

'No problem. This won't be the first time I've sued the wrong defendants.'

'It's strategy. A little sympathy won't hurt.'

Sandy placed his legal pad and the photos into his briefcase.

'Be careful,' Patrick said. 'As soon as you're identified as my lawyer, you'll attract all sorts of strange and nasty people.'

'The press?'

'Yeah, but not exactly what I had in mind. I've buried a lot of money, Sandy. There are people who'll do anything to find it.'

'How much of the money is left?'

'All of it. And then some more.'

'It may take that to save you, pal.'

'I have a plan.'

'I'm sure you do. See you in Biloxi.'

THIRTEEN

Through the vast web of leaks and sources, word came that yet another lawsuit would be filed late in the day, just before the clerk closed her office. The web had already been electrified with the confirmed reports that Patrick himself would be arriving around noon tomorrow.

Sandy asked the reporters to wait in the foyer of the courthouse while he filed the suit. He then distributed copies to the dozen or so bloodhounds gathered and jostling for position. Most were newspaper reporters. There were two minicams. One radio station.

At first, it appeared to be just another lawsuit, filed by another lawyer anxious to see his face in print. Things changed dramatically when Sandy announced he represented Patrick Lanigan. The crowd grew and bunched together curious office clerks, local lawyers, even a janitor stopped to listen. Calmly, he informed them that his client was filing suit against the FBI for physical abuse and torture.

Sandy took his time with the allegations, then answered the barrage of questions thoughtfully, fully, looking directly at the cameras. He saved the best for last. He reached into his briefcase and removed the two color photos, now enlarged to twelve by sixteen inches, and mounted on foam board. 'This is what they did to Patrick,' he said dramatically.

The cameras lunged in for close-ups. The group teetered on the verge of unruliness.

'They drugged him, then stuck wires to his body. They tortured him until his flesh burned because he wouldn't, and couldn't, answer their questions. This is your government at work, ladies and gentlemen, torturing an American citizen. Government thugs who call themselves FBI agents.'

Even the most jaded reporters were shocked. It was a splendid performance.

The Biloxi affiliate ran it at six, after announcing it with a sensational lead-in. Almost half the newscast was Sandy and the photos. The other half was Patrick's return tomorrow.

By early evening, CNN began running it every half-hour, and Sandy was the lawyer of the moment. The allegations were just too juicy to downplay.

Hamilton Jaynes was enjoying a quiet drink with the boys in the lounge of a posh country club near Alexandria when he saw the news clip on a corner TV. He had played eighteen holes, during which he had forbidden himself from thinking about the Bureau and the countless headaches there.

Another headache had just found him. The FBI sued by Patrick Lanigan? He excused himself and walked to the empty bar where he punched numbers on his cell phone.

Deep inside the Hoover Building on Pennsylvania Avenue is a hallway lined with windowless rooms where technicians monitor television news broadcasts from around the world. In another set of rooms they listen to and record radio news programs. In another, they read magazines and newspapers. Within the Bureau, the entire operation is known simply as Accumulation.

Jaynes called the supervisor on duty in Accumulation, and within minutes had the full story. He left the country club and drove back to his office, on the third floor of the Hoover Building. He called the Attorney General, who, not surprisingly, had been trying to reach him. A vicious ass-chewing ensued, with Jaynes on the receiving end and being allowed to say little. He did manage to reassure the Attorney General that the FBI had absolutely nothing to do with the alleged abuse of Patrick Lanigan.

'Alleged?' asked the Attorney General. 'I've seen the burns, haven't I! Hell, the whole world has seen the burns.'

'We didn't do it, sir,' Jaynes said calmly, armed with the knowledge that this time he was repeating the truth.

'Then who did?' the Attorney General snapped back. 'Do you know who did?'

'Yes sir.'

'Good. I want a three-page report on my desk at nine in the morning.'

'It will be there.'

The phone was hung up loudly on the other end, and Jaynes cursed and gave his desk a hard kick. Then he made another call, the effect of which was that two agents emerged from the darkness and stood before the front door of Mr and Mrs Jack Stephano.

Jack had watched the reports throughout the night, and was not surprised to get a reaction from the feds. As the story unfolded, he sat on the patio chatting with his lawyer on a cell phone. It was actually funny, he'd decided; the FBI getting blamed for acts committed by his men. And it was a brilliant move by Patrick Lanigan and his lawyer.

'Good evening,' he said politely as he stood in the door. 'Lemme guess. You're selling doughnuts.'

'FBI, sir,' one said, fumbling for his pocket.

'Save it, kid. I recognize you boys by now. Last time I saw you, you were parked down at the corner reading a tabloid and trying to duck behind your steering wheel. Did you honestly think you'd be doing such exciting work when you were in college?'

'Mr Jaynes would like to see you,' the second one said.

'Why?'

'Don't know. He told us to come get you. He wants you to ride with us to his office.'

'So Hamilton is working late, is he?'

'Yes sir. Can you come with us?'

'Are you arresting me again?'

'Well, no.'

'Then what exactly are you doing? I have lots of lawyers, you know. Wrongful arrest or detention, and you boys could get yourselves sued.'

They looked at each other nervously.

Stephano was not afraid of meeting with Jaynes, or anybody else for that matter. He could certainly handle anything Jaynes could throw at him.

But he reminded himself that there were criminal charges pending against him. A little cooperation might help.

'Give me five minutes,' he said, then disappeared inside.

Jaynes stood behind his desk holding a thick report and flipping its pages when Stephano entered. 'Have a seat,' he said abruptly, waving at the chairs opposite his desk. It was almost midnight.

'A pleasant evening to you, Hamilton,' Stephano said with a grin.

Jaynes dropped the report. 'What on earth did you do to that boy down there?'

'I don't know. I guess one of the Brazilian boys got a little rough. He'll survive.'

'Who did it?'

'Do I need my lawyer here, Hamilton? Is this an interrogation?'

'I'm not sure what this is, okay? The Director is at home, on the phone, consulting with the Attorney General, who by the way is not taking this very well, and they call me every twenty minutes and peel off some more skin. This is serious stuff, okay, Jack? These allegations are hideous, and right now the whole country is looking at those damned pictures and wondering why we tortured an American citizen.'

'I'm terribly sorry.'

'I can tell. Now, who did it?'

'Some locals down there. A gang of Brazilians we hired when we got a tip he was there. I don't even know their names.'

'Where'd the tip come from?'

'Wouldn't you like to know?'

'Yes, I would.' Jaynes loosened his tie and sat on the edge of his desk, looking down at Stephano, who was looking up without the slightest trace of concern. He could bargain his way out of any trouble the FBI might send him. He had very good lawyers.

'I have a deal for you,' Jaynes said. 'And this just came down from the Director.'

'I can't wait.'

'We're prepared to arrest Benny Aricia tomorrow. We'll make a big deal out of it, leak it to the press and all, tell them how this guy who lost ninety million hired you to track down Lanigan. And when you caught him, you worked him over but still didn't find the money.'

Stephano listened hard, but revealed nothing.

'Then we'll arrest the two CEO's – Atterson at Monarch-Sierra Insurance and Jill at Northern Case Mutual. Those are the other two members of your little consortium, as we understand it. We'll march into their fancy offices with storm troopers, cameras won't be far behind, and we'll haul them out in handcuffs and throw them in black vans. Lots of leaks to the media, you understand. And we'll make sure that it's well reported that these guys helped Aricia fund your little mission into Brazil to drag out Patrick. Think of it, Stephano, your clients will all be arrested and placed in jail.'

Stephano wanted to ask just exactly how in hell the FBI identified the members of his little Patrick consortium, but then he figured it wasn't too difficult. They isolated the people who'd lost the most.

'It'll kill your business, you know,' Jaynes said, feigning sympathy.

'So what do you want?'

'Well, here's the deal. It's quite simple. You tell us everything – how you found him, how much he told you, etc., everything. We have lots of questions – and we'll drop the charges against you and lay off your clients.'

'It's nothing but harassment then.'

'Exactly. We wrote the book. Your problem is that we can humiliate your clients and put you out of business.'

'Is that all?'

'No. With a bit of luck on our end, you could also go to jail.'

There were lots of reasons to grab this deal, not the least of which was Mrs Stephano. She felt disgraced because word was out the FBI was watching her house at all hours. Her phones were bugged; she knew this for a fact because her husband made his calls in the backyard near the rosebushes. She was on the verge of a nervous breakdown. They were respectable people, she kept telling her husband.

By implying he knew more than he did, Stephano had placed the FBI precisely where he wanted them.

114

He could get his charges dismissed. He could protect his clients. And, most importantly, he would enlist the considerable resources of the feds to track down the money.

'I'll have to talk to my attorney.'

'You have until 5 P.M. tomorrow.'

Patrick saw his ghastly wounds on a late edition of CNN, in full color, as his man Sandy waved the pictures around like a boxer showing the world his newly won belt. It was about halfway through an hour wrap-up of the day's stories. There was no official response from the FBI, said a correspondent who was poised outside the Hoover Building in Washington.

Luis happened to be in the room when the report ran. He froze, listening to it, looking from the television to the bed where Patrick sat smirking. Things connected quickly. 'My pictures?' he asked in heavily accented English.

'Yes,' Patrick replied, ready to laugh.

'My pictures,' he repeated proudly.

The story about the American lawyer who faked his death, watched his burial, stole ninety million from his firm and got caught four years later living quietly in Brazil made for good light reading in most of the Western world. Eva read the latest episode in an American paper while sipping coffee under a canopy at Les Deux Garçons, her favorite sidewalk café in Aix. It was raining, a steady mist that soaked the tables and chairs not far from her.

The story was buried deep inside the front section. It described third-degree burns but did not run the photos. Her heart broke and she put on sunglasses to hide her eyes.

Patrick was going home. Wounded and chained like an animal, he would make the one journey he always knew was inevitable. And she would go. She would linger in the background, hiding and doing what he wanted, and praying for the safety of both of them. She would roam her room at night, just like Patrick, asking herself what had become of their future.

FOURTEEN

For his return home, Patrick chose a pair of aqua surgeon's scrubs, very baggy and loose-fitting because he wanted nothing to aggravate his burns. The flight would be nonstop, but still more than two hours, and he needed to be as comfortable as possible. The doctor gave him a small bottle of pain pills, just in case, and also a file with his medical records. Patrick thanked him. He shook hands with Luis and said good-bye to a nurse.

Agent Myers waited outside his door with four large uniformed Military Police. 'I'll make a deal with you, Patrick,' he said. 'If you behave, no handcuffs and leg chains now. Once we land, though, I have no choice.'

'Thanks,' Patrick said, and began walking gingerly down the hallway. His legs ached from toe to hip, and his knees were weak from lack of use. He held his head high, shoulders back, and nodded politely to the nurses as he walked past. Down the elevator to the basement, where a blue van waited with two more MP's, armed and scowling at the empty cars parked nearby. A strong hand under the arm, and Patrick was helped up and onto the middle bench. An MP handed him a pair of cheap aviator sunglasses. 'You'll need these,' he said. 'It's bright as hell out there.'

The van never left the base. It moved slowly over blistering asphalt, through half-guarded checkpoints, never reaching thirty miles per hour. Not a word was spoken inside the van. Patrick looked through the thick shades and through the tinted windows at rows of barracks, then rows of offices, then a hangar. He had been there four days, he thought. Maybe three. He couldn't be sure because the drugs blurred the earlier hours. An air conditioner roared from the dash and kept them cool. He gripped his medical file, the only physical thing he owned at the moment.

He thought of Ponta Porã, his home now, and wondered if he had been missed. What had they done to his house? Was the maid cleaning it? Probably not. And what about his car, the little red Beetle he loved so much? He knew only a handful of people in town. What were they saying about him? Probably nothing.

What difference did it make now? Regardless of the gossip in Ponta Porã, the folks in Biloxi had certainly missed him. The prodigal son returns. The most famous Biloxian on the planet comes home, and how will they greet him? With leg chains and subpoenas. Why not a parade down Highway 90, along the Coast, to celebrate this local boy who made good? He put them on the map; he made their town famous. How many of them had been shrewd enough to own ninety million dollars?

He almost chuckled at his own silliness.

What jail would they put him in? As a lawyer, he had, at various times, seen all the local jails – City of Biloxi, Harrison County, even a federal holding cell at Keesler Air Force Base in Biloxi. He wouldn't be that lucky.

Would he get a cell to himself, or share it with common thieves and crackheads? An idea hit. He opened the file and quickly scanned the doctor's release notes. There it was, in bold letters –

PATIENT SHOULD REMAIN HOSPITALIZED
FOR AT LEAST ANOTHER WEEK

God bless him! Why hadn't he thought of this before? The drugs. His poor system had been subjected to more narcotics in the past week than he'd taken in a lifetime. His lapses in memory and judgment could be blamed on the chemicals.

He needed desperately to get a copy of his release to Sandy so that a nice little bed could be prepared for him, preferably in a private room with nurses running back and forth. That was the incarceration he had in mind. Put ten cops by the door, he didn't care. Just fix him up with an adjustable bed and remote control, and by all means keep him away from the common criminals.

'I need to make a phone call,' he said, past the MP's, in the general direction of the driver. There was no response.

They stopped at a large hangar with a cargo jet parked in front of it. The MP's waited outside, in the sun, while Patrick and Agent Myers went inside the small office and haggled over whether there existed a constitutional right for an accused to not only make a phone call to his attorney but also to fax along a document.

Patrick prevailed after calmly threatening all sorts of vile litigation against Brent, and the doctor's release instructions were faxed to the law office of Sandy McDermott in New Orleans.

After a long visit to the men's room, Patrick rejoined his escorts and slowly climbed the steps into the Air Force cargo plane.

It landed at Keesler Air Force Base at twenty minutes before noon. Much to Patrick's surprise, and a little to his dismay, there were no festivities awaiting his arrival. No throng of cameras and reporters. No mob

119

of old friends rushing forth to offer assistance in his hour of need.

The landing field had been sealed off for the moment by higher orders. The press had been excluded. A large group congregated near the front gate, a mile and a half away, and for good measure taped and photographed the plane as it flew over. They were greatly disappointed, too.

Frankly, Patrick wanted the press to see him as he emerged from the plane in his carefully selected surgeon's scrubs, and awkwardly limped his way down the steps to the tarmac, and then shuffled like a crippled dog in leg chains and handcuffs. It could have been a powerful image, the first seen by all those potential jurors out there.

As expected, the Coast's morning paper had run the story of his lawsuit against the FBI on the front page, as the lead story, with the pictures large and in color. Only the meanest of souls couldn't muster a trace of sympathy for Patrick, at least at this moment. The other side – the government, the prosecutors, the investigators – had been softened by the blow. It was to have been a glorious day for law enforcement; the return of a master thief, and a lawyer at that! Instead, the local office of the FBI had its phones unplugged and doors locked to keep reporters out. Only Cutter ventured forth, and he did so secretively. It was his duty to meet Patrick as soon as he touched ground.

Cutter was waiting with Sheriff Sweeney, two Air Force officers from the base, and Sandy.

'Hello, Patrick. Welcome home,' the Sheriff said.

Patrick extended his hands, cuffed at the wrist, and tried to shake hands. 'Hello, Raymond,' he answered with a smile. They knew each other well, a common acquaintance between local cops and local lawyers. Raymond Sweeney had been the chief deputy of

Harrison County nine years earlier when Patrick arrived in town.

Cutter stepped forward to introduce himself, but as soon as Patrick heard 'FBI' he turned his face and nodded at Sandy. A navy van, one remarkably similar to the van that had just deposited him at the plane in Puerto Rico, was nearby. They piled in, with Patrick in the back next to his lawyer.

'Where are we going?' Patrick whispered.

'To the base hospital,' Sandy whispered back. 'For medical reasons.'

'Good job.'

The van puttered along at a snail's pace, past a checkpoint where the guard lifted his eyes from the sports page just for a second, then down a quiet street with officers' quarters on both sides.

Life on the run was filled with dreams, some at night during sleep, real dreams, and some when the mind was awake but drifting. Most were terrifying, the nightmares of the shadows growing bolder and larger. Others were pleasant wishes of a rosy future, free of the past. These were rare, Patrick had learned. Life on the run was life in the past. There was no closure.

Other dreams were intriguing musings of the return home. Who would be there to greet him? Would the Gulf air feel and smell the same? When would he return, in what season? How many friends would seek him, and how many would avoid him? He could think of a handful of people he wanted to see, but he was not sure if they wanted to see him. Was he a leper now? Or a celebrity to be embraced? Probably neither.

There was a certain, very small comfort in the end of the chase. Horrendous problems lay ahead, but for now he could ignore what was behind. The truth was, Patrick had never been able to completely relax and enjoy his new life. Not even the money could calm his fears. This very day was inevitable; he'd known it all along. He had stolen too much money. A lot less, and the victims might not have been so determined.

He noticed small things as he rode along. The driveways were paved, which was quite rare in Brazil, at least in Ponta Porã. And the children wore sneakers as they played. In Brazil, they were always barefoot, the soles of their feet as tough as rubber. He suddenly missed his quiet street, Rua Tiradentes, with the groups of boys dribbling soccer balls in search of a game.

'Are you okay?' Sandy asked.

He nodded, still wearing the aviator shades.

Sandy reached into his briefcase and removed a copy of the Coast paper. The headline screamed,

LANIGAN SUES FBI FOR TORTURE AND ABUSE

The two photos consumed half the front page.

Patrick admired it for a moment. 'I'll read it later.'

Cutter sat directly in front of Patrick, and of course he was listening to his prisoner breathe. Conversation was out of the question, which suited Patrick fine. The van entered the parking lot of the base hospital, and stopped at the emergency entrance. They took Patrick through a service door, then along a hallway where the nurses were waiting for a quick inspection of their new patient. Two lab technicians stopped ahead of them, and one actually said, 'Welcome home, Patrick.' A real smartass.

No red tape here. No preadmission forms. No questions about insurance or who's paying for what. He was taken straight to the third floor and placed in a room at the end of the hall. Cutter had a few banal comments and instructions, as did the Sheriff. Limited phone use, guards by the door, meals in the room. What else can you say to a prisoner? They left, and only Sandy remained.

Patrick sat on the edge of his bed, his feet dangling. 'I'd like to see my mother,' he said.

'She's on her way. She'll be here at one.'

'Thanks.'

'What about your wife and daughter?'

'I'd like to see Ashley Nicole, but not now. I'm sure she doesn't remember me. By now, she thinks I'm a monster. For obvious reasons, I'd rather not see Trudy.'

There was a loud knock on the door, and Sheriff Sweeney was back, now holding a rather thick stack of papers. 'Sorry to disturb, Patrick, but this is business. I thought it best to get this over with.'

'Sure, Sheriff,' Patrick said, bracing for the onslaught.

'I need to serve these on you. First, this here is an indictment returned by the grand jury of Harrison County for capital murder.'

Patrick took it and, without looking at it, handed it to Sandy.

'This here is a summons and a complaint for divorce, filed by Trudy Lanigan over in Mobile.'

'What a surprise,' Patrick said, as he took it. 'On what grounds?'

'I haven't read it. This is a summons and complaint filed by a Mr Benjamin Aricia.'

'Who?' Patrick asked, in a flat effort at humor. The Sheriff didn't crack a smile.

'This is a summons and complaint filed by your old law firm.'

'How much are they after?' Patrick asked, taking the summons and complaint.

'I haven't read it. This is a summons and complaint filed by Monarch-Sierra Insurance Company.'

'Oh yes. I remember those boys.' He passed it to Sandy, whose hands were now full while the Sheriff's were empty.

'Sorry, Patrick,' Sweeney said.

'Is that all?'

'For now. I'll stop by the clerk's office in town to see if any more suits have been filed.'

'Send 'em over. Sandy here works fast.'

They shook hands, this time without the intrusion of cuffs, and the Sheriff left.

'I always liked Raymond,' Patrick said, hands on hips, slowly bending at the knees. He made it halfway down before stopping and easing up. 'A long way to go, Sandy. I'm bruised to the bone.'

'Great. Helps our lawsuit.' Sandy flipped through the papers. 'Seems Trudy is really upset with you. She wants you out of her life.'

'I've tried my best. What are the grounds?'

'Abandonment and desertion. Mental cruelty.'

'Poor thing.'

'Are you planning to contest it?'

'Depends on what she wants.'

Sandy flipped another page. 'Well, just scanning here, it appears she wants a divorce, full custody of the child with the termination of all your parental rights, including the right of visitation, all real and personal property jointly owned at the time of your disappearance – that's what she's calling it, your disappearance – plus, oh yes, here it is, a fair and reasonable percentage of the assets you may have acquired since your disappearance.'

'Surprise, surprise.'

'That's all she wants, for now anyway.'

'I'll give her the divorce, Sandy, and gladly. But it won't be as easy as she thinks.'

'What do you have in mind?'

'We'll talk about it later. I'm tired.'

'We have to talk sometime, Patrick. Whether you realize it or not, we have many things to discuss.'

'Later. I need to rest now. Mom will be here in a minute.'

'Fine. By the time I drive, fight New Orleans traffic, park and walk, it takes two hours to get from here to my office. When, exactly, might you want to meet again?'

'I'm sorry, Sandy. I'm tired, okay? How about tomorrow morning? I'll get rested up, and we'll work all day.'

Sandy relaxed and placed the papers in his brief-case. 'Sure, pal. I'll be here at ten.'

'Thanks, Sandy.'

He left, and Patrick rested comfortably for about eight minutes before his room was suddenly filled with all sorts of health care professionals, an all-female team. 'Hi, I'm Rose, your head nurse. We need to examine you. Can we take off your shirt here?' It was not a request. Rose was already pulling on the shirt. Two other nurses, equally as thick as Rose, appeared on each side and began to undress Patrick. They seemed to enjoy it. Another nurse stood ready with a thermometer and a box of other dreadful instruments. A technician of some variety gawked from the end of the bed. An orderly in an orange coat hovered near the door.

They had invaded as a team, and for fifteen minutes performed various tasks upon his body. He closed his eyes and simply took it. They left as fast as they had come.

Patrick and his mother had a tearful reunion. He apologized only once, for everything. She lovingly accepted, and forgave him, as only a mother can do. Her joy at seeing him displaced any ill will and bitterness that had naturally crept up during the past four days.

Joyce Lanigan was sixty-eight years old, in reasonably good health with only high blood pressure to struggle with. Her husband, Patrick's father, had left her for a younger woman twenty years earlier, then promptly died of a heart attack. Neither she nor Patrick attended his funeral in Texas. The second wife was pregnant at the time. Her child, Patrick's half brother, killed two undercover narcotics officers when he was seventeen, and now sat on death row in Huntsville, Texas. This little bit of dirty family laundry was unknown in New Orleans and Biloxi. Patrick had never told Trudy, his wife of four years. Nor had he told Eva. Why should he?

What a cruel twist. Both sons of Patrick's father were now charged with capital murder. One had been convicted. The other was well on his way.

Patrick was in college when his father left, then died. His mother adjusted badly to the life of a divorced middle-aged woman with no professional skills and no history of employment. The divorce settlement allowed her to keep the house and provided her with barely enough money to live on without having to find a job. She occasionally worked as a substitute teacher in a local elementary school, but she preferred to stay at home, puttering in the garden, watching soap operas, drinking tea with old ladies in the neighborhood.

Patrick had always found his mother to be a depressing person, especially after his father left, an event that didn't particularly bother him because he wasn't much of a father anyway. And he wasn't much of a husband either. Patrick had encouraged his mother to get out of the house, find a job, find a cause, live a little. She had a new lease on life.

But she enjoyed the misery too much. Over the years, as Patrick got busier and busier with his lawyering, he spent less time with her. He moved to

Biloxi, married a woman his mother couldn't tolerate, and on and on.

He asked about aunts and uncles and cousins, people he had lost contact with long before his death; people he had hardly thought of in the past four years. He asked only because he was expected to ask. For the most part, they were doing fine.

No, he did not want to see any of them.

They were anxious to see him.

Odd. They'd never been anxious to see him before.

They were very concerned about him.

Odd, too.

They chatted warmly for two hours, and the passage of time was quickly erased. She scolded him about his weight. 'Sickly' was her word. She quizzed him about his new chin and nose, and his dark hair. She said all sorts of motherly things, then she left for New Orleans. He promised to keep in touch.

He had always promised that, she thought to herself as she drove away. But he'd rarely kept in touch.

FIFTEEN

Operating from a suite at the Hay-Adams Hotel, Stephano spent the morning playing telephone tag with harried corporate executives. It had been easy to convince Benny Aricia that he was about to be arrested, photographed, printed, and otherwise harassed by the FBI. Convincing egos like Paul Atterson at Monarch-Sierra Insurance and Frank Jill at Northern Case Mutual was another matter. Both were typical CEO's, serious white men with huge salaries and large staffs to keep away anything unpleasant. Arrests and prosecutions were for the lower classes.

The FBI proved quite helpful. Hamilton Jaynes dispatched agents to both headquarters – Monarch's in Palo Alto and Northern Case Mutual's in St Paul – with instructions to call on both men and ask a bunch of questions about the search and capture of one Patrick Lanigan.

Both threw in the towel by lunch. Call off the dogs, they said to Stephano. The search is over. Cooperate fully with the FBI, and for heaven's sakes do something to get these agents out of our headquarters. It was very embarrassing.

And so the consortium unraveled. Stephano had kept it together for four years, and in doing so earned himself almost a million dollars. He'd spent another 2.5 million of his clients', and he could claim success.

They'd found Lanigan. They had not found the ninety million, but it was still around. It had not been spent. There was a chance of recouping it.

Benny Aricia was in the suite with Stephano throughout the morning, reading papers, making calls of his own, listening as Stephano worked the phones. At one, he called his attorney in Biloxi and got the news that Patrick had arrived. And amid almost no fanfare. The local TV ran the story at noon, complete with a shot of the Air Force cargo plane roaring overhead as it landed at Keesler. That was as close as they were allowed. The local Sheriff confirmed that the boy was back.

He had listened to the torture tape three times, often stopping it to replay his favorite spots. Once, two days ago on a flight to Florida, he had listened to it with earphones as he sipped a drink in first class and smiled at the blood-curdling sounds of a man begging for mercy. But the smiles were rare for Benny these days. He was certain Patrick had told what he knew, and it wasn't enough. Patrick knew he would someday get caught; that's why he shrewdly placed the money with the girl, who then hid it from everyone, including Patrick. Brilliant. Nothing short of it.

'What will it take to find her?' he asked Stephano, as the two lunched on soup sent up by room service. The question had been asked many times already.

'What, or how much?'

'How much, I guess.'

'Can't answer that. We have no idea where she is, but we know where she's from. And we know she'll likely surface somewhere around Biloxi, now that her man's there. It can be done.'

'How much?'

'Just guessing, I'd say a hundred thousand, with no

guarantees. Put up the money, and when it's gone, we quit.'

'Any chance the feds will know we're still looking?'

'Nope.'

Benny stirred his soup – tomatoes and noodles. Down one point nine million already, it seemed foolish not to give it one last shot. The odds were long, but the reward could be enormous. It was the same game he'd played for four years now.

'And if you find her?' he asked.

'We'll make her talk,' Stephano said, and they exchanged grimaces at the unpleasant thought of doing to a woman what they'd done to Patrick.

'What about his lawyer?' Aricia finally asked. 'Can't we bug his office, tap his phones, somehow listen in when he talks to his client. Surely they'll talk about my money.'

'It's a possibility. Are you serious?'

'Serious? I got ninety million out there, Jack. Minus a third for those bloodsucking lawyers. Of course I'm serious.'

'It could be tricky. The lawyer's not stupid, you know. And his client's a cautious fellow.'

'Come on, Jack. You're supposed to be the best. You're certainly the most expensive.'

'We'll do a preliminary – trail him for a couple of days, see his layout. There's no rush. His client isn't moving for a while. Right now I'm more concerned with getting the feds outta my hair. I need to do a few trivial things like reopen my office and get the bugs outta my phones.'

Aricia waved him off. 'How much will it cost me?'

'I don't know. We'll talk about it later. Finish your lunch. The lawyers are waiting.'

Stephano left first, on foot, and waved politely to the two agents parked illegally on I Street, down from the hotel. He walked briskly to his lawyer's office, seven blocks away. Benny waited ten minutes and caught a cab.

They spent the afternoon in a conference room crowded with lawyers and paralegals. The agreements were faxed back and forth between the lawyers – Stephano's and the FBI's. Eventually both sides got what they wanted. The criminal charges against Stephano were dropped and would not be pursued against his clients. The FBI received his written promise to divulge everything he knew about the search and capture of Patrick Lanigan.

Stephano truly planned to tell most of what he knew. The search was over; thus there was no longer anything to hide. The interrogation had produced little, just the name of a Brazilian lawyer who had the money. Now she had vanished, and he seriously doubted the FBI had the time and desire to pursue her. Why should they? The money didn't belong to them.

And though he worked hard not to show it, he desperately wanted the FBI out of his life. Mrs Stephano was severely rattled, and the pressure at home was enormous. If he didn't reopen his office quickly, he'd be out of business.

So, he planned to tell them what they wanted to hear, most of it anyway. He'd take Benny's money, what was left of it, and chase the girl some more, maybe get lucky. And he'd send a crew to New Orleans to watch Lanigan's lawyer. The FBI didn't need to know these little details.

Since there wasn't an available square inch in the federal building in Biloxi, Cutter asked Sheriff Sweeney to find a spot at the county jail. Sweeney reluctantly agreed, though the idea of the FBI spending time in his offices was unsettling. He cleaned out a storage room and installed a table and some chairs. The Lanigan Room was christened.

There was little to store there. No one suspected murder when Patrick died, and so there was no effort at gathering physical clues, at least not for the first six weeks. When the money vanished, suspicions grew, but by then the trail was cold.

Cutter and Ted Grimshaw, the chief investigator for Harrison County, carefully examined and inventoried their meager evidence. There were ten large color photos of the burned-out Chevy Blazer, and they tacked these on one wall. They had been taken by Grimshaw.

The fire had been extremely hot; now they knew why. Patrick no doubt had loaded the interior with plastic containers of gasoline. That would account for the melted aluminum seat frames, the blown-out windows, the disintegrated dashboard, and the scant remains of the body. Six photos were of the corpse, such as it was – a small pile of charred matter with half a pelvic bone protruding. It had come to rest on the floorboard of the passenger's side. The Blazer had flipped several times after it left the highway and barreled down a ravine. It burned on its right side.

Sheriff Sweeney had kept it for a month, then sold it for scrap with three other abandoned wrecks. Later, he wished he hadn't.

There were half a dozen photos of the site around the vehicle, trees and shrubs burned black. The volunteers had fought the fire for an hour before extinguishing it.

How convenient that Patrick wanted to be cremated. According to Trudy (and they had a typed statement given by her a month after the funeral), Patrick had suddenly decided he wanted to be cremated with his ashes buried in Locust Grove, the loveliest cemetery in the county. This decision was made almost eleven months before he disappeared. He'd even changed his will and included language directing his executor, Trudy, or in the event she died with him his alternate executor, Karl Huskey, to carry out the cremation. He also included specific details about his funeral and burial.

His excuse for doing this had been the death of a client who had not planned well. The family had fought viciously about how to bury the client, and Patrick had been pulled into the fray. He even made Trudy pick out her cemetery plot. She picked one next to his, but both knew she would quickly move it if something happened to him first.

The mortician later told Grimshaw that ninety percent of the cremating had been done in the Blazer. When he weighed the ashes after cooking the remains for an hour at two thousand degrees, the scales registered just four ounces, by far the smallest amount he'd ever registered. He could tell nothing about the body – male, female, black, white, young, old, alive or dead before the fire. There was simply no way. He didn't really try, to be honest about the whole thing.

They had no corpse, no autopsy report, no idea who John Doe was. Fire is the surest way to destroy evidence, and Patrick had done a splendid job of covering his tracks.

He'd spent the weekend in an old hunting cabin near the small town of Leaf, up in Greene County, at the edge of the De Soto National Forest. He and a law school friend from Jackson had bought the cabin two years earlier with modest plans to make small improvements. It was quite rustic. They hunted deer in the fall and winter, and turkeys in the spring. With the ups and downs of his marriage, he was spending more and more weekends at the cabin. It was only an hour and a half away. He claimed to be able to work there. It was very remote and quiet. His friend, the co-owner, had all but forgotten about it.

Trudy pretended to resent his weekends away, but Lance was usually lurking nearby, just waiting for Patrick to leave town.

Sunday night, February 9, 1992, Patrick called to tell his wife he was leaving the cabin. He'd finished a complicated brief for an appeal, and he was tired. Lance lingered for another hour before easing into the darkness.

Patrick stopped at Verhall's Country Store on Highway 15 at the divide between Stone and Harrison counties. He bought twelve gallons of gas for fourteen dollars and twenty-one cents and paid for it with a credit card. He chatted with Mrs Verhall, an older lady he'd become acquainted with. She knew many of the hunters who passed through, especially the ones who liked to linger and brag of their exploits in the woods, like Patrick. She said later that he was in good spirits, though he claimed to be tired because he had worked all weekend. She remembered thinking that this was odd. An hour later she heard the police and fire trucks race by.

Eight miles down the road, Patrick's Blazer was found engulfed in a raging fire at the bottom of a steep ravine, eighty yards from the highway. A truck driver saw the fire first, and managed to get to within fifty feet of it before his eyebrows were singed. He radioed for help, then sat on a stump and watched helplessly as it burned. The Blazer was on its right side with its top facing away, and so it was impossible to see if anyone was in the vehicle. It wouldn't have made any difference. A rescue was utterly impossible.

By the time the first county deputy arrived, the fireball was so intense it was difficult to distinguish the outline of the Blazer. The grass and shrubs began to burn. A small volunteer pumper arrived, but it was low on water. More traffic stopped, and soon a nice crowd stood mutely, watching and listening to the roar down below. Since the driver of the Blazer was not among them, everyone believed that he or she was in there getting incinerated along with everything else.

Two larger trucks arrived, and the fire was eventually extinguished. Hours passed as Sheriff Sweeney waited for things to cool. It was almost midnight when he first spotted a blackened clump of something he thought might be a body. The coroner was nearby. The pelvic bone ended the speculation. Grimshaw took his photographs. They waited for the corpse to cool even more, then collected it and placed it in a cardboard box.

The raised lettering and numerals on the license plates were traced by flashlight, and at 3:30 A.M. Trudy received the phone call that made her a widow. For four and a half years, anyway.

The Sheriff decided not to move the car during the night. At dawn, he returned with five of his deputies to comb the area. They found ninety feet of skid marks on the highway, and they speculated that perhaps a deer had run in front of poor Patrick, causing him to lose control. Because the fire had spread in all directions, any possible clues as to what might have happened were destroyed. The only surprise was the discovery of a shoe a hundred and thirty-one feet from the Blazer. It was a lightly worn Nike Air Max running shoe, size ten, and Trudy readily identified it as being Patrick's. She wept profusely when they showed it to her.

The Sheriff speculated that the vehicle rolled and flipped a few times as it crashed through the ravine, and perhaps in the midst of all this the body was thrown around inside. The shoe came off, got thrown out during a flip, etc. It made as much sense as anything else.

They loaded the Blazer on a flatbed truck and took it away. By late afternoon, what was left of Patrick had been cremated. His memorial service was the next day, and it was followed by a brief graveside service, the one he watched through binoculars.

Cutter and Grimshaw looked at the lonely shoe in the center of the table. Beside it were various statements taken from witnesses – Trudy, Mrs Verhall, the coroner, the mortician, even Grimshaw and the Sheriff – all saying exactly what they were expected to say. Only one surprise witness came forward in the months after the disappearance of the money. A young lady who lived near Verhall's store gave a sworn statement in which she claimed to have seen a red 1991 Chevy Blazer parked beside the road, precisely near the point where the fire occurred. She saw it twice. Once on Saturday night, then about twenty-four hours later around the time of the fire.

Her statement was taken by Grimshaw at her home in rural Harrison County, seven weeks after Patrick's funeral. By then, the death was shrouded in suspicion because the money had disappeared.

SIXTEEN

The doctor was a young Pakistani resident named Hayani, who by nature was a caring and compassionate soul. His English was heavily accented, and he seemed content to simply sit and chat with Patrick for as long as the patient wanted. The wounds were healing fine.

But the patient was deeply troubled. 'The torture was something I could never accurately describe,' Patrick said, after they had been talking for almost an hour. Hayani had brought the conversation around to this topic. It was all over the papers, since the filing of the lawsuit against the FBI, and from a medical standpoint it was a rare opportunity to examine and treat one injured in such an awful manner. Any young doc would enjoy being this close to the center of the storm.

Hayani nodded gravely. Just keep talking, he pleaded with his eyes.

Today, Patrick was certainly willing to do so. 'Sleep is impossible,' he said. 'Maybe an hour at the most before I hear voices, then I smell my flesh burning, then I wake up in a pool of sweat. And it's not getting better. I'm here now, home and safe, I guess, but they're still out there, still after me. I can't sleep. I don't want to sleep, Doc.'

'I can give you some pills.'

'No. Not yet, anyway. I've had too many chemicals.'

'Your blood looks fine. Some residue, but nothing significant.'

'No more drugs, Doc. Not now.'

'You need some sleep, Patrick.'

'I know, but I don't want to sleep. I'll get tortured again.'

Hayani wrote something on the chart he was holding. A long silence followed in which both men occupied themselves with thoughts about what to say next. Hayani found it difficult to believe that this kind man was capable of killing another, and especially in such a ghastly way.

The room was lit only by a narrow ray of sunshine along the edge of the window. 'Can I be honest with you about something, Doc?' Patrick asked, his voice even lower.

'Of course.'

'I need to stay here as long as I can. Here, in this room. In a few days, they'll start making noises about moving me to the Harrison County Jail where I'll get a bunk in a small cell with two or three street punks, and there's no way I can survive.'

'But why do they want to move you?'

'It's pressure, Doc. They have to slowly increase the pressure on me until I tell them what they want. They put me in a bad cell with rapists and drug dealers, and the message will be conveyed that I'd better start talking because that is what I'm faced with for the rest of my life. Prison, at Parchman, the worst place in the world. You ever been to Parchman, Doc?'

'No.'

'I have. I had a client there once. It's hell, literally. And the county jail isn't much better. But you can keep me here, Doc. All you have to do is keep telling the Judge that I need to remain under your care, and I stay here. Please, Doc.'

'Of course, Patrick,' he said, then made one more entry on his chart. Another long pause as Patrick closed his eyes and breathed rapidly. Just the thought of jail and prison had upset him mightily.

'I'm going to recommend a psychiatric evaluation,' Hayani said, and Patrick bit his lower lip to suppress a smile.

'Why?' he asked, feigning alarm.

'Because I'm curious. Do you object?'

'I guess not. When?'

'Perhaps in a couple of days.'

'I'm not sure if I can do it so soon.'

'There's no hurry.'

'That's more like it. We shouldn't hurry anything around here, Doc.'

'I see. Of course. Perhaps next week.'

'Maybe. Or the week after.'

The boy's mother was Neldene Crouch. She now lived in a trailer park outside Hattiesburg, but at the time of her son's disappearance she lived, with him, in a trailer park outside Lucedale, a small town thirty miles from Leaf. According to her recollection, her son had been missing since Sunday, February 9, 1992, precisely the same day Patrick Lanigan died on Highway 15.

But according to Sheriff Sweeney's records, Neldene Prewitt (her married name then) had first called his office on February 13, 1992, with the news that her son was missing. She was calling all the surrounding sheriffs, as well as the FBI and the CIA. She was quite disturbed and at times near hysterics.

Her son's name was Pepper Scarboro – Scarboro being the name of her first husband, Pepper's alleged father, though she'd never been certain precisely who the father was. As for his first name, no one could remember exactly where Pepper came from. She had named him LaVelle at the hospital, a name he'd always hated. He'd picked up Pepper at a young age, and had vigorously asserted it as his legal name. Anything but LaVelle.

Pepper Scarboro was seventeen at the time of his disappearance. After successfully completing the fifth grade, after three attempts, he dropped out of school and pumped gas at a local station in Lucedale. An odd child who stuttered badly, Pepper discovered the great outdoors as a young teenager, and loved nothing better than to camp and hunt for days, usually alone.

Pepper had few friends, and his mother rode him constantly for an assortment of shortcomings. She had two smaller children and various men friends, and she lived with the rest of her family in a dirty trailer with no air conditioning. Pepper preferred to sleep in a pup tent deep in the woods. He saved his money and bought his own shotgun and camping gear. So Pepper spent as much time as possible in the De Soto National Forest, twenty minutes but a thousand miles away from his mother.

There was no clear evidence that Pepper and Patrick had ever met. Coincidentally, Patrick's cabin was situated in the general vicinity of the forest where Pepper liked to hunt. Patrick and Pepper were both white males, roughly the same height, though Patrick was much heavier. Of much greater interest was the fact that Pepper's shotgun, tent, and sleeping bag were found in Patrick's cabin in late February of 1992.

The two disappeared at approximately the same time, from about the same area. In the months after their joint disappearances, Sweeney and Cutter had determined that no other person in the state of Mississippi had turned up missing around February 9 and remained so for more than ten weeks. Several, most of them troubled teens, had been reported

140

missing in February of 1992, but by late spring all had been accounted for. In March, a housewife up in Corinth evidently fled a violent marriage and had yet to be seen.

Working with FBI computers in Washington, Cutter had determined that the nearest person reported missing shortly before Patrick's fire was a shiftless truck driver from Dothan, Alabama, seven hours away. He had simply vanished on Saturday, February 8, leaving behind a miserable marriage and lots of bills. After investigating this case for three months, Cutter was certain there was no connection between the truck driver and Patrick.

Statistically, there was strong evidence that the disappearances of Pepper and Patrick were related. If, by some chance, Patrick didn't perish in his Blazer, Cutter and Sweeney were now almost positive Pepper did. This evidence, of course, was much too speculative to be admitted in a court of law. Patrick could've picked up a hitchhiker from Australia, a hobo from parts unknown, a drifter from a bus station.

They had a list with eight other names, ranging from an elderly gentleman in Mobile who was last seen driving errantly out of town, in the general direction of Mississippi, to a young prostitute in Houston who told friends she was moving to Atlanta to start a new life. All eight had been declared missing months and even years before February of 1992. Cutter and the Sheriff had long since declared the list worthless.

Pepper remained their strongest prospect; they just couldn't prove it.

Neldene, however, thought she could, and she was quite anxious to share her views with the press. Two days after Patrick was caught she went to a lawyer, a local sleazeball who'd handled her last divorce for three hundred dollars, and asked his assistance in guiding her through the media maze. He quickly obliged, said in fact he'd do it for free, then did what most bad lawyers do when presented with a client with a story – he called a press conference at his office in Hattiesburg, ninety miles north of Biloxi.

He displayed his weeping client to the media, and said all sorts of vile things about the local Sheriff down there in Biloxi and the FBI and their lame efforts at locating Pepper. Shame on them for dragging their feet for over four years while his poor client lived in sorrow and uncertainty. He ranted and raved and made the most of his fifteen minutes of fame. He hinted at legal action against Patrick Lanigan, the man who obviously killed Pepper and burned his body to hide the evidence so he could make off with ninety million bucks, but he was vague on specifics.

The press, disregarding whatever caution it may have collectively possessed, if any, ate it up. They were given pictures of young Pepper, a simple-looking boy with nasty peach fuzz around his mouth and unkempt hair. A face was thus given to the faceless victim, and he became human. This was the boy Patrick had killed.

The Pepper story played well in the press. He was properly referred to as the 'alleged victim,' but the word 'alleged' was invariably mumbled under the breath. Patrick watched it alone in his dark room.

Shortly after Patrick disappeared, he learned that Pepper Scarboro was rumored to have been lost in the fire. He and Pepper had hunted deer together in January of 1992, and had eaten beef stew over a fire late one cold afternoon in the woods. He had been surprised to learn that the boy practically lived in the forest, preferring it to home, which he spoke of sparingly. His camping and survival skills were extraordinary. Patrick offered the use of the cabin porch in

142

the event of rain or bad weather, but to his knowledge the kid had never used it.

They had met several times in the woods. Pepper could see the cabin from the top of a wooded hill a mile away, and when Patrick's car was there he would hide nearby. He enjoyed tracking behind Patrick as he took long walks or made his way into the woods to hunt. He would toss pebbles and acorns at him until Patrick would yell and curse. They would then sit for a short talk. Conversation was not something Pepper thrived on, but he seemed to enjoy the break in solitude. Patrick took him snacks and candy.

He wasn't surprised by the assumption, then or now, that he had killed the kid.

Dr Hayani watched the evening news with great interest. He read the papers and talked in great detail to his new wife about his famous patient. They sat in bed and watched it all again on the late news.

The phone rang as they were turning off the lights and preparing for sleep. It was Patrick, full of apologies, but in pain, and scared, and just needing someone to talk to. Since he was technically a prisoner, his calls were restricted to his lawyer and his doctor, and only twice a day each. Did the doctor have a minute?

Of course. Another apology for calling so late, but sleep was impossible now, and he was deeply upset by all the news and especially the suggestion that he killed that young kid. Did the doctor see it on TV?

Yes, of course. Patrick was in his room with the lights off, huddled in his bed. Thank God those deputies were in the hallway because he was scared, he had to admit. He was hearing things, voices and noises that made no sense. The voices were not coming from the hall but from within the room. Could it be the drugs?

It could be a number of things, Patrick. The medicine, the fatigue, the trauma of what you've been through, the shock both physically and psychologically.

They talked for an hour.

SEVENTEEN

He didn't wash his hair for the third straight day. He wanted the oily look. He didn't shave either. For his outfit, he switched from the light cotton hospital gown he'd slept in back to the aqua surgeon's scrubs, which were very wrinkled. Hayani promised to get him new ones. But for today, he needed the wrinkles. He put a white sock on his right foot but there was a nasty rope burn just above his left ankle, and he wanted people to see this. No sock there. Just a matching black rubber shower sandal.

He would be displayed today. The world was waiting.

Sandy arrived at ten with two pairs of cheap pharmacy sunglasses, per his client's instructions. And a black New Orleans Saints cap. 'Thanks,' Patrick said, as he stood before the mirror in the bathroom and admired the sunglasses and prepared the cap.

Dr Hayani arrived minutes later, and Patrick introduced one to the other. Patrick was suddenly nervous and light-headed. He sat on the edge of his bed, ran his fingers through his hair, and tried to breathe slowly. 'I never thought this day would happen, you know,' he mumbled to the floor. 'Never.' His doctor and his lawyer looked at each other with nothing to say.

Hayani ordered a strong depressant, and Patrick

gulped down both pills. 'Maybe I'll sleep through it all,' he said.

'I'll do all the talking,' Sandy said. 'Just try and relax.'

'He's about to,' Hayani said.

A knock on the door, and Sheriff Sweeney entered with enough deputies to quell a riot. Stiff pleasantries were exchanged. Patrick put on his Saints cap and his new shades, large dark ones, and held out his wrists to be handcuffed.

'What are those?' Sandy demanded, pointing to a set of ankle irons a deputy was holding.

'Ankle irons,' said Sweeney.

'I don't think so,' Sandy said harshly. 'The man has burns on one ankle.'

'He certainly does,' Dr Hayani said boldly, anxious to enter the fray. 'See,' he insisted, pointing to Patrick's left ankle.

Sweeney pondered this for a moment, and his hesitation cost him. Sandy charged ahead: 'Come on, Sheriff, what are his chances of escape? He's injured, handcuffed, surrounded by all these people. What the hell's he gonna do? Break and run? You guys aren't that slow, are you?'

'I'll call the Judge, if necessary,' Dr Hayani said angrily.

'Well, he came here with ankle irons,' the Sheriff said.

'That was the FBI, Raymond,' Patrick said. 'And they were leg chains, not ankle irons. And they hurt like hell anyway.'

The ankle irons were put away, and Patrick was led into the hallway, where men in matching brown uniforms grew silent at the sight of him. They gathered around him and the mob moved slowly toward the elevator. Sandy stayed to his left, gently holding him by the elbow.

146

The elevator was too small for his entire entourage. The ones who didn't make it scurried down the staircase and met them in the lobby where they reorganized and shuffled past the front reception and through the glass doors, into the warm autumn air, where a regular parade of freshly waxed vehicles awaited them. They put him in a sparkling new black Suburban with Harrison County insignia plastered from bumper to bumper, and away they went, followed by a white Suburban carrying his armed protectors. It, in turn, was followed by three freshly cleaned patrol cars. In front, two more patrol cars, the newest additions to the fleet, led the invasion as it cleared military checkpoints and entered the civilian world.

Through the cheap thick sunglasses, Patrick saw everything outside. Streets he'd driven a million times. The houses looked familiar. They turned on to Highway 90 and there was the Gulf, its calm brown waters seemingly unchanged since he left. There was the beach, a narrow strip of sand between the highway and the water, too far from the hotels and condos on the other side of the highway.

The Coast had prospered during his exile, thanks wholly to the surprising arrival of casino gambling. There had been rumors of its coming when he left town, and now he was riding past large Vegas-style casinos with glitz and neon. The parking lots were filling, at nine-thirty in the morning.

'How many casinos?' he asked the Sheriff, seated to his right.

'Thirteen at last count. With more on the way.'

'Hard to believe.'

The depressant was quite effective. His breathing became heavy and his body relaxed. He felt like nodding off for a moment, then they turned on to Main Street and he was anxious again. Just a couple of blocks now. A few more minutes, and his past would come roaring back to greet him. By City Hall, to the left, quickly now, for a glimpse of the Vieux Marche, and in the middle of the old street lined with shops and stores, a fine large white building he once owned a piece of as a partner in Bogan, Rapley, Vitrano, Havarac, and Lanigan, Attorneys and Counselors-at-Law.

It was still standing, but the partnership was crumbling within.

Ahead was the Harrison County Courthouse, only a three-block walk from his old office. It was a plain, brick two-story building with a small green lawn in the front next to Howard Street. The lawn was covered with people milling about. The streets were lined with cars. Pedestrians hurried along the sidewalks, all headed for the courthouse it seemed. Cars ahead pulled over as Patrick and his caravan came through.

The horde in front of the courthouse moved in a frantic wave around both sides, but was stopped by police barricades at the rear where a section was cordoned off. Patrick had seen several notorious murderers rushed to and from court through the back door, and so he knew exactly what was happening. The parade stopped. Doors flew open and a dozen deputies spilled forth. They crowded around the black Suburban. Its door slid open slowly. Patrick eventually appeared, his aqua garb quite the contrast to the dark brown uniforms squeezing around him.

An impressive mob of reporters, photographers, and cameramen gathered breathlessly along the nearest barricade. Others behind them ran to catch up. Patrick was immediately aware of the spotlight, and he lowered his head and crouched among the deputies. They walked him quickly to the rear door, a barrage of idiotic questions flying over his head.

'Patrick, what's it like to be home!?'

'Where's the money, Patrick!?'

'Who burned up in the car, Patrick!?'

Through the door and up the back stairway, a brief journey Patrick had sometimes taken when he was in a hurry to catch a judge for a quick signature. The smell was suddenly familiar. The concrete steps had not been painted in four years. Through a door, through a short hallway with a crowd of courthouse clerks gathered at one end gawking at him. They put him in the jury room, which was next to the courtroom, and he took a seat in a padded chair by a coffeepot.

Sandy hovered over him, anxious to make sure he was okay. Sheriff Sweeney dismissed the deputies, and they moved into the hall to wait for the next transfer.

'Coffee?' Sandy asked.

'Please, black.'

'You okay, Patrick?' Sweeney asked.

'Yeah, sure, Raymond, thanks.' He sounded meek and scared. His hands and knees shook and he couldn't make them stop. He ignored the coffee, and despite both hands cuffed together adjusted his black sunglasses and pulled the bill of his cap further down. His shoulders sagged.

There was a knock on the door, and a pretty girl named Belinda eased her head through just long enough to say, 'Judge Huskey would like to meet with Patrick.' The voice was so familiar. Patrick raised his head, looked at the door, and said softly, 'Hello, Belinda.'

'Hello, Patrick. Welcome back.'

He turned away. She was a secretary in the clerk's office, and all the lawyers flirted with her. A sweet girl. A sweet voice. Had it really been four years?

'Where?' the Sheriff asked.

'In here,' she said. 'In a few minutes.'

'Do you want to meet with the Judge, Patrick?'

149

Sandy asked. It was not mandatory. Under normal circumstances, it would be downright unusual.

'Sure.' Patrick was desperate to see Karl Huskey. She left and the door clicked behind her.

'I'll step outside,' Sweeney said. 'I need a cigarette.'

Finally, Patrick was alone with his lawyer. He suddenly perked up. 'Couple of things. Any word from Leah Pires?'

'No,' Sandy said.

'She'll get in touch soon, so be ready. I've written her a long letter, and I'd like for you to get it to her.'

'Okay.'

'Second. There's an antibugging device called a DX-130, made by LoKim, a Korean electronics outfit. Costs about six hundred dollars; about the size of a portable Dictaphone. Get one, and bring it with you whenever we meet. We'll disinfect the room and the phones before each little conference. Also, hire a reputable surveillance firm in New Orleans to check your office twice a week. It's very expensive, but I'll pay for it. Any questions?'

'No.'

Another knock, and Patrick slouched again. Judge Karl Huskey entered the room alone, robeless, in shirt and tie with reading glasses perched halfway down his nose. His gray hair and wrinkled eyes made him appear much older and wiser than forty-eight, which was exactly what he wanted.

Patrick was looking up and already smiling when Huskey offered his hand. 'Good to see you, Patrick,' he said warmly as they shook hands, the cuffs rattling. Huskey wanted to reach down and hug him, but with judicial restraint he limited the contact to a soft handshake.

'How are you, Karl?' Patrick said, keeping his seat.

'I'm fine. And what about you?'

150

'I've had better days, but it is good to see you. Even under these circumstances.'

'Thanks. I can't imagine –'

'Guess I look different, don't I?'

'You certainly do. I'm not sure I would recognize you on the street.'

Patrick only smiled.

Like a few others who still professed some level of friendship for Patrick, Huskey felt betrayed, but even more so he felt great relief in knowing that his pal was not dead. He was deeply worried about the capital murder charge. The divorce and the civil suits could be dealt with, but not murder.

Because of their friendship, Huskey would not preside over the trial. He planned to handle the preliminary matters, then step aside long before the important rulings were due. There had already been a story about their history.

'I assume you will enter a plea of not guilty,' he said.

'Yes, that's correct.'

'Then it will be a routine first appearance. I'll deny bail since it's capital murder.'

'I understand, Karl.'

'Whole thing won't take ten minutes.'

'I've been here before. The chair will be different, that's all.'

In twelve years on the bench, Judge Huskey had often been astonished at the amount of sympathy he could muster for average people who'd committed heinous crimes. He saw the human side of their suffering. He saw guilt eat them alive. He'd sent to prison hundreds of people who, if given the chance, would have left his courtroom and never sinned again. He wanted to help, to reach out, to forgive.

But this was Patrick. His Honor was almost moved to tears at the moment. His old friend – bound and dressed in a clown suit, eyes covered, face altered, nervous and twitchy and scared beyond words. He'd like to take him home, feed him some good food, let him rest, and help him pull his life together.

He kneeled next to him, and said, 'Patrick, I can't hear this case, for obvious reasons. Right now I'll handle the preliminary stuff to make sure you're protected. I'm still your friend. Don't hesitate to call.' He patted him very gently on the knee, hoping he didn't touch a raw spot.

'Thanks, Karl,' Patrick said, biting his lip.

Karl wanted eye contact, but it was impossible with the sunglasses. He stood and headed for the door. 'Everything's routine today, Counselor,' he said to Sandy.

'Are there a lot of people out there?' Patrick asked.

'Yes, Patrick. Friends and enemies alike. They're all out there.' He left the room.

The Coast had a long and rich history of sensational murders and notorious criminals, so crowded court-rooms were not uncommon. No one could remember, though, such a packed house for a simple *first appearance*.

The press had arrived early and taken the good seats. Since Mississippi was one of the remaining few states with the good sense to ban cameras from the courtroom, the reporters would be forced to sit and watch and listen, then put in their own words what they saw. They would be forced to be real reporters, a task for which most of them were ill-equipped.

Every big trial attracted the regulars – clerks and secretaries from courthouse offices, bored paralegals, retired cops, local lawyers who hung around most of the day, sipping free coffee in the clerks' offices, gossiping, examining real estate deeds, waiting for a judge to sign an order, doing anything to stay away from the office – and Patrick attracted all these and more.

In particular, there were many lawyers present just to get a glimpse of Patrick. The papers had been filled with stories about him for four days now, but no one had seen a current photo. Rumors were rampant about his appearance. The torture story had elevated curiosity even more.

Charles Bogan and Doug Vitrano sat together in the middle of the pack, as close to the front as they could get. The damned reporters beat them to the courthouse. They wanted to be on the front row, near the table where the defendant always sat. They wanted to see him, to make eye contact, to whisper threats and vulgarities if at all possible, to spit as much bile as they could in this civilized setting. But they were five rows back, waiting patiently for a moment they thought would never come.

The third partner, Jimmy Havarac, stood along the back wall and chatted quietly with a deputy. He ignored the stares and glances from people he knew, many of whom were other lawyers who secretly had been delighted when the money vanished and the firm lost its fortune. It would have been, after all, the largest single fee earned by any firm in the history of the state. Jealousy was the natural tendency. He hated them, as he hated virtually everyone else in the courtroom. A bunch of vultures waiting for a carcass.

Havarac, the son of a shrimper, was still stout and crude and not beyond a barroom brawl. Five minutes alone with Patrick in a locked room, and he'd have the money.

The fourth partner, Ethan Rapley, was at home in the attic, as usual, working on a brief in support of some insipid motion. He would read about it tomorrow.

A handful of the lawyers were old buddies who

came to cheer Patrick on. Escape was a common, usually unspoken, dream of many small-town lawyers trapped in an overcrowded, boring profession where expectations were too high. At least Patrick had the guts to chase the dream. There was an explanation for the dead body, they were sure of that.

Arriving late and pushed into a corner was Lance. He had loitered around back with the reporters, taking the measure of the security. It was quite impressive, at least for now. But could the cops keep it up every day during a long trial? That was the question.

Many acquaintances were present, people Patrick had known only in passing but who now suddenly claimed to have been his dearest friends. Some in fact had never met Patrick, but that didn't stop their idle chatter about Patrick this and Patrick that. Likewise, Trudy suddenly had new friends who had stopped by to scowl at the man who had broken her heart and abandoned precious little Ashley Nicole.

They read paperbacks and scanned newspapers and tried to look bored, as if they didn't really want to be there. There was movement among the deputy clerks and bailiffs near the bench, and the courtroom instantly grew quiet. The newspapers were lowered in unison.

The door next to the jury box opened and brown uniforms poured into the courtroom. Sheriff Sweeney entered, holding Patrick by the elbow, then two more deputies, then Sandy brought up the rear.

There he was! Necks strained and stretched and heads bobbed and weaved. The courtroom artists went to work.

Patrick walked slowly across the courtroom to the defense table, his head down, though from behind the sunglasses he was searching the spectators. He caught a glimpse of Havarac on the rear wall, his scowling face speaking volumes. And just before he sat he saw

154

Father Phillip, his priest, looking much older but just as amiable.

He sat low, his shoulders sagging, chin down, no pride here. He did not look around because he could feel the stares from every direction. Sandy put his arm on his shoulder and whispered something meaningless.

The door opened again, and T.L. Parrish, the District Attorney, entered, alone, and walked to his table next to Patrick's. Parrish was a bookish sort with a small ego, a contained ego. No higher office was calling him. His trial work was methodical, absent of any trace of flamboyance, and lethal. Parrish currently carried the second-highest conviction rate in the state. He sat next to the Sheriff, who had moved from Patrick's table to where he belonged. Behind him were agents Joshua Cutter, Brent Myers, and two other FBI types Parrish couldn't even name.

The stage was set for a spectacular trial, yet it was at least six months away. A bailiff called them to order, made them stand while Judge Huskey entered and assumed his perch on the bench. 'Please sit,' were his first words, and everyone obeyed.

'The matter of *State versus Patrick S. Lanigan*, case number 96–1140. Is the defendant present?'

'Yes, Your Honor,' Sandy said, half-standing.

'Would you please rise, Mr Lanigan?' Huskey asked. Patrick, still handcuffed, slowly pushed his chair back and got to his feet. He was semi-bent at the waist, with his chin and shoulders down. And it was no act. The depressant had deadened most parts of his body, including his brain.

He stiffened a bit.

'Mr Lanigan, I'm holding a copy of an indictment returned against you by the grand jury of Harrison County, in which it is alleged you murdered one John Doe, a human being, and for this you have been charged with capital murder. Have you read this indictment?'

'Yes sir,' he announced, chin up, voice as strong as he could make it.

'Have you discussed it with your attorney?'

'Yes sir.'

'How do you wish to plead?'

'Not guilty.'

'Your plea of not guilty is accepted. You may sit down.'

Huskey shuffled some papers, then continued: 'The Court, on its own motion, hereby imposes a gag order on the defendant, the attorneys, the police and investigating authorities, any and all witnesses, and all court personnel, effective now and lasting until the trial is over. I have copies of this order for everyone to read. Any violation of it will result in contempt of court, and I will deal harshly with any violators. Not one word to any reporter or journalist without my approval. Any questions from the attorneys?'

His tone left little doubt that the Judge not only meant what he said, but relished the thought of going after violators. The lawyers said nothing.

'Good. I have prepared a schedule for discovery, motions, pretrial, and trial. It's available in the clerk's office. Anything else?'

Parrish stood and said, 'Just one small matter, Your Honor. We would like to get the defendant in our detention facility as soon as possible. As you know, he's now at the base in a hospital, and, well, we –'

'I just talked to his doctor, Mr Parrish. He's undergoing medical treatment. I assure you that as soon as he is released by his doctor, then we'll transfer him to the Harrison County Jail.'

'Thank you, Judge.'

'If nothing else, then we stand adjourned.'

He was rushed from the courtroom, down the back

stairs, into the black Suburban as the cameras clicked and rolled. Patrick nodded then napped as he was returned to the hospital.

EIGHTEEN

The only crimes Stephano possibly committed were
the kidnapping and assault of Patrick, and convictions
were unlikely. It happened in South America, far from
U.S. jurisdiction. The actual assault was conducted by
others, including some Brazilians. Stephano's lawyer
was confident that they would prevail if pressed to
trial.

But there were clients involved, and a reputation to
protect. The lawyer knew all too well the FBI's ability
to harass without actually prosecuting. It was his
advice that Stephano cut the deal – agree to spill his
guts in return for the government's promise to grant
immunity to him and his clients. Since no other crimes
were involved, what was the harm?

The lawyer insisted on sitting with Stephano while
his statement was taken. The sessions would last for
many hours over several days, but the lawyer wanted
to be there. Jaynes wanted it done in the Hoover
Building, by his men. Coffee and pastries were served.
Two video cameras were aimed at the end of the table
where Stephano sat calmly in his shirtsleeves, his
lawyer by his side.

'Would you state your name?' asked Underhill, the
first of the interrogators, each of whom had memor-
ized the Lanigan file.

'Jonathan Edmund Stephano. Jack.'

'And your company is?'

'Edmund Associates.'

'And what does your company do?'

'Lots of things. Security consulting. Surveillance. Personnel research. Locating of missing persons.'

'Who owns the company?'

'I do. All of it.'

'How many employees do you have?'

'It varies. As of now, eleven full-time. Thirty or so part-time, or freelancers.'

'Were you hired to find Patrick Lanigan?'

'Yes.'

'When?'

'March 28, 1992.' Stephano had files packed with notes, but he didn't need them.

'Who hired you?'

'Benny Aricia, the man whose money was stolen.'

'How much did you charge him?'

'The initial retainer was two hundred grand.'

'How much has he paid you to date?'

'One point nine million.'

'What did you do after you were hired by Benny Aricia?'

'Several things. I immediately flew to Nassau in the Bahamas to meet with the bank where the theft occurred. It was a branch of the United Bank of Wales. My client, Mr Aricia, and his former law firm, had established a new account there to receive the money, and, as we now know, someone else was waiting on the money, too.'

'Is Mr Aricia a U.S. citizen?'

'Yes.'

'Why did he establish an account offshore?'

'It was ninety million dollars, sixty for him, thirty for the lawyers, and nobody wanted the money to appear in a bank in Biloxi. Mr Aricia lived there at the time, and it was agreed by all that it would be a bad idea for anyone locally to see the money.'

'Was Mr Aricia trying to avoid the IRS?'

'I don't know. You'll have to ask him. That was none of my business.'

'Who did you talk to at the United Bank of Wales?'

The lawyer snorted his disapproval, but said nothing.

'Graham Dunlap, a Brit. A vice president of some sort with the bank.'

'What did he tell you?'

'Same thing he told the FBI. That the money was gone.'

'Where did it come from?'

'Here, in Washington. The wire began at nine-thirty on the morning of March 26, 1992, originating from D.C. National Bank. It was a priority wire, meaning it would take less than an hour for it to land in Nassau. At fifteen minutes after ten, the wire hit the United Bank, where it sat for nine minutes before it was wired to a bank in Malta. From there, it was wired to Panama.'

'How did the money get wired out of the account?'

The lawyer was irritated by this. 'This is a waste of time,' he interrupted. 'You guys have had this information for four years now. You've spent more time with the bankers than my client has.'

Underhill was unfazed. 'We have a right to ask these questions. We are simply verifying what we know. How did the money get wired out of the account, Mr Stephano?'

'Unknown to my client and his lawyers, someone, Mr Lanigan we presume, had accessed the new offshore account, and had prepared the Malta wiring instructions in anticipation of the money coming in. He prepared bogus wiring instructions from my client's lawyers, his old firm, and rerouted the money nine minutes after it landed. They, of course, thought he was dead, and had no reason to suspect anyone was after the money. The settlement which produced the ninety million in the first place was extremely secret, and no one, with the exception of my client, his lawyers, and a handful of people at the Justice Department, knew exactly when or where the money was wired.'

'As I understand it, someone was actually at the bank when the money arrived.'

'Yes. We're almost certain it was Patrick Lanigan. On the morning the money was wired, he presented himself to Graham Dunlap as Doug Vitrano, one of the partners in the law firm. He had perfect identification – passport, driver's license, etc. – plus he was well dressed and knew all about the money which was about to be wired from Washington. He had a notarized partnership resolution authorizing him to accept the money on behalf of the firm, then wire it to the bank in Malta.'

'I know damned well you have copies of the resolution and the wire transfer authorizations,' the lawyer said.

'We do,' Underhill said, flipping through his notes and paying little attention to the lawyer. The FBI had tracked the money to Malta, and from there to Panama, where all trails vanished. There was a blurred still shot taken from the bank's security camera of the man who presented himself as Doug Vitrano. The FBI and the partners were certain it was Patrick, though he was wonderfully disguised. He was much thinner, his hair was short and very dark, he had grown a dark mustache and worn stylish horn-rimmed glasses. He had flown in, he explained to Graham Dunlap, to personally monitor the receiving and transferring of the money because the firm and the client were quite nervous about the transaction. That was certainly not

161

unusual in Dunlap's view, and he was happy to oblige. He was sacked a week later and returned to London.

'So we went to Biloxi, and spent a month there looking for clues,' Stephano continued.

'And you found the law offices to be wired?'

'We did. For obvious reasons, we were immediately suspicious of Mr Lanigan, and our task was twofold: first, to find him and the money, and, second, to determine how he had pulled the heist. The remaining partners granted us access to their offices for one weekend, and our technical people picked the place apart. It was, as you say, infested. We found bugs in every phone, in every office, under every desk, in the hallways, even in the men's rest room on the first floor. There was one exception. The office of Charles Bogan was completely clean. He was fastidious about locking it. The bugs were high in quality; twenty-two in all. Their signals were gathered by a hub we found hidden in a storage file box in the attic, in a spot no one had touched in years.'

Underhill listened but didn't hear. This was, after all, being recorded on video, and his superiors could study it later. He was quite familiar with these preliminaries. He pulled out a technical summary which analyzed, in four dense paragraphs, the bugging scheme installed by Patrick. The microphones were state of the art – tiny, powerful, costly, and manufactured by a reputable firm in Malaysia. Illegal to buy or possess in the United States, they could be purchased with relative ease in any European city. Patrick and Trudy had spent New Year's in Rome, five weeks before his death.

The hub found in the attic storage box had impressed even the FBI experts. It was less than three months old when Stephano found it, and the FBI reluctantly admitted it was at least a year ahead of their latest wizardry. Made in Hungary, it could receive signals from all twenty-two bugs hidden in the offices below, keep them separate, then transmit them, one at a time or all at once, to a satellite dish nearby.

'Did you determine where the signals were being relayed to?' Underhill asked. It was a fair question because the FBI certainly didn't know.

'No. It has a range of three miles, in all directions, so it would be impossible to tell.'

'Any ideas?'

'Yes, a very good one. I doubt Lanigan was foolish enough to set up a receiving dish anywhere within three miles of downtown Biloxi. He would have to rent space, hide the dish, spend lots of time there monitoring hours of conversations. He has proven to be quite methodical. I've always suspected he used a boat. It would be much simpler and safer. The office is only six hundred yards from the beach. There are a lot of boats in the Gulf. A man could drop anchor two miles out and never speak to another soul.'

'Did he own a boat?'

'We couldn't find one.'

'Any evidence he used a boat?'

'Maybe.' Stephano paused here because he was now entering territory unknown to the FBI.

The pause quickly irritated Underhill. 'This is not a cross-examination, Mr Stephano.'

'I know. We talked to every charter outfit along the Coast, from Destin to New Orleans, and found only one possible suspect. A small company in Orange Beach, Alabama, leased a thirty-two-foot sailboat to a man on February 11, 1992, the day Lanigan was buried. Their rate was a thousand dollars a month. This guy offered twice that if the transaction could be done in cash with nothing in writing. They figured he was a doper, and said no way. The guy then offered a five-thousand-dollar deposit, plus two thousand a month for two months. Business was slow. The boat was insured against theft. They took a chance.'

Underhill listened without blinking. He took no notes. 'Did you show them a picture?'

'Yeah. Said it could've been Patrick. But the beard was gone, the hair was dark, baseball cap, eyeglasses, overweight. This was before he discovered Ultra Slim-Fast. Anyway, the guy couldn't make a positive ID.'

'What name did he use?'

'Randy Austin. Had a Georgia driver's license. And he refused to provide more identification. He was offering cash, remember, five thousand. The guy would've sold it to him for twenty.'

'What happened to the boat?'

'They got it back, eventually. The guy said he got real suspicious because Randy didn't seem to know much about sailboats. He asked questions, fished around. Randy said he was in the process of drifting south after a bad marriage in Atlanta, tired of the rat race, lots of money, that routine. Used to sail a lot, and now wanted to float down to the Keys and practice his skills along the way. Said he'd always keep the shore in sight. It was a nice story, and the guy felt somewhat better, but he was still suspicious. Next day, Randy appeared from nowhere, no car, no cab, as if he had walked or hitchhiked somehow to the dock, and, after a lot of preliminaries, he left with the boat. It had a big diesel engine of some sort and it would cruise at eight knots, regardless of the wind. He disappeared, going east, and the owner had nothing else to do, so he eased down the Coast, stopped at a couple of favorite bars along the way, and managed to keep an eye on Randy, who was a quarter of a mile out and doing a decent job of handling the boat. He docked it at a marina at Perdido Bay, and left in a rented Taurus with Alabama registration. This went on for a couple of days. Our guy kept an eye on the boat. Randy

164

played with it, a mile out at first, then he ventured farther. On the third or fourth day, Randy took it west, toward Mobile and Biloxi, and was gone for three days.

'He came back, then left, going west again. Never east or south, in the direction of the Keys. The guy stopped worrying about his boat because Randy stayed close to home. He would leave for a week at a time, but he always came back.'

'And you think it was Patrick?'

'I do. I'm convinced of it. Makes perfect sense to me. He was isolated on the boat. He could go for days without speaking to another person. He could gather his intelligence from a hundred different spots along the Biloxi-Gulfport shore. Plus, the boat was a perfect place to starve himself.'

'What happened to it?'

'Randy left it at the dock, and simply vanished without a word. The owner got his boat back, plus the five grand.'

'Did you examine the boat?'

'With a microscope. Nothing. The guy said the boat had never been so clean.'

'When did he disappear?'

'The guy wasn't certain because he stopped checking on the boat every day. He found it at the dock on March 30, four days after the money was stolen. We talked to a kid who was on duty at the dock, and, to the best of his recollection, Randy docked on either March 24 or March 25, and was never seen again. So the dates match up perfect.'

'What happened to the rental car?'

'We tracked it down later. It was rented from the Avis desk at the Mobile Regional Airport on Monday morning, February 10, about ten hours after the fire was put out. Rented by a man with no beard, clean-shaven, short dark hair, horn-rimmed glasses, wearing a coat and tie and claiming he just stepped off a commuter flight from Atlanta. We showed pictures to the clerk on duty, and she made a very tentative ID of Patrick Lanigan. Evidently, he used the same Georgia driver's license. He used a phony Visa Card, one with the name of Randy Austin and a number he stole from a legitimate account in Decatur, Georgia. Said he was a self-employed real estate developer in town to look at land for a casino. So he had no company name to put on the form. He wanted the car for a week. Avis never saw him again. Didn't see the car for fourteen months.'

'Why wouldn't he return the car?' Underhill asked, musing.

'Simple. When he rented it, his death had just happened, and had not been reported. But the next day, his face was on the front page of both the Biloxi and Mobile papers. He probably figured it was too risky to take the car back. They found it later in Montgomery, wrecked and stolen.'

'Where did Patrick go?'

'My guess is that he left the Orange Beach area on March 24 or 25. He assumed the identity of Doug Vitrano, his former partner. We learned that on the twenty-fifth he flew from Montgomery to Atlanta, then first class to Miami, then first class to Nassau. All tickets were in the name of Doug Vitrano, and he used the passport when he left Miami and again when he entered the Bahamas. The flight arrived in Nassau at eight-thirty on the morning of the twenty-sixth, and he was at the bank when it opened at nine. He presented the passport and other papers to Graham Dunlap. He diverted the money, said good-bye, caught a flight to New York, and landed at La Guardia at 2:30 P.M. At that point, he ditched the Vitrano papers and found some others. We lost him.'

*

166

When the bidding got to fifty thousand dollars, Trudy said yes. The show was 'Inside Journal,' a slash-and-burn tabloid with solid ratings and, apparently, lots of cash. They set up lights and covered windows and ran wires throughout the den. The 'journalist' was Nancy de Angelo, flown straight in from L.A. with her own band of hairdressers and makeup artists.

Not to be outdone, Trudy spent two hours in front of the mirror, and looked absolutely glorious when she appeared. Nancy said she looked too good. She was supposed to be wounded, hurt, broke, besieged, handcuffed by the court, angry at what her husband had done to her and her daughter. She retreated in tears and Lance had to console her for half an hour. She looked almost as good when she returned in jeans and a cotton pullover.

Ashley Nicole was used as a prop. She sat close to her mother on the sofa. 'Look real sad now,' Nancy told her as the technicians checked the lights. 'We need tears from you,' she said to Trudy. 'Genuine tears.'

They chatted for an hour about all the horrible things Patrick was doing to them. Trudy cried when she recalled the funeral. They had a picture of the shoe found at the site. She suffered through the months and years afterward. No, she had not remarried. No, she had not heard from her husband since he had returned. Wasn't sure if she wanted to. No, he had made no effort to see his daughter, and she broke down again.

She hated the thought of divorce, but what was she to do? And the lawsuit, how horrible! This nasty insurance company hounding her like she was a deadbeat.

Patrick was such a horrible person. If they found the money, did she expect to get any of it? Of course not! She was shocked by the suggestion.

It was edited to twenty minutes, and Patrick watched it in his dark hospital room. It made him smile.

NINETEEN

Sandy's secretary was clipping his photo and the story of yesterday's brief court appearance from the New Orleans paper when the call came. She immediately found him, extracted him from a crowded deposition, and put him on the phone.

Leah Pires was back. She said hello and immediately asked if he'd had his office checked for bugs. Sandy said yes, just yesterday. She was in a hotel suite on Canal, a few blocks over, and she suggested the meeting take place there. A suggestion from her carried more weight than a directive from a federal judge. Whatever she wanted. He was excited just to hear her voice.

She was in no hurry, so Sandy strolled leisurely down Poydras, then to Magazine, then to Canal. He refused to watch his back. Patrick's paranoia was understandable – poor guy had lived on the run until the ghosts finally caught him. But no one could ever convince Sandy that the same people would shadow him. He was a lawyer in a high-profile case. The bad guys would be crazy to tap his phones and stalk him. One bungled move, and serious damage could be done to the case against Patrick.

But he had contacted a local security firm and made an appointment to have his offices swept for bugs. This was his client's wish, not his.

Leah greeted him with a firm handshake and a quick smile, but he could tell instantly that she had many things on her mind. She was barefoot, in jeans and a white cotton tee shirt, very casual, the way most Brazilians probably are, he thought. He'd never been down there. The closet door was open; there weren't many clothes hanging. She was moving around quickly, living out of a suitcase, probably on the run just as Patrick had been until last week. She poured coffee for both of them, and asked him to sit at the table.

'How is he?' she asked.

'He's healing. The doctor says he'll be fine.'

'How bad was it?' she asked quietly. He loved her accent, slight as it was.

'Pretty rough.' He reached into his briefcase, removed a folder, and slid it to her. 'Here.'

She frowned at the sight of the first photo, then mumbled something in Portuguese. Her eyes watered as she looked at the second one. 'Poor Patrick,' she said to herself. 'Poor baby.'

She took her time with the photos, gently wiping tears with the back of her hand until Sandy found the presence of mind to get her a tissue. She wasn't ashamed to cry over the pictures, and when she was finished with them she placed them in a neat stack and put them back in the folder.

'I'm sorry,' Sandy said. He could think of nothing else to offer. 'Here's a letter from Patrick,' he finally said.

She finished her crying and poured more coffee. 'Are any of the injuries permanent?' she asked.

'The doctor thinks probably not. There will be scarring, but with time everything should heal.'

'Mentally, how is he?'

'He's okay. He's sleeping even less. He has nightmares constantly, both day and night. But with medication, he's getting better. I honestly can't imagine what he's going through.' He took a sip of coffee, and said, 'I guess he's lucky to be alive.'

'He always said they wouldn't kill him.'

There was so much to ask her. The lawyer in Sandy almost screamed out an endless barrage: Did Patrick know they were close behind him? Did he know the chase was about to end? Where was she when they were closing in? Did she live with him? How did they hide the money? Where is the money now? Is it safe? Please, tell me something. I'm the lawyer. I can be trusted.

'Let's talk about his divorce,' she said, abruptly changing the subject. She could sense his curiosity. She stood and walked to a drawer where she removed a thick file and placed it before him. 'Did you see Trudy on TV last night?' she asked.

'Yes. Pathetic, wasn't it?'

'She's very pretty,' Leah said.

'Yes, she is. I'm afraid Patrick made the mistake of marrying her for her looks.'

'He wouldn't be the first.'

'No, he wouldn't.'

'Patrick despises her. She is a bad person, and she was unfaithful to him throughout their marriage.'

'Unfaithful?'

'Yes. It's all in the file there. The last year they were together, Patrick hired an investigator to watch her. Her lover was a man named Lance Maxa, and they were seeing each other all the time. There are even some photographs of Lance coming and going from Patrick's house when he was away. There are pictures of Lance and Trudy sunbathing by Patrick's pool, naked of course.'

Sandy took the file and flipped quickly until he found the photographs. Naked as newborns. He smiled wickedly. 'This will add something to the divorce.'

'Patrick wants the divorce, you understand. He will not contest it. But she needs to be silenced. She's having a nice time saying all those bad things about Patrick.'

'This should shut her up. What about the child?'

Leah took her seat and looked him squarely in the eyes. 'Patrick loves Ashley Nicole, but there is one problem. He is not the father.'

He shrugged as if he heard this every day. 'Who is?'

'Patrick doesn't know. Probably Lance. It seems as if Lance and Trudy have been together for some time. It goes back to high school even.'

'How does he know he's not the father?'

'When the child was fourteen months old, Patrick obtained a small blood sample by pricking her finger. He sent it, along with a sample of his, to a lab where DNA tests were run. His suspicions were correct. He is definitely not the father of the child. The report is in the file.'

Sandy had to walk around a bit to sort things out. He stood in the window and watched the traffic on Canal. Another clue in the Patrick puzzle had just fallen into place. The question of the moment was this: How long had Patrick planned his departure from his old life? Bad wife, bastard child, horrible accident, no corpse, elaborate theft, take the money and run. The planning was astonishing. Everything had worked perfectly, until now of course.

'Then why fight the divorce?' he asked, still looking below. 'If he doesn't want the child, why bring up the trash?'

Sandy knew the answer, but he wanted her to explain it. In doing so, she would give the first glimpse of the rest of the master plan.

'You bring up the trash only to her lawyer,' she said.

172

'You show him the file, all of it. At that point, they'll be anxious to settle.'

'Settle, as in money.'

'Correct.'

'What type of settlement?'

'She gets nothing.'

'What is there to get?'

'Depends. It could be a small fortune, or a large one.'

Sandy turned and glared at her. 'I cannot negotiate a property settlement if I don't know how much my client has. At some point, you guys have to clue me in.'

'Be patient,' she said, thoroughly unruffled. 'With time, you'll know more.'

'Does Patrick really think he can buy his way out of this?'

'He'll certainly try.'

'It won't work.'

'Do you have a better idea?'

'No.'

'I didn't think so. It's our only chance.'

Sandy relaxed and leaned against the wall. 'It would be helpful if you guys would tell me more.'

'We will. I promise. But first, we'll take care of the divorce. Trudy has to relinquish all claims to his assets.'

'That should be easy. And fun.'

'Get it done, and we'll chat again next week.'

It was suddenly time for Sandy to leave. She was on her feet, gathering papers. He took his files and placed them in his briefcase. 'How long will you be here?' he asked.

'Not long,' she said, and handed him an envelope. 'That's a letter for Patrick. Tell him I'm fine, I'm moving around, and so far I haven't seen anyone behind me.'

Sandy took the envelope and tried to make eye contact. She was nervous and anxious for him to leave. He wanted to help her, or at least to offer, but he knew whatever he said at this point would be dismissed.

She forced a smile, and said, 'You have a job to do. So do it. Patrick and I will worry about the rest.'

While Stephano told his story in Washington, Benny Aricia and Guy set up camp in Biloxi. They leased a three-bedroom condo on the Back Bay, and installed phones and a fax.

The theory was that the girl would have to surface in Biloxi. Patrick was confined, and for the foreseeable future his life was fairly predictable. He wasn't going anywhere. She would have to come to him. And they had to catch her when she did.

Aricia had budgeted a hundred thousand for this last little campaign, and that would be the end of it, he swore to himself. Down almost two million, he simply had to stop burning money while he had some left. Northern Case Mutual and Monarch-Sierra, the other two members of his shaky partnership, had thrown in the towel. Stephano would keep the FBI happy with his tall tales, while hopefully Guy and the rest of the organization could find the girl. It was a longshot.

Osmar and his boys were still loitering in the streets of Rio, watching the same places each day. If she came back, they would see her. Osmar used a lot of men, but they worked cheap down there.

Returning to the Coast brought back bitter feelings in Benny Aricia. He had moved there in 1985 as an executive of Platt & Rockland Industries, a mammoth conglomerate which had sent him around the world for twenty years as a troubleshooter. One of the company's more profitable divisions was New Coastal Shipyards in Pascagoula, between Biloxi and Mobile.

In 1985, New Coastal received a twelve-billion-dollar Navy contract to build four Expedition Class nuclear submarines, and someone upstairs decided Benny needed a permanent home.

Raised in New Jersey, educated in Boston, and the husband, at the time, of a repressed socialite, he was miserable living on the Gulf Coast of Mississippi. He considered it a serious diversion from the corporate hierarchy he longed for. His wife left him after two years in Biloxi.

Platt & Rockland was a public company with twenty-one billion in stockholders' equity, eighty thousand employees in thirty-six divisions in a hundred and three countries. It retailed office supplies, cut timber, made thousands of consumer products, sold insurance, drilled for natural gas, shipped containerized cargo, mined copper, and among many other ventures, built nuclear submarines. It was a sprawling mass of decentralized companies, and as a rule, the left hand seldom knew what the right one was doing. It amassed huge profits in spite of itself.

Benny dreamed of streamlining the company, of selling off the junk and investing in the prosperous divisions. He was unabashedly ambitious, and through the ranks of upper managers it was well known that he wanted the top job.

To him, life in Biloxi was a cruel joke, a pit stop from the fast lane orchestrated by his enemies within the company. He detested contracting with the government, detested the red tape and bureaucrats and arrogance from the Pentagon. He hated the snail's pace with which the submarines were built.

In 1988, he asked to be transferred, and was denied. A year later, the rumors of serious cost overruns on the Expedition project surfaced. Construction came to a halt as government auditors and Pentagon brass descended on New Coastal Shipyards. Benny was on the hot seat, and the end was near.

As a defense contractor, Platt & Rockland had a rich history of cost overruns, overbilling, and false claims. It was a way of doing business, and when discovered, the company typically fired everybody near the controversy and negotiated with the Pentagon for a small repayment.

Benny went to a local attorney, Charles Bogan, the senior partner in a small firm which included a young partner named Patrick Lanigan. Bogan's cousin was a U.S. Senator from Mississippi. The Senator was a rabid hawk who chaired the subcommittee on military appropriations, and was dearly loved by the armed services.

Lawyer Bogan's mentor was now a federal judge, and thus the small firm was as politically well connected as any in Mississippi. Benny knew this, and carefully selected Bogan.

The False Claims Act, also known as the Whistle-Blower Law, was designed by Congress to encourage those with knowledge of overbilling in government contracts to come forward. Benny studied the act thoroughly, and even had an in-house lawyer dissect it for him before he went to Bogan.

He claimed he could prove a scheme by Platt & Rockland to overbill the government some six hundred million dollars on the Expedition project. He could feel the ax dropping, and he refused to be the fall guy. By squealing, he would lose any chance of ever finding comparable work. Platt & Rockland would flood the industry with rumors of his own wrongdoing. He would be blacklisted. It would be the end of Benny's corporate life. He understood very well how the game was played.

Under the act, the whistle-blower *may* receive

fifteen percent of the amount repaid to the government by the offending corporation. Benny had the documentation to prove Platt & Rockland's scheme. He needed Bogan's expertise and clout to collect the fifteen percent.

Bogan hired private engineers and consultants to review and make sense of the thousands of documents Aricia was feeding him from inside New Coastal Shipyards. The scheme was tied together nicely, and it turned out not to be so intricate after all. The company was doing what it had always done – charging multiple prices for the same materials, and fabricating paperwork. The practice was so ingrained at Platt & Rockland that only two upper managers at the shipyards knew it existed. Benny claimed to have stumbled upon it by accident.

A clear and convincing case was assembled by the lawyers, and they filed suit in federal court in September of 1990. The lawsuit alleged six hundred million dollars in fraudulent claims submitted by Platt & Rockland. Benny resigned the day the suit was filed.

The lawsuit was meticulously prepared and researched, and Bogan pressed hard. So did his cousin. The Senator had been placed in the loop long before the actual filing, and monitored it with great interest once it arrived in Washington. Bogan did not come cheap; nor did the Senator. The firm's fee would be the standard one third. One third of fifteen percent of six hundred million dollars. The Senator's cut was never ascertained.

Bogan leaked enough dirt to the local press to keep the pressure on in Mississippi, and the Senator did the same in Washington. Platt & Rockland found itself besieged by hideous publicity. It was pinned to the ropes, its money cut off, its stockholders angry. A dozen managers at New Coastal Shipyards were fired. More terminations were promised.

As usual, Platt & Rockland negotiated hard with Justice, but this time made no progress. After a year, it agreed to repay the six hundred million dollars, and to sin no more. Because two of the subs were half-built, the Pentagon agreed not to yank the contract. Thus, Platt & Rockland could finish what was planned as a twelve-billion-dollar project, but was now well on its way to twenty billion.

Benny got set to receive his fortune. Bogan and the other partners in the firm got set to spend theirs. Then Patrick disappeared, followed by their money.

TWENTY

Pepper Scarboro's shotgun was a Remington .12 gauge pump he purchased from a pawnshop in Lucedale when he was sixteen, too young to buy from a licensed dealer. He paid two hundred dollars for it, and, according to his mother, Neldene, it was his most beloved possession. Sheriff Sweeney and Sheriff Tatum, of Greene County, found the shotgun, along with a well-worn sleeping bag and a small tent, a week after Patrick's death as they were making a routine inventory of his cabin. Trudy had given permission for the search, which in itself was a major problem since she had no ownership interest in the cabin. Any effort to use the shotgun, sleeping bag, and tent as evidence in Patrick's murder trial would be met with fierce resistance since they were found without a search warrant. A valid argument could be made that the sheriffs weren't searching for evidence since there wasn't, at that time, a crime. They were simply gathering up Patrick's personal effects to hand over to his family.

Trudy didn't want the sleeping bag and the tent. She was adamant in her belief that they didn't belong to Patrick. She had never seen them before. They were cheap, unlike items Patrick would buy. And, besides, he didn't camp. He had the cabin to sleep in. Sweeney put labels on them and stored them in his evidence room, for lack of a better place. He planned to wait a year or two, then sell them at one of his annual Sheriff's sales. Six weeks later, Neldene Crouch burst into tears when confronted with Pepper's camping gear.

The shotgun was handled differently. It was found under a bed, along with the tent and the sleeping bag, in the room Patrick slept in. Someone had hurriedly slid the items under the bed, in Sweeney's opinion. His curiosity was immediately aroused because of the presence of the shotgun. An avid hunter himself, he knew that no hunter with a brain would leave a shotgun or hunting rifle in a remote cabin for thieves to take at their convenience. Nothing of value was ever left in a hunting cabin in these parts. He had carefully examined it on the spot, and noticed the serial number had been filed off. The gun had been stolen at some point since its manufacture.

He discussed it with Sheriff Tatum, and they made the decision to at least have it checked for fingerprints. Nothing would come of it, they were sure, but both were experienced and patient cops.

Later, after repeated promises of immunity, the pawnbroker in Lucedale admitted he had sold the gun to Pepper.

Sweeney and Ted Grimshaw, the chief investigator for Harrison County, politely knocked on Patrick's hospital door, and entered only when invited in. Sweeney had called ahead to alert Patrick of their visit, and to inform him of its purpose. Just routine procedures. Patrick had yet to be properly booked.

They photographed his face while he was sitting in a chair, wearing a tee shirt and gym shorts, his hair unruly and his expression sour. He held the booking numbers they had brought along. They took his fingerprints, with Grimshaw doing the work as Sweeney handled the conversation. Patrick insisted on standing over the small table while Grimshaw took the prints.

Sweeney asked a couple of questions about Pepper Scarboro, but Patrick quickly reminded him he had a lawyer, and his lawyer would be present during any interrogation. Furthermore, he had nothing to say about anything, with or without a lawyer.

They thanked him and left. Cutter and an FBI fingerprint expert from Jackson were waiting in the Lanigan Room at the jail. At the time it was found, Pepper's .12 gauge yielded more than a dozen full, usable prints. They had been lifted by Grimshaw after dusting, filed away in a vault, and now were spread on the table. The shotgun was on a shelf, next to the tent and the sleeping bag, and the jogging shoe and the photographs, and the few other sparse items of evidence to be used against Patrick.

They drank coffee from plastic cups and talked about fishing while the print expert compared the old with the new through a magnifying glass. It didn't take long.

'Several of these are perfect matches,' he said, still working. 'The gun stock was covered with Lanigan's prints.'

Certainly good news, they thought. Now what?

Patrick insisted on a different room for all future meetings with his attorney, and Dr Hayani was quick to make the necessary arrangements. He also requested a wheelchair to transport him to the room on the first floor. A nurse pushed him, past the two deputies sitting benignly in the hall outside his door, past Special Agent Brent Myers, and onto the elevator for the brief ride to the first floor. One of the deputies trailed along.

The room was one used by doctors for staff meetings. The hospital was small and the room appeared to be used sparingly. Sandy had ordered the antibugging scanner Patrick had mentioned, but it wouldn't be in for a few days.

'Please rush it,' Patrick said.

'Come on, Patrick. Surely you don't think they would bug this room. No one knew we would use it until an hour ago.'

'We can't be too careful.' Patrick stood from the wheelchair and walked around the long conference table, walked without any limp whatsoever, Sandy noted.

'Look, Patrick, I think you should try and relax a little. I know you've been on the run for a long time. You've lived in fear, always looking over your shoulder, I know all that. But those days are over. They caught you. Relax.'

'They're still out there, okay? They have me, but not the money. And the money is much more important. Don't forget that, Sandy. They won't rest until they have the money.'

'So who might be bugging us here? Good guys or bad? Cops or crooks?'

'The people who lost the money have spent a bloody fortune trying to find it.'

'How do you know?'

Patrick merely shrugged as if it were time to play games again.

'Who are they?' Sandy asked, and there was a long pause, one similar to those used by Leah when she wanted to change the subject.

'Sit down,' Patrick said. They sat on opposite sides of the table. Sandy removed the thick file Leah had given him four hours earlier; the dirt-on-Trudy file.

Patrick recognized it immediately. 'When did you see her?' he asked anxiously.

'This morning. She's fine, sends her love, says nobody's stalking her yet, and asked me to deliver this.' He slid the envelope across the table where Patrick grabbed it, ripped it open, and pulled out a three-page letter. He then proceeded to read it slowly, oblivious to his lawyer.

Sandy flipped through the file and settled on the nudie pictures of Trudy reclining by the pool with her gigolo sprawled nearby. He couldn't wait to show these to her lawyer in Mobile. They had a meeting scheduled in three hours.

Patrick finished the letter, carefully refolded it, and placed it in the envelope. 'I have another letter for her,' he said. He glanced across the table and saw the photos. 'Pretty good work, huh?'

'It's amazing. I've never seen this much proof in a divorce case.'

'Well, there was a lot to work with. We'd been married almost two years when I bumped into her first husband, quite by accident. It was at a party before a Saints game in New Orleans. We had a few drinks, and he told me about Lance. He's the tomcat in the pictures there.'

'Leah explained it.'

'Trudy was very pregnant at the time, so I said nothing. The marriage was slowly unraveling, and we hoped the child would make things perfect. She has an amazing capacity for deceit. I decided to play along, be a proud daddy and all that, but a year later I started gathering evidence. I wasn't sure when I would need it, but I knew the marriage was over. I left town every chance I got – business, hunting, fishing, weekends with the boys, whatever. She never seemed to mind.'

'I meet with her lawyer at 5 P.M.'

'Good. You'll have a great time. It's a lawyer's dream. Threaten everything, but walk away with the settlement. She has to sign away all rights, Sandy. She gets none of my assets.'

'When do we talk about your assets?'

'Soon. I promise. But there is something more pressing.'

Sandy removed his obligatory legal pad and poised himself to take notes. 'I'm listening,' he said.

'Lance is a nasty character. He grew up in the bars along Point Cadet, never finished high school, and served three years for smuggling dope. A bad seed. He has friends in the underworld. He knows people who'll do anything for money. There's another thick file, this one on him. I take it Leah didn't give it to you.'

'No. Just this one.'

'Ask her about it next time. I gathered dirt on Lance for a year with the same private detective. Lance is a small-time hood, but he's dangerous because he has friends. And Trudy has money. We don't know how much is left, but she probably hasn't spent it all.'

'And you think he's coming after you?'

'Probably. Think about it, Sandy. Trudy is the only person right now who still needs me dead. If I'm out of the way, she keeps the money she has left, and she doesn't worry about the insurance company getting what she now owns. I know her. The money and the lifestyle mean everything.'

'But how could he –'

'It can be done, Sandy. Believe me. It can be done.'

He said this with the calm assurance of one who had committed murder and gotten by with it, and for a second Sandy's blood ran cold.

'It can easily be done,' he said for the third time, his eyes glaring, the wrinkles around them pinched tightly.

'Okay, what am I supposed to do? Sit with the deputies in the hallway?'

'You create the fiction, Sandy.'

'I'm listening.'

'First, you tell her lawyer that your office has received an anonymous tip that Lance is in the market for a hit man. Do this at the end of your meeting today. By then, the guy will be shell-shocked and he'll believe anything you say. Tell him you plan to meet with the cops and discuss this. He'll no doubt call his client, who'll deny it vehemently. But her credibility with him will be shot. Trudy will recoil at the very idea that someone else suspects she and Lance have entertained such thoughts. Then, meet with the Sheriff and the FBI and tell the same story. Tell them why you're worried about my safety. Insist that they chat with Trudy and Lance about these rumors. I know her very well, Sandy. She'll sacrifice Lance to keep the money, but not if there's the chance she'll get caught too. If the cops are suspicious now, she'll back off.'

'You've given this some thought. Anything else?'

'Yes. The last thing you do is leak it to the press. You need to find a reporter –'

'That shouldn't be hard to do.'

'One that you can trust.'

'Much harder.'

'Not really. I've been reading the papers, and I have a couple of names for you. Check them out. Find one you like. Tell him to print the rumors, off the record, and in return you'll give him first shot at the real stories. That's the way these guys operate. Tell him the Sheriff is investigating reports of the wife attempting to procure the services of a contract killer so she can keep the money. He'll eat it up. He won't have to validate the story. Hell, they print rumors all the time.'

Sandy finished his notes and marveled at his client's preparation. He closed his file, tapped it with his pen, and asked, 'How much of this stuff do you have?'

'Dirt?'

'Yeah.'

'I'd guess fifty pounds. It's been locked in a mini-storage in Mobile ever since I disappeared.'

'What else is there?'

'More dirt.'

'On who?'

'My former partners. And others. We'll get to it later.'

'When?'

'Soon, Sandy.'

Trudy's lawyer, J. Murray Riddleton, was a jovial, thick-necked man of sixty who specialized in two types of law: big, nasty divorces, and financial advice aimed at cheating the government. He was a quick study in contrasts; successful but badly dressed, intelligent but plain-faced, smiling but vicious, mild-spoken but sharp-tongued. His large office in downtown Mobile was strewn with long neglected files and out-of-date law books. He politely welcomed Sandy, indicated a chair, and offered a drink. It was, after all, a few minutes after five. Sandy declined, and J. Murray drank nothing.

'So how's our boy?' J. Murray asked, flashing teeth.

'That would be?'

'Come on. Our boy Patrick. Have you found the money yet?'

'Didn't know I was looking for any.'

J. Murray found this hilarious and laughed a few seconds. There was no doubt in his mind that he was thoroughly in control of this meeting. The cards were heavily stacked on his side of the desk.

'I saw your client on TV last night,' Sandy said. 'That sleazy tabloid, what's it called?'

'"Inside Journal." Wasn't she marvelous? And the little girl, what a doll. Those poor people.'

'My client would like to request that your client refrain from any further public comment about their marriage and divorce.'

186

'Your client can kiss my client's ass. And you can kiss mine.'

'I'll pass, as will my client.'

'Look, son, I'm a First Amendment hawk. Say anything. Do anything. Publish anything. It's all protected right there by the Constitution.' He pointed to a wall of cobwebbed law books next to his window. 'Request denied. My client has the right to go public with anything she wants, anytime she wants. She's been humiliated by your client, and now faces a very uncertain future.'

'Fair enough. Just wanted to clear the air.'

'Is it clear enough?'

'Yes. Now, we really have no problems with your client's desire to get a divorce, and she can have custody of the child.'

'Gee thanks. You guys are being generous.'

'In fact, my client has no plans to seek visitation rights with the child.'

'Smart man. After abandoning the child for four years, he'd be hard-pressed to see her.'

'There is another reason,' Sandy said, as he opened the file and picked out the DNA test. He handed a copy across to J. Murray, who had stopped smiling and was squinting at the papers.

'What's this?' he asked, suspiciously.

'Why don't you read it?' Sandy said.

J. Murray yanked his reading glasses from a coat pocket, and stuck them to his rather round head. He pushed the report away, got it just right, then read it slowly. He glanced up with a blank look after page one, and his buoyant shoulders sagged a bit at the end of page two.

'Disastrous, isn't it?' Sandy said when J. Murray had finished.

'Don't patronize me. I'm sure this can be explained.'

'I'm sure it cannot. Under Alabama law, the DNA is conclusive proof. Now, I'm not quite the First Amendment hawk you are, but if this got published it would be very embarrassing for your client. Imagine, having someone else's child while pretending to be happily married to another. Wouldn't play well along the Coast, I'm afraid.'

'Publish it,' J. Murray said, with no conviction. 'I don't care.'

'Better check with your client first.'

'It's insignificant, under our law. Even if she committed adultery, he continued to live with her after he knew. Therefore, he accepted it. He's barred from using it as grounds for divorce.'

'Forget the divorce. She can have that. Forget the kid too.'

'Oh, I see then. It's extortion. She releases her claim to his assets, and he doesn't go public.'

'Something like that.'

'Your client's crazy as hell and so are you.' J. Murray's cheeks turned red and his fists clenched for a second.

Sandy, coolly, flipped through the file and extracted the next bit of damage. He slid a report across the desk.

'What is it?' J. Murray demanded.

'Read it.'

'I'm tired of reading.'

'Okay, it's a report by the private detective who followed your client and her boyfriend for a year prior to my client's disappearance. They were together, alone, at various places but primarily at my client's home, indoors, and we presume in bed, on at least sixteen occasions.'

'Big deal.'

'Check these out,' Sandy said, and flung two eight-by-ten color photos, two of the nude ones, on top of

188

the report. J. Murray glanced, then grabbed them for a more in-depth study.

Sandy decided to be helpful. 'Those were taken by the pool at my client's home while he was attending a seminar in Dallas. Recognize anyone?'

J. Murray managed a slight grunt.

'There are many more,' Sandy promised, then waited for J. Murray to stop his gawking. 'And I also have three other reports from private detectives. Seems my client was quite suspicious.'

Before Sandy's eyes, J. Murray was transformed from a hardnosed advocate to a soulful mediator, a chameleon-like conversion common among lawyers who suddenly found themselves stripped of ammunition. He exhaled heavily, defeated, and sat low in his leather swivel. 'They never tell us everything, do they,' he said. It was suddenly us versus them. Lawyers versus their clients. He and Sandy were really together now, and what were they to do?

Sandy, though, was not ready for the tag team. 'Again, I'm not the First Amendment hawk you claim to be, but if these found their way into the tabloids, then it sure would be embarrassing for Trudy.'

J. Murray waved him off, and glanced at his watch. 'Sure you don't want a drink?'

'I'm sure.'

'What's your boy got?'

'I honestly don't know, yet. And that's not the important question. What matters is what he will have left when the dust settles, and right now no one knows.'

'Surely he's got most of the ninety million.'

'He's being sued for much more than that. Not to mention the possibility of a long prison sentence and maybe an execution. This divorce, Mr Riddleton, is the least of his worries.'

'Then why are you threatening us?'

'He wants her to shut up, to get her divorce and go away, and to release all future claims against him. He wants it done now.'

'If not?' J. Murray loosened his tie and sunk an inch lower. The day was suddenly late; he needed to go home. He thought for a long minute, then said, 'She'll lose everything, does he know that? The life insurance company will wipe her out.'

'There are no winners here, Mr Riddleton.'

'Let me speak to her.'

Sandy gathered his things and made a slow retreat to the door. J. Murray managed another sad smile, and just as they were shaking hands to depart, Sandy, as if he had almost forgotten it, mentioned the anonymous tip his office had received in New Orleans about Lance searching for a hit man. He didn't know if he believed it, but he felt compelled to discuss it with the Sheriff and the FBI anyway.

They discussed it briefly. Riddleton promised to mention it to his client.

TWENTY-ONE

Dr Hayani's last stop was Patrick's room. It was almost dark, long past time to leave for the day, and he found his famous patient sitting in his gym shorts in a chair at a makeshift desk in the only empty corner of his room. The desk was a small table, with a lamp Patrick had conned out of an orderly. A plastic water cup held pens and pencils. Another held the beginning of a collection of paper clips, rubber bands, push pins, all donated by the nursing staff. He even had three legal pads.

Patrick was in business. An impressive collection of legal documents occupied one corner, and he was reviewing one of the numerous lawsuits filed against him when his doc popped in, for the third time of the day.

'Welcome to my office,' Patrick said. A bulky TV hung not far above his head. The back of his chair was a foot from the end of his bed.

'Nice,' Hayani said. Rumors in hospitals flew faster than in law offices, and throughout the last two days there had been amused whispers about the new firm being established in Room 312. 'I hope you don't sue doctors.'

'Never. In thirteen years of practicing law, I never sued a doctor. Nor a hospital.' He stood as he said this and turned to face Hayani.

191

'I knew I liked you,' the doctor said as he gently examined the burns on Patrick's chest. 'How are you doing?' he asked, for the third time that day.

'I'm fine,' Patrick repeated, for the umpteenth time that day. The nurses, starstruck and curious, barged in at least twice an hour with any one of a hundred errands, and always with a chirping, 'How ya feeling?'

'I'm fine,' he always answered.

'Did you nap today?' Hayani asked, squatting and poking along the left thigh.

'No. It's hard to sleep without pills, and I really hate to take anything during the day,' Patrick answered. In truth, napping was impossible with the parade of nurses and orderlies.

He sat on the edge of the bed and looked sincerely at his doctor. 'Can I tell you something?' he asked.

Hayani stopped scribbling on a chart. 'Certainly.'

Patrick cast his eyes to the left and to the right as if there could be ears everywhere. 'When I was a lawyer,' he began softly, 'I had this client, a banker, who got caught embezzling. He was forty-four years old, married, three teenaged kids, a great guy who did a dumb thing. He was arrested at home, late at night, and taken to the county jail. It was crowded, and he got thrown into a cell with a couple of young street punks, black guys, mean as hell. They gagged him first so he couldn't scream. They beat him, then they did things you don't want to know about. Two hours after he was sitting in his den watching a movie, he was half-dead in a jail cell three miles from his home.' Patrick's chin hit his chest and he pinched the bridge of his nose.

Dr Hayani touched his shoulder.

'You can't let that happen to me, Doc,' Patrick said, his eyes watery, his voice strained.

'Don't worry, Patrick.'

192

'The thought of it horrifies me, Doc. I have nightmares about it.'

'You have my word, Patrick.'

'God knows I've been through enough.'

'I promise, Patrick.'

The next interrogator was a squirrely little man named Warren, who chain-smoked and viewed the world through thick, dark glasses. His eyes were invisible. His left hand worked the cigarette, his right one handled the pen, and nothing else moved, except his lips. He crouched behind his neat little piles of paper and shot questions to the other end, where Stephano fiddled with a paper clip and his lawyer fought with a laptop.

'When did you form your consortium?' Warren asked.

'After we lost his trail in New York, we pulled back and waited. We listened where we could listen. We covered old tracks. Nothing happened. The trail quickly ran cold, and we settled in for the long run. I'd met with Benny Aricia, and he was willing to finance the search. Then I also met with people from Monarch-Sierra and Northern Case Mutual, and they gave their tentative approval. Northern Case Mutual had just forked over two point five million to the widow. They couldn't sue to get it back because there was no conclusive evidence he was still alive. They agreed to put up a half a million. Monarch-Sierra was more complicated because they had not paid, at that time. Their exposure was four million.'

'Monarch carried the law firm's malpractice insurance?'

'Close. It was a separate crime rider, in addition to the customary Errors and Omissions policy. It protected the law firm from fraud and theft by its employees and partners. Since Lanigan stole from the firm, Monarch-Sierra was forced to pay up, to the tune of four million dollars.'

'But your client, Mr Aricia, received this money, correct?'

'Yes. He first sued the law firm for the entire sixty million he lost, but the firm had few assets. The firm agreed to hand over the proceeds from the policy. We all sat down at the table and struck a deal. Monarch-Sierra agreed to pay the money without a fight if Mr Aricia would use up to a million of it to find Lanigan. Mr Aricia agreed, but only if Monarch-Sierra would kick in another one million to finance the search.'

'So Aricia was in for a million, Monarch-Sierra for a million, and Northern Case Mutual for half a million. Total of two point five.'

'Yes, that was the initial agreement.'

'Where was the law firm?'

'They chose not to participate. Frankly, they didn't have the money, and they were too shocked to respond. Initially, they helped in other ways.'

'And the players paid up?'

'Yes. The money was wired to my firm's account.'

'Now that the search is over, how much of the money is left?'

'Almost none.'

'How much was spent?'

'Three and a half million, give or take a little. About a year ago, the funds ran out. The insurance companies said no. Mr Aricia kicked in another half a million, then another three hundred thousand. His total to date is one point nine.'

Actually, it was an even two million, now that Benny had reluctantly decided to go after the girl. The FBI, of course, would not know this.

'And how was the money spent?'

Stephano referred to his notes, but only for a glimpse.

194

'Almost a million in payroll, travel, and other expenses related to the search. One point five million in rewards. And an even million to my firm as fees.'

'You've been paid a million dollars?' Warren asked, still with no movement of muscle but with a slightly raised voice.

'Yes. Over a four-year period.'

'Tell me about the rewards.'

'Well, it goes to the heart of the search.'

'We're listening.'

'One of the first things we did was to establish a reward for any information about the disappearance of Patrick Lanigan. You guys knew about the reward, but you thought the law firm was backing it. We quietly went to the law firm and convinced Charles Bogan to announce the formation of a reward for information. He went public and promised fifty thousand, at first. Our deal with Bogan was that he would secretly notify us if there was any response.'

'The FBI was not informed of this.'

'No. The FBI knew about the reward, and approved it. But our agreement with Bogan was kept quiet. We wanted the first shot at any information. We didn't distrust the FBI, we simply wanted to find Lanigan and the money ourselves.'

'How many men did you have working on the case at this point?'

'Probably a dozen.'

'And where were you?'

'Here. But I went to Biloxi at least once a week.'

'Did the FBI know what you were doing?'

'Absolutely not. To my knowledge, the FBI never knew we were involved, until last week.'

The file in front of Warren certainly reflected this. 'Continue.'

'We heard nothing for two months, three months, four. We raised the reward money to seventy-five, then to a hundred. Bogan got hammered with all the nuts out there, and he passed this along to the FBI. Then in August of '92, he got a call from a lawyer in New Orleans who claimed to have a client who knew something about the disappearance. The guy sounded very legitimate, and so we went to New Orleans to meet with him.'

'What was his name?'

'Raul Lauziere, on Loyola Street.'

'Did you meet with him?'

'I did.'

'And who else from your firm?'

Stephano glanced at his lawyer, who had frozen for the moment and was deep in thought. 'This is a secretive business. I'd rather not mention the names of my associates.'

'He doesn't have to,' the lawyer pronounced loudly, and that was the end of the matter.

'Fine. Continue.'

'Lauziere appeared to be serious, ethical, and believable. He was also very prepared. He seemed to know everything about the disappearance of Patrick and the money. He had a file of all the press clippings. Everything was indexed and at his fingertips. He handed us a four-page, double-spaced narrative of what his client knew.'

'Just summarize it in detail. I'll read it later.'

'Certainly,' Stephano said, and recounted the narrative from memory: 'His client was a young woman named Erin who was struggling through med school at Tulane. She was recently divorced, broke, etc., and to help make ends meet she worked the late shift in a large bookstore in a mall, one of those big chains. Sometime in January of '92 she noticed a customer milling around the travel and language section. He was heavyset, dressed in a suit, neat black and gray beard, and appeared to be somewhat nervous. It was

196

almost nine at night, and the store was practically deserted. He finally picked out a language course with twelve cassettes, workbooks, etc., all in one slick box, and he was easing toward the checkout area where Erin worked when another man entered the store. The first man immediately withdrew between the racks and placed the language course back on the shelf. He then emerged on the other side, and attempted to slip past the second man, a person he obviously knew and didn't want to speak to. But he didn't make it. The second man glanced up, and said, 'Patrick, it's been a long time.' A brief conversation ensued in which the two men talked about their law careers. Erin puttered around the checkout stand and listened because there was nothing else to do. Evidently, she was keenly curious and watched everything.

'Anyway, the one called Patrick was anxious to leave, so he finally found the right moment and made a graceful getaway. Three nights later, at about the same time, he came back. Erin was putting up stock, not checking out. She saw him enter, recognized him, remembered he was called Patrick, and watched him. He made a point to look at the checkout clerk, and when he realized she was a different one, he loitered around the store until he stopped in the language and travel section. He picked out the same language course, slid to the counter, paid for it in cash, and left quickly. Almost three hundred bucks. Erin watched him leave. He never saw her, or if he did, he didn't recognize her.'

'So what's the language?'

'That, of course, was the big question. Three weeks later Erin saw in the paper where Patrick Lanigan was killed in a terrible auto accident, and she recognized his picture. Then, six weeks later the story broke about the stolen money from his old firm, the same picture was in the papers, and Erin saw it again.'

'Did the bookstore have security cameras?'

'No. We checked.'

'So what was the language?'

'Lauziere wouldn't tell us. At least at first he wouldn't. We were offering a hundred thousand dollars for solid information about Lanigan's whereabouts. He, and his client, quite naturally wanted all of the money for the name of the language. We negotiated for three days. He wouldn't budge. He allowed us to interrogate Erin. We spent six hours with her, and every aspect of her story checked out, so we agreed to pay the hundred grand.'

'Brazilian Portuguese?'

'Yes. The world suddenly shrunk.'

Like every lawyer, J. Murray Riddleton had been through it many times before, unfortunately. The airtight case suddenly springs leaks. The tables get turned in the blink of an eye.

Just for the fun of it, and with no small measure of enjoyment, he allowed Trudy to puff and posture for a bit before he lowered the ax.

'Adultery!' she gasped, with all the self-righteousness of a Puritan virgin. Even Lance pulled off a look of shock. He reached across and took her hand.

'I know, I know,' J. Murray said, playing along. 'Happens in almost every divorce. These things do get nasty.'

'I'll kill him,' Lance grunted.

'We'll get to that later,' J. Murray said.

'With whom?' she demanded.

'With Lance here. They claim the two of you were getting it on before, during, and after the marriage. In fact, they claim it goes all the way back to high school.'

Ninth grade, actually. 'He's an idiot,' Lance said, without conviction.

Trudy nodded and agreed with Lance. Preposterous. Then she asked nervously, 'What proof does he claim to have?'

'Do you deny it?' J. Murray asked, completing the setup.

'Absolutely,' she snapped.

'Of course,' added Lance. 'The man is a living lie.'

J. Murray reached into a deep drawer and withdrew one of the reports Sandy had given him. 'Seems Patrick was suspicious throughout most of the marriage. He hired investigators to snoop around. This is a report from one of them.'

Trudy and Lance looked at each other for a second, then realized they had been caught. Suddenly, it was difficult to deny a relationship that was now more than twenty years old. They both became smug at the same instant. So what? Big deal.

'I'll just summarize it,' J. Murray said, then clicked off dates, times, and places. They weren't ashamed of their activities, but it was discomforting to know that things were so well documented.

'Still deny it?' J. Murray asked when he finished.

'Anybody can write that stuff,' Lance said. Trudy was silent.

J. Murray pulled out another report, this one covering the seven months prior to Patrick's disappearance. Dates, times, places. Patrick left town, bam, Lance moved in. Every time.

'Can these investigators testify in court?' Lance asked when J. Murray finished.

'We're not going to court,' J. Murray said.

'Why not?' Trudy asked.

'Because of these.' J. Murray slid the eight-by-ten color glossies across his desk. Trudy grabbed one and gasped at the sight of herself lounging by the pool, naked, her stud next to her. Lance was shocked too, but managed a tiny grin. He sort of liked them.

They swapped the photos back and forth without a word. J. Murray relished the moment, then said, 'You guys got too careless.'

'Skip the lecture,' Lance said.

Predictably, Trudy started to cry. Her eyes watered, her lip quivered, her nose sniffled, and then she cried. J. Murray had seen it a thousand times. They always cried, not for what they had done, but for the wages of their sins.

'He's not getting my daughter,' she said angrily through the tears. She lost it, and they listened to her bawl for a while. Lance, ever vigilant, pawed at her and tried to console.

'I'm sorry,' she finally said, wiping tears.

'Relax,' J. Murray said without the slightest trace of compassion. 'He doesn't want the kid.'

'Why not?' she asked, the tear ducts shutting down instantly.

'He's not the father.'

They squinted, thought hard, tried to assemble things.

J. Murray reached for yet another report. 'He took a blood sample from the child when she was fourteen months old, and had a DNA test run on it. No way he's the father.'

'Then who ...' Lance started to ask, but couldn't complete the thought.

'Depends on who else was around,' J. Murray said, helpfully.

'No one else was around,' she said, mocking him angrily.

'Except me,' Lance volunteered, then slowly closed his eyes. Fatherhood descended heavily upon his shoulders. Lance despised children. He tolerated Ashley Nicole only because she belonged to Trudy.

'Congratulations,' J. Murray said. He reached into a

drawer, pulled out a cheap cigar and tossed it to Lance. 'It's a girl,' he said, and laughed loudly.

Trudy fumed and Lance toyed with the cigar. When J. Murray finished humoring himself, she asked, 'So where are we?'

'It's simple. You waive any right to his assets, whatever they may be, and he gives you the divorce, the kid, everything else you want.'

'What are his assets?' she asked.

'His lawyer is not sure right now. We may never know. The man is headed for death row, and the cash might stay buried forever.'

'But I'm about to lose everything,' she said. 'Look at what he's done to me. I got two and a half million when he died, now the insurance company is ready to bankrupt me.'

'She deserves a helluva lot of money,' Lance piped in on cue.

'Can I sue him for mental distress, or fraud, or something like that?' she pleaded.

'No. Look, it's very simple. You get the divorce and the kid, and Patrick keeps whatever money is out there. And everything is kept quiet. Otherwise, he'll leak all this to the press.' J. Murray tapped the reports and the photos when he said this. 'And you'll be humiliated. You've gone public with your dirty laundry; he's quite anxious to return the favor.'

'Where do I sign?' she said.

J. Murray fixed them all a vodka, and before too long he was mixing another round. He finally brought up the subject of those silly rumors about Lance looking for a hit man. The denials came fast and furious, and J. Murray confessed that he really didn't believe the trash anyway.

There were so many rumors racing up and down the Coast.

TWENTY-TWO

They began tracking Sandy McDermott as he left New Orleans at 8 A.M. and worked his way through the traffic on Interstate 10. He was followed until the congestion thinned near Lake Pontchartrain. They called ahead and reported he was on his way to Biloxi. Following him was easy. Listening would be another matter. Guy had bugs for Sandy's office and home phones, even one for his car, but the decision to install them had not yet been made. The risks were significant. Aricia especially was wary. He argued with Stephano and with Guy that Sandy might well expect his phones to get tapped, and might feed them all sorts of useless or even damaging gossip. His client had so far proved quite proficient at seeing around corners. And so they argued.

Sandy wasn't looking over his shoulder. Nor was he seeing much in front of him. He was simply driving, moving forward while avoiding contact, his mind, as usual, many miles away.

From a strategic point of view, the various Lanigan battles were in good shape. The civil suits filed by Monarch-Sierra, the law firm, and Aricia had been placed on dockets already densely crowded. Formal responses by Sandy were a month away. Discovery wouldn't start for three months and would last for a year. Trials were two years away at the earliest.

Likewise for Patrick's suit against the FBI; it would one day be amended to bring in Stephano and his consortium. It would be a delightful case to try, but Sandy doubted he would ever get the chance.

The divorce was under control.

The capital murder charge, clearly the center of attention, was another matter. Obviously the most serious of Patrick's problems, it was also the speediest. By law, the state had to try Patrick within two hundred and seventy days of the indictment, so the clock was ticking.

In Sandy's opinion, a conviction based on the evidence would be a longshot. For the moment, crucial elements of proof were missing – significant facts such as the identity of John Doe, and the manner in which he died, and the certainty that Patrick killed him. It was a tenuous circumstantial case at best. Large assumptions would be called for.

However, a conviction based on public sentiment was foreseeable. By now everyone within a hundred miles of Biloxi knew most of the details, and you couldn't find a literate breathing soul who didn't think Patrick killed someone to fake his death so he could lie in ambush and steal ninety million dollars. Patrick had a few admirers, those who also dreamed of a new life with a new name and plenty of dough. But they would not be on his jury. Most folks, it seemed through the informal polling of coffee shop talk and courthouse gossip, felt he was guilty and should spend time in prison. Very few favored the death penalty. Leave that for rapists and cop killers.

Most pressing, though, at the moment, was keeping Patrick alive. The file on Lance, hand-delivered last night by the lovely Leah in yet another hotel room, portrayed a quiet man with a hair-trigger temper and a penchant for violence. He liked guns, and had once been indicted by a federal grand jury for fencing them through a pawnshop. The charges were later dismissed. In addition to his three-year stint for smuggling pot, he had been sentenced to sixty days for his part in a barroom brawl in Gulfport, though the time was suspended due to an overcrowded jail. There were two other arrests – one for another fight and one for a DUI.

Lance could be cleaned up and made presentable. He was lanky and handsome, and well admired by the ladies. He knew how to dress and carry on amusing chitchat over cocktails. But his forays into society were temporary. His heart was always in the street, just above the gutter, where he hung out with loan sharks and bookies and fences and reputable drug dealers, the smart white-collar boys of local crime. These were his friends, the guys from his neighborhood. Patrick had found them too, and the file contained no fewer than a dozen little biographies of Lance's pals, all with criminal records.

Sandy at first had been skeptical of Patrick's paranoia. Now he believed it. Though he knew little of the underworld, the nature of his profession occasionally brought him into contact with criminals. He had heard many times that for five thousand bucks you could get anyone killed. Maybe even less along the Coast.

Lance certainly had more than five thousand bucks. And he had a wonderful motive to eliminate Patrick. The life insurance policies that made Trudy rich didn't exclude any particular causes of death, other than suicide. A bullet to the head was treated just like a car wreck, or a heart attack, or anything else. Dead was dead.

The Coast was not Sandy's turf. He didn't know the sheriffs and their deputies, the judges and their quirks, the other members of the bar. He suspected this was precisely why Patrick picked him.

Sweeney had been less than hospitable on the phone. He was very busy, he said, and besides, meetings with lawyers were usually a waste of time. He could spare a few minutes, starting at nine-thirty and barring an emergency. Sandy arrived early, and poured his own coffee from a pot he found next to the watercooler. Deputies milled about. The sprawling jail was in the rear. Sweeney found him and led him through to his office, a spartan room with government hand-me-down furniture and fading photos of smiling politicians on the wall.

'Have a seat,' Sweeney said, pointing to a ratty chair as he sat behind his desk. Sandy did as he was told.

'Mind if I record?' Sweeney asked, already punching the button on a large tape recorder in the center of his desk. 'I tape everything,' he said.

'Sure,' Sandy said, as if he had a choice. 'Thanks for working me in.'

'No problem,' Sweeney said. He had yet to smile or offer anything other than the impression of being bothered by this. He lit a cigarette and sipped steaming coffee from a Styrofoam cup.

'I'll get right to the point,' Sandy said, as if idle conversation were an option. 'My office has received a tip that Patrick's life may be in danger.' Sandy hated the lying, but he had little choice under the circumstances. This was what his client wanted.

'Why would someone tip your office that your client was in danger?' Sweeney asked.

'I have investigators working on the case. They know lots of people. Some gossip got passed along, and one of my investigators tracked it down. That's the way these things happen.'

Sweeney showed neither belief nor disbelief. He smoked his cigarette and thought about it. In the past week, he had heard every conceivable species of rumor about the adventures of Patrick Lanigan. People were talking about nothing else. The hit man stories were of several varieties. Sweeney figured his network was better than the lawyer's, especially one from New Orleans, so he would let him talk. 'Got any suspects?'

'Yes. His name is Lance Maxa; I'm sure you know him.'

'We do.'

'He took Patrick's place with Trudy not long after the funeral.'

'Some would say Patrick took his place,' Sweeney said, with his first smile. Sandy was indeed on foreign turf. The Sheriff knew more than he.

'Then I guess you know all about Lance and Trudy,' Sandy said, a little rattled.

'We do. We take good notes around here.'

'I'm sure you do. Anyway, Lance, as you know, is a nasty sort, and my men got a rumor that he was looking for a contract killer.'

'How much is he offering?' Sweeney asked skeptically.

'Don't know. But he has the money, and he has the motive.'

'I've already heard this.'

'Good. What do you plan to do?'

'About what?'

'About keeping my client alive.'

Sweeney took a deep breath and decided to hold his tongue. He struggled with his temper. 'He's on a military base, in a hospital room with my deputies guarding his door and FBI agents down the hall. I'm not sure what else you have in mind.'

'Look, Sheriff, I'm not trying to tell you how to do your job.'

'Really?'

'No. I promise. Please try and understand that my

client is a very frightened man right now. I'm here acting on his behalf. He's been stalked for over four years. He's been caught. He hears voices we don't hear. He sees shadows we don't see. He's convinced people will try to kill him, and he expects me to protect him.'

'He's safe.'

'For now. What if you talked to Lance, and you grilled him pretty good and told him about the rumors. If he knew you were watching, he'd be stupid to try something.'

'Lance is stupid.'

'Maybe, but Trudy is not. If she thinks she might get caught, she'll yank Lance back where he belongs.'

'Been yanking him all his life.'

'Precisely. She will not run the risk.'

Sweeney lit another cigarette, and glanced at his watch. 'Anything else?' he asked, suddenly anxious to get up and leave. He was a Sheriff, not an office manager with a desk and Rolodex.

'Just one thing. And again, I'm not trying to tend to your business. Patrick has enormous respect for you. But, well, he thinks he's much safer where he is.'

'What a surprise.'

'Jail could be dangerous for him.'

'He shoulda thought about that before he killed Mr Doe.'

Sandy ignored this, and said, 'He'll be easier to protect in the hospital.'

'Have you been to my jail?'

'No.'

'Then don't lecture me about how unsafe it is. I've been doing this for a long time, got it?'

'I'm not lecturing.'

'The hell you're not. You got five more minutes. Anything else?'

'No.'

207

'Good.' Sweeney bolted to his feet and left the room.

The Honorable Karl Huskey arrived at Keesler Air Force Base late in the afternoon, and slowly made his way through security to the hospital. He was in the middle of a one-week drug trial, and he was tired. Patrick had called and asked him to stop by, if possible.

Himself a pallbearer, Karl had sat next to Sandy McDermott at Patrick's funeral. Unlike Sandy, though, Huskey had been a recent friend of Patrick's. The two had met during a civil case Patrick had tried not long after he arrived in Biloxi. They became friendly, the way lawyers and judges often do when they see each other every week. They chatted over bad food at the monthly bar luncheons, and once drank too much at a Christmas party. They played golf twice a year.

It was an easy acquaintance, but not a close friendship, at least not for the first three years Patrick was in Biloxi. But they grew closer in the months before he disappeared. With the benefit of hindsight, though, it was easy to look back and see a change in Patrick.

In the months after his disappearance, those in the legal community who knew him best, including Karl, liked to gather over drinks at the Lower Bar at Mary Mahoney's Restaurant on Friday afternoons and piece together the Patrick puzzle.

Trudy took her share of the blame, though she was too easy a target, in Karl's opinion. On the surface, the marriage didn't appear to be that bad. Patrick certainly didn't discuss it with anybody, at least no one who drank with them at Mary Mahoney's. Trudy's actions after the funeral, especially the red Rolls and

the live-in toyboy and the go-to-hell attitude she
adopted as soon as the life insurance was collected,
had soured everyone and made objectivity impossible.
No one was certain that she was sleeping around
before Patrick left. In fact, Buster Gillespie, the
Chancery Clerk and a regular at those sessions,
professed admiration for Trudy. She'd once worked
with his wife at a charity ball of some variety, and he
always felt compelled to say something nice about her.
He was about the only one. Trudy was easy to talk
about and easy to criticize.

Job pressure was certainly a factor in pushing
Patrick to the brink. The firm was rolling in those
days, and he desperately wanted to become a partner.
He worked long hours, and he took the difficult cases
his partners didn't want. Not even the birth of Ashley
Nicole kept him home. He had made partner three
years after joining as an associate, but few people
outside the firm knew it. He had whispered it to Karl
one day after court, but Patrick was not the least bit
boastful.

He was tired and stressed, but then so were most of
the lawyers who entered Karl's courtroom. The oddest
changes in Patrick were physical. He was an even six
feet tall, and he said he had never been thin. He
claimed to have been quite a jogger in law school, at
one point doing forty miles a week. But as a busy
lawyer, who had the time? His weight crept up, then
ballooned the last year he was in Biloxi. He seemed
oblivious to the jokes and comments from the courthouse crowd. Karl had chided him more than once,
but he kept eating. A month before he disappeared, he
told Karl over lunch that he weighed two hundred and
thirty pounds, and that Trudy was raising hell about it.
She, of course, aerobicized two hours a day with Jane
Fonda and was as thin as a model.

He said his blood pressure was up, and he promised

to go on a diet. Karl had encouraged this. He found out later that Patrick's blood pressure had been normal.

The weight gain, and its overnight loss, made perfect sense now that they thought about it.

The beard too. He had grown it around November of 1990, said it was his deer hunting beard. Such growth was not unusual among non-rednecks and lawyers in Mississippi. The air was cool. The testosterone was up. It was a boy thing. He didn't shave it, and Trudy bitched about that too. The longer he kept it, the grayer it became. His friends got accustomed to it. She did not.

He let his hair grow a bit and started wearing it thicker on top and halfway down the ears. Karl called it the Jimmy Carter look from 1976. Patrick claimed to have lost his hairstylist and couldn't find one he trusted.

He wore nice clothes and carried his weight well, but he was too young to let himself go.

Three months before he checked out of Biloxi, Patrick succeeded in convincing his partners that the firm needed its own brochure. It was a small project, but one he embraced with great vigor. Though Patrick wasn't supposed to know it, the firm was getting closer to the Aricia settlement, and the money was almost in sight. Egos were expanding daily. A very serious firm was about to become a very wealthy one, so why not impress themselves with a professionally done brochure. It was a way to humor Patrick. Each of the five sat for a professional photographer, then they spent an hour on the group shot. Patrick printed five thousand, and received high marks from the other partners. There he was on page two, fat, bearded, bushy-headed, and looking nothing like the Patrick they found in Brazil.

The photo was used by the press when his death was

reported. It was by far the most recent, and, coincident-ally, Patrick had sent a brochure to the local paper, just in case the firm decided to advertise. They had laughed about this over drinks at Mary Mahoney's. They could envision Patrick orchestrating the photo-graphy in the firm's conference room. They could see Bogan and Vitrano and Rapley and Havarac in the darkest navy suits and their most serious smiles, and all the while Patrick was laying the groundwork for his exit.

In the months after he left them, the gang at Mary Mahoney's had toasted Patrick many times and played the game of 'Where could he be?' They had wished him well and thought about his money. Time passed and so did the shock of his disappearance. Once they had thoroughly analyzed his life, the sessions came further apart and finally stopped. Months became years. Patrick would never be found.

Karl still found it difficult to believe. He entered the elevator in the lobby and rode alone to the third floor.

He wondered if he had ever given up on Patrick. The mysteries were too rich to escape. A bad day on the bench, and he would think of Patrick on a sun-drenched beach reading a novel, sipping a drink, watching the girls. Another year without a pay raise, and he would wonder what the ninety million was doing. The latest rumor on the demise of the Bogan firm, and he would shame Patrick for the misery he had caused. No, the truth was, Karl had thought of Patrick, for one reason or another, at least once a day, every day, since he left.

There were no nurses or other patients in the hall. The two deputies stood. One said, 'Evenin', Judge.' He greeted them and entered the darkened room.

TWENTY-THREE

Patrick was sitting in bed watching 'Jeopardy' with his shirt off and the blinds drawn. A dim table light was on. 'Sit here,' he told Karl, pointing to the end of his bed. He waited just long enough for Karl to see the burns on his chest, then quickly slipped on a tee shirt. The sheet was up to his waist.

'Thanks for coming,' he said. He turned the TV off, and the room grew even darker.

'Pretty nasty burns, Patrick,' Karl said as he sat on the edge of the bed, as far away as possible, his right foot hanging off the edge. Patrick pulled his knees to his chest. Under the sheet, he still looked painfully thin.

'It was ugly,' he said, his hands wrapped tightly around his knees. 'Doc says they're healing okay. But I'll need to stay here for a while.'

'I have no problem with that, Patrick. No one is screaming for you to be moved to the jail.'

'Not yet. But I bet the press will start soon.'

'Relax, Patrick. That decision will be made by me.'

He seemed relieved. 'Thanks, Karl. You know I can't survive in jail. You've seen it.'

'What about Parchman? It's a hundred times worse.'

There was a long pause as Karl wished he could

212

take back the words. It was instantaneous, and cruel. 'I'm sorry,' he said. 'That was uncalled for.'

'I'll kill myself before I go to Parchman.'

'I don't blame you. Let's talk about something pleasant.'

'You can't keep this case, can you, Karl?'

'No. Of course not. I'll have to recuse myself.'

'When?'

'Pretty soon.'

'Who'll get it?'

'Either Trussel or Lanks, probably Trussel.' Karl stared at him intently as he spoke. Patrick was having trouble with eye contact. Karl was waiting for a telling flicker from the eyes, followed by a grin, then a laugh as Patrick broke down and bragged about his escapades. 'Come on, Patrick,' Karl wanted to say. 'Let's hear it. Tell me the whole story.'

But the eyes were distant. This was not the same Patrick.

Karl felt compelled to try. 'Where'd you get that chin?'

'Bought it in Rio.'

'And the nose?'

'Same place, same time. You like it?'

'It's handsome.'

'In Rio, they have drive-through plastic surgery shops.'

'I hear they have beaches.'

'Unbelievable beaches.'

'Did you meet any girls down there?'

'A couple.'

Sex was not a subject Patrick had ever dwelt on. He enjoyed a long, admiring gaze at an attractive woman, but, to Karl's knowledge, he had remained faithful to Trudy throughout their marriage. Once, at deer camp, they had compared notes about their wives. Patrick

213

had admitted it was a challenge to keep Trudy satisfied.

A long pause, and Karl realized Patrick was in no hurry to talk. The first minute passed in silence, and the second one dragged on. Karl was happy to visit, even delighted to see his friend, but there was a limit to how long he could sit in a dark room and stare at the walls.

'Look, Patrick, I will not hear your case, so I'm not here as your Judge. I'm not your lawyer. I'm your friend. You can talk to me.'

Patrick reached for a small can of orange juice with a straw in it. 'Would you like something to drink?'

'No.'

He took a short drink, and put the can back on the table. 'I guess it sounds romantic, doesn't it? The dream of simply walking away, vanishing into the night and when the sun comes up you're somebody new. All your problems are left behind – the drudgery of work, the heartbreak of a bad marriage, the pressure of becoming more and more affluent. You have that dream, don't you, Karl?'

'I guess everybody does at some point. How long did you plan it?'

'A long time. I seriously doubted that the baby was mine. I decided –'

'I beg your pardon.'

'It's true, Karl. I'm not the father. Trudy slept around throughout our marriage. I loved the child as best I could, but I was miserable. I gathered evidence and promised myself I would confront Trudy, but it was easy to put off. Oddly enough, I sort of got used to the idea that she had a lover. I was planning to leave, but I just didn't know how to do it. So I read a couple of underground books on how to change identities and obtain new papers. It's not complicated. Just takes a little thought and planning.'

214

'So you grew a beard and gained fifty pounds.'

'Yeah, I was amazed at how different I looked with the beard. That was right about the time I made partner, and I was already burned out. I was married to a woman who wasn't faithful, playing with a child who wasn't mine, working with a bunch of people I couldn't stand. Something clicked, Karl. I was driving one day along Highway 90, headed somewhere important but stuck in traffic, and I looked out across the Gulf. There was a lonely little sailboat barely moving on the horizon. And I wanted so desperately to be on it, to sail away to some place where no one knew me. I sat there, watching it move, aching so badly to swim out to it. I cried, Karl. Can you believe that?'

'We all have days like that.'

'Then I snapped, and I was never the same afterward. I knew I would vanish.'

'How long did it take?'

'I had to be patient. Most people get in a hurry when they decide to disappear, and they make mistakes. I had time. I wasn't broke or running from creditors. I bought a two-million-dollar life insurance policy, and that took three months. I knew I couldn't leave Trudy and the baby with nothing. I started gaining the weight, eating like a maniac. I changed my will. I convinced Trudy that we should make our funeral and burial arrangements, and I did it without arousing suspicions.'

'Cremation was a nice touch.'

'Thanks. I highly recommend it.'

'Makes it impossible to determine cause of death and identity, a few important things like that.'

'Let's not talk about that.'

'Sorry.'

'Then I got wind of Mr Benny Aricia, and his little war with the Pentagon and Platt & Rockland Industries. Bogan kept him under wraps. I dug deeper and found out that Vitrano and Rapley and Havarac were all in on the deal. All the partners but me. They changed, Karl, all of them. They became secretive and devious. Sure I was the new guy, but I was a partner after all. They had voted unanimously to make me a full partner, and two months later they were dodging me while they conspired with Aricia. Suddenly, I was the guy doing all the traveling, which worked out just beautifully for everyone. Trudy could arrange her little trysts. The partners could meet with Aricia without hiding. They sent me everywhere, which was fine with me too because I was making plans. Once I went to Fort Lauderdale for three days of depositions, and while I was there I found a guy in Miami who could do perfect papers. Two thousand bucks and I had a new driver's license, passport, Social Security card, and voter registration papers from right here in Harrison County. Carl Hildebrand was my name, in honor of you.'

'I'm touched.'

'In Boston, I tracked down a guy who can get you lost. For a thousand bucks I had my own one-day seminar on how to vanish. In Dayton, I hired a surveillance expert who taught me about bugs and mikes and dirty little devices like that. I was patient, Karl. Very patient. I stayed at the office at odd hours, and gathered as much of the Aricia story as I could get. I listened hard, quizzed secretaries, rummaged through the garbage. Then I began wiring offices, just a couple at first to learn how it's done. I wired Vitrano's, and I couldn't believe what I heard. They were going to kick me out of the firm, Karl. Can you believe it? They knew their cut from the Aricia settlement would be around thirty million, and they were planning to split it four ways. But the pieces would not be equal. Bogan, of course, would get more, something close to ten million. He had to take care of some people in Washington. The other three would get five million, and the rest would be spent on the firm. I, as it was planned, would be on the streets.'

'When was this?'

'Throughout most of '91. Aricia's claim got tentative Justice approval to settle on December 14, 1991, and at that time it was taking about ninety days to get the money. Not even the Senator could speed things along.'

'Tell me about the car wreck.'

Patrick shifted his weight, then kicked his legs from under the sheet and got out of bed. 'A cramp,' he mumbled as he stretched his back and legs. He stood by the bathroom door, rocking gently from one foot to the other, looking down at Karl. 'It was a Sunday.'

'February ninth.'

'Right. February ninth. I spent the weekend at my cabin, and as I was driving home I had a wreck, got killed, and went to heaven.'

Karl watched him closely and never smiled. 'Try it again,' he said.

'Why, Karl?'

'Morbid fascination.'

'Is that all?'

'I promise. It was such a masterful job of deceit, Patrick. How'd you do it?'

'I may have to skip a few of the details.'

'I'm sure you will.'

'Let's take a walk. I'm tired of this place.'

They entered the hall, and Patrick explained to his guards that he and the Judge needed a stroll. The deputies followed at a distance. A nurse smiled and asked if she could bring anything. Two Diet Cokes, Patrick said politely. Patrick walked very deliberately, saying nothing until they came to the end of the hallway, where plate-glass windows overlooked the parking lot. They sat on a vinyl bench, looking back

217

down the hall, where the deputies waited fifty feet away with their backs turned to them.

Patrick wore scrub pants, no socks, leather sandals. 'Have you seen pictures of the crash site?' he asked, very quietly.

'Yes.'

'I found it the day before. The ravine is fairly steep, and I thought it was the perfect place to have the accident. I waited until about ten, Sunday night, and left the cabin. I stopped at a little store at the county line.'

'Verhall's.'

'Right, Verhall's. I filled the tank.'

'Twelve gallons, fourteen dollars and twenty-one cents, paid with a credit card.'

'That sounds right. I chatted with Mrs Verhall, then left. There wasn't much traffic. Two miles away, I turned onto a gravel road and went a mile to a spot I had picked out. I stopped, opened the trunk, and proceeded to get dressed. I had a set of gear used by dirt bikers – a helmet, shoulder pads, knee and hand pads, the works. I quickly put it on over my clothing, everything but the helmet, then returned to the highway, where I drove south. The first time, there was a car behind me. The second time, there was a car coming toward me in the distance. I braked hard anyway, leaving skid marks. There was no traffic the third time. I put the helmet on, took a deep breath, and left the road. It was scary as hell, Karl.'

Karl figured that at this point there was another body somewhere in the car, either dead or alive, but he wouldn't ask. At least not now.

'I was only doing about thirty when I left the road, but thirty feels like ninety when you're airborne and trees are flying by. I was bouncing, snapping small trees. The windshield cracked. I was steering right and left, dodging as best I could, but a big pine tree caught

218

the left front. The airbag exploded, and for a second I was knocked out. There was a tumbling sensation, then all was still. I opened my eyes, and felt a sharp pain in my left shoulder. No blood. I was dangling somehow, and I realized that the Blazer had come to rest on its right side. I began crawling out. By the time I got out of the damned thing, I knew I was lucky. My shoulder wasn't broken, just jammed. I walked around the Blazer and was amazed at how well I had wrecked it. The roof had caved in just above my head. Another six inches and I'm not sure I could've gotten out.'

'That seems incredibly risky. You could've been killed or badly injured. Why not simply push the car down the ravine?'

'Wouldn't work. It had to look real, Karl. The ravine was not steep enough. This is flat country, remember.'

'Why not put a brick on the accelerator and jump out of the way?'

'Bricks don't burn. If they'd found a brick in the car, maybe they would've been suspicious. I thought of everything, and I decided I could drive it into the trees and walk away. I had a seat belt, an airbag, a helmet.'

'Evel Knievel himself.'

The nurse brought the Diet Cokes, and wanted to chat for a moment. She finally left. 'Where was I?' Patrick asked.

'I think you were about to torch it.'

'Right. I listened for a moment. The left rear wheel was spinning, and that was the only sound. I couldn't see the highway, but I looked up in its direction and heard nothing. Absolutely nothing. It was a clean exit. The nearest house was a mile away. I was certain no one had heard the crash, but still I was in a hurry. I stripped off the helmet and the pads and threw them in the Blazer, then I ran farther down the ravine to a spot where I had hidden the gasoline.'

'When?'

'Earlier in the day. Very early. At dawn. I had four two-gallon plastic jugs of gas, and I quickly hauled them up to the Blazer. It was dark as hell and I couldn't use a flashlight, but I had marked off a little path. I placed three of the containers in the Blazer, stopped, listened. Nothing from the highway. Not a sound anywhere. The adrenaline was pumping and my heart was in my throat. The last container I splashed inside and out, then threw it in with the rest. I backed off thirty feet or so, and lit a cigarette I had in my pocket. I threw it, backed up even farther, and ducked behind a tree. It landed on the Blazer, then the gas exploded. Sounded like a bomb. In an instant it was roaring from all the windows. I climbed up the steepest side of the ravine and found a vantage point probably a hundred feet away. I wanted to watch without getting caught. The fire was howling; I had no idea it would make so much noise. Some brush started to burn, and I thought maybe I had started a forest fire. Luckily it had rained on Friday, a hard rain that soaked the trees and ground cover.' He took a drink of his soda. 'I just realized I forgot to ask you about your family. I'm sorry, Karl. How's Iris?'

'Iris is fine. We can talk about the family later. Right now, I'd like to hear the story.'

'Sure. Where was I? I'm so scatterbrained. It's all those drugs.'

'Watching the car burn.'

'Right. So the fire gets really hot, then the gas tank explodes and it's another bomb. I thought for a second I might get scorched. Debris flies through the air, and rattles through the trees as it falls. Finally, I hear something from the highway. Voices. People yelling. I can't see anybody, but there's a commotion. A long time passes and the fire spreads around the car. It's coming at me now, so I leave. I can hear a siren coming. I'm trying to find a creek I'd come across the day before a hundred yards or so through the woods. I'm going to follow it. And I'm looking for my dirt bike.'

Karl hung on every word, absorbed every scene, made every step along the way with Patrick. This escape route had been the subject of many fierce debates in the months after the disappearance, and no one had a clue. 'A dirt bike?'

'Yeah. An old one. I bought it for five hundred dollars cash from a used car dealer in Hattiesburg several months earlier. I played with it some in the woods. Nobody knew I had it.'

'No title or registration?'

'Of course not. I gotta tell you, Karl, as I ran through the woods, looking for the creek, still scared but in one piece, and I heard the fire and voices fade behind me and the siren getting louder, I knew I was running to freedom. Patrick was dead, and he took with him a bad life. He would get honored and buried properly, and everyone would say good-bye. And before long people would start to forget about him. But me, I was running wildly to a new life. It was exhilarating.'

What about the poor guy burning in the car, Patrick? While you were running joyously through the woods someone else was dying in your place. Karl almost asked. Patrick seemed oblivious to the fact that he had committed murder.

'Then suddenly, I'm lost. The woods are dense, and somehow I stumble the wrong way. I get a small flashlight, and I figure it's safe to use it. I roam and backtrack until I can no longer hear the siren. At one point, I sit down on a stump and make myself get a grip. I'm in a panic. Wouldn't this be great? Survive the wreck only to die of starvation and exposure. I start walking again, get lucky and find the creek. Before long, I find the dirt bike. I push it a hundred yards, up the side of a hill, to an old logging trail, and of course by now my two-hundred-and-thirty-pound lumbering fat ass is practically dead. There's not a house within two miles, so I start the bike and follow the logging trail. I've ridden the area several times on the bike, so I know it well. I find a gravel road, and see the first house. I've got the bike jerry-rigged with aluminum tubes that act to muffle the engine, so I'm not making much noise. Before long, I'm on a paved road in Stone County. I stay away from the main highway, and stick to the back roads. A couple of hours later, I make it back to the cabin.'

'Why did you go back to the cabin?'

'I had to regroup.'

'Weren't you afraid of being seen by Pepper?'

Patrick didn't flinch at the question. Karl had timed it perfectly, and he watched for a reaction. None. Patrick studied his feet for a few seconds, then said, 'Pepper was gone.'

TWENTY-FOUR

Underhill was back. Fresh from eight hours of watching videos and reviewing notes in another room. He walked in, gave a generic hello in the general direction of Stephano and his lawyer, then got to work. 'If we could pick up where you left off yesterday, Mr Stephano.'

'Where might that be?'

'Your invasion of Brazil.'

'Right. Well, let's see. It's a big country. A hundred and sixty million people, more square miles than the lower forty-eight, and a history of being a marvelous place to hide, especially if you're on the run. Nazis favored it for years. We put together a dossier on Lanigan, had it translated into Portuguese. We had a police artist work with some computer people to develop a series of color-enhanced renderings of what Lanigan looked like now. We spent hours with the sailboat charter captain in Orange Beach, as well as with the bankers in Nassau, and together they helped us develop a series of detailed sketches of Lanigan. We even met with the partners in the firm and went over the sketches. They, in turn, showed them to the secretaries. One of the partners, Mr Bogan, even took the best rendering to the widow Lanigan for her opinion.'

'Now that you've caught him, were your photos close?'

'Fairly close. The chin and the nose threw us off a bit.'

'Please continue.'

'We hurried to Brazil, and found three of the best private investigative firms in the country. One in Rio, one in São Paulo, and one in Recife, in the northeast. We were paying top dollar, so we hired the very best. We put them together as a team, and gathered them in São Paulo for a week. We listened to them. They developed the story that Patrick should be an American fugitive wanted for the kidnap and murder of the daughter of a wealthy family, a family now offering a reward for information about his whereabouts. The murder of a child was, of course, designed to arouse more sympathy than stealing money from a bunch of lawyers.

'We went straight to the language schools, flashing pictures of Lanigan and offering cash. The reputable schools slammed their doors. Others looked at the pictures but couldn't help. By this time, we had a lot of respect for Lanigan, and we didn't think he'd run the risk of studying in a place where questions were asked and records were kept. So we targeted the private tutors, of which there are only about a million in Brazil. It was tedious work.'

'Did you offer cash up front?'

'We did what our Brazilian agents wanted to do, which was to show the pictures, tell the story of the murdered child, then wait for a reaction. If there was a nibble, then we'd gently drop the hint about some reward money.'

'Any nibbles?'

'A few, here and there. But we never paid any money, at least not to language tutors.'

'To others?'

Stephano nodded as he glanced at a sheet of paper. 'In April of '94, we found a plastic surgeon in Rio who showed some interest in Lanigan's pictures. He toyed with us for a month, and finally convinced us he had worked on Lanigan. He had some photos of his own, before and after shots. He played us perfectly, and we eventually agreed to pay him a quarter of a million dollars, cash, offshore, for his entire file.'

'What was in the file?'

'Just the basics. Clear frontal photos of our man before and after the surgery. It was really odd because Lanigan had insisted on no photos. He wanted no trail whatsoever, just hard cash for the alterations. Wouldn't give his real name, said he was a business-man from Canada who suddenly wanted to look younger. The surgeon heard this all the time, and he knew the guy was on the run. He kept a hidden camera in his office, thus the photos.'

'Could we see them?'

'Certainly.' The lawyer was aroused for the moment and slid a manila envelope down the table to Under-hill, who opened it and only glanced at the photos.

'How did you find the doctor?'

'At the same time we were checking language schools and tutors, we were also pursuing other professions. Forgers, plastic surgeons, importers.'

'Importers?'

'Yeah, there's a Portuguese word for these guys, but "importers" is a very rough translation. They're a shady group of specialists who can get you into Brazil and then get you lost – new names, new papers, the best places to live and hide. We found them to be impenetrable. We had pretty much the same bad luck with the forgers. They can't afford to talk about their clients. It's very bad for business.'

'But the doctors were different?'

'Not really. They don't talk. But we hired a plastic

surgeon as a consultant, and he gave us the names of some of his sleazier brethren who worked on the nameless. That's how we found the doctor in Rio.'

'This was over two years after Lanigan disappeared.'

'That's correct.'

'Was this the first evidence that he was actually in the country?'

'The very first, yes.'

'What did you do for the first two years?'

'Spent a lot of money. Knocked on a lot of doors. Chased a lot of worthless leads. As I said, it's a big country.'

'How many men were working for you in Brazil?'

'At one point, I was paying sixty agents. Thankfully, they're not as expensive as Americans.'

If the Judge wanted a pizza, then the Judge got a pizza. It was fetched from Hugo's, an old family bistro on Division Street, near the Point and far away from the fast-food places lining the beach. It was delivered by a deputy to Room 312. Patrick smelled it as it left the elevator. He stared at it when Karl opened the box at the foot of his bed. He closed his eyes and sucked in the heavenly aroma of black olives, portobello mushrooms, Italian sausage, green peppers, and six different cheeses. He had eaten a thousand pizzas from Hugo's, especially during the last two years of his old life, and he had been dreaming of this one for a week now. Home did have certain advantages.

'You look like death warmed over. Eat up,' Karl said.

Patrick devoured his first slice of pizza without a word, then went for a second.

'How did you get so skinny?' Karl asked, chomping away.

'Can we get some beer?' Patrick asked.

'No. Sorry. You're in jail, remember.'

'Losing weight is between the ears. Make up your mind, it's easy. I suddenly had plenty of motivation to starve myself.'

'How fat did you get?'

'The Friday before I disappeared, I weighed two hundred thirty-six pounds. I dropped forty-seven pounds the first six weeks. This morning I weighed one-sixty.'

'You look like a refugee. Eat.'

'Thanks.'

'You were at the cabin.'

Patrick wiped his chin with a paper napkin and placed his slice back in the box. He sipped from his Diet Coke. 'Yeah, I was at the cabin. It was around eleven-thirty. I entered through the front door, and didn't turn on any lights. There's another cabin a half a mile away, up on a ridge and visible from mine. It's owned by some people from Hattiesburg, and while I didn't think they were there that weekend, I had to be careful. I covered the small bathroom window with a dark towel, turned on the light, and quickly shaved. Then I cut my hair. Then I dyed it, a dark brown, almost black.'

'Sorry I missed that.'

'It was quite becoming. It was odd. I even felt like a different person as I stared at the mirror. Then I cleaned up my mess, wiped up all the hair and whiskers because I knew they would go through the place with a fine-tooth comb, and I packed away the dye box and tubes. I changed into heavy clothing. I made a pot of strong coffee, and drank half of it. The other half went in a thermos for my journey. At 1 A.M., I left the cabin in a hurry. I didn't expect the cops to show up that night, but there was always the chance. I knew it would take time to identify the Blazer and call Trudy, and someone might suggest that they go to the cabin for some reason. I didn't expect this to happen, but by 1 A.M. I was anxious to leave.'

'Did you have any concern for Trudy?'

'Not particularly. I knew she would handle the shock well, and that she would do a marvelous job of getting me buried. She'd be a model widow for about a month, and then she would get the life insurance money. It would be her finest hour. Lots of attention, lots of money. No, Karl, I had no love for the woman. Nor any concern.'

'Did you ever go back to the cabin?'

'No.'

Karl could not, would not, hold the next question. 'Pepper's shotgun and camping gear were found under one of the beds. How'd they get there?'

Patrick glanced up for a second as if surprised, then he looked away. Karl absorbed this reaction, because he would think about it many times over the next few days. A jolt, then a glance, and then unable to answer truthfully, a diversion to the wall.

The line from the old movie said, 'When you commit a murder you make twenty-five mistakes. If you can think of fifteen of them, you're a genius.' Perhaps Patrick, in all his meticulous scheming, had simply forgotten about Pepper's things. In the rush of the moment, he had hurried a bit too much.

'I don't know,' he said, almost grunting it, still looking at the wall.

Karl had got what he wanted, and he pressed on. 'Where did you go?'

'The bike ride from hell,' Patrick said, perking up and anxious to move on. 'It was forty degrees, which on a motorcycle going down a highway at night feels like twenty below. I stayed on the back roads, away from traffic, moving slowly because the wind cut through me like a knife. I crossed into Alabama, and again kept off the main roads. A dirt bike on a highway at three in the morning might give a bored cop something to do, so I avoided towns. I finally made it to the outskirts of Mobile around four in the morning. A month earlier I had found a small motel where they took cash and asked no questions. I sneaked into the parking lot, hid the bike behind the motel, and walked in the front door as if I had just gotten out of a cab. Thirty bucks for a room, cash, no paperwork. It took an hour to thaw out. I slept for two hours and woke up with the sun. When did you hear about it, Karl?'

'I guess about the time you were dirt-biking through the countryside. Doug Vitrano called me at a few minutes after three. Woke me up, which really ticks me off now. Losing sleep and grieving while you were playing Easy Rider and rambling off to the good life.'

'I wasn't home free.'

'No, but you certainly weren't worried about your friends.'

'I feel bad about that, Karl.'

'No you don't.'

'You're right, I don't.' Patrick was relaxed, animated, into his story, grinning now.

'You woke up with the sun. A new man in a new world. All your worries and problems left behind.'

'Most of them. It was terribly exciting, and also frightening. Sleep was difficult. I watched television until eight-thirty, saw nothing about my death, then showered, changed into fresh clothes –'

'Wait. Where was the hair dye box and tubes?'

'I threw them in a dumpster somewhere in Washington County, Alabama. I called a cab, which in Mobile is not the easiest thing to do. The driver parked outside my room, and I left. No checkout. I left the dirt bike behind the motel and went to a mall which I knew opened at nine. I went to a department store and bought a navy jacket, some slacks, and a pair of loafers.'

'How did you pay for them?'

'Cash.'

'You didn't have a credit card?'

'Yes, I had a phony Visa I'd procured from a source in Miami. It was good for only a handful of charges, then it had to be discarded. I saved it for the rental car.'

'How much cash did you have?'

'About twenty thousand.'

'Where did it come from?'

'I'd been saving it for a while. I was making good money, though Trudy was doing her best to spend it faster than I could make it. I told the bookkeeper in the firm that I needed to reroute some money to keep it away from my wife. She said she did this all the time for the lawyers. It went to another account. I cashed it periodically, and stuffed it in a drawer. Satisfied?'

'Yes. You had just bought a pair of loafers.'

'I went to another store and bought a white shirt and a tie. I changed in a small rest room, and presto, I looked like any one of a million traveling salesmen. I bought some more clothes and accessories, put them in a new canvas bag, and called another cab. This one took me to the Mobile airport, where I ate breakfast and waited on a Northwest Airlink flight from Atlanta. It arrived. I fell in with the other commuters, all very busy and anxious to attack Mobile, and I stopped with two other guys at the Avis desk. They had reserved cars. Mine was a bit more complicated. I had a perfect driver's license from Georgia, along with my passport, just in case. I used the Visa, and I was very scared. The card number was a valid one – some poor guy in Decatur, Georgia, and I was terrified a computer would catch it and alarms would go off. But nothing happened. I filled out the paperwork, and left in a hurry.'

'What was your name?'

'Randy Austin.'

'Big question, Randy,' Karl said as he took a bite of pizza and chewed it slowly. 'You were in the airport. Why didn't you simply get on a plane and leave?'

'Oh, I thought about it. As I was eating breakfast, I watched two planes take off, and I wanted so badly to hop on and leave. But there was unfinished business. It was a very tough decision.'

'What was the unfinished business?'

'I think you know. I drove to Gulf Shores, then along the Coast east to Orange Beach, where I rented a small condo.'

'One you had already checked out.'

'Of course. I knew they would take cash. It was February, and cold, business was slow. I took a mild sedative and slept for six hours. I watched the evening news and saw where I'd died a fiery death. My friends were just devastated.'

'You ass.'

'I drove to the grocery and bought a bag of apples and some diet pills. After dark, I walked the beach for three hours, something I did every night while I was hiding around Mobile. Next morning, I sneaked into Pascagoula and got a newspaper, saw my fat smiling face on the front page, read about the tragedy, saw the touching little blurb you offered, and also saw that the funeral would be that afternoon at three. I went to Orange Beach and rented a sailboat. Then drove to Biloxi in time for my service.'

'The papers have said you watched your own burial.'

'True. I hid in a tree in the woods beyond the cemetery, and watched through binoculars.'

'That seems like an incredibly dumb thing to do.'

'It was. Absolutely idiotic. But I was drawn to the place. I had to make certain, to see for myself that my

231

trick had worked. And I guess by then, I was convinced I could get by with anything.'

'I guess you had picked out the tree, the perfect spot.'

'No. In fact, I wasn't sure I would do it. I left Mobile and drove west on the interstate, and I kept telling myself not to do it. Not to get near Biloxi.'

'Your big ass climbed a tree?'

'I was motivated. It was an oak with thick branches.'

'Thank God for that. I wish a limb had cracked and you'd fallen on your head.'

'No you don't.'

'Yes I do. We're huddled around the grave fighting back tears and consoling the widow, and you're perched on a limb like a fat frog laughing at us.'

'You're just trying to be angry, Karl.'

And he was right. Four and a half years had eliminated any anger Karl had felt. The truth was, he was delighted to be sitting there on the end of the hospital bed, eating pizza with Patrick and soaking up the coveted details.

However, the funeral was as far as they would get. Patrick had talked enough, and they were now back in his room, a place he didn't completely trust. 'Tell me, how are Bogan and Vitrano and the boys?' he said, and relaxed on his pillows, already relishing what he was about to hear.

TWENTY-FIVE

Paulo Miranda's last phone call from his daughter had been two days earlier. She was in a hotel in New Orleans, still traveling on her legal work for her mysterious new client, still warning him of people who might be looking for her and watching him because her client had enemies in Brazil. As with the previous calls, she was brief and vague and scared, though trying desperately not to show it. He had become angry and pressed for details. She had been more concerned with his safety. He wanted her to come home. He exploded and revealed for the first time that he had met with her former partners and knew that she had been terminated. She had calmly explained that she was on her own now, a solo practitioner with a rich client in international trading, and that extended travel like this would become routine.

He hated to argue with her on the phone, especially since he was so worried about her.

Paulo was also tired of the shady little men lurking around his street and following him as he walked to the market or drove to his office at the Pontificia Universidade Católica. He watched for them; they were always nearby. He had nicknames for them. Paulo had spoken several times to the manager of Eva's apartment building, and the same shifty creatures were watching there too.

His last class, a survey of German philosophy, ended at one. He met in his office for thirty minutes with a struggling student, then left for the day. It was raining and he had forgotten his umbrella. His car was parked in a small faculty lot behind a classroom building.

Osmar was waiting. Paulo was deep in thought as he left the building, his eyes down, with a newspaper on top of his head, his mind a million miles away as he walked under a dripping shade tree and stepped in a puddle near his car. Next to it was a small red Fiat delivery van. The driver emerged, but Paulo didn't notice. The driver opened the rear door of the van, but Paulo neither heard nor saw anything. He was reaching for his keys when Osmar shoved him from the side, and knocked him roughly into the van. His briefcase fell to the ground.

The door slammed. In the darkness, the barrel of a gun was placed between Paulo's eyes, and a voice told him to be silent.

The driver's door of his car was opened, and papers from his briefcase were strewn from the front seat to the rear tires.

The van raced away.

A phone call to the police informed them of the kidnapping.

For an hour and a half, they drove Paulo out of the city, then into the countryside, though he had no idea where he was. The van was hot – no windows, no lights. There were the silhouettes of two men sitting close to him, both with guns. They stopped behind a sprawling farmhouse, and Paulo was led inside. His quarters were in the rear; a bedroom, a bath, a parlor with a television. There was plenty of food. He would not be harmed, he was told, unless of course he made the mistake of trying to escape. He would be held for a week or so, then released, if he behaved himself.

234

He locked his door and peeked from a window. Two men sat under a tree, laughing and drinking tea with submachine guns nearby.

Anonymous calls were made to Paulo's son in Rio, to the manager of Eva's apartment, to her old law firm, and to one of her friends who worked at a travel agency. The message was the same; Paulo Miranda had been kidnapped. The police were investigating.

Eva was in New York, staying for a few days in a suite at the Pierre Hotel, shopping along Fifth Avenue, spending hours in museums. Her instructions were to keep on the move, to pop in and out of New Orleans. She had received three letters from Patrick, and she had written him twice, all correspondence being passed through Sandy. Whatever physical abuse he had suffered had certainly not affected his attention to details. His letters were specific – plans and checklists and emergency procedures.

She called her father, and there was no answer. She called her brother, and the sky came crashing down. She had to return immediately, he insisted. Her brother was a delicate type, unaccustomed to pressure and adversity. He cracked easily. The difficult family decisions were always left to Eva.

She kept him on the phone for half an hour as she tried to calm both of them. No, there had been no ransom demand. Not a word from the kidnappers.

Against his specific instructions, she called him. Fidgeting at a pay phone in La Guardia, looking over her shoulder through thick sunglasses and tugging nervously at her hair, she dialed his room number, and spoke in Portuguese. If they were listening, at least they would have to find a translator.

'Patrick, it's Leah,' she said, with as little emotion as possible.

'What's wrong?' he asked, also in Portuguese. He hadn't heard her wonderful voice for some time, and he was not pleased to hear it now.

'Can we talk?'

'Yes. What's the matter?' Patrick checked the phone in his room for bugs every three or four hours. He was bored. He also scanned every possible hiding place with the bugging sensor Sandy had found him. With guards posted around the clock, he had learned to relax somewhat. But the outside lines still worried him.

'It's my father,' she said, then blurted out the story of Paulo's disappearance. 'I have to go home.'

'No, Leah,' he said calmly. 'It's a trap. Your father is not a wealthy man. They are not asking for money. They want you.'

'I cannot abandon my father.'

'And you can't find him either.'

'This is all my fault.'

'No. The blame lies with me. But don't make matters worse by rushing into their trap.'

She twirled her hair and watched the parade of people rushing by. 'So what do I do?'

'Go to New Orleans. Call Sandy when you get there. Let me think.'

She bought a ticket, then walked to her gate and found a seat in a corner where she could hide her face next to the wall and behind a magazine. She thought of her poppa and the horrible things they could be doing to him. The only two men she loved had been kidnapped by the same people, and Patrick was still in the hospital because of his wounds. Her father was older and not as strong as Patrick. They were hurting him because of her. And there was nothing she could do.

After a day of searching, a Biloxi policeman saw Lance's car leaving the Grand Casino at 10:20 P.M.

Lance was stopped and detained for no valid reason until Sweeney arrived. He and Lance conferenced in the backseat of a flashing patrol car in the parking lot of a Burger King.

The Sheriff asked how the dope trade was going, and Lance said business was good.

'How's Trudy?' the Sheriff asked, toothpick between his lips. It was a massive struggle in the backseat to see who could be the coolest. Lance even put on his newest Ray-Bans.

'She's fine. How's your woman?'

'I don't have one. Look, Lance, we've picked up some pretty serious tips that you're in the market for a trigger.'

'Lies, lies, total lies.'

'Yeah, well, we don't think so. You see, Lance, all your pals are just like you. Either just off probation or working hard to get back on. Scum, you know. Just scum. Always looking for a dirty buck, always one step ahead of trouble. They hear a good rumor, they can't wait to whisper it to the feds. Might help them with their probation.'

'That's nice, real nice. I like that.'

'And so we know you got some cash, you got this woman who's about to lose a bundle, and everything would be great if Mr Lanigan sorta remained dead.'

'Who?'

'Yeah. So here's what we're doing. Us and the feds. We're puttin' you under surveillance, you and the woman, and we're watching and listening real hard. You make a move, we'll get you. Both you and Trudy will get yourselves in more trouble than Lanigan's in.'

'I'm supposed to be frightened by this?'

'If you had a brain you would be.'

'Can I go now?'

'Please.'

Both doors were opened from the outside, and Lance was taken back to his car.

At the same time, Agent Cutter rang Trudy's doorbell, hoping she was asleep. He had been sitting in a coffee shop in Fairhope, waiting for word that Lance had been detained.

Trudy was awake. She unbolted the front door and spoke through the chain. 'What do you want?' she demanded as Cutter flashed his badge and emphasized the 'FBI.' She recognized him.

'Can I come in?'

'No.'

'Lance is in police custody. I think we should talk.'

'What!'

'The Biloxi police have him.'

She unlocked the chain and opened the door. They stood in the foyer, facing each other. Cutter was thoroughly enjoying himself.

'What's he done?' she asked.

'I think he'll be released soon.'

'I'll call my lawyer.'

'Fine, but there's something I should tell you first. We have it from a good source that Lance has been trying to locate a hit man to take out your husband, Patrick Lanigan.'

'No!' She covered her mouth with a hand. The surprise seemed real.

'Yes. And you could be implicated. It's your money Lance is trying to protect, and I'm sure you'll be considered a co-conspirator. If something happens to Lanigan, we'll come here first.'

'I haven't done anything.'

'Not yet. We're watching you very closely, Mrs Lanigan.'

'Don't call me that.'

'Sorry.'

Cutter left her standing in the foyer.

Sandy parked in a lot off Canal around midnight, and darted down Decatur and into the heart of the French Quarter. His client had lectured him sternly about security, especially when meeting Leah. Only Sandy could lead them to her, and so he must be extremely cautious. 'She's in grave danger, Sandy,' Patrick had told him an hour before. 'You can't be too careful.'

He walked around one block three times, and when he was certain no one could possibly be behind him, he ducked into an open bar, where he drank a soda and watched the sidewalk. Then he walked across the street to the Royal Sonesta. He milled about the lobby with the tourists, then he rode the elevator to the third floor. Leah opened the door, and locked it behind him.

Not surprisingly, she looked tired and wrung out.

'I'm sorry about your father,' Sandy said. 'Have you heard anything?'

'No. I've been traveling.' There was a tray of coffee on top of the television. Sandy poured a cup and stirred in sugar. 'Patrick told me about it,' he said. 'Who are these people?'

'There's a file over there,' she said, nodding at a small table. 'Please sit.' She was pointing at the end of the bed. Sandy sat with his coffee and waited. It was time for a talk.

'We met two years ago, in 1994, after his surgery in Rio. Patrick said he was a Canadian businessman who needed a lawyer with experience in trade matters. But he really needed a friend. I was a friend for two days, then we fell in love. He told me everything about his past, everything. He had done a perfect job of escaping, and he had lots of money, but Patrick could not forget his past. He was determined to know who was chasing him, and how close they were. In August of 1994, I came to the U.S., and I made contact with a private security firm in Atlanta. It's an odd name, the Pluto Group, a bunch of ex-FBI types Patrick had found before he disappeared. I gave them a false name, told them I was from Spain, and that I needed information about the search for Patrick Lanigan. I paid them fifty thousand dollars. They, in turn, sent people to Biloxi, where they at first made contact with Patrick's old law firm. They pretended to have some vague information about his whereabouts, and the lawyers very quietly referred them to a man in Washington named Jack Stephano. Stephano is a high-priced sleuth who specializes in corporate espionage and the locating of missing people. They met with him in Washington. He was very secretive and told them little, but it was obvious he was running the search for Patrick. They met with him several times, and the prospect of a reward popped up. They offered to sell their information, and Stephano agreed to pay fifty thousand dollars if it led to Patrick. In the course of these meetings, they learned that Stephano had good reason to believe Patrick was in Brazil. This, of course, terrified Patrick and me.'

'This was Patrick's first hint that they knew he was in Brazil?'

'Absolutely. He had been there for over two years. When he told me the truth about his past, he had no idea if his pursuers were on the right continent. To learn they were in Brazil was devastating.'

'Why didn't he run again?'

'Lots of reasons. He thought about it. We talked about it forever. I was willing to leave with him. But in the end, he was convinced he could disappear even farther into the country. He knew it well – the language, the people, the endless places to hide. Plus, he didn't want me to leave my home. I guess we should've run to China or some place.'

240

'Maybe you couldn't run.'

'Maybe. I kept in touch with the Pluto Group. They were hired to monitor the Stephano investigation as best they could. They contacted his client, Mr Benny Aricia, with the same story about possible information. They also contacted the insurance companies. All calls were referred to Jack Stephano. I flew in every three or four months, always from some place in Europe, and they would tell me what they had discovered.'

'How did Stephano find him?'

'I can't tell you that story now. Patrick will have to do it.'

Another black hole, and a rather significant one. Sandy placed his coffee on the floor and tried to sort things out. It would certainly be easier if these two would tell him everything. Start at the beginning, bring it forward to the present, so that he, the lawyer, could help them with their immediate future. Perhaps they didn't need any help.

So Patrick knew how he'd been found.

She handed him the thick folder from the table. 'These are the people who have my father,' she said.

'Stephano?'

'Yes. I'm the only person who knows where the money is, Sandy. The kidnapping is a trap.'

'How does Stephano know about you?'

'Patrick told them.'

'Patrick?'

'Yes. You've seen the burns, haven't you?'

Sandy stood and tried to clear his head. 'Then why didn't Patrick tell them where the money is?'

'Because he didn't know.'

'He gave it all to you.'

'Something like that. I have control of it. Now I'm being chased, and my poor father is caught in the middle.'

'What am I supposed to do?'

She opened a drawer and removed a similar but thinner file. 'This contains information about the FBI investigation of Patrick. We didn't learn much, for obvious reasons. The agent in charge is a man named Cutter, in Biloxi. As soon as I knew Patrick had been captured, I called Cutter. It probably saved Patrick's life.'

'Slow down. This is hard to follow.'

'I told Cutter that Patrick Lanigan had been found, and that he was in the custody of people working for Jack Stephano. We assume the FBI went straight to Stephano and threatened him. His operatives in Brazil tortured Patrick for a few hours, almost killed him, then handed him over to the FBI.'

Sandy absorbed every word with his eyes closed hard. 'Go on,' he said.

'Two days later, Stephano was arrested in Washington and his offices were locked up.'

'How do you know this?'

'I'm still paying a lot of money to the men at Pluto. They're very good. We suspect that Stephano is talking to the FBI, while at the same time quietly pursuing me. And my father.'

'What am I supposed to tell Cutter?'

'First, tell him about me. Describe me as a lawyer who is very close to Patrick, that I'm making decisions for him, and that I know everything. Then, tell him about my father.'

'And you think the FBI will lean on Stephano?'

'Maybe, maybe not. But we have nothing to lose.'

It was almost one, and she was very tired. Sandy gathered the files and headed for the door.

'We have a lot to talk about,' she said.

'It would be nice to know everything.'

'Just give us time.'

'You'd better hurry.'

TWENTY-SIX

Dr Hayani began his morning rounds promptly at seven. Because Patrick had such trouble sleeping, he eased into his dark room each morning just for a peek. The patient was usually asleep, though later in the day he would often explain the ordeals of the night. This morning, Patrick was awake, and seated in a chair before the window. He wore only his white cotton boxers. He stared at the blinds closed tightly before him, stared at nothing because there was nothing to see. The dim light came from the table by his bed.

'Patrick, are you okay?' Hayani asked as he stood beside him.

He didn't answer. Hayani glanced down at the table in the corner where Patrick did his legal work. It was neat, with no books open or files out of place.

Finally, he said, 'I'm fine, Doc.'

'Did you sleep?'

'No. Not at all.'

'You're safe now, Patrick. The sun is up.'

He said nothing; didn't move or speak. Hayani left him as he found him, gripping the chair arms and watching the shades.

Patrick heard the pleasant voices in the hallway, the doc speaking again to the bored deputies, and the nurses as they hurried by. Breakfast would arrive shortly, not that food held much interest for him. After four and a half years of near starvation, he had mastered his desire to eat. A few bites of this and that, with sliced apples and carrots when hunger hit. The nurses at first had felt challenged to fatten him up, but Dr Hayani intervened and imposed a diet low in fat, free of sugar, and heavy on steamed vegetables and breads.

He rose from his chair and walked to the door. He opened it and quietly said good morning to the deputies, Pete and Eddie, two of the regulars.

'Did you sleep well?' Eddie asked, as he did every morning.

'I slept safe, Eddie, thanks,' Patrick said, part of the ritual. Down the hall on a bench by the elevator he saw Brent Myers, the useless FBI agent who had escorted him from Puerto Rico. He nodded, but Brent was involved with the morning paper.

Patrick withdrew to his room, and began a set of gentle knee bends. His muscles were healed, but the burns were still sore and stiff. Push-ups and sit-ups were out of the question.

A nurse knocked on the door as she pushed it open. 'Good morning, Patrick,' she chirped happily. 'It's time for breakfast.' She sat the tray on a table. 'How was your night?'

'Wonderful. Yours?'

'Wonderful. Anything I can get for you?'

'No thanks.'

'Just call,' she said, leaving. The routine varied little from day to day. As boring as it had become, Patrick had not lost sight of how bad things could be. Breakfast at the Harrison County Jail would be served on metal trays stuck through narrow slots in the bars and eaten in the presence of various cellmates, the mixture of which changed daily.

He took his coffee and entered his little office in the

corner, under the television. He turned the lamp on and stared at his files.

He had been in Biloxi a week. His other life had ended thirteen days ago, on a narrow dusty road that was now a million miles away. He wanted to be Danilo again, Senhor Silva, with his quiet life in his simple house, where the maid spoke to him in melodic Portuguese heavily tinted with her Indian roots. He yearned for the long walks along the warm streets of Ponta Porã, and the long runs into the countryside. He wanted to speak again to the old men lounging under cool trees sipping their green tea and anxious to chat up anyone willing to linger. He missed the bustle of the market downtown.

He missed Brazil, Danilo's home, with its vastness and beauty and stark contrasts, its teeming cities and backward villages, its gentle people. He ached for his beloved Eva; the softness of her touch, the beauty of her smile, the wonders of her flesh, the warmth of her soul. He would not live without her.

Why can't a man have more than one life? Where was it written that you couldn't start over? And over? Patrick had died, and Danilo had been captured.

He had survived both the death of the first and the seizure of the second. Why couldn't he escape again? A third life was calling, this one, though, without the sorrow of the first or the shadows of the second. This would be the perfect life with Eva. They would live somewhere, anywhere, as long as they were together and the past couldn't catch them. They would live in a grand home and reproduce like rabbits.

She was strong, but she had limits, like everyone. She loved her father, and home was a powerful magnet. All true Cariocas love their city, and consider it specially created by the Almighty.

He had placed her in danger, and now he must protect her.

Could he do it again? Or had his luck run out?

Cutter agreed to an eight o'clock meeting only because Mr McDermott insisted it was urgent. The federal building was creaking to life as a meager handful of bureaucrats arrived at such an early hour. The throng would get there at nine.

Cutter was not abrupt, but certainly not hospitable. Chats with pushy lawyers ranked low on his list of favorite chores. He fixed scalding coffee in Styrofoam cups, and cleared some of the debris from his tiny desk.

Sandy thanked him nicely for agreeing to see him, and Cutter softened a bit. 'You remember that phone call you received thirteen days ago?' Sandy asked. 'The lady from Brazil?'

'Sure.'

'I've met with her a few times. She's a lawyer for Patrick.'

'Is she here?'

'She's around.' Sandy blew hard into his cup, then ventured a sip. He quickly explained most of what he knew about Leah, though he never called her by name. Then he asked how the Stephano investigation was proceeding.

Cutter grew cautious. He scribbled some notes with a cheap pen, and tried to arrange the players. 'How do you know about Stephano?'

'My co-counsel, the lady from Brazil, knows all about Stephano. Remember, she gave you his name.'

'How did she know about him?'

'It's a very long, complicated story, and I don't know most of it.'

'Then why bring it up?'

'Because Stephano is still after my client, and I'd like to stop him.'

More scribbling by Cutter, another sip of steaming

coffee. A rough flow chart evolved as he tried to arrange who had said what to whom. He knew most of what was happening in Washington with the Stephano tell-all, but there were gaps. It had certainly been established that Stephano would stop his chase. 'And how do you know this?'

'Because his men in Brazil have kidnapped the father of my co-counsel.'

Cutter couldn't keep his lips together, nor his head exactly straight. His eyes wandered to the ceiling as this rattled around his brain. Then it made some sense. 'Could it be that this Brazilian lawyer might possibly know where the money is?'

'That's a possibility.'

Perfect sense now.

Sandy continued, 'The kidnapping is an effort to lure her back to Brazil, where they'd like to snatch her and give her some of the same medicine they gave Patrick. It's all about money.'

Cutter's words were ponderous, but not by choice. 'When did the kidnapping occur?'

'Yesterday.' A paralegal in Sandy's office had pulled a story off the Internet two hours earlier. It was a short report on page six of *O Globo*, a popular Rio daily. It gave the victim's name as Paulo Miranda. Sandy still had no idea of Leah's real name, and it was safe to assume the FBI could identify her if and when it got the story. Frankly, he saw no harm in telling the FBI her name. Trouble was, he didn't know it.

'There's not much we can do about it.'

'The hell there isn't. Stephano's behind it. Put pressure on him. Tell him my co-counsel is not about to be sucked into his trap, and that she's preparing to go to the Brazilian authorities with the name of Jack Stephano.'

'I'll see what I can do.' Cutter had not forgotten the fact that Sandy McDermott had filed a multi-million-dollar lawsuit against the Bureau for crimes it did not commit. Nothing would be gained by discussing the lawsuit at this point. Maybe later.

'Stephano cares about nothing but the money,' Sandy said. 'If the old man gets hurt, he'll never see a dime.'

'Are you implying there's room for negotiation here?'

'What do you think? You're facing death row or life in prison, wouldn't you be willing to negotiate?'

'So what do we tell Stephano?'

'Tell him to release the old man, and then we might talk about the money.'

Stephano's day began early. The meeting, his fourth, was scheduled to last all day and bring to an end his tales of adventure in the search for Patrick. His lawyer was absent, away in court with an unavoidable conflict. Stephano didn't need a lawyer to hold his hand, and, frankly, he was tired of paying $450 an hour. The interrogator was a new one. Oliver something or other. It didn't matter. They were all from the same school.

'You were talking about the plastic surgeon,' Oliver said, as if the two men had simply been interrupted by a phone call. The two men had never met, and it had been thirteen hours since Jack had spoken to anyone about Patrick.

'Yes.'

'And that was April of '94?'

'Correct.'

'Continue, then.'

Stephano settled into his chair and got himself comfortable. 'The trail ran cold for a while. For a long time, actually. We worked hard, but months passed with nothing, absolutely nothing. Not a clue. Then, late in '94, we were contacted by an investigative firm in Atlanta, the Pluto Group.'

'Pluto?'

'Yes, the Pluto Group. We referred to them as the boys from Pluto. Good boys. Some of your ex-agents. They asked questions about the search for Patrick Lanigan, said they might have some information. I met with them a couple of times here in Washington. They had a mysterious client who claimed to know something about Lanigan. Obviously, I was interested. They were in no hurry because their client seemed quite patient. The client, not surprisingly, wanted lots of money. Oddly enough, this was encouraging.'

'How so?'

'If their client knew enough to expect a fat reward, then the client had to know that Lanigan still had plenty of money. In July of '95, the boys from Pluto approached me with a scheme. What if, they said, their client could lead us to a place in Brazil where Lanigan had recently lived? I said sure. They said, how much? And we agreed on the sum of fifty thousand dollars. I was desperate. The money changed hands by way of a wire transfer to a bank in Panama. I was then told to go to the small city of Itajaí in the state of Santa Catarina, in the deep south of Brazil. The address they gave us led to a small apartment building in a nice part of town. The manager was cordial, especially after we greased his palm. We showed him our pictures of Lanigan post-op, and he said maybe. More grease in the palm, and he made a definite I.D. Jan Horst was the man's name, a German, he thought, with good Portuguese. He had rented a three-room apartment for two months, paid in cash, kept to himself, and spent little time there. He was friendly, and liked to drink coffee with the manager and his wife. She also made a positive I.D. Horst said he was a travel writer who was working on a book about the immigration of

Germans and Italians to Brazil. When he left, he said he was going to the city of Blumenau to study the Bavarian architecture there.'

'Did you go to Blumenau?'

'Of course we did. And quickly. We covered the town, but after two months gave it up. After the initial excitement, we settled back into the tedium of hanging around hotels and markets, showing the photos and offering small bribes.'

'What about the boys from Pluto, as you called them?'

'They cooled off considerably. I was anxious to talk to them, but they had little to say. I think their client got scared, or maybe was happy just to get the fifty grand. Anyway, six months passed with little word from Pluto. Then, in late January of this year, they came back in a rush. Their client needed money, and was finally ready to sell out. We shadowboxed for a few days, then they dropped the bomb that for a million dollars we could learn the exact location of our man. I said no. It wasn't that I didn't have the money, it was just too risky. Their client was not willing to talk until the money was paid, and I was not willing to pay until their client talked. There was no way whatsoever to ascertain whether their client knew anything. In fact, for all I knew there wasn't a client anymore. Tempers flared and talks broke down.'

'But you kept talking?'

'Yes, eventually. We had to. Their client had to have the money. We had to have Lanigan. Another deal was proposed whereby we would, for another fifty thousand bucks, get the name and location of a place Lanigan had lived after he left Itajaí. We agreed, because from our point of view the fifty thousand was cheap and there was always the chance of getting lucky and stumbling over another tip. From their point of view, it was smart because it strengthed their client's

250

credibility. And, of course, it was another step toward the million bucks. There was a brain at work behind Pluto, and I was desperate to play ball. I would gladly pay the million bucks. I just needed some reassurance.'

'Where was the second town?'

'São Mateus, in the state of Espírito Santo, north of Rio on the coast. It's a small town of sixty thousand, a pretty place with friendly people, and we spent a month there mingling and showing our photos. The apartment arrangement was similar to the one in Itajaí – two months' cash paid by a man named Derrick Boone, a Brit. Without being bribed, the owner positively identified Boone as our man. Seems as if Boone stayed over for a week without paying, so there was a bit of a grudge. Unlike Itajaí, though, Boone kept to himself and the owner knew nothing about his doings. Nothing else turned up, and we left São Mateus in early March of this year. We regrouped in São Paulo and Rio, and made new plans.'

'What were the new plans?'

'We withdrew from the north and concentrated on the smaller towns in the states near Rio and São Paulo. Here in Washington, I got more aggressive with the boys from Pluto. Their client was stuck on a million. My client was unwilling to pay without verification. It was a logjam, with both sides playing hardball but willing to keep talking.'

'Did you ever learn how their client knew so much about Lanigan's movements?'

'No. We speculated for hours. One theory was that their client was also chasing Lanigan, for some unknown reason. It could've been someone in the FBI who needed cash. That, of course, was a longshot, but we thought of everything. The second theory, and the most likely, was that their client was someone Lanigan knew and trusted, who was willing to sell him out.

251

Regardless, my client and I decided we could not allow the opportunity to escape. The search was now almost four years old, and going nowhere. As we had learned, there are a million wonderful places to hide in Brazil, and Lanigan seemed to know what he was doing.'

'Did you break the logjam?'

'They did. In August of this year, they ambushed us with another offer: current photos of Lanigan, in exchange for another fifty grand. We said yes. The money was wired offshore. They handed me the photos in my office here in Washington. There were three, black-and-white eight-by-tens.'

'Could I see them, please?'

'Sure.' Stephano pulled them from his perfectly organized briefcase, and slid them down the table. The first was a shot of Lanigan in a crowded market, obviously taken at long range. He wore sunglasses, and was holding what appeared to be a tomato. The second was taken either a moment before or a moment after as he walked along a sidewalk with a bag of something in his hand. He wore jeans and looked no different from any Brazilian. The third was the most telling; Patrick in shorts and a tee shirt washing the hood of his Volkswagen Beetle. The license plates could not be seen, nor could much of the house. The sunglasses were off, and it was a clear shot of his face.

'No street names, no license plates,' Oliver said.

'Nothing. We studied them for hours, but found nothing. Again, as I said, there was a brain at work.'

'So what did you do?'

'Agreed to pay the million dollars.'

'When?'

'In September. The money was placed in escrow with a trust agent in Geneva, to be held until both sides gave notice to move it. Under our deal, their client had fifteen days to give us the name of the town,

252

and the street address where he lived. We chewed our nails for the entire fifteen days, then on the sixteenth, after verbal warfare, they came through. The town was Ponta Porã, the street was Rua Tiradentes. We raced to the town, then sneaked into it. We had great respect for Lanigan by now, and we figured he was brilliant at moving forward while watching his back. We found him, then watched him for a week just to make sure. His name was Danilo Silva.'

'A week?'

'Yeah, we had to be patient. He picked Ponta Porã for a reason. It's a wonderful place to hide. Local officials are cooperative if the money is right. The Germans discovered it after the war. One bad move, the cops get tipped, and they step in to protect him. So we waited and schemed and finally grabbed him outside of town, on a small road with no witnesses. A clean getaway. We sneaked him into Paraguay to a safe house.'

'And there you tortured him?'

Stephano paused, took a sip of coffee, and stared at Oliver. 'Something like that,' he said.

TWENTY-SEVEN

Patrick paced and stretched at one end of the doctors' conference room while Sandy sat and listened and doodled on a legal pad. A nurse had brought a tray of cookies, still untouched. Sandy admired the cookies and asked himself how many capital murder prisoners got cookies delivered to them? How many had their own team of bodyguards lurking nearby? How many had the Judge stopping by for pizza?

'Things are changing, Sandy,' Patrick said without looking at him. 'We have to move fast.'

'Move where?'

'She won't stay here as long as her father is missing.'

'As usual, I'm thoroughly confused. The gaps are getting wider and the two of you speak in tongues. But I'm just the lawyer. Why should I know anything?'

'She has the files and records, and the story. You have to go see her.'

'I just saw her last night.'

'She's waiting on you.'

'Really? Where?'

'There's a beach house at Perdido. She's there.'

'Let me guess. I'm supposed to drop everything, and race over right now.'

'It's important, Sandy.'

'So are my other clients,' he said angrily. 'Why can't you give me a little notice here?'

'I'm sorry.'

'I have court this afternoon. My daughter's got soccer. Is it asking too much for some warning?'

'I couldn't anticipate a kidnapping, Sandy. You've got to admit the circumstances are somewhat unusual. Try and understand.'

Sandy took a deep breath and scribbled something. Patrick sat on the edge of the table, very near him. 'I'm sorry, Sandy.'

'What might we discuss at the beach house?'

'Aricia.'

'Aricia,' he repeated, then looked away. He knew the basics, at least what he'd read in the papers.

'It will take some time, so I'd pack for overnight.'

'Am I expected to stay at the beach house?'

'Yes.'

'With Leah?'

'Yes. It's a big house.'

'And what exactly am I supposed to tell my wife? That I'm shacked up in a beach house with a beautiful Brazilian woman?'

'I wouldn't. Just tell her you're meeting with the rest of my defense team.'

'That's nice.'

'Thanks, Sandy.'

Underhill joined Oliver after a coffee break. They sat next to each other with the video camera behind them, all eyes aimed down the table at Stephano.

'Who interrogated Patrick?' Underhill asked Stephano.

'I'm not required to give the names of my associates.'

'Did this person have any experience with physical interrogation?'

'Limited.'

'Describe the means used.'

'I'm not sure –'

'We've seen the photos of the burns, Mr Stephano. And we, the FBI, have been sued for injuries inflicted by your men. Now, tell us how you did it.'

'I wasn't there. I didn't plan the interrogation because I have little experience in that field. I knew in general terms that a series of electrical shocks would be applied to various points on Mr Lanigan's body. That is what happened. I had no idea it would cause serious burns.'

There was a pause as Underhill glanced at Oliver and Oliver glanced at Underhill. Blatant disbelief. Stephano simply sneered at them.

'How long did this go on?'

'Five to six hours.'

They looked at a file and whispered something. Underhill asked him some questions about the identification process, and Stephano described the fingerprinting. Oliver struggled with the time sequences, and spent almost an hour pinning down exactly when they grabbed him and how far they drove him and how long they interrogated him. They grilled Stephano about the trip out of the jungle to the airstrip at Concepción. They probed and fished and covered everything else, then they huddled for a moment and returned to the crucial question.

'During the interrogation of Mr Lanigan, what did you learn about the money?'

'Not much. He told us where the money had been, but it had been moved.'

'Can we assume he told you this under extreme duress?'

'Safe assumption.'

'Are you convinced he didn't know where the money was at that time?'

'I wasn't there. But the man who conducted the interrogation has told me that, without a doubt, he believes that Mr Lanigan did not know the exact location of the money.'

'The interrogation wasn't recorded either by video or audio?'

'Of course not,' Jack said, as if he had never thought about it.

'Did Mr Lanigan mention an accomplice?'

'Not to my knowledge.'

'What does that mean?'

'Means I don't know.'

'How about the man who conducted the interrogation? Did he hear Mr Lanigan mention an accomplice?'

'Not to my knowledge.'

'So, as far as you know, Mr Lanigan never mentioned an accomplice?'

'That's correct.'

They shuffled files again, and whispered between themselves, then took a long pause, one that became profoundly unsettling for Stephano. He had told two lies in a row – no recording and no accomplice – and he still felt safe with them. How could these guys know what was said in the jungles of Paraguay? But they were the FBI. So he fidgeted, and waited.

The door opened suddenly, and Hamilton Jaynes walked through it, followed by Warren, the third interrogator. 'Hello, Jack,' Jaynes said loudly as he took a seat on one side of the table. Warren sat near his buddies.

'Hello, Hamilton,' Stephano said, fidgeting even more.

'Been listening in the next room,' Jaynes said with a smile. 'And I'm suddenly wondering if you're being truthful.'

'Of course I am.'

'Of course. Look, ever heard the name Eva Miranda?'

Stephano repeated it slowly, as if totally confused by it. 'Don't think so.'

'She's a lawyer in Rio. A friend of Patrick's.'

'Nope.'

'Well, see, that's what bothers me, Jack, because I think you know precisely who she is.'

'I've never heard of her.'

'Then why are you trying to find her?'

'I don't know what you're talking about,' Stephano said, rather weakly.

Underhill spoke first. He was looking directly at Stephano, but he spoke to Jaynes. 'He's lying.'

'He certainly is,' said Oliver.

'No question about it,' Warren added.

Stephano's eyes darted from voice to voice. He started to say something, but Jaynes showed him his palms. The door opened, and one more comrade from the Underhill-Oliver-Warren school walked in just far enough to say, 'The voice analysis shows sufficient proof of lying.' His announcement over, he withdrew immediately.

Jaynes picked up a single sheet of paper and summarized from it. 'This is a story appearing in a Rio paper this morning. It tells of the kidnapping of a Mr Paulo Miranda. His daughter is Patrick's friend, Jack. We've checked with the authorities in Rio. No ransom demand. Nothing from the kidnappers.' He slid the paper in the direction of Stephano, but it stopped out of his reach.

'So where is Mr Miranda?'

'I don't know. I don't know what you're talking about.'

Jaynes looked at the other end of the table.

'Still lying,' Underhill said. Oliver and Warren nodded their agreement.

'We had a deal, Jack. You would tell us the truth, and we would drop the charges against you. And, as I recall, we agreed not to arrest your clients. Now what am I supposed to do, Jack?'

Stephano was looking at Underhill and Oliver, who seemed ready to pounce on his next utterance. They, in turn, stared coldly at him, missing nothing.

'She knows where the money is,' Stephano said in resignation.

'Do you know where she is?'

'No. She fled Rio when we found Patrick.'

'No sign of her?'

'No.'

Haynes looked at his truth squad. Yes, he had stopped the lying.

'I agreed to tell you everything,' Jack said. 'I did not agree to do anything else. We can still look for her.'

'We didn't know about her.'

'Too bad. If necessary, we can review our agreement. I'll be happy to call my lawyer.'

'Yes, but we've already caught you lying.'

'I'm sorry. It won't happen again.'

'Lay off the girl, Jack. And release her father.'

'I'll think about it.'

'No. You'll do it now.'

The beach house was a modern tri-level in a row of seemingly identical structures along a freshly developed strip of the Coast. October was off-season. Most of the houses appeared to be empty. Sandy parked behind a shiny generic four-door with Louisiana plates, a rental car, he presumed. The sun was low on the horizon, inches off the top of the flat water. The Gulf was deserted; not a boat or a ship could be seen. He climbed the steps and followed the wraparound deck until he found a door.

Leah answered his knock with a smile, a short one forced through because she was at heart a warm person, not given to the dark mood swings which now plagued her. 'Come in,' she said softly, and locked the door behind him. The living room was large and vaulted, with glass on three sides and a fireplace in the center.

'Nice place,' he said, then caught a delicious aroma floating in from the kitchen. He had skipped lunch, thanks to Patrick.

'Are you hungry?' she asked.

'Starving.'

'I'm cooking a little something.'

'Wonderful.'

The authentic hardwood floors creaked a little as he followed her to the dining room. On the table was a cardboard box, and beside it were papers neatly arranged. She had been working. She paused by the table and said, 'This is the Aricia file.'

'Prepared by whom?'

'Patrick, of course.'

'Where has it been for the past four years?'

'In storage. In Mobile.'

Her answers were short, and each gave rise to a dozen quick questions Sandy would have loved to throw at her. 'We'll get to it later,' she said, and dismissed it with a casual wave.

In the kitchen, there was a whole roasted chicken on the cutting board by the sink. A pan of brown rice mixed with vegetables was steaming on the stove. 'It's pretty basic,' she said. 'I find it hard to cook in someone else's kitchen.'

'Looks delicious. Whose kitchen is this?'

'It's just a rental. I have it for the month.'

She sliced the chicken and directed Sandy to pour the wine, a fine pinot noir from California. They sat at a small table in the breakfast nook, with a splendid view of the water and the remains of the sunset.

'Cheers,' she said, raising her glass.

'To Patrick,' Sandy said.

'Yes, to Patrick.' She made no effort to address her food. Sandy stuffed a large slice of chicken breast into his mouth.

'How is he?'

He chewed rapidly so he wouldn't disgust this delightful young woman with a mouthful of food. A sip of wine. Napkin to the lips. 'Patrick's okay. The burns are healing nicely. A plastic surgeon examined him yesterday, and said that no grafts will be necessary. The scars will be with him for a few years, but they will eventually fade. The nurses bring him cookies. The Judge brings him pizza. No less than six armed men guard him around the clock, so I'd say Patrick is doing better than most capital murder defendants.'

'This is Judge Huskey?'

'Yes, Karl Huskey. Do you know him?'

'No. But Patrick spoke of him often. They were good friends. Patrick told me once that if he was captured, he hoped it would happen while Karl Huskey was still the Judge.'

'He's retiring soon,' Sandy said. What fortunate timing, he thought.

'He can't hear Patrick's case, can he?' she asked.

'No. He'll recuse himself very soon.' Sandy ate a much smaller piece of chicken, still eating alone because she had yet to touch her knife and fork. She held the glass of wine near her head, and looked at the orange and violet clouds on the horizon.

'I'm sorry. I forgot to ask about your father.'

'No word. I talked to my brother three hours ago, and there's still no word.'

'I'm very sorry, Leah. I wish I could do something.'

'And I wish I could do something. It's frustrating. I can't go home, and I can't stay here.'

'I'm sorry,' Sandy said again, because he could think of nothing better to offer.

He continued his meal in silence. She played with her rice and watched the ocean.

'This is delicious,' he said, twice.

'Thanks,' she said with a sad grin.

'What does your father do?'

'He's a university professor.'

'Where?'

'In Rio. At the Catholic University.'

'Where does he live?'

'In Ipanema, in the apartment I grew up in.'

Her father was a delicate subject, but at least Sandy was getting answers to his questions. Maybe it helped her to talk about him. He asked more questions, all very general and all far away from the kidnapping.

She never touched her food.

When he finished, she asked, 'Would you like some coffee?'

'We'll probably need it, won't we?'

'Yes.'

They removed the plastic rental dishes from the table and left them in the kitchen. Leah made coffee while Sandy inspected the house. They met in the dining room, where the coffee was served and the polite talk, such as it was, came to an end. They sat facing each other across the glass table.

'How much do you know about the Aricia matter?' she asked.

'He was the client whose ninety million got snatched by Patrick, if you believe the papers. He was an executive with Platt & Rockland, who had squealed on the company for overbilling. He filed a charge under the False Claims Act. Platt & Rockland got caught to the tune of something like six hundred million. His reward, under the act, was fifteen percent of that. His lawyers were Bogan and company, where our pal Patrick worked. That's about it. The basics.'

'That's pretty good. What I'm about to tell you can all be verified by these documents and tapes. We'll go through them, as it will be necessary for you to know this material inside and out.'

'I've actually done this before, you know.' He smiled, but she didn't. No more lame efforts at humor.

'The Aricia claim was fraudulent from the very beginning.' She spoke deliberately; there was no hurry. She waited until he absorbed this, which took a few seconds. 'Benny Aricia is a very corrupt man who conceived a scheme to defraud both his company and his government. He was assisted by some very capable lawyers, Patrick's old firm, and some powerful people in Washington.'

'That would be Senator Nye, Bogan's first cousin.'

'Primarily, yes. But, as you know, Senator Nye has considerable influence in Washington.'

'So I've heard.'

'Aricia carefully planned his scheme, then took it to Charles Bogan. Patrick was a new partner then, but he knew nothing of Aricia. The other partners were brought into the conspiracy, everyone but Patrick. The law firm changed, and Patrick knew something was different. He started digging and eavesdropping and eventually found out that this new client named Aricia was the cause for all the secrecy. He was patient. He pretended to notice nothing, and all the time he was gathering evidence. A lot of it is in here.' She touched the box when she said this.

'Let's go back to the beginning,' Sandy said. 'Explain how the claim was fraudulent.'

'Aricia ran New Coastal Shipyards in Pascagoula. It's a division of Platt & Rockland.'

'I know all that. Big defense contractor with a shady past, a bad reputation for bilking the government.'

'That's it. Aricia took advantage of its size to

263

implement his plan. New Coastal was building the Expedition nuclear submarines, and things were already over budget. Aricia decided to make matters worse. New Coastal submitted fraudulent labor records, thousands of hours at union scale for work that was never done, for employees who never existed. It procured materials at grossly inflated prices – lightbulbs for sixteen dollars each, drinking cups at thirty dollars each, and on and on. The list is endless.'

'Is the list in this box?'

'Only the big items. Radar systems, missiles, weapons, things I've never heard of. The lightbulbs are insignificant. Aricia had been with the company long enough to know exactly how to avoid detection. He created a ton of paperwork, little of it with his name on it. Platt & Rockland had six different divisions involved with defense contracting, and so the home office was a zoo. Aricia took advantage of this. For every bogus claim he submitted to the Navy, he had written authorization signed by some executive at the home office. Aricia would subcontract for the inflated materials, then request approval from a higher-up. It was an easy system to work, especially for a shrewd man like Aricia, who was planning on screwing the company anyway. He kept meticulous records, and later gave them to his lawyers.'

'And Patrick got them?'

'Some of them.'

Sandy looked at the box. The top flaps were closed. 'And this has been in hiding since he disappeared?'

'Yes.'

'Did he ever come back to check on it?'

'No.'

'Did you?'

'I came two years ago to renew the rental at the storage facility. I looked in the box, but didn't have the time to examine the contents. I was scared and

264

nervous, and I didn't want to come. I was convinced these materials would never be needed because he would never be caught. But Patrick always knew.'

The cross-examiner in Sandy was ready to burst with another round of questions unrelated to Aricia, but he let the moment pass. Relax, he told himself, don't appear eager and maybe the questions will get answered eventually. 'So Aricia's scheme worked, and at some point he approached Charles Bogan, whose cousin is an ass-kicker in Washington and whose old boss is a federal judge. Did Bogan know Aricia had caused the overruns?'

She stood, reached into the box, and removed a battery-operated tape player and a rack of neatly labeled mini-cassettes. She picked through the cassettes with a pen until she found the one she wanted. She inserted it in the tape player. It was obvious to Sandy that she had done this many times before.

'Listen,' she said. 'April 11, 1991. The first voice is Bogan, the second is Aricia. Aricia had placed the call, and Bogan took it in the conference room on the second floor of the firm's offices.'

Sandy leaned forward on his elbows. The tape began to play.

BOGAN: I gotta call from one of Platt's New York lawyers today. A guy named Krasny.

ARICIA: I know him. Typical New York ass.

BOGAN: Yes, he wasn't very friendly. He said they might have proof that you knew about the double-billing on the Stalker screens New Coastal bought from RamTec. I asked him to show me the proof. He said it would be a week or so.

ARICIA: Relax, Charlie. There's no way they can prove that because I didn't sign anything.

BOGAN: But you knew about it?

ARICIA: Of course I knew about it. I planned it. I set it in motion. It was another one of my wonderful ideas. Their problem, Charlie, is that they can't prove it. There are no documents, no witnesses.

The cassette went silent, and Leah said, 'Same conversation, about ten minutes later.'

ARICIA: How's the Senator?

BOGAN: Doing well. Yesterday he met with the Secretary of the Navy.

ARICIA: How'd it go?

BOGAN: Went well. They're old friends, you know. The Senator expressed his strong desire to punish Platt & Rockland for its greed, yet not harm the Expedition project. The Secretary feels the same, and said he would push for a stiff penalty against Platt & Rockland.

ARICIA: Can he speed things up?

BOGAN: Why?

ARICIA: I want the damned money, Charlie. I can feel it. I can taste it.

Leah pushed a button and the recording stopped. She removed the cassette and placed it back in the rack. 'Patrick started recording early in '91. Their plans were to cut him out of the firm at the end of February, on the grounds that he was not generating enough business.'

'Is that box full of tapes?'

'There are about sixty of them, all carefully edited by Patrick, so you can listen to everything in three hours.'

Sandy glanced at his watch.

'We have a lot of work to do,' she said.

TWENTY-EIGHT

Paulo's request for a radio was declined, but when they realized he simply wanted music they brought him a well-used tape player and two cassettes of the Rio Philharmonic Orchestra. Classical was his preference. Paulo turned the volume low and flipped through a stack of old magazines. His request for books had been taken under consideration. The food so far was more than adequate; they seemed anxious to keep him happy. His captors were young men working for someone else, someone Paulo knew he would never see. If they in fact released him, the young men would flee and prosecution would be impossible.

His second day passed slowly. Eva was too wise to rush into their trap. One day soon this would make sense. He could wait as long as they could.

His Honor brought the pizza with him on the second night. He had enjoyed the first so much, he had called Patrick during the afternoon to see if they could do it again. Patrick was anxious for company.

Huskey reached into a small briefcase and withdrew a stack of envelopes which he tossed on Lawyer Lanigan's worktable. 'A lot of people want to say hello, mostly the courthouse gang. I told them they could write.'

'I didn't realize I had so many friends.'

'You don't. These are bored office workers with plenty of time to write letters. It's as close as they can get to the action.'

'Gee thanks.'

Huskey pulled a chair close to Patrick's bed and propped his feet on a drawer opened from the night table. Patrick had eaten almost two pieces of pizza, and was now finished.

'I'll have to recuse myself soon,' Huskey said, almost apologetically.

'I know.'

'I talked with Trussel this morning at length. I know you're not crazy about him, but he is a good judge. He's willing to take the case.'

'I prefer Judge Lanks.'

'Yes, but unfortunately, you don't get your choice. Lanks is having trouble with his blood pressure, and we've tried to keep the big cases away from him. As you know, Trussel has more experience than Lanks and myself combined, especially in death penalty cases.'

Patrick managed a slight flinch, a sudden squinting around the eyes, and a momentary sag of the bony shoulders when his friend finished the last sentence. A death penalty case. It seized him, as often happened when he dragged himself to the mirror for a long look. Huskey caught every tiny movement.

As they say, anybody is capable of murder, and Huskey had chatted with many killers during his twelve years as a judge. Patrick, however, just happened to be his first friend to face death row.

'Why are you leaving the bench?' Patrick asked.

'The usual reasons. I'm bored with it, and if I don't quit now I'll never be able to. Kids are getting closer to college, and I need to make more money.' Huskey paused for a second, then asked, 'Just curious, how

268

did you know I was leaving the bench? It's not something I've broadcast.'

'Word gets around.'

'To Brazil?'

'I had a spy, Karl.'

'Someone here?'

'No. Of course not. I couldn't run the risk of contacting anyone here.'

'So it was someone down there?'

'Yes, an attorney I met.'

'And you told him everything?'

'Her. And yes, I told her everything.'

Huskey tapped his fingers together, and said, 'I guess that makes sense.'

'I highly recommend it, next time you're down there disappearing.'

'I'll remember that. This attorney, where is she now?'

'Close by, I think.'

'Now I see. She must be the one who has the money.'

Patrick smiled, then chuckled. The ice was broken, finally. 'What do you want to know about the money, Karl?'

'Everything. How'd you steal it? Where is it? How much is left?'

'What's the best courthouse rumor you've heard about the money?'

'Oh, there are hundreds. My favorite is that you've doubled the money and buried it in vaults in Switzerland, that you were just passing time in Brazil and in a few more years you would leave and go play with your cash.'

'Not bad.'

'Remember Bobby Doak, that little pimple-faced weasel who does divorces for ninety-nine bucks and resents any lawyer who charges more?'

'Sure, advertises in church bulletins.'

'That's him. He was drinking coffee in the clerk's office yesterday and telling how he had it from an inside source that you'd blown the money on drugs and teenaged prostitutes, and that was why you were living like a peasant in Brazil.'

'That sounds like Doak.'

The levity passed quickly as Patrick grew quiet. Huskey wasn't about to lose the moment. 'So where's the money?'

'I can't tell you, Karl.'

'How much is left?'

'A ton.'

'More than you stole?'

'More than I took, yes.'

'How'd you do it?'

Patrick swung his feet from the other side of the bed, and walked to the door. It was closed. He stretched his back and legs, and took a drink from a bottle of water. Then he sat on the edge of the bed, looking down at Karl.

'I got lucky,' he said, almost in a whisper. But Karl heard every syllable.

'I was leaving, Karl, with or without the money. I knew the money was coming to the firm, and I had a plan to get it. But if that had fallen through, I was still leaving. I couldn't take another day with Trudy. I hated my job, and I was about to get my throat cut at the firm anyway. Bogan and those boys were in the midst of a gigantic fraud, and I was the only person outside the firm who knew it.'

'What fraud?'

'Aricia's claim. We'll talk about that later. So I slowly planned my escape, and I got lucky and got away. The luck followed me until two weeks ago. Incredible luck.'

'We got as far as the burial.'

270

'Right. I went back to the little condo I had rented at Orange Beach. I stayed there a couple of days, indoors, listening to language tapes and memorizing Portuguese vocabulary. I also spent hours editing the conversations I had recorded around the office. There were a lot of documents to organize. I actually worked quite hard. At night, I walked the beach for hours, working up a sweat, trying to melt the pounds off as quickly as possible. I completely disassociated myself from food.'

'What kind of documents?'

'The Aricia file. I ventured out in the sailboat. I knew the basics, and suddenly I was motivated to become a good sailor. The boat was big enough to live on for days at a time, and soon I was hiding out there on the water.'

'Here?'

'Yes. I'd anchor close to Ship Island, and watch the shoreline of Biloxi.'

'Why did you want to do that?'

'I had the office wired, Karl. Every phone, every desk, except for Bogan's. I even had a mike in the men's room on the first floor between Bogan's office and Vitrano's. The mikes transmitted to a hub I had hidden in the attic. It's an old firm in an old building with a million old files stashed away in the attic. Nobody ever went up there. There was an old TV antenna attached to the chimney on top of the building, and I ran my wires through it. The receiver then transmitted to a ten-inch dish I had on the sailboat. This was high-tech, state-of-the-art stuff, Karl. I bought it on the black market in Rome, cost me a ton of money. With binoculars, I could see the chimney, and the signals were easy to collect. Every conversation within earshot of a mike was beamed to me on the sailboat. I recorded all of them, and did my editing at night. I knew where they were eating lunch and what moods their wives were in. I knew everything.'

'That's incredible.'

'You should've heard them trying to sound serious after my funeral. On the phone, they took all these calls, all these condolences, and sounded so grave and proper. But among themselves, they joked about my death. It saved a nasty confrontation. Bogan had been elected to deliver the news to me that I was being booted from the firm. The day after the funeral he and Havarac drank Scotch in the conference room and laughed about how lucky I was to have died at such an opportune time.'

'Do you have these tapes?'

'Of course. Get this. I have the tape of the conversation between Trudy and Doug Vitrano, in my old office, just hours before my funeral, when they open my lockbox and find the surprise life insurance policy for two million dollars. It's hilarious. It took Trudy about twenty seconds before she asked, 'When do I get the money?''

'When can I hear it?'

'I don't know. Soon. There were hundreds of tapes. The editing took twelve hours a day for several weeks. Imagine all the phone calls I had to wade through.'

'Were they ever suspicious?'

'Not really. Rapley once made the remark to Vitrano that my timing was incredible, since I had purchased the two-million-dollar policy only eight months before my death. And there was a comment or two about how strange I had been acting, but it was harmless. They were so thrilled that I was gone and out of the way.'

'Did you tap Trudy's phones?'

'I thought about it, but then why bother? Her behavior was predictable. She couldn't help me.'

'But Aricia could.'

'Certainly. I knew every move they made for Aricia. I knew the money was going offshore. I knew which bank, and when it would get there.'

'So how'd you steal it?'

'Again, lots of luck. Though Bogan was calling the shots, Vitrano was doing most of the talking with the bankers. I flew to Miami with a fresh set of papers declaring me to be Doug Vitrano. I had his Social Security number and other vitals. This guy in Miami has a computer catalog with a million faces in it, and you simply point to the one you want, and presto, that face is on your driver's license. I picked a face that was somewhere between mine and Vitrano's. From Miami I flew to Nassau, and that's where it got sticky. I presented myself to the bank, the United Bank of Wales. The main guy Vitrano had been talking to was a chap named Graham Dunlap. I presented all my fake papers, including a forged partnership resolution, on firm stationery of course, which directed me to wire the money out as fast as it came in. Dunlap had not expected Mr Vitrano, and he was quite surprised, even flattered, that someone from the firm would make the journey for such a routine matter. He fixed me coffee and sent a secretary out for croissants. I was eating one in his office when the wire came in.'

'He never thought about calling the firm?'

'No. And listen, Karl, I was prepared to bolt. If Dunlap had been the least bit suspicious, I would have slugged him, run from the building, grabbed a cab, and raced to the airport. I had three different tickets for three different flights.'

'Where would you have gone?'

'Well, I was still dead, remember. Probably to Brazil. I would've found a job as a bartender and spent the rest of my days on the beach. In retrospect, I might have been better off without the money. I had it, and they had to come after it. That's why I'm here now.

Anyway, Dunlap asked the right questions and my answers came out beautifully. He confirmed the wire was in, and I immediately authorized the wire out, to a bank in Malta.'

'All of it?'

'Almost all of it. Dunlap hesitated for a moment when he realized all the money was leaving his bank. I almost swallowed my tongue. He mentioned something about an administrative fee for his services, and I asked him what was customary. He turned into a slimy little twerp, said fifty thousand would be appropriate, and I said fine. Fifty thousand stayed in the account and was later transferred to Dunlap. The bank is in downtown Nassau –'

'Was in downtown Nassau. It folded six months after you robbed it.'

'Yeah, so I heard. Too bad. When I left through the front door, my feet hit the sidewalk, and it was difficult to keep from sprinting like a madman through the traffic. I wanted to scream and leap from street to street, but I controlled myself. I jumped into the first empty cab, told the driver I was late for a flight, and off we went. The plane to Atlanta left in an hour. The one to Miami was an hour and a half. The one to La Guardia was boarding, so I flew to New York.'

'With ninety million bucks.'

'Minus fifty thousand for old Dunlap. It was the longest flight of my life, Karl. I knocked down three martinis and was still nothing but nerves. I would close my eyes and see customs agents with machine guns waiting on me at the gate. I just knew Dunlap had gotten suspicious and called the firm, and that somehow they had tracked me to the airport and onto the flight. I have never wanted to get off a plane so badly in my life. We landed, taxied to the terminal, got off the plane. A camera flashed as we stepped into the gate area, and I thought, This is it! They've got me! It was some kid with a Kodak. I practically ran to the men's room, where I sat on the toilet for twenty minutes. Next to my feet was a canvas overnight bag with all my worldly possessions.'

'Don't forget the ninety million.'

'Oh yeah.'

'How'd the money get to Panama?'

'How do you know it went to Panama?'

'I'm the Judge, Patrick. The cops talk to me. It's a small town.'

'It was in the wiring instructions from Nassau. The money went into a new account in Malta, then quickly on to Panama.'

'How'd you become such a wizard at wiring money?'

'Just took a little research. I worked on it for a year. Tell me, Karl, when did you hear that the money was missing?'

Karl laughed and reclined even farther. He clasped his hands behind his head. 'Well, your pals at the firm did a poor job of keeping their little settlement quiet.'

'I'm shocked.'

'In fact, the whole town knew they were about to be filthy rich. They acted so serious about the secrecy, yet they were spending money like crazy. Havarac bought the biggest, blackest Mercedes ever made. Vitrano's architect was in the final stage of designing their new home – eleven thousand square feet. Rapley signed a contract to buy an eighty-foot sailboat; said he was contemplating retirement. I heard the private jet talk a few times. Thirty million in legal fees would be hard to hide around here, but they didn't really try. They wanted people to know.'

'Sounds like a bunch of lawyers.'

'You struck on a Thursday, right?'

'Right. March twenty-sixth.'

'The next day, I was preparing to proceed with a

civil trial when one of the lawyers got a call from the office. The news was that there were problems with the big settlement over at Bogan, Rapley, Vitrano, Havarac, and Lanigan. The money vanished. All of it. Stolen by someone offshore.'

'Was my name mentioned?'

'Not the first day. It didn't take long, though. Word got out that the bank's security cameras had captured someone vaguely resembling you. Other pieces fell into place, and the gossip roared around town.'

'Did you believe I did it?'

'At first, I was too shocked to believe anything. All of us were. We had buried you, put you to rest, said our prayers. It was impossible to believe. But, as the days passed, the shock wore off and the puzzle came together. The new will, the life insurance, the cremated corpse – we started getting suspicious. Then they found the office crawling with bugs. The FBI was questioning everyone around here. A week after it happened, it was pretty well accepted that you had pulled it off.'

'Were you proud of me?'

'I wouldn't say I was proud. Astonished maybe. Perhaps stunned. There was, after all, a dead body. Then, I was intrigued.'

'Not the slightest hint of admiration?'

'I don't remember it that way, Patrick. No, an innocent person had been murdered so you could steal the money. Plus, you left behind a wife and daughter.'

'The wife got a bundle. The child isn't mine.'

'I didn't know that at the time. No one did. No, I don't think you were admired around here.'

'What about my pals at the firm?'

'No one saw them for months. They got sued by Aricia. Other litigation followed. They had grossly overspent, so bankruptcy got them. Divorces, booze, it was awful. They self-destructed in textbook fashion.'

276

Patrick crawled onto his bed and gently folded his legs. He savored this with a nasty smile. Huskey stood and walked to the window. 'How long did you stay in New York?' he asked, peeking through the shades.

'About a week. I didn't want any of the money coming back into the States, so I arranged to have it wired to a bank in Toronto. The bank in Panama was a branch of the Bank of Ontario, so it was easy to wire in as much as I needed.'

'You started spending?'

'Not much. I was a Canadian now, with good papers, a transplant from Vancouver, and the money allowed me to purchase a small apartment and obtain credit cards. I found a Portuguese instructor and studied the language six hours a day. I went to Europe several times so my passport would get used and scrutinized. Everything worked perfectly. After three months, I put the apartment on the market and went to Lisbon, where I studied the language for a couple of months. Then, on August 5, 1992, I flew to São Paulo.'

'Your independence day.'

'Absolute freedom, Karl. I landed in that city with two small bags. I got in a cab and I was soon lost in a sea of twenty million people. It was dark and raining, traffic was standing still, and I was in the back of a cab thinking to myself that no one in the world knew where I was. And no one would ever find me. I almost cried, Karl. It was sheer, unbridled freedom. I looked at the faces of the people racing down the sidewalks, and I thought to myself, I'm now one of them. I'm a Brazilian named Danilo, and I'll never be anybody else.'

TWENTY-NINE

Sandy slept three hours on a hard mattress in a loft somewhere above the den, far away from her, and awoke with the early sun beaming through slits beneath the blinds. It was six-thirty. They had said good night at three, after seven hours of intensely scouring documents and listening to dozens of surreptitious talks Patrick had amazingly captured.

He showered and dressed, and found his way down to the kitchen, where Leah sat in the breakfast nook with fresh coffee and a surprisingly alert face. She fixed him wheat toast with jam as he glanced at the newspapers. Sandy was ready to leave, to return to his office with the Aricia mess and sort it out on his own turf.

'Any word from your father?' he asked. The early voices were quiet, the words scarce.

'No. But I can't call from here. I'll go to the market later and use a pay phone.'

'I'll say a prayer for him.'

'Thanks.'

They loaded the entire Aricia file into the trunk of his car, and said good-bye. She promised to call him within twenty-four hours. She would not be leaving anytime soon. Their client's problems had gone from serious to urgent.

The early air was cool. It was October after all, and

even the Coast felt a hint of autumn. She put on a parka and went for a walk on the beach, barefoot and bare-legged, with one hand in a pocket and the other holding her coffee. She hid behind sunglasses, which annoyed her. The beach was deserted. Why was she compelled to hide her face?

Like all Cariocas, she had spent a great deal of her life on the beach, the center of culture. Her childhood home had been her father's apartment in Ipanema, the poshest of Rio's neighborhoods, where every kid grew up on the beach.

She was unaccustomed to long walks near the water without being surrounded by a million people happily sunning and playing. Her father had been one of the first to organize efforts against the unbridled development of Ipanema. He despised the increase of population and haphazard construction, and worked tirelessly with neighborhood groups. Such actions went against the typical Carioca attitude of live and let live, but with time came to be admired and even welcomed. As a lawyer, Eva still donated time to preservation groups in the neighborhoods of Ipanema and Leblon.

The sun crept behind clouds, and the breeze picked up. She returned to the house as the seagulls followed and squawked overhead. She locked every door and window, and drove two miles to a supermarket, where she planned to buy shampoo and fruit, and to find the nearest possible pay phone.

She didn't see the man at first, and when she finally noticed him he seemed to have been standing beside her forever. She was holding a bottle of hair conditioner when he sniffed, as if he had a cold. She turned, glanced from behind the sunglasses, and was startled by his sustained eye contact. He was thirty or forty, white, unshaven, but she didn't have time to notice anything else.

He was staring at her, with rabid green eyes that glowed in the middle of a beach-bronzed face. She coolly walked away, down the aisle with the conditioner. Maybe he was just a local character, a harmless pervert who lurked in the grocery and scared pretty vacationers. Perhaps everyone in the store knew his name and made excuses for him because he wouldn't harm an insect.

Minutes later, she saw him again, this time hiding near the bakery with his face behind a pizza crust but his metallic eyes watching every move she made. Why was he hiding, covering his face? He wore shorts and sandals, she noticed.

Panic hit hard through her chest and sent waves down her legs. Her first thought was to run, but she kept her cool long enough to find a small shopping basket. She had been spotted by whoever he was, and it was to her advantage to watch him as much as he was watching her. Who knew when she might see him again? She loitered in the produce department, next picked her way through the cheeses, and didn't see him for a long time. Then she saw him with his back to her, holding a gallon of milk.

A few minutes later, she caught sight of him through the large front windows, walking through the parking lot, his head cocked to one side, talking into a cell phone, carrying nothing. What happened to the milk? She would've raced through a back door, but her car was parked in the front. She paid for the items as calmly as possible, but her hands shook as she took her change.

There were thirty cars, including her rental, in the parking lot, and she knew she couldn't inspect them all. Not that she wanted to. He was in one of them. She simply wanted to leave without being followed. She quickly got in her car, left the lot, and turned in the direction of the beach house, though she knew she could never go back there. She drove a half a mile, then made an abrupt U-turn, just in time to see him behind her, three cars back, driving a new Toyota. His green eyes glanced away at the last second. Odd, she thought, that he wasn't covering them.

Everything seemed odd, at the moment. How odd that she was driving along a foreign highway in a foreign country with a fake passport proclaiming her to be someone she never wanted to be, and going to a place that she had yet to determine. Yes, everything was odd and blurred and frightening as hell, and what Eva needed and desperately wanted was to see Patrick so she could scream at him for an hour, and throw rocks as well. This was not part of the deal. It was one thing for Patrick to be hunted for his past, but she had done nothing wrong. Not to mention Paulo.

Being Brazilian, she normally drove with one foot on the gas and the other on the brake, and the traffic along the beach badly needed a good dose of her native driving. But she had to be calm. You don't panic when you're on the run, Patrick had said many times. You think, you watch, you plan.

She watched the cars behind her. She obeyed all highway rules.

'Always know where you are,' Patrick had told her. She had studied the road atlas for hours. She turned north and stopped at a gas station to see what she attracted. Nothing. The man with the green eyes was not behind her, but this was of no comfort. He knew she had seen him. He'd been caught. He'd simply called ahead with his little cell phone and now the rest of them were watching.

An hour later, she entered the airport terminal in Pensacola and waited eighty minutes for a flight to Miami. Any flight would have suited her. The one to Miami happened to be the soonest. It would prove to be disastrous.

She waited behind a magazine in a coffee bar and watched everything that moved. A security guard enjoyed looking at her, and she found him difficult to ignore. Otherwise, the airport was almost devoid of human activity.

The flight to Miami was by turboprop commuter, and seemed to take forever. Eighteen of the twenty-four seats were vacant, and the other five passengers looked harmless. She even managed a brief nap.

In Miami, she hid in an airport lounge for an hour, sipping expensive water and watching the throngs come and go. At the Varig counter, she bought a first-class ticket to São Paulo, one way. She wasn't sure why. São Paulo wasn't home, but it was certainly in the right direction. Maybe she would hide there in a nice hotel for a few days. She'd be closer to her father, wherever he was. Planes were leaving for a hundred destinations. Why not visit her country?

As it routinely does, the FBI issued an alert to customs and immigration personnel, as well as to the airlines. This one specified a young woman, age thirty-one, traveling under a Brazilian passport, real name of Eva Miranda but probably using an alias. Having learned the identity of her father, getting her real name was a simple matter. When Leah Pires walked through a passport checkpoint at Miami International, she wasn't expecting trouble in front of her. She was still looking for the men behind her.

Her Leah Pires passport had proven quite reliable in the past two weeks.

But the customs agent had seen the alert an hour earlier during a coffee break. He pushed an alarm button on his scanner while he slowly examined every word of the passport. The hesitation at first was annoying, then Leah realized something was wrong. The travelers at the other booths were breezing through, barely slowing long enough to open their passports and having the approvals nodded back at them. A supervisor in a navy jacket appeared from nowhere and huddled with the agent. 'Could you step in here, Ms Pires?' he asked politely but with no room for discussion. He was pointing at a row of doors down the wide corridor.

'Is there a problem?' she insisted.

'Not really. Just a few questions.' He was waiting for her. A uniformed guard with Mace and a gun on his waist was waiting too. The supervisor was holding her passport. Dozens of passengers behind her were watching.

'Questions about what?' she demanded as she walked with the supervisor and the guard to the second door.

'Just a few questions,' he repeated, opening the door and escorting her into a square room with no windows. A holding room. She noticed the name of Rivera on his lapel. He didn't look to be Hispanic.

'Give me the passport,' she demanded as soon as they were alone and the door was closed.

'Not so fast, Ms Pires. I need to ask you a few questions.'

'And I don't have to answer them.'

'Please, relax. Have a seat. Can I get you some coffee or water?'

'No.'

'Is this a valid address in Rio?'

'It certainly is.'

'Where did you arrive from?'

'Pensacola.'

'Your flight?'

'Airlink 855.'

'And your destination?'

'São Paulo.'

'Where in São Paulo?'

'Maybe that's a private matter.'

'Business or pleasure?'

'Why does it matter?'

'It matters. Your passport lists your home in Rio. So where will you be staying in São Paulo?'

'A hotel.'

'And the name of the hotel?'

She hesitated as she struggled to grab the name of a hotel, and the little interval was deadly. 'Uh, the – the – Inter-Continental,' she finally said, without the slightest hint of truthfulness.

He wrote it down, then said, 'And we can assume the room there is reserved in the name of Leah Pires?'

'Of course,' she said, snapping back nicely. But one quick phone call would prove she was lying.

'Where is your luggage?' he asked.

Another crack in the facade, and this one even more revealing. She hesitated, glanced away, and said, 'I'm traveling light.'

Someone knocked on the door. Rivera opened it slightly, took a sheet of paper, and whispered to his unseen colleague. Leah sat down and tried to relax. The door closed and Rivera studied his evidence.

'According to our records, you entered the country eight days ago, here in Miami, on a flight from London which originated in Zurich. Eight days, and no luggage. Seems odd, doesn't it?'

'Is it a crime to travel light?' she asked.

'No, but it is a crime to use a false passport. At least here, in the U.S.'

She looked at the passport lying on the table near him, and she knew it was as phony as could be. 'It's not a false passport,' she said indignantly.

'Do you know a person by the name of Eva Miranda?' Rivera asked, and Leah couldn't keep her chin up. Her heart stopped and her face fell, and she knew the chase was over.

Rivera knew they had snared another one. 'I'll have to contact the FBI,' he said. 'It will take some time.'

'Am I under arrest?' she asked.

'Not yet.'

'I'm a lawyer. I –'

'We know. And we have the right to detain you for questioning. Our offices are on the lower level. Let's go.'

She was led away hurriedly, clutching her purse, her eyes still covered.

The long table was piled with papers and files, with crumpled sheets from legal pads and napkins and empty cups and even half-eaten sandwiches from the hospital cafeteria. Lunch had been five hours earlier but neither lawyer had thought of dinner. Time was being kept outside the room. Inside, it didn't matter.

Both men were barefoot. Patrick wore a tee shirt and gym shorts. Sandy wore a very wrinkled cotton button-down, khakis, no socks, the same attire he'd put on hours earlier in the beach house.

The Aricia box was empty in a corner, its contents all on the table.

The door opened while it was being knocked on, and Agent Joshua Cutter entered before he was asked. He stayed by the door.

'This is a private meeting,' Sandy said, very near Cutter's face. The documents on the table could not be seen by anyone. Patrick walked to the door and helped shield the view.

'Why don't you knock before you enter?' he said angrily.

'Sorry,' Cutter said calmly. 'I'll just be a minute. Just thought you'd want to know that we have Eva Miranda in custody. Caught her sneaking through the Miami airport, on her way home to Brazil, fake passport and all.'

Patrick froze and tried to think of something to say.

'Eva?' Sandy asked.

'Yeah, also known as Leah Pires. That's what her fake passport calls her.' Cutter was looking at Patrick while answering Sandy.

'Where is she?' Patrick asked, stunned.

'Jail, in Miami.'

Patrick turned and walked along the table. Jail would be horrible anywhere, but jail in Miami had a particularly ominous ring to it.

'Do you have a number where we can call her?' Sandy asked.

'No.'

'She has the right to a telephone.'

'We're working on it.'

'Get me a number, okay.'

'We'll see.' Cutter continued to watch Patrick and ignore Sandy. 'She was in a hurry. No luggage, not one bag. Just trying to sneak back to Brazil, leaving you behind.'

'Shut up,' Patrick said.

'You can leave now,' Sandy said.

'Just thought you'd want to know,' Cutter said with a smile, and left.

Patrick sat down and gently massaged his temples. His head had been aching before Cutter arrived, now it was splitting. He and Eva had gone over and over the three scenarios which she would face if they caught him. First, and the one according to plan, was that she would remain in the shadows, assisting Sandy and moving at will. Second, she might be caught by Stephano and Aricia, which was by far the most frightening possibility. Third, the FBI could catch her, which was not nearly as terrifying as the second, but did pose enormous problems. At least she was safe.

They had not discussed this fourth scenario, her

286

return to Brazil without him. He would not believe it was abandonment.

Sandy quietly gathered files and cleaned up the table.

'What time did you leave her?' Patrick asked.

'About eight. She was fine, Patrick. I told you that.'

'No mention of Miami or Brazil?'

'No. None whatsoever. I left with the impression she would be at the beach house for a while. She told me she leased it for a month.'

'Then she got scared. Why else would she run?'

'I don't know.'

'Find a lawyer in Miami, Sandy. And quickly.'

'I know a couple.'

'She must be scared to death.'

THIRTY

It was after six, so Havarac was probably in a casino at the blackjack table, sipping free whiskey and looking for women. Rumors about his gambling debts were abundant. No doubt Rapley was locked away in his attic, a place the rest of the world preferred him to be. The secretaries and paralegals were gone. Doug Vitrano locked the front door of the building and walked to the rear office, the largest and nicest one, where Charlie Bogan was waiting behind his desk with his sleeves rolled up.

Patrick had managed to bug every office except the senior partner's, a fact Bogan had relied on heavily during the roaring brawls that followed the loss of the money. If Bogan wasn't in his office, or somewhere in the very near vicinity, it was locked with a deadbolt. His partners had been much too careless, he had reminded them repeatedly. Especially Vitrano, whose phone had been used during those last fateful chats with Graham Dunlap offshore, which was how Patrick had learned the direction of the money. This had been rehashed to the point of near fistfights.

Bogan could not, in all fairness, claim he suspected espionage in his own firm. If so, why hadn't he warned his more indifferent partners? He'd simply been cautious, and lucky. Important conversations were held in Bogan's office. It took only seconds to engage the deadbolt. He kept the only key. Not even the janitors could get in without Bogan's presence.

Vitrano closed the door firmly and dropped into the soft leather chair across the desk.

'I saw the Senator this morning,' Bogan said. 'He called me to his house.' Bogan's mother and the Senator's father were siblings. The Senator was ten years older than Bogan.

'Is he in a good mood?' Vitrano asked.

'I wouldn't call it that. He wanted an update on Lanigan, and I told him what I knew. Still no sign of the money. He's very nervous about what Lanigan might know. I assured him, as I've done many times, that all communications with him were done in this office, and that this office was clean. So, he shouldn't worry about what Lanigan might know.'

'But he's worried?'

'Of course he's worried. He asked me again if there was any document tying him to Aricia, and I again said no.'

'Which of course is true.'

'Yes. There are no documents with the Senator's name. Everything with him was verbal. Most of it was done on the golf course. I've told him this a thousand times, but he wanted to hear it again, in light of Patrick's return.'

'You didn't tell him about the Closet?'

'No.'

They both watched the dust on Bogan's desk and relived what happened in the Closet. In January of 1992, a month after the Justice Department approved the Aricia settlement, and about two months before they were to receive the money, Aricia had popped in one day, unscheduled and unannounced and in a foul mood. Patrick was still around, though his funeral was only three weeks away. The firm had already begun an extensive renovation of its offices, and for this reason

Bogan couldn't meet with Aricia in his office. Painters were on ladders. Drop cloths covered the furniture. They got the combative Aricia into a small meeting room across the hall from Bogan's, a room everyone referred to simply as the Closet because of its size. A small square table with a chair on each side. No windows. The ceiling was slanted because a stairway ran above it.

Vitrano was fetched because he was second in command, and a meeting of sorts commenced. It didn't last long. Aricia was chafed because the lawyers were about to earn thirty million dollars. Now that his settlement had been approved, reality had hit hard, and he thought thirty million in legal fees was obscene. Things turned nasty quickly as Bogan and Vitrano held their ground. They offered to find their contract for legal services, but Aricia cared nothing for it.

In the heat of the moment, Aricia asked how much of the thirty million the Senator would get. Bogan grew hostile and said it was none of his business. Aricia claimed that it was his business, because, after all, the money was his, and then he launched into a windy diatribe attacking the Senator and all politicians in general. He made much of the fact that the Senator had been working so hard in Washington to pressure the Navy, the Pentagon, and the Justice Department to settle his claim. 'How much will he get?' he kept asking.

Bogan kept slipping the punches. He would say only that the Senator would be taken care of. He reminded Aricia that he had carefully chosen the firm because of its political connections. And he hotly added that sixty million in Aricia's pocket was not such a bad deal, considering how the claim was bogus to begin with.

Too much was said.

Aricia proposed a fee of only ten million. Bogan and

290

Vitrano rejected it outright. He stormed out of the Closet, swearing every step of the way.

There were no phones in the Closet, but two mikes were found. One was under the table, hidden in a corner where two brackets joined, stuck in place by black putty. The second was placed between two dusty ancient law books on the only shelf in the room. The books were for decorative purposes.

After the shock of the vanishing fortune, and the subsequent discovery by Stephano of all the bugs and wires, Bogan and Vitrano didn't discuss the Closet meeting for a long time. Maybe it would just disappear. They never spoke to Aricia about it, primarily because he had sued them so quickly and now hated the mention of their names. The incident faded from their memories. Maybe it never happened after all.

Now that Patrick was back, they had been forced to timidly confront it. There was always the chance that the mikes had malfunctioned or that Patrick in his haste had missed it. There were certainly enough other bugs for him to absorb and assimilate. In fact, they had decided there was a very good chance the Closet meeting had been missed by Patrick.

'Surely he wouldn't keep the tapes for four years, would he?' Vitrano asked.

But Bogan didn't answer. He sat with his fingers locked over his stomach and watched the dust settle on his desk. Oh, what could've been. He would get five million, the Senator the same. No bankruptcy, no divorce. He would still have his wife and family, his home and his stature. He could've taken the five and made it ten by now, and twenty before long, serious big money and the freedom to do anything. It was all there, a feast on a table, then Patrick snatched it.

The giddiness of finding Patrick had lasted a couple of days, then vanished slowly when it became obvious that the money was not following him back to Biloxi.

With each passing day, the money actually seemed farther away.

'Do you think we'll get the money, Charlie?' Vitrano asked, barely audible, his eyes on the floor. He hadn't called him Charlie in years. Such familiarity was unheard of in a firm with so much hatred.

'No,' he said. There was a long pause. 'We'll be lucky if we're not indicted.'

With an hour of serious phone work ahead of him, Sandy made the most troubling one first. Sitting in his parked car in the hospital lot, he called his wife and told her he'd be in very late, so late that he might be forced to stay in Biloxi. His son was playing in a junior high football game. He apologized, blamed everything on Patrick, and said he'd explain later. She took it much better than expected.

He caught a secretary working late at his office, and collected phone numbers from her. He knew two lawyers in Miami, neither of whom happened to be at the office at seven-fifteen. The home number for one went unanswered. The other had a private listing. He made a series of calls to lawyers he knew in New Orleans, and finally got the home number of Mark Birck, a highly regarded criminal defense specialist in Miami. Birck was not delighted at receiving the call during dinner, but he listened anyway. Sandy gave the ten-minute version of the Patrick saga, including the latest development with Eva in jail somewhere in Miami. Thus the call. Birck showed an interest, and claimed a thorough knowledge of immigration law as well as criminal procedure. He would make two calls, after dinner. Sandy agreed to phone him back in an hour.

It took three calls to locate Cutter, and twenty minutes of wheedling before he would agree to meet for coffee at a doughnut shop. Sandy drove there, and while waiting for Cutter called Birck again.

Birck reported that Eva Miranda was indeed in custody in a federal detention center in Miami. She had not yet been formally charged with any crime, but it was early. There was no way to see her tonight, and it would be difficult to see her tomorrow. Under the law, the FBI and the U.S. Customs Service can hold an alien caught traveling under a bogus passport for up to four days before a release can be applied for. Makes sense, Birck explained, considering the circumstances. These people tend to disappear quickly.

Birck had been in the detention center several times visiting clients, and, as these places went, it was not bad. She was in her own private cell, and generally safe. With luck, she would have access to a telephone in the morning.

Without providing too much detail, Sandy stressed that there was no rush in getting her released. There were people looking for her on the outside. Birck promised to pull strings early in the morning, and try to see her.

His fee would be ten thousand dollars, which Sandy agreed to pay.

He hung up as Cutter swaggered into the doughnut shop and sat at a table by the front window, as promised. Sandy locked his car and followed him in.

Dinner was packaged food, microwaved and served on a well-worn plastic tray. Though she was hungry, the thought of eating it hardly crossed her mind. It was delivered to her cinder-blocked cell by two heavy women in uniform, keys dangling from chains around their waists. One asked how she was doing. She mumbled something in Portuguese and they left her alone. The door was thick metal with a small square hole in it. Voices of other women prisoners could occasionally be heard, but the place was generally quiet.

She had never been in jail before, not even as a lawyer. Other than Patrick, she couldn't recall a friend who'd been incarcerated. The initial shock yielded to fear, then to humiliation at being caged like a criminal. Only the thought of her poor father kept her focused during the first hours. No doubt his conditions were far worse than hers. She prayed that they were not hurting him.

The praying came easier in jail. She prayed for her father, and she prayed for Patrick. She resisted the temptation to blame him for her troubles, though it would've been easy. Most of the blame rested with her. She had panicked and run too quickly. Patrick had taught her how to move without leaving a trail, how to vanish. The mistake was her fault, not his.

The false passport charges were minor, she decided, and could be dealt with in short order. In a violent country without enough jail cells, surely such a simple offense from such a noncriminal could be handled swiftly with a small fine and a quick deportation.

She found comfort in the money. Tomorrow she would demand an attorney, a good one with clout. Phone calls would be made to officials in Brasília; she knew their names. If necessary, the money could be used to bully everyone in sight. She would be out before long, then back home to rescue her father. She would hide somewhere in Rio; it would be simple.

The cell was warm, and locked, and guarded by lots of people with guns. It was a safe place, she decided. The men who hurt Patrick and now had her father couldn't touch her.

She turned off the ceiling light and stretched out on the narrow bunk. The FBI would be anxious to tell Patrick that she was in custody, so he probably knew by now. She could see him with his legal pad, running lines here and there, analyzing this latest development from an amazing variety of angles. By now, Patrick had conceived no fewer than ten ways to rescue her. And he wouldn't sleep until he had the list pared down to the best three plans.

The fun was in the planning, he always said.

Cutter ordered a caffeine-free soda and a chocolate doughnut. He was off-duty, so the standard dark suit and white shirt were replaced by jeans and short sleeves. Smirking came naturally for him. Now that they had found the girl and locked her up, he was especially cocky.

Sandy ate a ham sandwich in four bites. It was almost 9 P.M. Lunch had been hospital food with Patrick, a long time ago. 'We need to have a serious talk,' he said. The shop was packed and his voice was low.

'I'm listening,' Cutter said.

Sandy swallowed, wiped his mouth, leaned even closer and said, 'Don't take this the wrong way, but we need to include other people.'

'Like who?'

'Like the people above you. People in Washington.'

Cutter pondered this for a minute as he watched the traffic move along Highway 90. The Gulf was a hundred yards away.

'Sure,' he said. 'But I gotta tell them something.'

Sandy glanced around. Not a single person was even casually looking their way. 'What if I can prove that the Aricia claim against Platt & Rockland was completely fraudulent; that he conspired with the Bogan firm to defraud the government, and that Bogan's cousin, the Senator, was a part of the conspiracy and was to have received several million bucks under the table?'

'A wonderful story.'

'I can prove it.'

'And if we believe it, then we're supposed to allow Mr Lanigan to make some type of restitution and walk away.'

'Perhaps.'

'Not so fast. There's still the matter of the dead body.'

Cutter casually took a bite of his doughnut and chewed it thoughtfully. Then, 'What kind of proof?'

'Documents, recorded phone calls, all sorts of things.'

'Admissible in court?'

'Most of it.'

'Enough for convictions?'

'A box full.'

'Where's the box?'

'In the trunk of my car.'

Cutter instinctively looked over his shoulder in the general direction of the parking lot. Then he stared at Sandy. 'This is stuff Patrick gathered before he split?'

'Correct. He got wind of the Aricia matter. The firm was planning to kick him out, so he very patiently collected the dirt.'

'Bad marriage, etc., etc., so he took the money and ran.'

'No. He ran, then took the money.'

'Whatever. So now he wants to cut a deal, huh?'

'Of course. Wouldn't you?'

'What about the murder?'

'That's a state matter, not really your concern. We'll deal with it later.'

'We can make it our concern.'

'I'm afraid not. You've got the indictment for the theft of the ninety million. The state of Mississippi has the indictment for the murder. Unfortunately for you, the feds can't come in now and charge murder.'

Cutter hated lawyers for that very reason. They didn't bluff easily.

Sandy continued. 'Look, this meeting is a formality. I'm just going through channels, don't want to overstep here. But I'm perfectly ready to start making calls to Washington first thing in the morning. I thought we'd have this chat, and I hoped you would be convinced we're ready to deal. Otherwise, I'm on the phone.'

'Who do you want?'

'Someone with complete authority, FBI and Justice. We'll meet in a large room somewhere and I'll lay out the case.'

'Let me talk to Washington. But this better be good.'

They shook hands stiffly, and Sandy left.

THIRTY-ONE

Mrs Stephano was sleeping again. Those bothersome young men in matching dark suits had left their street, and the neighbors had stopped calling with their nosy questions. The gossip over bridge had returned to more normal topics. Her husband was relaxed.

She was sleeping soundly when the phone rang at 5:30 A.M. She grabbed it from the night table. 'Hello.'

A stout, firm voice said, 'Jack Stephano, please.'

'Who's calling?' she demanded. Jack was moving under the covers.'

'Hamilton Jaynes, FBI,' came the reply.

And she said, 'Oh my God!' She placed a hand over the receiver. 'Jack, it's the FBI again.'

Jack turned on a light, glanced at the clock, took the phone. 'Who is it?'

'Good morning, Jack. This is Hamilton Jaynes. Hate to call so early.'

'Then don't.'

'Just wanted you to know that we've got the girl, Eva Miranda, in custody. She's safe and secure, so you boys can call off your dogs.'

Stephano swung his feet out of the bed and stood next to the table. Their last hope was gone. The search for the money was finally over. 'Where is she?' he asked, not expecting any meaningful answer.

'We have her, Jack. She's with us.'

'Congratulations.'

'Look, Jack, I've sent some men down to Rio to monitor the situation with her father. You have twenty-four hours, Jack. If he is not released by five-thirty tomorrow morning, then I'll have a warrant for your arrest, and the arrest of Aricia. Hell, I'll probably arrest Mr Atterson at Monarch-Sierra and Mr Jill at Northern Case Mutual, you know, just for the hell of it. I've really wanted to talk to those boys, along with Aricia.'

'You enjoy the harassment, don't you?'

'Love it. We'll help the Brazilians extradite you guys down to Brazil, you know, and that should take a coupla months. No bail with an extradition, so you and your sleazy clients would spend Christmas in jail. Who knows, extradition might work for a change, and you'd get to go to Rio. I hear the beaches are lovely. Are you there, Jack?'

'I hear you.'

'Twenty-four hours.' The phone clicked and the line was dead. Mrs Stephano was in the bathroom with the door locked, too rattled to face him.

Jack went downstairs and made coffee. He sat at the kitchen table, in the semidarkness, waiting for the sun to rise. He was tired of Benny Aricia.

He had been hired to find Patrick and the money, not to ask questions about how the money got created. He knew the basics of Benny Aricia's history with Platt & Rockland, and he had always suspected there was much more to the story. He had probed once or twice, but Aricia showed no interest in discussing the events which preceded Patrick's disappearance.

From the beginning, Jack had suspected the law firm's offices had been wired for two reasons. The first was to gather dirt on the other partners and their clients, specifically Aricia. The second was to lead Patrick to the money after his funeral. What was unknown to everyone, except to maybe Aricia and the partners, was how much damaging evidence had been taped and stored by Patrick. Stephano suspected that plenty of dirt had been gathered.

When the money vanished, and Stephano began his search, the law firm chose not to join the consortium. It had thirty million dollars at stake, yet chose to lick its wounds and go home. The reason given was lack of money. The partners were basically broke, things were about to get much worse, and they simply couldn't afford to participate. This had some logic at the time, but Stephano also sensed a reluctance to find Patrick.

Something was on the tapes. Patrick had caught them red-handed. As miserable as their lives had become, the actual capture of Patrick could be their worst nightmare.

Same for Aricia. He'd wait an hour, then call him.

By six-thirty, the office of Hamilton Jaynes was crawling with people. Two agents sat on a sofa and studied the latest report from their contacts in Rio. One stood beside Jaynes' desk and waited to give an update on Aricia's whereabouts; he was still at the rented condo in Biloxi.

Another stood nearby with an update on Eva Miranda. A secretary carried a box of files into the office. Jaynes was in his chair, on the phone, haggard and coatless, ignoring everyone.

Joshua Cutter entered, also worn and wrinkled. He'd slept two hours in the Atlanta airport waiting for a flight to Washington, D.C., where an agent met him for the drive to the Hoover Building. Jaynes immediately hung up, and ordered everyone from his office.

'Get us some coffee, lots of it,' he barked at the secretary. The room cleared and Cutter sat rigidly before the grand desk. Though mightily fatigued, he tried hard to be alert. He'd never been near the Deputy Director's office before.

'Let's hear it,' Jaynes growled.

'Lanigan wants to cut a deal. He claims to have enough evidence to convict Aricia, the lawyers, and an unnamed U.S. Senator.'

'What kind of evidence?'

'A box full of documents and tapes, stuff Lanigan accumulated before he skipped out.'

'Did you see the box?'

'No. McDermott said it was in the trunk of his car.'

'And what about the money?'

'We never got that far. He wants to meet with you and somebody at Justice to discuss settlement possibilities. I got the impression he thinks they can buy their way out of it.'

'That's always a possibility when you steal dirty money. Where does he want to meet?'

'Down there, somewhere in Biloxi.'

'Let me call Sprawling at Justice,' Jaynes said almost to himself, as he lunged for the phone. The coffee arrived.

Mark Birck tapped his designer pen on the table as he waited in the visitors' room of the federal detention center. It was not quite nine, much too early for lawyers to see their clients, but he had a friend in administration. Birck explained it was an emergency. The table had privacy panels on both sides and a thick glass plate down the center. He would talk to her through a small screened opening.

For thirty minutes he tapped and fidgeted. She was finally brought from around the corner, dressed in a yellow one-piece jumpsuit with faded lettering stamped in black across the chest. The guard removed the handcuffs and she rubbed her wrists.

When they were alone, she sat in her chair and

looked at him. He slid a business card through a tiny slot. She took it and examined every letter.

'Patrick sent me,' he said, and she closed her eyes. 'Are you okay?' he asked.

She leaned forward on her elbows and spoke through the screened opening. 'I'm fine. Thanks for coming. When do I get out?'

'Not for a few days. The feds can do one of two things. First, and the most serious, they can indict you for traveling under a false passport. This is a longshot because you're a foreigner and you have no criminal record. Second, and most likely, they'll simply deport you with your promise never to return. Either way, it'll take them a few days to decide. In the meantime, you're stuck here because we can't get bail right now.'

'I understand.'

'Patrick is very concerned about you.'

'I know. Tell him I'm fine. And I'm very concerned about him.'

Birck adjusted his legal pad, and said, 'Now, Patrick wants a detailed account of exactly how you were caught.'

She smiled and seemed to relax. Of course Patrick would want the details. She started with the man with the green eyes, and slowly told the story.

Benny had always laughed at the Biloxi beach. Just a narrow strip of sand bordered on one side by a highway too dangerous to cross on foot, and on the other by dull brown water too brackish to swim in. During the summer it attracted low-budget vacationers, and on weekends students threw Frisbees and rented jet-skis. The casino boom brought more tourists to the beach, but they seldom lingered long before returning to their gambling.

He parked at the Biloxi pier, lit a long cigar, removed his shoes, and walked the beach anyway. It

302

was much cleaner now, another benefit from the casinos. It was also deserted. A few fishing boats drifted out to sea.

Stephano's call an hour earlier had ruined his morning, and, for the most part, altered the remainder of his life. With the girl locked away, he had no chance of finding the money. She couldn't lead him to it now, nor could she be used as leverage with Lanigan.

The feds had an indictment hanging over Patrick's head. Patrick, in turn, had the money and the evidence. One would be swapped for the other, and Aricia would get caught in the crossfire. When the pressure was applied to his co-conspirators, Bogan and the rest of those pansy-ass lawyers, they would sing in an instant. Benny was the odd man out, and he knew this perfectly well. Had known it, in fact, for a long time. His dream had been to somehow find the money, then disappear with it, just like Patrick.

But his dream was over now. He had a million bucks left. He had friends in other countries, and contacts around the world. It was time to split, just like Patrick.

Sandy kept a scheduled 10 A.M. meeting with T.L. Parrish, in the D.A.'s office, though he'd been tempted to postpone it and spend the morning working on the documents. When he left his office at 8:30, his entire staff and both of his partners were making copies and enlarging crucial pages.

Parrish had requested the meeting. Sandy was certain he knew why. The state's case had major holes in it, and now that the thrill of the indictment had passed, it was time to talk business. Prosecutors tend to try the airtight cases, and there is never a shortage of them. But a high-profile case with gaping holes is serious trouble.

Parrish wanted to fish, but first he puffed and

postured and talked about venue. A jury anywhere would not be sympathetic to a lawyer who murdered for money. Sandy just listened, at first. Parrish recited his favorite statistics about his conviction rate and the fact that he'd never lost a capital murder trial. Got eight of 'em on death row, he said, not bragging.

Sandy really had better things to do. He needed to have a serious conversation with Parrish, but not today. He asked how he would prove the murder occurred in Harrison County. And he followed it by the cause of death – how could that be proven? Patrick certainly wouldn't testify and help them out. And the big one, who was the victim? According to Sandy's research, there was not a single reported murder conviction in the state with an unidentified victim.

Parrish anticipated these troublesome inquiries, and did an adequate job of evading concrete answers. 'Has your client considered a plea bargain?' he finally asked, as if in deep pain.

'No.'

'Would he?'

'No.'

'Why not?'

'You ran to the grand jury, got your capital murder indictment, waved it in front of the press, now you have to prove it. You didn't bother to wait and assess your evidence. Forget it.'

'I can get a conviction for manslaughter,' Parrish said angrily. 'That carries twenty years.'

'Maybe,' Sandy said nonchalantly. 'But my client has not been charged with manslaughter.'

'I can do that tomorrow.'

'Fine. Go do it. Dismiss the capital murder charges, refile for manslaughter, then we'll talk.'

THIRTY-TWO

It was labeled the Camille Suite, and it occupied one third of the top floor of the Biloxi Nugget, the newest, gaudiest, largest, and most successful of all the Vegas-style casinos popping up along the Coast. The boys from Vegas thought it clever to name the Nugget's suites and banquet rooms after the worst hurricanes to hit the Coast. For an average Joe who came in from the street and simply wanted spacious quarters, it rented for $750 a day. That's what Sandy agreed to pay. For a high-roller flown in from afar, the suite would be complimentary. But gambling was the last thing on Sandy's mind. His client, less than two miles away, had approved the expense. The Camille had two bedrooms, a kitchen, den, and two parlors – plenty of places to meet with separate groups. It also had four incoming phone lines, a fax, and a VCR. Sandy's paralegal brought the PC and the technical machinery from New Orleans, along with the first batch of Aricia documents.

The first visitor to Mr McDermott's temporary law offices was J. Murray Riddleton, Trudy's thoroughly defeated divorce lawyer. He sheepishly handed over a proposed settlement of property rights and child visitation. They discussed it over lunch. The terms of surrender were dictated by Patrick. And since he was now calling the shots, Sandy found numerous details to nitpick through. 'This is a good first draft,' he said repeatedly as he continued to mark it up with red ink. Riddleton took the thrashing like a pro. He argued every point, bitched about the amendments, but both lawyers knew the settlement would be changed to suit Patrick's whim. The DNA test and nude photos ruled supreme.

The second visitor was Talbot Mims, Biloxi counsel for Northern Case Mutual, a hyper and jovial man who traveled in a very comfortable van, complete with a fast driver, leather seats and interior, a small worktable, two phones, a fax, beeper, television and VCR so Mims could study video depositions, a laptop and a PC, and a sofa for quick naps, though he succumbed only after the most arduous days in court. His entourage included a secretary and a paralegal, both of whom kept cell phones in their pockets, and an obligatory associate hauled along for extra billing purposes.

The four hurriedly presented themselves at the Camille Suite, where Sandy met them in jeans and offered soft drinks from the mini-bar. All declined. The secretary and the paralegal immediately found matters to discuss on their cell phones. Sandy led Mims and the unnamed associate to a parlor, where they sat before a huge window with a splendid view of the Nugget's parking garage, and beyond that the first steel pillars of yet another garish casino.

'I'll get right to the point,' Sandy said. 'Do you know a man by the name of Jack Stephano?'

Mims thought quickly. 'No.'

'I didn't think so. He's a super-sleuth out of D.C. He was hired by Aricia, Northern Case Mutual, and Monarch-Sierra to find Patrick.'

'So?'

'So take a look at these,' Sandy said with a smile as he slid a set of gory color photos from a file. Mims spread them out on the table – Patrick's horrid burns in all their glory.

'These were in the newspaper, right?' he said.

'Some of them.'

'Yeah, I think you spread them around when you sued the FBI.'

'The FBI didn't do this to my client, Mr Mims.'

'Oh really.' Mims released the photos and waited for Sandy.

'The FBI didn't find Patrick.'

'Then why did you sue them?'

'Publicity stunt, designed to arouse some sympathy for my client.'

'Didn't work.'

'Maybe not with you, but you won't be on the jury, will you? Anyway, these injuries were the result of prolonged torture, inflicted by men working for Jack Stephano, who was working for several clients, one of whom happened to be Northern Case Mutual, a very proud publicly owned company with a solid reputation for corporate responsibility and six billion in stockholders' equity.'

Talbot Mims was extremely practical. He had to be. With three hundred open files in his office and eighteen large insurance companies as clients, he didn't have time to play games. 'Two questions,' he said. 'First, can you prove this?'

'Yes. The FBI can confirm it.'

'Second. What do you want?'

'I want a high-ranking Northern Case Mutual executive here in this room tomorrow, someone with unquestioned authority.'

'These are busy people.'

'We're all busy. I'm not threatening a lawsuit, but think of how embarrassing this could be.'

'Sounds like a threat to me.'

'Take it any way you want.'

'What time tomorrow?'

'Four P.M.'

'We'll be here,' Mims said, reaching forward to shake hands. He then left in a rush, his minions racing behind.

Sandy's own crew arrived mid-afternoon. A secretary answered the phone, which by then was ringing every ten minutes. Sandy had placed calls to Cutter, T.L. Parrish, Sheriff Sweeney, Mark Birck in Miami, Judge Huskey, a handful of lawyers in Biloxi, and Maurice Mast, the U.S. Attorney for the Western District of Mississippi. On a personal level, he called his wife twice to get reports on the family, and he called the principal of his third-grader's lower school.

He had spoken to Hal Ladd twice by phone, but met him for the first time at the Camille Suite. Ladd represented Monarch-Sierra. He arrived alone, which Sandy found shocking because insurance defense lawyers *always* traveled in pairs. Regardless of the task at hand, there had to be two of them before the work began. Both listened, both looked, spoke, took notes, and, most important, both billed the client for the same work.

Sandy knew of two large, rich firms in New Orleans that, not surprisingly, had adopted a threesome approach to the practice of insurance defense.

Ladd was a serious sort in his late forties, and by reputation didn't need the assistance of another lawyer. He politely took a diet cola and sat in the same seat Mr Mims had occupied.

Sandy asked him the same question. 'Do you know a man by the name of Jack Stephano?'

He didn't, and so Sandy delivered the standard brief bio. Then he laid the color photos of Patrick's wounds on the table, and they discussed them for a moment. The burns were not inflicted by the FBI, Sandy explained. Ladd read between the lines. Having represented insurance companies for many years, he had long since ceased to be surprised by the depths to which they could sink.

Even so, this was shocking. 'Assuming you can prove this,' Ladd said, 'I'm sure my client would prefer to keep it quiet.'

'We're prepared to amend our lawsuit, drop the FBI, and name as defendants your client, Northern Case Mutual, Aricia, Stephano, and anybody else responsible for the torture. It's an American citizen intentionally wounded and scarred by American defendants. The case is worth millions. We'll go to trial right here in Biloxi.'

Not if Ladd had anything to do with it. He agreed to call Monarch-Sierra immediately and demand that the chief in-house lawyer drop everything and fly to Biloxi. He appeared angry that his client had funded the search without informing him. 'If it's true,' he said, 'I'll never represent them again.'

'Trust me. It's true.'

It was almost dark when Paulo was blindfolded and handcuffed and led from the house. No guns were poked at him, no threats made. No voices whatsoever. He rode in the backseat of a small car, by himself, for an hour or so. The radio played classical music.

When the car stopped, the two front doors opened, and Paulo was helped from the back. 'Come with me,' came a voice at his shoulder, and a large hand took him by the elbow. The road under his feet was gravel. They walked a hundred meters or so, then stopped. The voice said, 'You are on a road twenty kilometers from Rio. To your left, three hundred meters, is a farmhouse with a telephone. Go there for help. I have a gun. If you turn around, I will have no choice but to kill you.'

'I won't turn around,' Paulo said, his body shaking.

'Good. I will remove the handcuffs first, then I will remove the blindfold.'

'I won't turn around,' Paulo said.

The handcuffs were removed. 'Now, I will remove the blindfold. Walk forward quickly.'

The blindfold was yanked off, and Paulo lowered his head and began jogging down the road. There was no sound behind him. He didn't dare glance around. He called the police at the farmhouse, then he called his son.

THIRTY-THREE

The court reporters arrived promptly at eight. Both were named Linda – one with an *i* and one with a *y*. They produced business cards and followed Sandy to the center of the suite, where the furniture had been shoved to the walls and chairs added. He placed Y at one end of the room, with her back to the window with the shades pulled tightly, and sat I at the other end, in a nook next to the bar with a clear view of all the players. Both desperately needed one last smoke. He sent them into the far bedroom.

Jaynes arrived next with his group. He had a driver, an aging FBI agent who also served as bodyguard, lookout, and errand boy; he had an FBI lawyer; and he had Cutter and Cutter's immediate supervisor. From the Attorney General's office, he had Sprawling, an intense dark-eyed veteran who said little but gathered every sound. All six men wore either black or navy suits; all produced business cards, which Sandy's paralegal collected. Sandy's secretary took their coffee orders while the men shuffled as a group through the small parlor and into the den.

Next came Maurice Mast, the U.S. Attorney for the Western District of Mississippi, traveling light with only one assistant. He was followed by T.L. Parrish, alone, and the meeting was ready to begin.

The pecking order took care of itself. Jaynes' driver

and Mast's assistant stayed in the parlor, where they found a platter of doughnuts and the morning papers.

Sandy closed the door, offered a cheerful 'Good morning,' and thanked them all for coming. They were seated around the room. No one smiled, yet they were not unhappy to be there. It was quite intriguing.

Sandy introduced both court reporters, and explained that their dual transcripts of the meeting would be kept by him and considered extremely confidential. This seemed to satisfy everyone. There were no questions or comments at this point because they weren't sure what the meeting was about.

Sandy held a legal pad with his notes neatly arranged, his case organized for a dozen pages or so. He could've been in front of a jury. He sent greetings from his client, Patrick Lanigan, and said the burns were healing nicely. Then he recapped the charges pending against Patrick; capital murder levied by the state; theft, wire fraud, and flight charged by the United States. Capital murder could mean death. The others could tally up to thirty years.

'The federal charges are serious,' he said gravely. 'But they pale in comparison to capital murder. Frankly, and with all due respect, we'd like to get rid of the feds so we can concentrate on the murder charges.'

'Do you have a plan to get rid of us?' Jaynes asked.

'We have an offer.'

'Does it include the money?'

'It does indeed.'

'We have no claim to the money. It wasn't stolen from the federal government.'

'That's where you're wrong.'

Sprawling was itching to say something. 'Do you really think you can buy your way out of this?' It was more of a challenge. His gruff voice was flat, his words efficient.

The jury was barking back at him, but Sandy was determined to follow his script. 'Just wait,' he said. 'If you'll allow me to present my case, then we'll discuss the options. Now, I'm assuming that we're all familiar with Mr Aricia's 1991 claim against his former employer under the False Claims Act. It was prepared and filed by the Bogan firm here in Biloxi, a firm which, at that time, included a new partner by the name of Patrick Lanigan. The claim was fraudulent. My client found out about it, and then learned that the firm planned to kick him out after the claim was approved by Justice but before the money arrived. Over the course of many months, my client covertly gathered evidence which proves, clearly and convincingly, that Mr Aricia and his lawyers conspired to screw the government out of ninety million dollars. The evidence is in the form of documents and taped conversations.'

'Where is this evidence?' asked Jaynes.

'It's under the control of my client.'

'We can get it, you know. We can get a search warrant and take the evidence anytime we want.'

'And what if my client doesn't honor your search warrant? What if he destroys the evidence, or simply hides it again? What will you do then? Lock him up? Indict him for something else? Frankly, he's not afraid of you and your search warrants.'

'And what about you?' asked Jaynes. 'If it's in your possession, we can get a search warrant for you.'

'I won't produce. Anything my client gives me is privileged and confidential, you know that. It's called attorney's work product. Don't forget that Mr Aricia has sued my client. All documents in my possession are privileged. I will not, under any circumstances, hand over the documents until my client tells me to.'

'What if we get a court order?' asked Sprawling.

'I'll ignore it, then I'll appeal it. You can't win on

this one, gentlemen.' And with that they seemed to accept their defeat. No one was surprised.

'How many people were involved?' asked Jaynes.

'The four partners at the firm and Mr Aricia.'

There was a heavy pause as they waited for Sandy to announce the name of the Senator, but he didn't. Instead, he looked at his notes and continued. 'The deal is quite simple. We'll hand over the documents and tapes. Patrick will return the money, all of it. In exchange, the federal charges are dropped so we can concentrate on the state's. The IRS agrees to leave him alone. His Brazilian attorney, Eva Miranda, is released immediately.' He clicked off these terms fluidly because they had been well rehearsed, and his jury absorbed every word. Sprawling took careful notes. Jaynes looked at the floor, neither smiling nor frowning. The rest were noncommittal, but each had many questions.

'And it has to be done today,' Sandy added. 'There is a sense of urgency.'

'Why?' asked Jaynes.

'Because she's locked up. Because you're all here, and you have the authority to make the decision. Because my client has set a deadline of 5 P.M. today to strike the deal, or he'll just keep the money, destroy the evidence, serve his time, and hope one day he gets out.'

With Patrick, they doubted nothing. He had thus far managed to spend his incarceration in a rather cushy private room with a staff at his beck and call.

'Let's talk about the Senator,' Sprawling said.

'Great idea,' Sandy said. He opened a door to the parlor and said something to a paralegal. A table with speakers and tape deck was rolled into the center of the room, and Sandy closed the door again. He looked at his notes, said, 'The date was January 14, 1992, about three weeks before Patrick disappeared. The

314

conversation took place in the law firm, on the first floor, in a room known as the Closet, sort of an all-purpose room sometimes used for very small meetings. The first voice you'll hear is that of Charlie Bogan, then Benny Aricia, then Doug Vitrano. Aricia had arrived at the firm unannounced, and, as you'll see, was not in a good mood.'

Sandy stepped to the table and examined the various buttons. The tape deck was new and had two expensive speakers wired to it. They watched him carefully, most of them pushing forward just a little.

Sandy said, 'Again, Bogan first, then Aricia, then Vitrano.' He pushed a button. There was a ten-second gap of complete silence, then voices came sharply from the speakers. Edgy voices.

BOGAN: We agreed on a fee of one third, that's our standard fee. You signed the contract. You've known for a year and a half that our fee was a third.

ARICIA: You don't deserve thirty million dollars.

VITRANO: And you don't deserve sixty.

ARICIA: I want to know how the money will be split.

BOGAN: Two thirds, one third. Sixty, thirty.

ARICIA: No, no. The thirty million that comes in here. Who gets how much?

VITRANO: That's none of your business.

ARICIA: The hell it's not. It's money I'm paying as a fee. I'm entitled to know who gets how much.

BOGAN: No you're not.

ARICIA: How much does the Senator get?

BOGAN: None of your business.

ARICIA: (Shouting) It is my business. This guy's spent the last year in Washington twisting arms, leaning on people at Navy and the Pentagon and Justice. Hell, he's spent more time working on my file than he has working for his constituents.

VITRANO: Don't yell, okay, Benny.

ARICIA: I want to know how much the slimy little

crook's getting. I have a right to know how much you're shoveling under the table, because it's my money.

VITRANO: It's all under the table, Benny.

ARICIA: How much?

BOGAN: He'll be taken care of, Benny, okay. Why are you so hung up on this? This is nothing new.

VITRANO: I think you picked this firm specifically because of our connections in Washington.

ARICIA: Five million, ten million? How expensive is he?

BOGAN: You'll never know.

ARICIA: The hell I won't. I'll call the sonofabitch up and ask him myself.

BOGAN: Go ahead.

VITRANO: What's with you, Benny? You're about to get sixty million bucks, and now you're getting greedy.

ARICIA: Don't preach to me, especially about greed. When I came here you guys were working for two hundred bucks an hour. Now look at you, trying to justify a fee of thirty million bucks. Already redoing your offices. Already ordering new cars. Next it'll be boats and airplanes and all the other toys of the seriously rich. And all with my money.

BOGAN: Your money? Aren't we missing something here, Benny? Help me out. Your claim was as bogus as a three-dollar bill.

ARICIA: Yeah, but I made it happen. I, not you, set the trap for Platt & Rockland.

BOGAN: Then why did you hire us?

ARICIA: A helluva question.

VITRANO: You got a bad memory, Benny. You came here because of our clout. You needed help. We put the claim together, spent four thousand hours working on it, and we pulled the right strings in Washington. All with your full knowledge, I might add.

ARICIA: Let's cut the Senator out. That should save

316

us ten million. Shave another ten million, and that leaves you boys with ten million for yourselves. That's a much fairer fee, in my opinion.

VITRANO: (Laughing) That's a great deal, Benny. You get eighty, we get ten.

ARICIA: Yeah, and we screw the politicians.

BOGAN: No way, Benny. You're forgetting something very important. If not for us and the politicians, you wouldn't be getting a dime.

Sandy pushed the button. The tape stopped, but the voices seemed to rattle around the room for a full minute. The players looked at the floor, the ceiling, the walls, each trying to savor and record for later the best of what had been said.

With a vulgar smile, Sandy said, 'Gentlemen, this is just a sample.'

'When do we get the rest?' asked Jaynes.

'Could happen within hours.'

'Will your client testify before a federal grand jury?' asked Sprawling.

'Yes, he will. But he won't promise to testify at trial.'

'Why not?'

'He doesn't have to explain. That's just his position.' Sandy rolled the table to the door, knocked, and gave it back to the paralegal. He addressed his group again. 'You fellas should talk. I'll step outside. Make yourselves comfortable.'

'We're not talking in here,' Jaynes said, jumping to his feet. There were too many wires, and given Patrick's history, no room was safe. 'We'll go to our room.'

'Whatever,' Sandy said. They were all rising and grabbing briefcases. They filed through the door, through the parlor, and finally out of the suite. Lynda and Linda raced to the rear bedroom for a smoke and a pee.

Sandy fixed a coffee, and waited.

They reassembled two floors below in a double room that immediately became cramped. Jackets were removed and thrown across the pillows of both beds. Jaynes asked his driver to wait in the hall with Mast's assistant. Matters too sensitive for their lowly ears were about to be discussed.

The deal's biggest loser would be Maurice Mast. If the federal charges were dropped, he would have nothing to prosecute. A rather grand trial would vanish, and he felt compelled to at least register his objection before the others got started. 'We'll look foolish if we allow him to buy his way out,' he said, primarily in the direction of Sprawling, who was trying vainly to relax in a flimsy wooden chair.

Sprawling was only one level down from the Attorney General himself, and this placed him several levels above Mast. He would listen politely for a few minutes to the opinions of the underlings, then he and Jaynes would make the decision.

Hamilton Jaynes looked at T.L. Parrish, and asked, 'Are you reasonably confident you can convict Lanigan of murder?'

T.L. was a cautious type, and he knew full well any promises made to this group would be long remembered. 'Murder might have some problems. Manslaughter is a lock.'

'How much time on a manslaughter?'

'Twenty years.'

'How much would he serve?'

'Five, more or less.'

Oddly, this seemed to please Jaynes, a career man who thought trespassers should serve time. 'You agree, Cutter?' he asked, pacing along the edge of the bed.

'There's not much evidence,' Cutter said. 'We can't

318

prove who, how, what, when, or where as far as the murder goes. We think we know why, but the trial could be a nightmare. Manslaughter is much easier.'

Jaynes asked Parrish, 'How about the Judge? Will he sentence him to the maximum?'

'If convicted of manslaughter, I would expect the Judge to sentence him to twenty years. Parole is determined by the prison authorities.'

'Can we safely assume that Lanigan will spend the next five years behind bars?' Jaynes asked, looking around the room.

'Yes, certainly,' said Parrish, defensively. 'And we're not backing off the capital murder. We intend to make a strong argument that Lanigan killed another person so he could steal the money. The death penalty is a longshot, but if he's convicted of simple murder, he could face life in prison.'

'Does it really make any difference to us whether he spends time at Parchman prison or in a federal facility?' Jaynes asked. It was obvious it didn't make any difference to him.

'I'm sure Patrick has an opinion on the matter,' Parrish said, and got a few weak grins.

T.L. especially liked the deal because he would become the sole remaining prosecutor. Mast and the FBI would make a hasty exit from the case. There was a gap, and he decided to shove Mast a bit closer to the edge of the cliff. 'I have no doubt Patrick will serve time, at Parchman,' he said, helpfully.

Mast wouldn't go quietly. He shook his head and frowned gravely. 'I don't know,' he said. 'I think we look bad if we do this. You can't rob a bank, then get caught, then offer to give the money back if the charges are dropped. Justice is not for sale.'

'It's a bit more complicated than that,' Sprawling said. 'We suddenly have bigger fish to catch, and Lanigan is the key. The money he stole was contaminated. We're simply retrieving it and returning it to the taxpayers.'

Mast wasn't about to argue with Sprawling.

Jaynes looked at T.L. Parrish, and said, 'With all due respect, Mr Parrish, could I ask you to step outside for just a moment. Us federal boys need to discuss something.'

'Sure,' Parrish said. He walked to the door and stepped into the hallway.

Enough of the chitchat. It was time for Sprawling to close the deal. 'Gentlemen, it's very simple. There are some very important people in the White House who are watching things closely. Senator Nye has never been a friend of the President's, and, frankly, a good scandal down here would make the administration happy. Nye's up for reelection in two years. These allegations will keep him busy. And if they're true, then he's dead.'

'We'll do the investigation,' Jaynes said to Mast. 'And you'll get to prosecute.'

It was suddenly obvious to Mast that this meeting was for his benefit. The decision to cut a deal with Patrick had been made by people with far more clout than Sprawling and Jaynes. They were just trying to keep him happy, since he was, after all, the U.S. Attorney for the district.

The idea of indicting and prosecuting a U.S. Senator had enormous potential, and Mast warmed to it immediately. He could see himself in a crowded courtroom playing Patrick's tapes, the jurors and spectators hanging on every word. 'So we're gonna take the deal?' he said, shrugging as if he couldn't have cared less.

'Yes,' said Sprawling. 'It's a no-brainer. We look good by getting the money back. Patrick stays in jail for a long time. We nail even bigger crooks.'

320

'Plus the President wants it done,' Mast said, smiling, though no one else did so.

'I didn't say that,' Sprawling said. 'I haven't talked to the President about this. My bosses talked to his people. That's all I know.'

Jaynes retrieved T.L. Parrish from the hall, and they spent almost an hour walking through Patrick's offer and examining each of its components. The girl could be released with an hour's notice. Patrick would also have to pay interest on the money, they decided. What about the lawsuit he'd filed against the FBI? Jaynes made a list of points to cover with Sandy.

In Miami, Mark Birck personally delivered to Eva the wonderful news that her father had been released. He had not been harmed; in fact, had been treated quite well.

He told her that with a little luck, she might be released herself in a day or two.

THIRTY-FOUR

Solemn-faced and noncommittal, they returned to the Camille Suite and took their same seats. Most had left their jackets in the other room, and had rolled up their sleeves and loosened their ties, as if all manner of hard work was under way. By Sandy's watch, they had been gone for almost an hour and a half. Sprawling was now their spokesman.

'About the money,' he began, and Sandy instantly knew they had a deal. It was just a matter of the details. 'About the money, how much is your client willing to return?'

'All of it.'

'All of it being?'

'All ninety million.'

'What about interest?'

'Who cares about interest?'

'We do.'

'Why?'

'Well, it's only fair.'

'Fair to whom?'

'Uh, the taxpayers.'

Sandy practically laughed at him. 'Come on. You guys work for the federal government. Since when do you worry about protecting the taxpayers?'

'It's standard in cases involving theft and embezzlement,' Maurice Mast added.

'How much?' Sandy asked. 'At what rate?'

'Prime is nine percent,' Sprawling said. 'That would be fair, I think.'

'Oh you do? What does the IRS pay when it determines I've paid too much and it sends me a refund?'

No one could answer. 'Six percent,' Sandy said. 'Six lousy percent is what the government pays.'

Sandy, of course, had had the benefit of planning this. He had anticipated the questions and had crafted the answers, and it was enormous fun watching them squirm as they tried to catch up.

'So, are you offering six percent?' Sprawling asked. His words were careful and slow.

'Of course not. We have the money; we'll determine how much we'll pay. It's the same principle used by the government. We figure the money'll simply go back into the black hole at the Pentagon.'

'We can't control that,' Jaynes said. He was already tired and in no mood for a lecture.

'Here's the way we see the money,' Sandy said. 'It would've been lost entirely, paid to some very slick crooks and never seen again. My client prevented this, has held the money, and is now willing to return it.'

'So we give him a reward?' asked Jaynes.

'No. Just back off the interest.'

'We have to sell this to some people in Washington,' Sprawling said, not pleading but needing help. 'Give us something to work with.'

'We'll pay half the IRS rate, and not a penny more.'

With a serious poker face, Sprawling said, 'I'll run it by the Attorney General. I just hope he's in a good mood.'

'Give him my regards,' Sandy said.

Jaynes looked up from his notetaking, and asked, 'Three percent, right?'

323

'That's right. From March 26, 1992, until November 1, 1996. Total comes to a hundred and thirteen million, plus some change, which we'll ignore. One hundred thirteen million, even.'

The figure had a nice ring to it, and it certainly sounded good to the government boys. They each wrote it on their legal pads. It looked large. Who could argue with a deal that brought so much back into the hands of the taxpayers?

To offer this much meant only one thing: Patrick had taken the ninety and invested well. Sprawling's boys had crunched some numbers earlier. Assuming Patrick placed all the money in investments earning eight percent a year, the loot would now be worth a hundred and thirty-one million. Ten percent, and the value would be one hundred and forty-four million. Tax free, of course. Apparently, Patrick hadn't spent much of it, so he would remain a very wealthy man.

'We're also concerned about this lawsuit you filed on behalf of Mr Lanigan,' Sprawling said.

'We'll dismiss the FBI from the lawsuit, but I'll need a quick favor from Mr Jaynes. We can discuss it later. It's a minor point.'

'All right. Moving right along. When will your client be prepared to testify before the grand jury?'

'Whenever you need him. Physically, he's able to do it anytime.'

'We intend to move quickly with this.'

'The sooner the better for my client.'

Sprawling circled items on his checklist. 'We will insist on confidentiality. No press whatsoever. This deal will be subject to a lot of criticism.'

'We're not saying a word,' Sandy promised.

'When would you like for Ms. Miranda to be released?'

'Tomorrow. And she needs to be escorted from the

324

jail in Miami to the private air terminal. We would like FBI protection until she is on the plane.'

Jaynes shrugged as if he didn't understand. 'No problem,' he said.

'Anything else?' Sandy asked, rubbing his hands together as if the fun was about to start.

'Nothing from the government,' Sprawling said.

'Good. Here's what I suggest,' Sandy said, as if they had a choice. 'I have two secretaries here with PC's. We have already prepared a rough draft of a settlement agreement and order of dismissal. It shouldn't take too long to hammer out the finer points, then you guys can sign off. I will then drive it over to my client, and hopefully within a couple of hours we'll be finished. Mr Mast, I suggest you contact the federal Judge and arrange a conference call as soon as possible. We'll fax him the order of dismissal.'

'When do we get the documents and tapes?' asked Jaynes.

'If everything gets signed and approved in the next few hours, you can have them at 5 P.M. today.'

'I need a phone,' Sprawling said. So did Mast and Jaynes. They scattered throughout the suite.

Regular inmates received an hour each day outdoors. It was late October, a cool and cloudy day, and Patrick decided to demand his constitutional rights. The deputies in the hallway said no; it had not been authorized.

Patrick called Karl Huskey and got everything approved. He also asked Karl if he could stop by Rosetti's on Division Street near the Point and pick up a couple of Vancleave Specials – crabmeat and cheese po'boys – and join him for lunch, outside. Karl said he would be delighted.

They ate on a wooden bench, not far from a small fountain and a sad little maple. The various wings of the hospital surrounded them. Karl had brought po'boys for the deputies as well, and they sat nearby, just out of earshot.

Karl knew nothing of the meeting under way at the hotel suite, and Patrick didn't tell him. Parrish was there, and before long he would tell His Honor.

'What are people saying about me?' Patrick asked after he finished a third of his sandwich and put it away.

'The gossip has died down. Things are back to normal. Your friends are still your friends.'

'I'm writing letters to some of them. Would you deliver them?'

'Of course I will.'

'Thanks.'

'I hear they caught your lady friend in Miami.'

'Yeah. But she'll be out soon. Just a small problem with her passport.'

Huskey took a large bite of his sandwich and chewed in silence. He was growing accustomed to the long quiet intervals in their dialogue. He struggled with what to say next. Patrick did not.

'The fresh air is nice,' he finally said. 'Thanks.'

'You have a constitutional right to fresh air.'

'You ever been to Brazil?'

'No.'

'You should go.'

'Like you, or with my family?'

'No, no. Go visit sometime.'

'The beaches?'

'No. Forget the beaches, and forget the cities. Go to the heart of the country, to the open spaces where the sky is clear and blue, the air is light, the land is beautiful, the people are gentle and uncomplicated. It's my home, Karl. I can't wait to go back there.'

'Might be a while.'

'Maybe, but I can wait. I'm not Patrick anymore,

326

Karl. Patrick is dead. He was trapped and unhappy. He was fat and miserable and, thankfully, he went away. I'm Danilo now, Danilo Silva, a much happier person with a quiet life in another country. Danilo can wait.'

And with a beautiful woman and a large fortune, Karl wanted to say, but he let it pass.

'How does Danilo get back to Brazil?' Karl asked.

'I'm still working on that.'

'Look, Patrick – I guess it's okay if I call you Patrick and not Danilo.'

'Sure.'

'I think it's time for me to step down and give the case to Judge Trussel. Some motions will soon be due, and rulings will have to be issued. I've done all I can do to help you.'

'Are you taking some heat?'

'A little, but nothing that worries me. I don't want to hurt you, and I'm afraid if I keep your case much longer, people might resent it. Everybody knows we're friends. Hell, you even picked me as one of your pallbearers.'

'Did I ever thank you for serving?'

'No. You were dead at the time, so don't mention it. It was fun.'

'Yeah, I know.'

'Anyway, I've talked to Trussel, and he's ready to take the case. I've also told him about your heinous injuries, and how important it is for you to stay here for as long as possible. He understands.'

'Thanks.'

'But you have to be realistic. At some point, you're gonna be put in jail. And you might be there for a long time.'

'Do you think I killed that boy, Karl?'

Karl dropped the remains of his sandwich into a bag and drank his iced tea. He was not inclined to lie about this. 'It looks suspicious. First, there were human remains in the car, so somebody was killed. Second, the FBI has done an exhaustive computer analysis of all persons who became missing on or shortly before February 9, 1992. Pepper is the only person within three hundred miles who has not been heard from.'

'But that's not enough to convict me.'

'Your question was not about getting a conviction.'

'Fine. Do you think I killed him?'

'I don't know what to think, Patrick. I've been a judge for twelve years, and I've seen people stand before me and confess to crimes that they still couldn't believe they committed. Under the right circumstances, a man can do just about anything.'

'So you believe it?'

'I don't want to. I'm not sure what I believe.'

'You think I could kill someone?'

'No. But I didn't think you could fake your death and swipe ninety million bucks either. Your recent history is full of surprises.'

Another long pause. Karl glanced at his watch. Patrick left him on the bench and walked slowly around the courtyard.

Lunch in the Camille Suite was an array of bland sandwiches served on plastic trays, and it was interrupted by a return call from the federal Judge who had been assigned Patrick's case four years earlier. The Judge was in the middle of a trial in Jackson, and had only a minute. Mast described the cast of players assembled in the suite, and the Judge consented to being placed on a speakerphone. Mast then gave a hurried summary of the proposed agreement. The Judge wanted to hear Sandy's version next, and he delivered it. Sprawling was asked a few questions, and the short phone conference became a lengthy one. At

328

one point, Sprawling left the room to chat privately with the Judge. He conveyed the urgent wishes of higher-ups in Washington to cut the deal with Mr Lanigan so bigger fish could be caught. The Judge also talked privately with T.L. Parrish, who gave the same assurances that Lanigan was not walking away, that he would indeed face the more serious charges, and in all likelihood, though no guarantees were given, spend many years in jail.

The Judge was reluctant to act in such a hurry, but with pressure from those so intimately involved with the case, and given the stature of those present in Biloxi, he relented and agreed to sign the order dismissing all federal charges against Patrick. The order was promptly faxed to him, and he promptly signed it and faxed it back.

As they finished lunch, Sandy left them briefly for a quick drive to the hospital. Patrick was in his room, writing a letter to his mother, when Sandy burst in. 'We did it!' He threw the agreement on Patrick's worktable.

'We got everything we wanted,' he said.

'Full dismissal?'

'Yep. The Judge just signed it.'

'How much money?'

'Ninety, plus three percent.'

Patrick closed his eyes and clenched his fists. The fortune had just taken a major hit, but there was plenty left; enough for him and Eva to one day settle down somewhere safe and have a house full of kids. A large house. And many kids.

They scanned the agreement. Patrick signed it, then Sandy raced back to the hotel.

The crowd had thinned by 2 P.M., when the second meeting got started. Sandy welcomed Talbot Mims and his client, a senior VP for Northern Case Mutual

329

named Shenault, who brought with him two in-house lawyers whose names Sandy missed. For good measure, Mims also brought one of his partners and an associate, both nameless too. Sandy collected their business cards and escorted them into the same parlor where the first meeting had taken place. The court reporters took their positions.

Jaynes and Sprawling were next door in the den, on the phone to Washington. They had sent the rest of their entourage down to the casino for an hour of leisure, no alcohol.

The squad from Monarch-Sierra was much smaller, just Hal Ladd, one of his associates, and the chief in-house lawyer for the company, a dapper little man named Cohen. Stiff introductions were made around the room, and they all settled in to listen to Sandy. He had packets for them, thin folders which he distributed and asked them to flip through. Each contained a copy of the lawsuit filed by Patrick against the FBI for his injuries, and each had a set of color pictures of the burns. The insurance boys had been prepped by their lawyers, so none of this was a surprise.

Sandy summarized what he had alleged yesterday – that the injuries to his client had not been inflicted by the FBI because the FBI didn't find Patrick. Stephano did. And Stephano was working for three clients: Benny Aricia, Northern Case Mutual, and Monarch-Sierra. All three had serious exposure in a civil liability suit to be filed by Patrick.

'How do you plan to prove this Stephano business?' asked Talbot Mims.

'Just a second,' Sandy said. He opened the door that led to the den and asked Jaynes if he had a minute. Jaynes entered the room, and identified himself to the group. With great pleasure he described in detail the things Stephano had told them about the search for Patrick; the financing of the consortium, the rewards,

330

the tips, the hunt in Brazil, the plastic surgeon, the boys from Pluto, the capture, and the torture. Everything. And all done with money provided by Aricia, Monarch-Sierra, and Northern Case Mutual. And all done solely for their benefit.

It was a dazzling performance, one Jaynes himself enjoyed immensely.

'Any questions for Mr Jaynes?' Sandy asked happily as the narrative came to a close.

There were none. In the past eighteen hours, neither Shenault of Northern Case Mutual nor Cohen of Monarch-Sierra had been able to determine who in their companies had authorized the hiring of Jack Stephano. It was unlikely they would ever know, now that tracks were being erased.

Both companies were large and rich, with lots of shareholders and big ad budgets used to protect their good corporate names. Neither wanted this headache.

'Thank you, Mr Jaynes,' Sandy said.

'I'm next door if you need me,' Jaynes said, as if he would like nothing better than to return and do some more coffin-nailing.

His presence was baffling and ominous. Why was the Deputy Director of the FBI in Biloxi, and why did he seem so eager to place blame on them?

'Here's the deal,' Sandy said when the door was shut. 'It's simple, quick, non-negotiable. First, Mr Shenault, as to Northern Case Mutual, your client's last assault in this little war is an effort to recoup its two and a half million paid to Trudy Lanigan. We prefer that you simply go back home. Dismiss the lawsuit, forget about Trudy, let her live in peace. She has a child to raise, and, besides, most of the money has been spent anyway. Dismiss, and my client will not pursue his claim for personal injuries against your company.'

'Is that all?' Talbot Mims asked in disbelief.

'Yes. That's it.'

'Done.'

'We'd like a moment to consult,' Shenault said, still hard-faced.

'No we don't,' Mims said to his client. 'It's a great deal. It's on the table. We take it. Just like that.'

Shenault said, 'I'd like to analyze –'

'No,' Mims said, bristling at Shenault. 'We take the deal. Now, if you want someone else to represent you, fine. But as long as I'm your lawyer, we're taking the deal, right now.'

Shenault went speechless.

'We'll take it,' Mims said.

'Mr Shenault?' Sandy said.

'Uh, sure. I guess we'll agree to it.'

'Great. I have a proposed settlement agreement waiting on you in the room next door. Now, if you gentlemen will leave us for a few minutes, I need to talk with Mr Ladd and his client in private.'

Mims led his crew out. Sandy locked the door behind them and turned to address Mr Cohen, Hal Ladd, and his associate. 'Your deal is a bit different from theirs, I'm afraid. They get off lightly because there is a divorce. It's messy and complicated, and my client can use his claim against Northern Case Mutual to his advantage in the divorce proceedings. You, unfortunately, are not in the same position. They put up a half a million for Stephano, you put up twice that much. You have more liability, more exposure, and, as we all know, a helluva lot more cash than Northern Case Mutual.'

'How much do you have in mind?' Cohen asked.

'Nothing for Patrick. He's very concerned, however, about the child. She's six, and her mother burns money. That's one reason Northern Case Mutual collapsed so quickly – it'll be very difficult to collect from Mrs Lanigan. Patrick would like a modest amount to go into a trust fund for the child, money out of the mother's reach.'

'How much?'

'A quarter of a million. Plus the same amount to cover his legal fees. Total of a half a million, paid very quietly so your client won't be embarrassed by those pictures.'

The Coast had a history of generous verdicts in personal injury and wrongful death cases. Hal Ladd had advised Cohen that he could see a multi-million-dollar verdict against Aricia and the insurance companies for what was done to Patrick. Cohen, from California, certainly understood this. The company was quite anxious to settle and leave town.

'All litigation is dismissed,' Cohen said. 'And we pay a half a million?'

'That's it.'

'We'll do it.'

Sandy reached into a file and removed some papers. 'I have a proposed settlement agreement, which I'll leave with you.' He handed copies to them, and left them.

THIRTY-FIVE

The psychiatrist was a friend of Dr Hayani's. Patrick's second session with him lasted for two hours and was as unproductive as the first. It would be the last.

Patrick asked to be excused, and returned to his room in time for dinner. He ignored most of it as he watched the evening news. His name was not mentioned. He paced the floor and spoke to his guards. Sandy had called throughout the afternoon with updates, but he wanted to see documents. He watched 'Jeopardy' and tried to read a thick paperback.

It was almost eight when he heard Sandy speak to the guards and ask how the prisoner was doing. Sandy enjoyed referring to him as 'the prisoner.'

Patrick met him at the door. His lawyer was exhausted, but smiling. 'It's all done,' he said as he handed Patrick a stack of paperwork.

'What about the documents and tapes?'

'We handed them over an hour ago. There must've been a dozen FBI agents swarming around. Jaynes told me they would work through the night.'

Patrick took the settlement agreements and sat at his worktable in the corner, under the television. Carefully, he read every word. Sandy's dinner was fast food from a bag, and he ate it standing beside the bed, watching muted rugby from Australia on ESPN.

'Did they squawk at the half a million?' Patrick asked, without looking up.

'Not for a minute. Nobody squawked at anything.'

'Guess we should've asked for more.'

'I think you have enough.'

Patrick flipped a page, then signed his name. 'Good work, Sandy. A masterful job.'

'We had a good day. Federal charges are all dismissed, the litigation is settled. Attorneys' fees are taken care of. The kid's future is secure. Tomorrow we'll finish with Trudy. You're on a roll, Patrick. Too bad you've got this dead body in your way.'

Patrick left the papers on the table and stepped to the window, his back to the room. The shades were open, the window was cracked six inches.

Sandy kept eating and watching him. 'You have to tell me sometime, Patrick.'

'Tell you what?'

'Well, let's see. Why don't we start with Pepper?'

'Okay. I didn't kill Pepper.'

'Did someone else kill Pepper?'

'Not to my knowledge.'

'Did Pepper kill himself?'

'Not to my knowledge.'

'Was Pepper alive when you disappeared?'

'I think so.'

'Dammit, Patrick! I've had a long day! I'm not in the mood for games.'

Patrick turned around and politely said, 'Please, don't yell. There are cops out there, straining to hear every word. Sit down.'

'I don't want to sit down.'

'Please.'

'I can hear better standing up. I'm listening.'

Patrick shut the window, pulled the shades, checked the locked door, and turned off the television. He resumed his customary position on his bed, sitting,

335

with the sheet pulled to his waist. Once situated, he said, in a low voice, 'I knew Pepper. He came to the cabin one day asking for food. It was just before Christmas of '91. He told me he lived in the woods most of the time. I cooked bacon and eggs for him and he ate like a refugee. He stuttered, and was very shy and uncomfortable around me. Obviously, I was intrigued. Here was this kid, he said he was seventeen but looked younger, who was reasonably clean and dressed and had a family twenty miles away, yet lived in the woods. I made him talk. I asked about his family, and got the sad story. When he finished eating, he was ready to go. I offered him a place to sleep, but he insisted on returning to his campsite.

'The next day, I was deer hunting, alone, and Pepper tracked me down. He showed me his little tent and sleeping bag. He had cooking utensils, an ice chest, a lantern, a shotgun. He said he hadn't been home in two weeks. Said his mother had a new boyfriend, who was the worst one in years. I followed him deep into the woods to a deer stand he'd found. An hour later, I killed a ten-point buck, my biggest ever. He said he knew the woods inside and out, and offered to show me the best places to hunt.

'A couple of weeks later, I was back at the cabin. Life with Trudy was unbearable, and she and I both lived for the weekends so I could leave. Pepper showed up not long after I arrived. I cooked a stew and we ate like hogs – I had an appetite back then. He said he'd gone home for three days, and left after a fight with his mother. The more he talked, the less he stuttered. I told him I was a lawyer and before long he told me his legal troubles. His last job had been pumping gas at a station in Lucedale. Some money came up missing from the cash register. Because everybody thought he was retarded, they blamed it on him. He, of course, had nothing to do with it. It was another very good reason to stay in the woods. I promised to check into the matter.'

'And so the setup began,' Sandy said.

'Something like that. We saw each other a few more times in the woods.'

'It was getting close to February ninth.'

'Yes, it was. I told Pepper that the cops were about to arrest him. This was a lie. I hadn't made a single call. Couldn't afford to. But the more we talked, the more convinced I became that he knew something about the missing money. He was scared, and leaning heavily on me. We discussed his options, one of which was to simply disappear.'

'Gee, that sounds familiar.'

'He hated his mother. Cops were after him. He was a scared boy who couldn't live in the woods for the rest of his life. He liked the idea of going out West and working as a hunting guide in the mountains. We hatched a plan. I watched the newspapers until I saw this terrible story of a high school sophomore getting killed in a train wreck outside New Orleans. His name was Joey Palmer; had a nice generic ring to it. I called a forger in Miami, who got Joey's Social Security number, and presto! – within four days I had a nice set of papers for Pepper. Louisiana driver's license, complete with a very close photo, Social Security number, birth certificate, even a passport.'

'You make it sound so easy.'

'No, it's easier than I make it sound. Just takes a little cash and some imagination. Pepper liked his new papers, and loved the idea of riding a bus off to the mountains. No kidding, Sandy, the kid had no hesitation whatsoever about leaving his mother in the dark. There was not one trace of concern.'

'Your kinda guy.'

'Yeah, well, anyway, on Sunday, February ninth –'

'The date of your death.'

337

'Yes, as I recall it now. I drove Pepper to the Greyhound bus station in Jackson. I gave him every opportunity to turn back, but he was determined. No, he was excited. The poor kid had never left the state of Mississippi. Just the ride to Jackson was a thrill. I made it clear that he could never come back, under any circumstances. He never mentioned his mother. Three hours in the car, and he never mentioned his mother.'

'Where was he headed?'

'I'd located a logging camp north of Eugene, Oregon, and I'd checked the bus routes and schedules. I wrote it all down for him, then we practiced it a dozen times on the way to the bus station. I gave him two thousand dollars in cash, and dropped him off two blocks from the bus station. It was almost 1 P.M., and I couldn't run the risk of being seen. The last time I saw Pepper he was jogging away with a smile on his face and a stuffed backpack slung over his shoulder.'

'His shotgun and camping gear were found in the cabin.'

'Where else could he put it?'

'Just another piece of the puzzle.'

'Of course. I wanted them to think Pepper burned up in the car.'

'Where is he now?'

'I don't know, and it's not important.'

'That's not what I asked, Patrick.'

'It's not important, really.'

'Stop playing games with me, dammit. If I ask a question, then I deserve an answer.'

'I'll give an answer when I feel like it.'

'Why are you so evasive with me?'

Sandy's voice was louder, and edgy, and Patrick paused a moment to let him calm down. They both breathed slower, both tried to get a grip.

'I'm not being evasive, Sandy,' Patrick said evenly.

'The hell you're not. I fight like hell to solve one riddle, and ten more mysteries hit me in the face. Why can't you tell me everything?'

'Because you don't need to know everything.'

'It would certainly be nice.'

'Really? When was the last time a criminal defendant told you everything?'

'Funny, I don't think of you as a criminal.'

'Then what am I?'

'A friend, maybe.'

'Your job will be easier if you think of me as a criminal.'

Sandy lifted the settlement agreements from the table and started for the door. 'I'm tired and I'm going to rest. I'll be back tomorrow, and you'll tell me everything.'

He opened the door and left.

The tail had first been noticed two days earlier by Guy as they were leaving a casino. A familiar face turned away a little too quickly. Then a car followed them a bit too aggressively. Guy had experience in such matters, and he mentioned it to Benny, who happened to be driving. 'It's gotta be the feds,' Guy had said. 'Who else would care?'

They made plans to leave Biloxi. The phone lines were disconnected in the rented condo. They sent the other boys away.

They waited until dark. Guy left in one car, headed east to Mobile, where he would spend the night watching his rear and then catch a plane in the morning. Benny went west, along the Coast on Highway 90, then across Lake Ponchartrain into New Orleans, a city he knew well. He watched closely, but saw nothing behind him. He ate oysters in the French Quarter, then caught a cab to the airport. He flew to Memphis, then to O'Hare, where he hid most of the night in an airport lounge. Then on to New York at dawn.

The FBI was in Boca Raton, watching his home. His Swedish live-in was still there. She would bolt soon, they figured, and be much easier to follow.

THIRTY-SIX

No release had ever gone as smoothly. Eva walked out of the detention center a free woman at 8:30 A.M., in the same jeans and button-down she'd worn into the place. The guards were nice; the clerks were surprisingly efficient; the supervisor even wished her well. Mark Birck whisked her to his car, a handsome old Jaguar he'd scrubbed inside and out for the occasion, and nodded to their two escorts. 'Those are FBI agents,' he said to her, pointing with his head at two gentlemen waiting in a car nearby.

'I thought we were through with them,' she said.

'Not quite.'

'Am I supposed to wave hello or something?'

'No. Just get in the car.' He opened the door for her, closed it gently, for a second admired the fresh wax job on the long, sloping hood, then scampered around to the driver's side.

'Here's a letter faxed to me from Sandy McDermott,' he said as he cranked the engine and backed away. 'Open it.'

'Where are we going?' she asked.

'To the airport, general aviation. There's a small jet waiting for you there.'

'To take me where?'

'New York.'

'And then to where?'

'London, on the Concorde.'

They were on a busy street, with the FBI agents behind them. 'Why are they behind us?' she asked.

'Protection.'

She closed her eyes and rubbed her forehead, and thought of Patrick in his small room at the hospital, bored, with little to do but think of places to send her. Then she noticed the car phone. 'May I?' she said, lifting it.

'Sure.' Birck was driving carefully, watching his mirrors as if he were chauffeuring the President.

Eva called Brazil and, switching to her native tongue, had a tearful reunion with her father, via satellite. He was well, and so was she. Both were liberated, though she didn't tell him where she'd spent the last three days. Kidnapping wasn't such a harsh ordeal after all, he joked. He had been treated superbly; not a single bruise. She promised to be home soon. Her legal work in the United States was almost over, and she was very homesick.

Birck listened without trying to, though he couldn't understand a word. When she hung up and finished wiping her eyes, he said, 'There are some phone numbers in the letter, in case you get stopped again by customs. The FBI has lifted its alert, and they've agreed to allow you to travel under your passport for the next seven days.'

She listened but said nothing.

'There's also a phone number in London, if something happens at Heathrow.'

She finally opened the letter. It was from Sandy, on his letterhead. Things were proceeding nicely, and rapidly, in Biloxi. Call him at the hotel suite when she arrived at JFK. He would have further instructions.

In other words, he would tell her things Mr Birck here shouldn't hear.

They arrived at the busy general aviation terminal

342

on the north side of Miami International. The agents stayed with their car as Birck escorted her inside. The pilots were waiting. They pointed to a handsome little jet parked just outside, ready to take her anywhere she wanted. 'Take me to Rio,' she almost said. 'Please, Rio.'

She shook hands with Birck, thanked him for being so nice, and boarded her flight. No luggage. Not a stitch of extra clothing. Patrick would pay dearly for this. Let her get to London; give her a day along Bond and Oxford. She'd have more clothes than this little jet could carry.

At such an early hour, J. Murray looked especially tired and disheveled. He managed to grunt a hello to the secretary who opened the door, and he said yes to coffee, strong and black. Sandy greeted him, took his wrinkled blazer, and showed him to a parlor where they sat and reviewed the property settlement agreement.

'This is much better,' Sandy said when he finished. Trudy had already signed off on the deal. J. Murray couldn't endure another visit by her and her slimy gigolo. She and Lance had fought yesterday in his office. J. Murray had been doing dirty divorces for years, and he'd bet good money that Lance's days were numbered. The financial strain was gnawing at Trudy.

'We'll sign it,' Sandy said.

'Why wouldn't you? You're getting everything you want.'

'It's a fair settlement, under the circumstances.'

'Yeah, yeah.'

'Look, Murray, there's been a significant development involving your client and her lawsuit with Northern Case Mutual.'

'Do tell.'

'Yes, there's a lot of background which is really not relevant to your client, but the bottom line is this: Northern Case Mutual has agreed to drop its lawsuit against Trudy.'

J. Murray just sat there for a few seconds, then his bottom lip slowly departed from his top. Was this a joke?

Sandy reached for some papers, a copy of the settlement agreement with Northern Case Mutual. He had already blacked out sensitive paragraphs, but there was plenty for J. Murray to read.

'You're kidding,' he mumbled as he took the agreement. He scanned past the blackened lines without the least bit of curiosity, and came to the heart of the matter, two paragraphs beautifully untouched by censors. He read clear and precise language which called for the immediate dismissal of the lawsuit against his client.

He didn't care why it was happening. An impenetrable shroud of mystery surrounded Patrick, and he wasn't about to start asking questions.

'What a pleasant surprise,' he said.

'I thought you'd like it.'

'She keeps everything?'

'Everything she has left.'

J. Murray read it again, slowly. 'Can I keep this?' he asked.

'No. It's confidential. But a motion to dismiss will be filed today, and I'll fax you a copy.'

'Thanks.'

'There's one other item,' Sandy said. He handed J. Murray a copy of the Monarch-Sierra settlement, equally as censored. 'Look on page four, third paragraph.'

J. Murray read the sentences establishing a trust to be funded to the tune of two hundred and fifty thousand dollars, for the benefit of little Ashley Nicole

344

Lanigan. Sandy McDermott would act as trustee. The money was to be used only for the health and education of the child, and any unused funds would be paid to the child upon her thirtieth birthday.

'I don't know what to say.' But he was already thinking of how this might play back in his office.

Sandy waved him off as if it were nothing.

'Anything else?' J. Murray asked with a bright smile. Any more goodies?

'That's it. The divorce is settled. It's been a pleasure.'

They shook hands and J. Murray left, his step a bit quicker. He rode the elevator alone, his mind racing wildly. He'd tell her how he'd played hardball with the rascals, how he'd finally just had it up to here with their outrageous demands, how he had barged into the meeting and threatened a vicious trial unless they yielded and made concessions. He had tried many such cases, was in fact known to be quite a courtroom brawler.

Damn the adultery charges! Damn the nudie pictures! His client was wrong but was still entitled to fairness. There was a poor innocent child to protect here!

He'd tell her how they'd broken and run in full retreat. He had demanded a trust fund for the child, and Patrick had collapsed under the weight of his own guilt. Here, they insisted, take a quarter of a million dollars.

And he'd fight like hell, fight them forever to protect the assets of his client, who had done nothing wrong by taking the two point five million. Out of fear, they had folded and scrambled to find a way to save Trudy's money. These details were murky at the moment, but he had an hour's worth of driving to work on the story.

345

By the time he got to his office, it would be a magnificent victory.

Eyebrows were raised at the Concorde counter at JFK because she had no luggage. A supervisor was called and a huddle ensued as Eva fought to control her nerves. She couldn't take another arrest. She loved Patrick, but this was far above and beyond the call of romance. Not long ago she'd had a promising career as a lawyer in a city she loved. Then Patrick came along.

Suddenly there were warm British smiles everywhere. She was directed to the Concorde lounge, where she had coffee and called Sandy's number in Biloxi.

'Are you okay?' he asked when he heard her voice.

'I'm fine, Sandy. I'm at JFK, en route to London. How's Patrick?'

'Wonderful. We've cut the deal with the federal folks.'

'How much?'

'A hundred and thirteen million,' he replied, and waited to hear a response. Patrick had been perfectly noncommittal when he'd been told the size of the repayment. She followed the same script.

'When?' was all she said.

'I'll have instructions when you get to London. There's a room at the Four Seasons in the name of Leah Pires.'

'That's me again.'

'Call me when you get there?'

'Tell Patrick I still love him, even after going to jail.'

'I'll see him tonight. Be careful.'

'*Tchau.*'

With such heavyweights in town, Mast couldn't resist the opportunity to impress them. The evening before, after they had taken possession of the documents and tapes, he'd arranged for his staff to call every member of the sitting grand jury and inform them of an emergency session. With five of his assistant U.S. attorneys, he had worked with the FBI in scouring and indexing the documents. He had left his office at three in the morning, and returned five hours later.

The federal grand jury meeting was at noon, with lunch provided. Hamilton Jaynes decided to hang around long enough to sit through it, as did Sprawling from the Attorney General's office. Patrick would be the only witness.

Pursuant to their agreement, he was not transported in handcuffs. He was hidden in the back of an unmarked Bureau car, and sneaked through a side door of the federal courthouse in Biloxi. Sandy was at his side. Patrick wore large khakis, sneakers, a sweatshirt; clothing Sandy had purchased for him. He was pale and thin, but walked with no visible impairment. Actually, Patrick felt great.

The sixteen grand jurors sat around a long, square table, so that at least half of them had their back to the door when Patrick walked through with a smile. Those not facing him quickly turned around. Jaynes and Sprawling sat in a corner, intrigued by their first glimpse of Mr Lanigan.

Patrick sat at the end of the table, in a chair used by witnesses, and seized the moment. He needed little prodding from Mast to tell his story, or at least some of it. He was relaxed and lively, in part because this panel could no longer touch him. He had managed to free himself of the tentacles of any federal law.

He started with the law firm, the partners, their personalities, clients, work habits, and slowly built his way to Aricia.

Mast stopped him, and handed over a document which Patrick identified as the contract between the firm and Aricia. It was four pages long, but could be reduced to a basic agreement of the firm getting one third of anything Aricia got by filing his claim against Platt & Rockland Industries.

'And how did you get this?' Mast asked.

'Mr Bogan's secretary typed it. Our computers were interfaced. I simply pulled it off.'

'Is that why this copy is unsigned?'

'That's correct. The original is probably in Mr Bogan's file.'

'Did you have access to Mr Bogan's office?'

'Limited,' Patrick answered, and explained Bogan's zealousness for secrecy. That led to a digression about access to the other offices, then to the fascinating story of Patrick's adventures in the world of sophisticated surveillance. Because he was very suspicious of Aricia, he set out to gather as much information as possible. He educated himself on electronic surveillance. He monitored the other PC's in the firm. He listened for gossip. He quizzed secretaries and paralegals. He went through the wastepaper in the copy room. He worked odd hours in hopes of finding open doors.

After two hours, Patrick asked for a soft drink. Mast declared a fifteen-minute break. The time had gone so fast because the audience was enthralled.

When the witness returned from the rest room, they settled in quickly, anxious to hear more. Mast asked some questions about the claim against Platt & Rockland, and Patrick described it in general terms. 'Mr Aricia was quite skillful. He set up a scheme for double billing, yet was able to pass the blame on to people in the home office. He was the secret moving force behind the cost overruns.'

Mast placed a stack of documents at Patrick's side. He took one, and with only a glance knew everything about it. 'This is a sample of the fictitious labor New Coastal Shipyards was paid for. It's a computerized

348

labor summary for one week in June of 1988. It lists eighty-four employees, all bogus names, and gives their wages for the week. The total is seventy-one thousand dollars.'

'How were these names selected?' asked Mast.

'At the time, there were eight thousand employees at New Coastal. They selected real names that were common – Jones, Johnson, Miller, Green, Young – and changed the first initial.'

'How much labor was falsified?'

'According to Aricia's filing, it was nineteen million dollars over a four-year period.'

'Did Mr Aricia know it was falsified?'

'Yes, he implemented the scheme.'

'And how do you know this?'

'Where are the tapes?'

Mast handed him a sheet of paper on which the tapes of over sixty conversations had been cataloged. Patrick studied it for a minute. 'I think it's tape number seventeen,' he said. The assistant U.S. attorney in charge of the box of tapes produced number seventeen, and inserted it into a player in the center of the table.

Patrick said, 'This is Doug Vitrano talking to Jimmy Havarac, two of the partners, in Vitrano's office, on May 3, 1991.'

The player was turned on, and they waited for the voices.

FIRST VOICE: How do you pad nineteen million dollars in bogus labor?

'That's Jimmy Havarac,' Patrick said quickly.

SECOND VOICE: It wasn't difficult.

'And that's Doug Vitrano,' Patrick said.

VITRANO: The labor was running fifty million a year. For four years it was over two hundred million. So they were just tacking on a ten percent increase. It got lost in the paperwork.

HAVARAC: And Aricia knew about it?

VITRANO: Knew about it? Hell, he implemented it.

HAVARAC: Come on, Doug.

VITRANO: It's all bogus, Jimmy. Every aspect of his claim is bogus. The labor, the inflated invoices, the double and triple billing for expensive hardware. Everything. Aricia planned this from the beginning, and he just happened to work for a company with a long history of screwing the government. He knew how the company worked. He knew how the Pentagon worked. And he was shrewd enough to set up the scheme.

HAVARAC: Who told you this?

VITRANO: Bogan. Aricia's told Bogan everything. Bogan's told the Senator everything. We keep our mouths shut and play along, and we'll all be millionaires.

The voices went silent as the tape, well edited by Patrick years ago, came to the end.

The grand jurors stared at the tape player.

'Could we hear some more?' one of them asked.

Mast shrugged and looked at Patrick, who said, 'I think that's a marvelous idea.'

With Patrick's play-by-play commentary and sometimes colorful analysis, it took almost three hours to listen to the tapes. The Closet tape was saved for last, and played four times before the grand jurors would let it go. At six, they ordered dinner from a nearby deli.

At seven, Patrick was allowed to leave.

While they ate, Mast discussed some of the more telling documents. He addressed the various federal laws involved. With the voices of the crooks captured so vividly on the tapes, the conspiracy was laid bare.

At eight-thirty, the grand jury voted unanimously to indict Benny Aricia, Charles Bogan, Doug Vitrano, Jimmy Havarac, and Ethan Rapley for conspiring to commit fraud under the False Claims Act. If convicted, each could face up to ten years, and be fined up to five hundred thousand dollars.

Senator Harris Nye was named as an unindicted co-conspirator, a temporary designation that would most likely change for the worse. Sprawling, Jaynes, and Maurice Mast fashioned a strategy of first indicting the smaller fish, then pressuring them to cut a deal and squeal on the big one. They would aggressively go after Rapley and Havarac because of their hatred of Charles Bogan.

The grand jury adjourned at nine. Mast met with the U.S. Marshal, and planned the arrests for early the next morning. Jaynes and Sprawling found late flights from New Orleans back to D.C.

THIRTY-SEVEN

'I handled a car wreck once, just after I joined the firm. It happened on 49, up in Stone County, near Wiggins. Our clients were going north when a flatbed truck pulled out from a county road, right in front of them. A big wreck. Three people were in our car, the driver was killed, his wife was severely injured, a kid in the backseat had a broken leg. The flatbed truck was owned by a paper company, heavily insured, and so the case had potential. They gave it to me, and I jumped in gung ho because I was new. There was no doubt the truck was at fault, but its driver, who was not hurt, claimed our car was speeding. This became the big issue – how fast was our dead driver going? My accident reconstructionist estimated his speed at sixty miles per hour, which was not too bad. The highway was posted for fifty-five; everybody does at least sixty. My clients were driving to Jackson to visit family, and were in no hurry.

'The accident reconstructionist hired by the truck's insurance company estimated my guy's speed at seventy-five, and this, of course, would've seriously hurt our case. Any jury will frown on twenty miles over the speed limit. We found a witness, an old man who was either the second or third person on the scene. His name was Mr Clovis Goodman, age eighty-one, blind in one eye and couldn't see out of the other.'

'Seriously?' Sandy asked.

'No, but his vision was somewhat impaired. He was still driving, and on that day he was puttering down the highway in his 1968 Chevrolet pickup when our car passed him. Then, just over the next hill, old Clovis happened upon the wreck. Clovis was a very tender old man, lived alone, no close family, forgotten and neglected, and seeing this horrible accident moved him deeply. He tried to help the victims, and hung around for a while, then he left. He didn't say anything to anybody. He was too upset. He told me later he didn't sleep for a week.

'Anyway, we got word that one of the later arrivals had actually videoed the accident scene while the ambulances and cops and fire trucks were there. Traffic was backed up, people were bored, and, hell, they'll video anything, so we borrowed the tape. A paralegal analyzed it and took down all the license plate numbers. Then he found the owners, trying to find witnesses. That's how we found Clovis. He said he practically saw the wreck, but was too upset to talk about it. I asked him if I could come out for a visit, and he said yes.

'Clovis lived in the country, out from Wiggins, in a small whiteframe house he and his wife had built back before the war. She had been dead for many years. So had his only child, a son who'd gone astray. He had two grandchildren; one lived in California and the other near Hattiesburg. He hadn't seen either in years. I learned all this within the first hour. Clovis was a lonely old man, gruff at first, as if he didn't trust lawyers and resented wasting time, but not long into the first visit he was boiling hot water for instant coffee and telling family secrets. We sat on the porch, in rocking chairs with a dozen old cats swarming under our feet, and talked about everything but the wreck. Fortunately, it was a Saturday, so I could waste time and not worry about the office. He was a wonderful storyteller. The Depression was a favorite topic, as was the war. After a couple of hours, I finally mentioned the car wreck, and he went quiet and looked pained and informed me softly that he just couldn't talk about it yet. Said he knew something important, but it wasn't the right time. I asked him how fast he was driving when our car went by. He said he never got above fifty. I asked him if he could estimate how fast our car was going, and he just shook his head.

'Two days later, I stopped by late one afternoon, and we settled back on the porch for another round of war stories. Promptly at six, Clovis said he was hungry, said furthermore that he loved catfish, and asked if I would like to join him for dinner. I was single at the time, and so Clovis and I left for dinner. I drove, of course, and he talked. We had greasy catfish at six bucks for all you can eat. Clovis ate real slow, his chin just inches above the pile of fish. The waitress put the check on the table and Clovis never saw it. It sat there for ten minutes. He kept talking with a mouthful of hush puppies. I figured the dinner was money well spent if Clovis ever came through with his testimony. We eventually left, and driving back to his house he announced he needed a beer, just one beer for his bladder, and at that moment we just happened to be nearing a country store. I parked. He didn't move, and so I bought the beer too. We drove and drank, and he said he'd like to show me where he grew up. It wasn't far away, he said. One county road led to the next, and after twenty minutes I had no idea where I was. Clovis couldn't see very well. He needed another beer, also for his bladder. I asked directions from a store clerk, and Clovis and I set sail again. He pointed this way and that, and we finally found the town of Necaise

354

Crossing in Hancock County. Once we found it, he said we could turn around. He forgot the part about his childhood home. More beer. More directions from the store clerks.

'When we got near his house, I realized where we were, and I started asking questions about the car wreck. He said it was still too painful to talk about. I helped him into the house and he fell onto the sofa, snoring. It was almost midnight. This went on for about a month. Rocking on the front porch. Catfish on Tuesdays. Road trips for his bladder. The insurance policy had limits of two million. Our case was worth every bit of that, and, though Clovis didn't know it, his testimony was getting more crucial by the day. He assured me no one else had contacted him about the accident, so it was critical that I nail down his facts before the insurance boys found him.'

'How much time had passed since the accident?' Sandy asked.

'Four or five months. I finally pressed him one day. I told him that we had reached an important point in the lawsuit, and it was time for him to answer some questions. He said he was ready. I asked him how fast our car was going when it passed him. He said it sure was awful, seeing those people hurt like that, crushed and bleeding, especially the little boy. The poor old man had tears in his eyes. A few minutes later, I asked him again, "Clovis, can you estimate how fast the car was going when it passed you?" He said he sure would like to help the family. I said they would certainly appreciate that. And then he looked me square in the eyes, and said, "How fast do you think it was going?"

'I said that in my opinion it was going about fifty-five miles an hour. Clovis said, "Then that's what it was. Fifty-five miles an hour. I was doing fifty, and they just barely eased past me."

'We went to trial, and Clovis Goodman was the best

355

witness I've ever seen. He was old, humble, but wise and thoroughly believable. The jury ignored all the fancy accident reconstruction testimony and hung their verdict on Clovis. They gave us two point three million dollars.

'We kept in touch. I did his will for him. He didn't have much; just the house and six acres, seven thousand dollars in the bank. When he died, he wanted everything sold and the money given to the Daughters of the Confederacy. Not one relative was mentioned in his will. The grandson in California had been gone for twenty years. The granddaughter in Hattiesburg hadn't made contact since he received an invitation to her high school graduation in 1968. He neither attended nor sent a gift. He seldom mentioned them, but I knew Clovis longed for some connection with his family.

'He got sick and couldn't live by himself, so I moved him into a nursing home in Wiggins. I sold his house and farm, and handled all of his financial affairs. At the time, I was his only friend. I sent him cards and gifts, and every time I went to Hattiesburg or Jackson I would stop and visit for as long as I could. At least once a month, I would go get him and take him to the Catfish Cabin. Then we'd take a road trip. After a beer or two he'd start with his stories. I took him fishing one day, just me and Clovis in a boat for eight hours, and I've never laughed so hard in my life.

'He caught pneumonia in November of '91, and almost died. It scared him. We fixed his will again. He wanted to leave some of the money to his local church, the rest to the remnants of the Confederacy. He picked out his cemetery plot, made his burial arrangements. I brought up the idea of a living will, so he wouldn't be kept alive by machines. He liked it, and he insisted that I be designated as the person to pull the plug, in consultation with his doctors, of course.

Clovis was tired of the nursing home, tired of the loneliness, tired of life. He said his heart was right with God, and he was ready to go.

'The pneumonia came back with a fury in early January of '92. I had him transferred to the hospital here in Biloxi so I could watch him. I went by every day, and I was the only visitor old Clovis ever had. No other friends. No relatives. No minister. Not one single person but me. He deteriorated slowly, and it became apparent he would never leave. He lapsed into a coma, never to return. They put him on a respirator, and after about a week of that the doctors said he was brain dead. We, myself and three doctors, read his living will together, then turned off the respirator.'

'What day was it?' Sandy asked.

'February 6, 1992.'

Sandy exhaled, closed his eyes tightly, and slowly shook his head.

'He didn't want a church service because he knew no one would come. We buried him in a cemetery outside Wiggins. I was there, as a pallbearer. Three old widows from the church were there, crying, but you got the impression they had cried over every burial in Wiggins in the past fifty years. The minister was there, and he dragged with him five elderly deacons to act as pallbearers. Two other folks were there, for a total of twelve. After a brief service, Clovis was laid to rest.'

'It was a pretty light casket, wasn't it?' Sandy said.

'Yes it was.'

'Where was Clovis?'

'His spirit was rejoicing with the saints.'

'Where was his body?'

'On the porch of my cabin, in a freezer.'

'You sick puppy.'

'I didn't kill anybody, Sandy. Old Clovis was

singing with the angels when his remains got burned up. I figured he wouldn't mind.'

'You have an excuse for everything, don't you, Patrick?'

Patrick's legs hung from the side of his bed. His feet were six inches from the floor. He didn't respond.

Sandy paced around a bit, then leaned on the wall. He was only slightly relieved to learn his friend had not killed anyone. The thought of burning a corpse seemed almost as repulsive.

'Let's hear the rest of it,' Sandy said. 'I'm sure you have everything mapped out.'

'I've had time to think about it, yes.'

'I'm listening.'

'There's a Mississippi penal statute on grave-snatching, but it wouldn't apply to me. I didn't steal Clovis from the grave. I took him from his casket. There's another statute dealing with mutilating a corpse, and it's the only one Parrish can stick on me. It's a felony, and carries up to one year in jail. I figure that if that's all they can use, then Parrish will push very hard for the one year.'

'He can't let you walk away.'

'No, he can't. But here's the catch. He won't know about Clovis unless I tell him, but I have to tell him before he'll drop the murder charges. Now, telling him about Clovis is one thing, but testifying in court is another. He can't make me testify in court if he tries me for mutilation. He'll be pressured to try me for something, because, as you say, he can't allow me to walk away. He can try me, but he can't convict me because I'm the only witness and there's no way to prove the burned body was that of Clovis.'

'Parrish is screwed from all sides.'

'Correct. The federal charges are gone, and when we drop this bomb Parrish will feel enormous heat to nail me for something. Otherwise, I walk.'

'So what's the plan?'

'Simple. We take the pressure off Parrish and allow him to save face. You go to Clovis' grandchildren, tell them the truth, offer them some money. They'll certainly have the right to sue me once the truth is known, and you can assume they'll do it. Their suit isn't worth much because they ignored the old man most of their lives, but it's a safe bet they'll sue anyway. We cut them off at the pass. We settle with them quietly, and in return for the money they agree to pressure Parrish not to press charges.'

'You scheming bastard.'

'Thank you. Why won't it work?'

'Parrish can prosecute you regardless of the family's wishes.'

'But he won't because he can't convict me. The worst scenario for Parrish is to take me to trial and lose. It's much safer for him to hit the back door now, use the family as an excuse, and avoid the embarrassment of losing a high-profile case.'

'Is this what you've been thinking about for the past four years?'

'It has crossed my mind, yes.'

Sandy began pacing along the foot of the bed, deep in thought, his mind clicking away and trying to keep up with his client's. 'We have to give Parrish something,' he said, almost to himself, still walking.

'I'm more concerned with myself than Parrish,' Patrick said.

'It's not just Parrish. It's the system, Patrick. If you walk away, then you've effectively bought your way out of jail. Everybody looks bad but you.'

'Maybe I'm only concerned with me.'

'So am I. But you can't humiliate the system and expect to ride off into the sunset.'

'Nobody made Parrish run and get a capital murder indictment. He could've waited a week or two. No one made him announce it to the press. I have no sympathy for him.'

'Neither do I. But this is a hard sell, Patrick.'

'Then I'll make it a bit easier. I'll plead guilty to the mutilation, but with no jail time. Not one single day. I'll go to court, plead guilty, pay a fine, let Parrish get credit for a conviction, but then I'm outta here.'

'You'll be a convicted felon.'

'No, I'll be free. Who in Brazil will care if I get a slap on the wrist?'

Sandy stopped the pacing and sat on the bed beside him. 'So you'll go back to Brazil?'

'It's home, Sandy.'

'And the girl?'

'We'll either have ten kids, or eleven. We haven't decided.'

'How much money will you have?'

'Millions. You gotta get me out of here, Sandy. I have another life to live.'

A nurse barged through the door, flipped on a light switch, and said, 'It's eleven o'clock, Patty. Visiting hours are over.' She touched his shoulder. 'You okay, sweetie?'

'I'm fine.'

'You need anything?'

'No thanks.'

She left as fast as she came. Sandy picked up his briefcase. 'Patty?' he said.

Patrick shrugged.

'Sweetie?'

Another shrug.

Sandy thought of something else when he got to the door. 'A quick question. When you drove the car off the road, where was Clovis?'

'Same place as always. Strapped in the passenger's seat. I put a beer between his legs and wished him farewell. He had a smile on his face.'

360

THIRTY-EIGHT

By 10 A.M. in London, the wiring instructions for the return of the loot had not yet arrived. Eva left her hotel and took a long walk along Piccadilly. With no particular destination and no schedule, she drifted with the crowd, gazed at the store windows, and enjoyed life on the sidewalk. Three days in solitary had sharpened her appreciation for the sounds and voices of people hurrying about. Lunch was a warm goat cheese salad in the corner of a crowded ancient pub. She absorbed the light, happy voices of people who had no clue as to who she was. And they didn't care.

Patrick had told her his first year in São Paulo was often exhilarating because not a single person knew his name. Sitting in the pub, she felt more like Leah Pires than Eva Miranda.

She began shopping on Bond Street, first for the necessities – undergarments and perfume – but before long it was Armani and Versace and Chanel, with little regard for price. She was a very wealthy woman at the moment.

It would have been simpler, and certainly less dramatic, to wait until nine and arrest them at the office. But then their work habits were erratic, and one, Rapley, seldom left home.

A predawn raid was chosen. So what if it scared

them and humiliated them in front of their families. So what if the neighbors were drawn to the commotion. Catch 'em while they're sleeping or in the shower, that would be the best tactic.

Charles Bogan answered the door in his pajamas, and began crying quietly when a U.S. Marshal, a man he knew, produced handcuffs. Bogan had lost his family, so at least he was spared some of the shame.

Doug Vitrano's wife answered the door and was immediately hostile. She slammed it in the faces of two young FBI agents, who waited patiently as she ran upstairs to get her husband out of the shower. Thankfully, the kids were asleep when they put Doug in the back of the car, handcuffed like a common criminal, and left her on the front steps in her nightgown, cursing them and crying at the same time.

As usual, Jimmy Havarac had gone to bed blind drunk and the doorbell proved inadequate. They called him from a cell phone as they sat in his driveway, and he was eventually aroused and arrested.

Ethan Rapley was in the attic when the sun rose, working on a brief, oblivious to day or time. He heard nothing below. His wife was awakened by the knocking on the door, and she climbed the steps to deliver the bad news. First, though, she hid his gun. He kept it in a drawer in his dresser. He looked for it twice as he searched for the right pair of socks. But he wouldn't ask her for it. He was afraid she would tell him where it was.

The lawyer who founded the Bogan firm had been promoted to the federal bench thirteen years earlier. He had been nominated by Senator Nye, and once he left the firm Charles took over. The firm had strong connections with all five sitting federal judges, and so it was no surprise that the phones were ringing even before the partners were reunited at the jail. At eight-thirty, they were transported in separate cars to the federal courthouse in Biloxi for a hastily arranged appearance before the nearest federal Magistrate.

Cutter was irritated by the speed and ease with which Bogan pulled strings. While he didn't expect the four to stay in jail pending their trials, neither could he accept the sudden hearing before a Magistrate barely out of bed. And so Cutter tipped the local newspaper, and then he tipped the TV station.

The paperwork was prepared and signed quickly, and the four left the courthouse, on foot, unshackled, free to walk the three blocks to their offices. They were followed by a large, clumsy boy fumbling with a minicam and a young, green reporter who wasn't sure what the story was, but had been told it was huge. No comments from the stern faces. They made it to their office building on Vieux Marche, and locked the door behind them.

Charles Bogan went straight to the phone to call the Senator.

The private investigator, the one recommended by Patrick, found the woman in less than two hours, using nothing but the phone. She lived in Meridian, two hours north and east of Biloxi. Her name was Deena Postell, and she ran the deli and worked the second cash register of a brand-new convenience store on the edge of town.

Sandy found the place and walked inside. He pretended to admire a fresh rack of fried chicken breasts and deep-fried potato logs while he surveyed the employees hustling behind the counters. A wide, squatty woman with frosted hair and a loud voice caught his attention. Like all employees, she wore a red-and-white-striped shirt, and when she got close enough, Sandy could see her nameplate. It said Deena.

To build trust, he wore jeans and a navy blazer, no tie.

'Can I help you?' she said with a smile.

It was almost 10 A.M., much too early for a potato log. 'A large coffee, please,' Sandy said, also with a smile, and there was a twinkle in her eye. Deena enjoyed flirting. She met him at the cash register. Instead of handing over the money, Sandy gave her a business card.

She took one glance at it, then dropped it. For a woman who had raised three juvenile delinquents, a surprise like this only meant trouble. 'A dollar-twenty,' she said, punching buttons and glancing down the counter to see if anyone was watching.

'I have nothing but good news for you,' Sandy said, reaching for the money.

'What do you want?' she said, almost under her breath.

'Ten minutes of your time. I'll wait over there at a table.'

'But what do you want?' She took his money, and got the change.

'Please. You'll be happy you gave me the time.'

She loved men, and Sandy was a nice-looking guy, much better dressed than most of the traffic she endured. She fiddled with the rotisserie chicken, made some more coffee, then told her supervisor she was taking her break.

Sandy was waiting patiently at a table in the small dining section, next to the beer cooler and the ice machine. 'Thanks,' he said as she sat down.

She was in her mid-forties, with a round face generously adorned with cheap cosmetics.

'A lawyer from New Orleans, huh?' she said.

'Yeah. I don't suppose you've read or heard about that case down on the Coast where they caught the lawyer who stole all that money?'

She was shaking her head before he finished. 'I don't read nothin', honey. I work sixty hours a week here, and I got two grandbabies livin' with me. My husband keeps 'em. He's disabled. Bad back. I don't read nothin', watch nothin', do nothin' but work here and change dirty diapers when I'm home.'

Sandy was almost sorry he asked. How depressing!

As efficiently as possible, he told Patrick's story. She found it amusing, but her interest waned toward the end.

'Give 'im the death penalty,' she said during a pause.

'He didn't kill anybody.'

'Thought you said there was a body in his car.'

'There was. But the body was already dead.'

'Did he kill it?'

'No. He just sort of stole it.'

'Hummm. Look, I gotta get back to work. If you don't mind me askin', what's all this got to do with me?'

'The body he took was Clovis Goodman, your dear departed grandfather.'

Her head rolled to the right. 'He burned up Clovis!'

Sandy nodded.

Her eyes narrowed as she tried to arrange the proper emotions. 'What for?' she asked.

'He had to fake a death, okay?'

'But why Clovis?'

'Patrick was his lawyer and friend.'

'Some friend.'

'Yeah, look, I'm not trying to make sense of all this. It was done four years ago, long before you and I entered the picture.'

She tapped the fingers of one hand and chewed the nails of the other. The guy across from her seemed to be a pretty sharp lawyer, so the onset of drippy feelings

365

about her beloved old gramps probably wouldn't work. This was confusing. Let him do the talking.

'I'm listening,' she said.

'It's a felony to mutilate a corpse.'

'It should be.'

'It's also actionable at civil law. That means the family of Clovis Goodman can sue my client for destroying the corpse.'

Ah, yes. Her back stiffened as she took a deep breath, then smiled, then said, 'Now I see.'

Sandy smiled too. 'Yes. That's why I'm here. My client would like to offer a very quiet settlement with Clovis' family.'

'What does family mean?'

'Surviving spouse, children, and grandchildren.'

'I guess I'm the family.'

'What about your brother?'

'Nope. Luther died two years ago. Drugs and alkyhall.'

'Then you're the only person with a right to sue.'

'How much?' she blurted out, unable to hold it, then was embarrassed by it.

Sandy leaned a bit closer. 'We're prepared to offer twenty-five thousand dollars. Right now. The check's in my pocket.'

She was leaning down too, getting lower and closer to his face, when the money hit and stopped her cold. Her eyes watered and her bottom lip quivered. 'Oh my God,' she said.

Sandy glanced around. 'That's right, twenty-five thousand bucks.'

She ripped a paper napkin from the holder and in doing so knocked over the salt shaker. She dabbed her eyes, then blew her nose. Sandy was still glancing around, hoping to avoid a spectacle.

'All mine?' she managed to say. Her voice was hoarse and low, her breathing rapid.

'All yours, yes.'

She wiped her eyes again, then said, 'I need a Coke.'

She drank a 44-ounce Big Gulp without a word. Sandy sipped his bad coffee and watched the foot traffic come and go. He was in no hurry.

'The way I figure it,' she finally said, clear-eyed now, 'is that if you walk in here and offer twenty-five thousand right off the bat, then you're probably willing to pay more.'

'I'm in no position to negotiate.'

'If I sue, it might look bad for your client, you know what I mean? The jury will look at me, and think about poor old Clovis getting burned up so your client could steal ninety million dollars.'

Sandy sipped and nodded. He had to admire her.

'If I got me a lawyer, I could probably get a lot more money.'

'Maybe, but it might take five years. Plus, you have other problems.'

'Such as?' she asked.

'You were not close to Clovis.'

'Maybe I was.'

'Then why didn't you go to his funeral? That might be hard to sell to a jury. Look, Deena, I'm here ready to settle. If you don't want to, then I'll get in my car and go back to New Orleans.'

'What's your top dollar?'

'Fifty thousand.'

'It's a deal.' She stuck forth her beefy right hand, still moist from the Big Gulp, and squeezed his.

Sandy pulled a blank check from his pocket and filled it in. He also produced two documents; one was a short settlement agreement, the other was a letter from Deena to the prosecutor.

The paperwork took less than ten minutes.

*

367

Finally, there was movement on the canal in Boca. The Swedish lady was seen hurriedly shoving luggage into the trunk of Benny's BMW. She sped away. They tracked her to Miami International, where she waited two hours before boarding a plane to Frankfurt.

They would be waiting in Frankfurt. They would patiently watch her until she made a mistake. Then they would find Mr Aricia.

THIRTY-NINE

The presiding judge's last official act in the matter was an impromptu hearing of an undetermined variety, in his office, and without the accused's attorney present. Nor the prosecutor. The file would indicate no record of the meeting. Patrick was rushed through the rear of the courthouse by three escorts, up the back stairs, and quietly into Huskey's chambers, where His Honor waited, robeless. No trial was in session, and on an otherwise typical day the courthouse would have been peaceful. But four prominent lawyers had been arrested that morning, and the gossip was bouncing along the hallways at full throttle.

His wounds were still bandaged and prevented tight clothing. The aqua surgeon's scrubs were nice and baggy, and they also reminded people that he was hospitalized, not jailed like a criminal.

When they were alone and the door was locked, Karl handed him a single sheet of paper. 'Take a look at this.'

It was a one-paragraph order, signed by Judge Karl Huskey, in which he, upon his own motion, recused himself in the matter of *State versus Patrick S. Lanigan*. Effective at noon, an hour away.

'I spent two hours with Judge Trussel this morning. In fact, he just left.'

'Will he be nice to me?'

369

'As fair as possible. I told him that, in my opinion, it's not a capital murder trial. He was very relieved.'

'There's not going to be a trial, Karl.'

Patrick looked at a calendar on the wall, the same kind Karl had always used. Each day for the month of October was packed with more hearings and trials than any five judges could handle. 'Haven't you bought a computer yet?' he asked.

'My secretary uses one.'

They had first met in this room, years earlier when Patrick arrived as a young, unknown lawyer representing a family devastated by a car wreck. Karl was presiding. The trial lasted for three days, and the two became friends. The jury awarded Patrick's client two point three million dollars, at that time one of the largest verdicts on the Coast. Against Patrick's wishes, the Bogan firm agreed to settle the case for an even two million dollars during appeal. The lawyers took a third, and after the firm paid some debts and made some purchases, the remaining fee was split four ways. Patrick was not a partner at the time. They reluctantly gave him a bonus of twenty-five thousand dollars.

It was the trial in which Clovis Goodman was the star.

Patrick picked at Sheetrock peeling in a corner. He examined a brown water spot on the ceiling. 'Can't you get the county to paint this room. It hasn't changed a bit in four years.'

'I'm leaving in two months. Why should I care?'

'Remember the Hoover trial? My first in your courtroom, and my finest hour as a trial lawyer.'

'Of course.' Karl crossed his feet on his desk, his hands locked behind his head.

Patrick told him the Clovis story.

A firm rap on the door interrupted the narrative near the end. Lunch had arrived, and it would not wait. A deputy walked in with a cardboard box, and the aroma floated from it. Patrick stood close by as it was unloaded on Karl's desk: gumbo and crab claws.

'It's from Mahoney's,' Karl said. 'Bob sent it over. He said hello.'

Mary Mahoney's was more than a Friday afternoon watering hole for lawyers and judges. It was the oldest restaurant on the Coast, with delicious food and legendary gumbo.

'Tell him I said hello too,' Patrick said, reaching for a crab claw. 'I want to eat there soon.'

At precisely noon, Karl turned on the small television mounted in the center of a set of bookshelves, and they watched without comment the frenzied coverage of the arrests. It was a mum bunch. No comments from anybody; certainly the lawyers, in fact their office doors were locked; Maurice Mast surprisingly had nothing to say; nothing from the FBI. Nothing of any substance, so the reporter did what she'd been trained to do. She lapsed into gossip and rumor, and that's where Patrick entered the piece. Unconfirmed sources told her that the arrests were part of an ever-widening investigation in the Lanigan matter, and to prove this she flashed up uncontroverted footage of Patrick entering the Biloxi courthouse for his appearance. An earnest colleague appeared on the screen, informed them in hushed tones that he was standing outside the door of the Biloxi office of Senator Harris Nye, first cousin to Charles Bogan, in case anybody had missed the connection. The Senator was off in Kuala Lumpur on a trade mission to bring more minimum-wage jobs back to Mississippi, and thus unavailable for comment. None of the eight people in the office knew anything about anything; thus they had nothing to say.

The story ran uninterrupted for ten minutes.

'Why are you smiling?' Karl asked.

'It's a wonderful day. I just hope they have the guts to nail the Senator.'

'I hear the feds have dropped everything against you.'

'That's correct. I testified before the grand jury yesterday. It was great fun, Karl, finally unloading all this baggage I've been keeping secret for years.'

Patrick had stopped eating during the news story, and was suddenly bored with food. According to Karl's observations, he had eaten two crab claws and hardly touched the gumbo. 'Eat. You look like a skeleton.'

Patrick took a saltine and walked to the window.

'So let me get this straight,' Karl said. 'The divorce is settled. The feds have dropped all charges and you've agreed to pay back the ninety million, plus a little interest.'

'Total of a hundred and thirteen.'

'The capital murder is about to collapse because there wasn't a murder. The state can't charge you with theft because the feds have already done so. The lawsuits filed by the insurance companies have been dismissed. Pepper is still alive, out there somewhere. Clovis took his place. That leaves one lousy little charge of grave tampering.'

'Close. It's called mutilating a corpse, should you care to check the criminal code. You should know this stuff by now.'

'Right. A felony, I believe.'

'A light felony.'

Karl stirred his gumbo and admired his skinny friend gazing out the window, nibbling on a cracker, no doubt plotting his next maneuver.

'Can I go with you?' he asked.

'To where?'

'To wherever you're going. You walk outta here,

meet the girl, pick up the dough, hit the beach, live on a yacht. I'd just like to tag along for the ride.'

'I'm not there yet.'

'You're getting closer every day.'

Karl turned off the television and moved his food aside. 'There's a gap I'd like to fill in,' he said. 'Clovis died, then he was buried, or he wasn't buried. But what happened in between?'

Patrick chuckled, and said, 'You like the details, don't you?'

'I'm a Judge. The facts are important.'

Patrick took a seat and propped his bare feet on the desk. 'I almost got caught. It's not easy to steal a corpse, you know?'

'I'll take your word for it.'

'I had insisted that Clovis make his funeral arrangements. I even added a codicil to his will giving directions to the funeral home – no open casket, no visitation, no music, an overnight wake, a simple wood coffin, and a simple graveside service.'

'A wooden coffin?'

'Yeah, Clovis was big on the ashes-to-ashes-dust-to-dust routine. Cheap wooden casket, no vault. That was the way his grandfather was buried. Anyway, I was at the hospital when he died, and I waited for the mortician from Wiggins to arrive with the hearse. Rolland was his name, a real card. Owns the only funeral home in town. Black suit, the works. I gave him a copy of Clovis' instructions. The will gave me authority to do what needed to be done, and Rolland didn't care. It was around three in the afternoon. Rolland said he would do the embalming in a few hours. He asked me if Clovis had a suit to be buried in. We hadn't thought of that. I said no, I had never seen Clovis in a suit. Rolland said he kept a few old ones around, and he'd take care of it.

'Clovis wanted to be buried on his farm, but I

373

explained to him many times that in Mississippi you can't do that. Has to be in a registered cemetery. His grandfather fought in the Civil War, and had been quite the hero, according to Clovis. When he was seven years old his grandfather died, and they had one of those old-fashioned wakes that lasted for three days. They placed his grandfather's casket on a table in the front parlor and folks trooped by and looked at him. Clovis liked that. He was determined to do something similar. He made me swear that I would do a small wake for him. I explained this to Rolland. He said something to the effect that he'd seen everything. This was no surprise.

'Just after dark, I was sitting on Clovis' front porch when the hearse pulled up. I helped Rolland roll the casket down the driveway. We manhandled it up the steps, over the porch, and into the den, where we parked it in front of the television. I remember thinking how light it was. Clovis had shriveled up to a hundred pounds.

'"You the only one here?" Rolland said, looking around.

'"Yep. It's a small wake," I said.

'I asked him to open the casket. He hesitated, and I told him that I had forgotten to include some Civil War memorabilia that Clovis wanted to be buried with. While I watched, he opened the casket with his church key, a small generic wrench which will open any casket in the world. Clovis looked the same. On his waist, I placed his grandfather's infantryman's cap and a tattered regimental banner from the Seventeenth Mississippi. Rolland closed the casket again, and left.

'No one showed up for the wake. Not a soul. I turned the lights off around midnight and locked the doors. Church keys are nothing more than Allen wrenches, and I had purchased a full set. It took less than a minute to open the casket. I removed Clovis; he was light, stiff as a board, and shoeless. I guess for three thousand bucks you don't get a pair of shoes. I laid him gently on the sofa, then I placed four concrete cinder blocks in the coffin, and closed it.

'Clovis and I left and drove to my hunting cabin. He was lying in the backseat, and I was driving very carefully. It would've been difficult to answer questions from a highway patrolman.

'A month earlier, I had bought an old freezer and put it on the screened porch of the cabin. I had just managed to get Clovis stuffed in the freezer when I heard something in the woods. It was Pepper, sneaking up on the cabin. Two o'clock in the morning, and Pepper caught me. I told him my wife and I had just finished a big fight, I was in a foul mood, and would he please leave. I don't think he saw me wrestling the corpse up the steps of the cabin. I locked the freezer with log chains, put a tarp over it, then some old boxes. I waited until dawn because Pepper was out there somewhere. Then I sneaked off, drove home, changed clothes, and was back at Clovis' by ten. Rolland arrived in a chirpy mood and wanted to know how the wake went. Just perfect, I said. The grieving had been held to a minimum. We pushed and pulled and loaded the casket back into the hearse, then went to the cemetery.'

Karl listened with his eyes closed, his lips curled into a smile, his head shaking slowly in disbelief. 'You devious bastard,' he said, almost to himself.

'Thanks. On Friday afternoon, I went to the cabin for the weekend. I worked on a brief, scouted turkeys with Pepper, checked on old Clovis, who seemed to be resting comfortably. Sunday morning, I left before sunrise and positioned the dirt bike and the gasoline. Later, I drove Pepper to the bus station in Jackson. After dark, I removed Clovis from the freezer, sat him up next to the fireplace so he'd thaw, then around ten put him in my trunk. An hour later, I was dead.'

'No remorse?'

'Of course. It was a terrible thing to do. But I made the decision to vanish, Karl, and I had to figure out a way. I couldn't kill anybody, but I needed a body. It actually makes sense.'

'Perfectly logical.'

'And when Clovis died, it was time for me to leave. A lot of it was luck. So many things could've gone wrong.'

'Your luck continues.'

'So far.'

Karl looked at his watch, and took another crab claw. 'How much of this do I tell Judge Trussel?'

'Everything but Clovis' name. We'll save that for later.'

FORTY

Patrick sat at the end of the table. His space was clear, unlike his attorney to the right, who had two files and a short stack of legal pads arranged like weapons poised for battle. To his left sat T.L. Parrish, with only one legal pad but also armed with a bulky tape recorder, which Patrick had allowed him to set up. No associates or flunkies to complicate things, but since all good lawyers need verifiers, they agreed to the taping.

Now that the federal charges had disintegrated, the pressure was on the state to extract justice from Patrick. Parrish felt it. The feds had dumped this defendant on him so they could chase a Senator; off to bigger things. But this defendant had new twists to add to the story, and Parrish was at his mercy.

'You can forget capital murder, Terry,' Patrick said. Though nearly everyone called him Terry, it grated a bit coming from a defendant he'd barely known years before in a prior life. 'I didn't kill anyone.'

'Who burned in the car?'

'A person who had been dead for four days.'

'Anybody we know?'

'No. It was an old person nobody knew.'

'How did this old person die?'

'Old age.'

'Where did this old person die of old age?'

'Here, in Mississippi.'

Parrish drew lines and made squares on his pad. The door had opened when the feds collapsed. Patrick was walking through it; no shackles, no handcuffs, nothing, it seemed, could stop him.

'So you burned a corpse?'

'That's correct.'

'Don't we have a statute on that?'

Sandy slid a sheet of paper across the table. Parrish read it quickly, and said, 'Forgive me. It's not something we prosecute every day.'

'It's all you have, Terry,' Patrick said, with all the cool confidence of someone who'd planned this meeting for years.

T.L. was convinced, but no prosecutor folded this easily. 'Looks like a year in jail,' he said. 'A year in Parchman should do you good.'

'Sure, except that I'm not going to Parchman.'

'Where do you plan to go?'

'Somewhere. And I'll get there with a first-class ticket.'

'Not so fast. We have this body.'

'No, Terry. You don't have a body. You have no clue who got cremated, and I'm not telling until we cut the deal.'

'The deal being?'

'Drop the charges. Give it up. Both sides pack up and go home.'

'Oh, that'll look nice. We catch the bank robber, he gives the money back, we drop the charges, and wave good-bye to him. That'll send the right message to the other four hundred defendants I have under indictment. I'm sure their lawyers will understand. A real shot in the arm for law and order.'

'I don't care about the other four hundred, and they certainly don't care about me. This is the criminal process, Terry. It's every man for himself.'

'But not everybody is on the front page.'

'Oh, I see. You're worried about the press. When is reelection. Next year?'

'I'm unopposed. I'm not too worried about the press.'

'Of course you are. You're a public official. It's your job to be worried about the press, which is precisely the reason why you should dismiss the charges against me. You can't win. You're worried about the front page? Imagine your picture there after you lose.'

'The family of the victim does not wish to press charges,' Sandy said. 'And the family is willing to go public.' He lifted a piece of paper and waved it. The message was delivered: we have the proof, we have the family, we know who they are and you don't.

'That'll look good on the front page,' Patrick said. 'The family begging you not to prosecute.'

How much did you pay them, he started to ask, then let it go. It was not relevant. More doodling on the legal pad. More appraising his sinking options as the tape recorder captured the silence.

With his opponent on the ropes, Patrick moved in for the knockout. 'Look, Terry,' he said sincerely. 'You can't prosecute me for murder. That's gone. You can't prosecute me for mutilating a corpse, because you don't know who got mutilated. You have nothing. I know it's a bitter pill to swallow, but you can't change the facts. You'll take some heat, but, hell, that's part of your job.'

'Gee thanks. Look, I can indict you for mutilating the corpse. We'll call him John Doe.'

'Why not Jane Doe?' Sandy asked.

'Whatever. And we'll pull the records of every old codger who died in early February of 1992. We'll go to the families, see if they've talked to you. We might even get a court order, dig up a few graves. We'll take our time. Meanwhile, you'll get transferred to the

Harrison County Jail, where I'm sure Sheriff Sweeney will see the need to give you a few good cellmates. We'll oppose bail, and no judge will grant it because of your propensity to flee. Months will go by. Summer will come. The jail has no air conditioning. You'll lose some more weight. We'll keep digging, and with a little luck we'll find the empty grave. And in exactly nine months, two hundred and seventy days after the indictment, we'll go to trial.'

'How are you going to prove I did it? There are no witnesses, nothing but some circumstantial evidence.'

'It'll be close. But you miss my point. If I drag my feet getting the indictment, I could add two months to your sentence. That's almost a year you'll spend in the county jail before trial. That's a long time for a man with plenty of money.'

'I can handle it,' Patrick said, staring into Parrish's eyes, hoping he didn't blink first.

'Maybe, but you can't run the risk of getting convicted.'

'What's your bottom line?' Sandy asked.

'You gotta look at the big picture,' Parrish said, spreading his hands wide above his head. 'You can't make fools out of us, Patrick. The feds have hit the back door. The state doesn't have much left. Give us a notch for our belts, something.'

'I'll give you a conviction. I'll walk into a courtroom, face the Judge, listen to your routine, and I'll plead guilty to the felony charge of mutilating the corpse. But I get no jail time. You can explain to the Judge that the family does not want to prosecute. You can recommend a suspended sentence, probation, fines, restitution, credit for time served. You can talk about the torture and what I've been through. You can do all that, Parrish, and you'll look very good. Bottom line is this: no jail.'

380

Parrish tapped his fingers and analyzed it. 'And you'll reveal the name of the victim?'

'I will, but only after we have a deal.'

'We have authorization from the family to open the casket,' Sandy said, waving another document briefly before returning it to the file.

'I'm in a hurry, Terry. I have places to go.'

'I need to speak with Trussel. He'll have to approve this, you know.'

'He will,' Patrick said.

'Do we have a deal?' Sandy asked.

'As far as I'm concerned we do,' Parrish said, then turned off the recorder. He gathered his weapons and stuffed them into his briefcase. Patrick winked at Sandy.

'Oh, by the way,' Parrish said as he stood. 'I almost forgot. What can you tell us about Pepper Scarboro?'

'I can give you his new name and Social Security number.'

'So he's still with us?'

'Yes. You can track him down, but you can't disturb him. He's done nothing wrong.'

The D.A. left the room without another word.

Her two o'clock appointment was with a senior vice president of DeutscheBank, London branch. He was a German with perfect English, an impeccably tailored navy double-breasted suit, rigid manners, and a fixed smile. He gazed for one split second at her legs, then got down to business. The wire from his bank, Zurich branch, would be for one hundred and thirteen million dollars, sent immediately to the AmericaBank, Washington branch. She had the account numbers and routing instructions. Tea and biscuits were brought in as he excused himself to have a private chat with Zurich.

'No problem, Ms Pires,' he said, smiling warmly

now as he returned and took a biscuit for himself. She
certainly hadn't expected any problems.

His computer hissed with quiet efficiency, and a
printout emerged. He handed it to her. After the wire,
the balance in DeutscheBank would be one point nine
million dollars and change. She folded it and put it in
her purse, a sleek new Chanel.

Another Swiss account had a balance of three
million. A Canadian bank on Grand Cayman held six
point five million. A money manager in Bermuda was
investing over four million for them, and seven point
two million was currently parked in Luxembourg, but
was about to be moved.

When her business was complete, she left the bank
and found her car and driver parked nearby. She
would call Sandy, and pass along her next movements.

Benny's stint as a federal fugitive was brief. His
girlfriend spent the night in Frankfurt, then flew to
London, landing at Heathrow around noon. Since
they knew she was coming, the customs officer
double-checked her passport and made her wait. She
wore dark sunglasses and her hands shook. It was all
captured on video.

At the cab stand, she was unknowingly detained by
a policeman who appeared to be in charge of whistling
for taxis. He asked her to stand over there, next to
those other two ladies, while he worked the traffic. Her
driver was a true cabbie, but only seconds earlier had
been briefed and given a small radio.

'Athenaeum Hotel on Piccadilly,' she said. He eased
away from the terminal in heavy traffic, and nonchalantly gave the destination on the radio.

He took his time. An hour and a half later, he
deposited her at the door of the hotel. She waited
again at the registration desk. The assistant manager
apologized for the delay, but the computer was down.

When word came that the phone in her room was adequately tapped, they gave her a key and a bellman took her away. She tipped him lightly, locked and chained her door, and went straight for the phone.

The first words they heard her say were, 'Benny, it's me. I'm here.'

'Thank God,' said Benny. 'Are you okay?'

'I'm fine. Just scared.'

'Did anyone follow you?'

'No. I don't think so. I was very careful.'

'Great. Look, there's a little coffee bar on Brick Street near Down, two blocks from your hotel. Meet me there in an hour.'

'Okay. I'm scared, Benny.'

'Everything's fine, dear. I can't wait to see you.'

Benny wasn't at the coffee bar when she arrived. She waited for an hour before panicking and running back to her hotel. He didn't call, and she didn't sleep.

The next morning, she gathered up the morning papers in the lobby and read them over coffee in the dining room. Deep in the *Daily Mail* she finally found a two-paragraph blip about the capture of an American fugitive, one Benjamin Aricia.

She packed her bags and booked a flight to Sweden.

FORTY-ONE

With Judge Karl Huskey whispering into the ear of his colleague Judge Henry Trussel, it was established that the Lanigan matter should take precedence until it was put to rest. Rumors of a deal were floating throughout the legal community in Biloxi, rumors chased and being chased by even more gossip about the poor Bogan firm. In fact, nothing else was being discussed in the courthouse.

Trussel began the day by calling in T.L. Parrish and Sandy McDermott for a quick update, which eventually lasted for hours. Patrick was brought into the discussion on three occasions by use of Dr Hayani's cell phone. The two, patient and doctor, were playing chess in the hospital cafeteria.

'I don't think he's cut out for jail,' Trussel mumbled after the second call to Patrick. He was visibly and verbally reluctant to let Patrick off the hook with such ease, but a conviction was a long-shot. With a docket filled with drug dealers and child molesters, he wasn't about to waste time with a high-profile corpse mutilator. All the evidence was circumstantial, and given Patrick's current reputation for meticulous planning, Trussel doubted a conviction.

The terms of the plea agreement were hammered out. The paperwork began with a joint motion to reduce the charges against Patrick. Then an agreed order to substitute new charges was prepared, followed by an agreed order accepting the guilty plea. In the course of the first meeting, Trussel spoke by phone to Sheriff Sweeney, Maurice Mast, Joshua Cutter, and Hamilton Jaynes in Washington. He also chatted twice with Karl Huskey, who was next door, just in case.

The two judges, along with Parrish, were subject to voter recall every four years in the general election. Trussel had never had an opponent and considered himself politically immune. Huskey was quitting. Parrish was sensitive, though being a good politician he presented the traditional facade of making the tough decisions without regard for public reaction. The three had been involved in politics for a long time, and each had learned a basic lesson: when contemplating an action which might be unpopular, do it quickly. Get it over with. Hesitation allows the issue to fester. The press grabs it, creates a controversy before the action, and certainly throws gasoline on the fire afterward.

The Clovis issue was simple, once Patrick explained it to everybody. He would submit the name of the victim, along with authorization from the family to dig up the grave, open the casket, look inside. If it was in fact empty, then the plea agreement would be complete. Since there would always be doubt until they opened the grave, if by some chance the casket was occupied, then the plea agreement would be ripped up and Patrick would still face capital murder charges. Patrick was supremely confident when he talked of the victim, and everyone believed without a doubt that the grave would be empty.

Sandy drove to the hospital, where he found his client in bed, surrounded by nurses as Dr Hayani cleaned and dressed his burns. It was urgent, Sandy said, and Patrick apologized and asked them to leave. Alone, they walked through each motion and order, read every word aloud, then Patrick signed his approval.

Sandy noticed a cardboard box on the floor next to Patrick's temporary desk. In it were some of the books he'd loaned his client. The client was already packing.

For Sandy, lunch was a quick sandwich at the hotel suite, eaten while standing and watching over the shoulder as a secretary retyped a document. Both paralegals and a second secretary were back in the office in New Orleans.

The phone rang, and Sandy grabbed it. The caller identified himself as Jack Stephano, from D.C.; maybe Sandy had heard of him. Yes, in fact, he had. Stephano was in the lobby downstairs and would like to talk for a few minutes. Certainly. Trussel had asked the lawyers to return around two.

They sat in the small den and looked at each other across a cluttered coffee table. 'I'm here out of curiosity,' Stephano said, and Sandy didn't believe him.

'Shouldn't you start with an apology?' Sandy said.

'Yes, you're right. My men got a little carried away down there, and, well, they shouldn't have been so rough with your boy.'

'Is that your idea of an apology?'

'I'm sorry. We were wrong.' It lacked sincerity.

'I'll pass it along to my client. I'm sure it'll mean a lot to him.'

'Yes, well, moving along here, I, of course, no longer have a dog in this fight. My wife and I are on our way to Florida for a vacation, and I wanted to take this little detour. I'll just be a minute.'

'Have they caught Aricia?' Sandy asked.

'Yes. Just hours ago. In London.'

'Good.'

'I no longer represent him, and I had nothing to do with all that Platt & Rockland business. I was hired

386

after the money disappeared. My job was to find it. I tried, I got paid, I've closed the file.'

'So why this visit?'

'I'm extremely curious about something. We found Lanigan in Brazil only after someone squealed on him. Someone who knew him very well. Two years ago we were contacted by an Atlanta firm called the Pluto Group. They had a client from Europe who knew something about Lanigan, and this client wanted money. We happened to have some at the time, and so a relationship developed. The client would offer us a clue, we would agree to pay a reward, the money changed hands, and the client was always accurate. This person knew an awful lot about Lanigan – his movements, his habits, his aliases. It was all a setup – there was a brain at work. We knew what was coming, and, frankly, we were quite anxious. Finally, they popped the big one. For a million bucks, the client would tell us where he lived. They produced some very nice photos of Lanigan, one washing his car, a Volkswagen Beetle. We paid the money. We got Lanigan.'

'So who was the client?' Sandy asked.

'That's my question. It's gotta be the girl, right?'

Sandy's reaction was delayed a bit. He grunted as if to laugh, but there was no humor in it. It came back to him slowly, her story about using Pluto to monitor Stephano, who of course was searching for Patrick.

'Where is she now?' Stephano asked.

'I don't know,' Sandy said. She was in London, but it was certainly none of his business.

'We paid a total of one million, one hundred and fifty thousand dollars to this mysterious client, and she, or he, delivered. Just like Judas.'

'It's over. What do you want from me?'

'As I said, I'm just curious. One of these days, if you learn the truth, I'd appreciate a call. I have nothing to

387

gain or lose, but I won't rest well until I know if she took our money.'

Sandy made a vague promise to perhaps one day give a call if he learned the truth, and Stephano left.

Sheriff Raymond Sweeney got wind of the deal during lunch, and didn't like it at all. He called Parrish and Judge Trussel, but both were too busy to talk to him. Cutter was out of the office.

Sweeney went to the courthouse to be seen. He parked himself in the hallway between the judges' offices, so that if a deal was struck he would somehow be in the middle of it. He whispered with the bailiffs and deputies. Something was coming down.

The lawyers showed up around two with tight lips and solemn faces. They gathered in Trussel's office behind a locked door. After ten minutes, Sweeney knocked on it. He crashed the meeting with a demand to know what was going on with his prisoner. Judge Trussel calmly explained that there would soon be a guilty plea, the result of a plea bargain, which, in his opinion, and in the collective opinions of everyone present, was in the best interests of justice.

Sweeney had his own opinion, which he readily shared. 'It makes us look like fools. Folks out there are hot about this. You catch a rich crook, and he buys his way outta jail. What are we, a bunch of clowns?'

'What do you suggest, Raymond?' Parrish asked.

'I'm glad you asked. First, I'd put him in the county jail and let him sit for a while, same as all prisoners. Then I'd prosecute him to the fullest extent.'

'For what crime?'

'He stole the damned money, didn't he? He burned up that dead body. Let the boy serve ten years in Parchman. That's justice.'

'He didn't steal the money here,' Trussel explained. 'We have no jurisdiction. It was a federal matter, and

388

the federal boys have already dismissed the charges.'
Sandy was in a corner, his eyes fixed on a document.

'Then somebody screwed up, didn't they?'

'It wasn't us,' Parrish said quickly.

'That's great. Go sell that to the people who elected
you. Blame it on the feds because they don't run for
office. What about burning the corpse? He gets to
walk after admitting he did it?'

'You think he should be prosecuted for it?' Trussel
asked.

'Damned right I do.'

'Good. How do you think we should prove our
case?' Parrish asked.

'You're the prosecutor. That's your job.'

'Yeah, but you seem to know everything. Tell me,
how would you prove the case?'

'He said he did it, didn't he?'

'Yeah, and do you think Patrick Lanigan will take
the witness stand in his own criminal trial and confess
to the jury that he burned a corpse? Is that your idea of
trial strategy?'

'He won't,' Sandy inserted helpfully.

Sweeney's neck and cheeks were red, and his arms
were flailing in all directions. He glared at Parrish,
then at Sandy.

And when he realized that these lawyers had all the
answers, he brought himself under control. 'When will
this happen?' he asked.

'Late this afternoon,' Trussel said.

Sweeney didn't like this either. He stuck his hands
deep in his pockets and headed for the door. 'You
lawyers take care of your own,' he said, just loud
enough for everyone to hear.

'One big happy family,' Parrish said, the sarcasm
heavy.

Sweeney slammed the door and huffed down the
hallway. He left the courthouse in his unmarked

cruiser. Using his car phone, he called his own personal informant, a reporter with the Coast daily.

Since the family, such as it was, had given blanket approval, as had Patrick, the executor of the estate, the digging up of the grave was a simple matter. Judge Trussel and Parrish and Sandy didn't miss the irony of having Patrick, Clovis' only friend, sign an affidavit granting permission to open the casket so that Patrick could be cleared. Every decision seemed to be layered with irony.

It was far different from an exhumation, a procedure that required a court order, after a proper motion and sometimes even a hearing. It was simply a look-see, a procedure unknown to the Mississippi Code, and therefore Judge Trussel took great latitude with it. Who could be harmed? Certainly not the family. Certainly not the casket; evidently it was serving little purpose anyway.

Rolland still owned the funeral home up in Wiggins. How well he remembered Mr Clovis Goodman and his lawyer, and the odd little wake out there in the county, at the home of Mr Goodman, where no one showed up but the lawyer. Yes, he recalled it well, he told the Judge on the phone. Yes, he'd read something about Mr Lanigan, and no, he hadn't made the connection.

Judge Trussel gave him a quick summary, which led immediately to Clovis' involvement in the plot. No, he had not opened the casket after the wake, had had no need to, never did in those situations. While the Judge talked, Parrish faxed to Rolland copies of the consents signed by Deena Postell and by Patrick Lanigan, the executor.

Rolland was suddenly eager to help. He'd never had a corpse stolen before, folks just didn't do those things in Wiggins, and, well, yes, he could certainly have the

390

grave opened in no time flat. He owned the cemetery too.

Judge Trussel sent his law clerk and two deputies to the cemetery. Under the handsome headstone:

CLOVIS F. GOODMAN
JANUARY 23, 1907, to FEBRUARY 6, 1992
GONE ON to GLORY

a backhoe carefully picked through the loamy soil as Rolland gave directions and waited with a shovel. It took less than fifteen minutes to reach the casket. Rolland and a helper stepped into the grave and shoveled away more dirt. The poplar had started to rot around the edges of the coffin. Rolland straddled the lower half of the casket and with dirty hands inserted the church key. He jerked and pried until the lid made a cracking sound, then he slowly opened it.

To no one's surprise, the casket was empty.

Except, of course, for the four cinder blocks.

The plan was to do it in open court, as required by law, but to wait until almost five, when the courthouse was closing and many of the county employees were leaving. Five o'clock sounded fine to everyone, especially to the Judge and the District Attorney, who were convinced they were doing the right and proper thing, but were nervous about it nonetheless. Throughout the day, Sandy had pushed hard for a quick disposal once the plea agreement had been reached and the casket opened. There was no reason to wait. His client was incarcerated, though this received little sympathy. The court was in the middle of a scheduled term. The timing was perfect. What could be gained by waiting?

Nothing, His Honor finally decided. Parrish did not object. He had eight trials scheduled over the next three weeks, and unloading Lanigan was a relief.

Five was most satisfactory for the defense. With a bit of luck, they could be in and out of the courtroom in less than ten minutes. Another bit of luck, and no one would see them. Five was perfect for Patrick. What else did he have to do?

He changed into a pair of loose-fitting khakis and a large white cotton shirt. He wore new Bass loafers, no socks because of the rope-burned ankle. He hugged Hayani and thanked him for his friendship. He hugged the nurses and thanked the orderlies, and promised them all he'd be back soon to visit again. He wouldn't, and everyone knew it.

After more than two weeks as a patient and prisoner, Patrick left the hospital, his lawyer at his side, his armed escorts following dutifully behind.

FORTY-TWO

Evidently five was a perfect time for everyone. Not a single courthouse employee left for home once word reached every corner of every office, a process that took only minutes.

A real estate secretary for a large law firm was busy checking a land title in the office of the Chancery Clerk when she overheard the latest Patrick report. She raced to the phone and called her office. Within minutes the entire legal community along the Coast knew that Lanigan was about to plead guilty in some strange deal, and would attempt to do so secretly at five in the main courtroom.

The notion of a clandestine hearing to complete a backroom deal made for a frenzy of phone calls; calls to other lawyers, to wives, to favorite reporters, to partners out of town. In less than thirty minutes, half the city knew Patrick was about to make an appearance and a deal, and most likely walk.

The hearing would have attracted less attention had it been advertised in the newspaper and posted on billboards. It was to be quick and secretive. Mystery engulfed it. It was the legal system protecting one of its own.

They grouped in pockets of hushed gossip in the courtroom, whispering while watching people stream in, and guarding their seats. The crowd grew and gave further credence to the hearsay. All these people couldn't be wrong. And when the reporters arrived, the rumors were immediately confirmed as facts.

'He's here,' someone said, a court clerk up near the bench, and the curious began finding seats.

Patrick smiled for the two cameramen rushing to meet him by the back door. He was led to the same jury room on the second floor, where the handcuffs were removed. His khakis were an inch too long, so he methodically rolled them up and cuffed them. Karl entered and asked the deputies to wait in the hall.

'So much for a quiet little appearance,' Patrick said.

'Secrets are hard to keep around here. Nice clothes.'

'Thanks.'

'This reporter I know from the Jackson paper asked me to ask you —'

'Absolutely not. Not a word to anybody.'

'That's what I figured. When are you leaving?'

'I don't know. Soon.'

'Where's the girl?'

'Europe.'

'Can I go with you?'

'Why?'

'Just want to watch.'

'I'll send you a video.'

'Gee thanks.'

'Would you really leave? If you had the chance to walk away, to vanish right now, would you do it?'

'With or without ninety million?'

'Either way.'

'Of course not. It's not the same. I love my wife, you didn't. I have three great kids, your situation was different. No, I wouldn't run. But I don't blame you.'

'Everybody wants to run, Karl. At some point in life, everybody thinks about walking away. Life's always better on the beach or in the mountains. Problems can be left behind. It's inbred in us. We're the products of immigrants who left miserable conditions and came here in search of a better life. And they kept moving west, packing up and leaving, always looking for the pot of gold. Now, there's no place to go.'

'Wow. I hadn't thought of it through a historical perspective.'

'It's a stretch.'

'I wish my grandparents had clipped someone for ninety million before they left Poland.'

'I gave it back.'

'I hear there might be a small nest egg left over.'

'One of many unfounded rumors.'

'So you're saying the next trend will be looting of clients' money, the burning of dead bodies, and the flight to South America, where, of course, there are beautiful women just waiting to be caressed?'

'It's working well so far.'

'Those poor Brazilians. All these crooked lawyers coming their way.'

Sandy entered the room with yet another sheet of paper for another signature. 'Trussel is really edgy,' he said to Karl. 'The pressure is getting to him. His phone is ringing off the hook.'

'What about Parrish?'

'Nervous as a whore in church.'

'Let's get it done before they get cold feet,' Patrick said as he signed his name.

A bailiff walked to the bar and announced that court was about to convene, so please have a seat. People hushed and moved hurriedly for empty spaces. Another bailiff closed the double doors. Spectators lined the walls. Every clerk in the courthouse had business near the bench. It was almost five-thirty.

Judge Trussel entered with his customary rigid dignity, and everybody stood. He welcomed them, thanked them for their interest in justice, especially at this late hour of the day. He and the District Attorney had agreed that a quick hearing would reek of a sleazy deal, so things would proceed deliberately. They had even discussed postponing it, but decided a delay would give the impression that they had been caught trying to sneak something through.

Patrick was led through the door by the jury box, and stood next to Sandy in front of the bench. He did not look at his audience. Parrish stood nearby, anxious to perform. Judge Trussel flipped through the file, inspecting every word on every page.

'Mr Lanigan,' he finally said, deeply and slowly. For the next thirty minutes, everything would be said in slow motion. 'You have filed several motions.'

'Yes, Your Honor,' Sandy said. 'Our first is a motion to reduce the charges from capital murder to mutilating a corpse.'

The words echoed through the still courtroom. Mutilating a corpse?

'Mr Parrish,' His Honor said. It had been agreed that Parrish would do the bulk of the talking. The burden would be his to explain to the court, for the record, and, more important, for the press and the citizenry listening out there.

He did a wonderful job of detailing recent developments. Wasn't a murder, after all, but something far less. The state did not oppose the reduction of charges, because it no longer believed that Mr Lanigan killed anyone. He paced around the courtroom in his best Perry Mason routine, unshackled by the customary rules of etiquette and procedure. He was the spin doctor for all sides.

'Next, we have a motion by the defendant for this court to accept a plea of guilty to the charge of mutilating a corpse. Mr Parrish?'

The second act was similar to the first, with Parrish relishing the story of poor old Clovis. Patrick could feel the heated stares as Parrish delighted in as many details as Sandy had given them. 'At least I didn't kill anyone!' Patrick wanted to scream.

'How do you plead, Mr Lanigan?' His Honor asked.

'Guilty,' Patrick said, firmly but with no pride.

'Does the state have a recommended sentence?' the Judge asked the prosecutor.

Parrish walked to his table, fumbled through his notes, paced back toward the bench, and along the way finally said, 'Yes, Your Honor. I have a letter from a Ms Deena Postell of Meridian, Mississippi. She is the only surviving grandchild of Clovis Goodman.' He handed a copy to Trussel as if it were something brand new. 'In the letter, Ms Postell pleads with this court not to prosecute Mr Lanigan for burning her grand-father's corpse. He's been dead for over four years, and the family cannot survive any more suffering and agony. Evidently, Ms Postell was quite close to her grandfather, and took his death very hard.'

Patrick cut his eyes at Sandy. Sandy wasn't about to look at Patrick.

'Have you spoken with her?' the Judge asked.

'Yes. About an hour ago. She became quite emo-tional on the phone, and pleaded with me not to reopen this sad case. She vowed that she would not testify in any trial, nor would she cooperate with the prosecution in any way.' Parrish again walked to his table and rifled through some more papers. He spoke to the Judge but addressed the courtroom. 'Given the feelings of the family, it is the recommendation of the state that the defendant be sentenced to serve twelve months in jail, that the incarceration be suspended pending good behavior, that he pay a fine of five thousand dollars and all court costs, and be placed on probation.'

'Mr Lanigan, do you agree with this sentence?' Trussel asked.

'Yes, Your Honor,' Patrick said, barely able to lift his head.

'It is so ordered. Anything further?' Trussel picked up his gavel, and waited. Both lawyers shook their heads.

'We are adjourned,' he said, rapping it loudly.

Patrick turned and made a quick exit from the courtroom. Gone again, vanished before their very eyes.

He waited with Sandy for an hour in Huskey's office while darkness settled in and the last of the courtroom stragglers reluctantly gave it up and went home. Patrick was anxious to leave.

At seven, he said a long, fond good-bye to Karl. He thanked him for being there, for standing by him, for everything, and he promised to keep in touch. On his way out the door, he also thanked him again for serving as one of his pallbearers.

'Anytime,' Karl said. 'Anytime.'

They left Biloxi in Sandy's Lexus – Sandy at the wheel, Patrick sitting low in the passenger's seat, subdued and taking in for the last time the lights along the Gulf. They passed the casinos on the beaches at Biloxi and Gulfport, the pier at Pass Christian, and then the lights spread out as they crossed the Bay of St Louis.

Sandy handed him the phone number, and he called her hotel. It was 3 A.M. in London, but she grabbed the phone as if she were watching it. 'Eva, it's me,' he said, with restraint. Sandy almost stopped the car so he could get out while they talked. He tried not to listen.

'We're leaving Biloxi now, on the way to New Orleans. Yes, I'm fine. I've never felt better. And you?'

He listened for a long time, his eyes closed, his head leaning back.

'What's today?' he asked.

'Friday, November sixth,' Sandy said.

'I'll meet you in Aix, at the Villa Gallici, on Sunday. Right. Yes. I'm fine, dear. I love you. Go back to sleep, and I'll call you in a few hours.'

They crossed into Louisiana in silence, and somewhere over Lake Pontchartrain, Sandy said, 'I had a very interesting visitor this afternoon.'

'Really, who?'

'Jack Stephano.'

'Here, in Biloxi?'

'Yes. He found me at the hotel, said he was finished with the Aricia case and was on his way to Florida for a vacation.'

'Why didn't you kill him?'

'He said he was sorry. Said his boys got a little carried away down there when they caught you, wanted me to pass along his apologies.'

'What a guy. I'm sure he didn't stop by just to apologize.'

'No, he didn't. He told me about the mole in Brazil, about the Pluto Group and the rewards, and he asked me point-blank if the girl, Eva, was your Judas. I said I had no idea.'

'Why does he care?'

'Good question. He said his curiosity has the best of him. He paid over a million bucks in rewards, got his man, but didn't get the money, and he said he won't be able to sleep until he knows. I sort of believed him.'

'Sounds reasonable.'

'He doesn't have a dog in the fight anymore, or something like that. His words, not mine.'

Patrick put his left ankle on his right knee, and gently touched the burn. 'What does he look like?' he asked.

'Fifty-five, very Italian, lots of groomed gray hair, black eyes, a handsome man. Why?'

'Because I've seen him everywhere. For the last three years, half the strangers I've seen in the outback of Brazil have been Jack Stephano. I've been chased in my sleep by a hundred men, all of whom turned out to be Jack Stephano. He has ducked in alleys, hidden behind trees, followed on foot at night in São Paulo, tagged behind me on motor scooters and chased me in cars. I've thought about Stephano more than I have my own mother.'

'The chase is over.'

'I finally got tired of it, Sandy. I gave up. Life on the run is quite an adventure, very thrilling and romantic, until you learn that someone is back there. While you're sleeping, someone is trying to find you. While you're having dinner with a wonderful woman in a city of ten million, someone is knocking on doors, quietly showing your photo to a clerk, offering small bribes for information. I stole too much money, Sandy. They had to come after me, and when I learned they were already in Brazil, I knew the end would come.'

'What do you mean, you gave up?'

Patrick breathed heavily and shifted his weight. He looked through his window at the waters below, and tried to organize his thoughts. 'I gave up, Sandy. I got tired of running, and I gave up.'

'Yeah, I've already heard that.'

'I knew they would find me, so I decided to do it on my terms, not theirs.'

'I'm listening.'

'The rewards were my idea, Sandy. Eva would fly to Madrid, then to Atlanta, where she would meet with the boys from Pluto. They were paid to contact Stephano and handle the flow of information and money. We milked the money out of Stephano, and eventually led him to me, to my little house in Ponta Porã.'

Sandy turned slowly, his face blank, mouth open and crooked to one side, his eyes vacant.

'Watch where you're going,' Patrick said, pointing to the road.

Sandy jerked the wheel and brought the car back into the right lane. 'You're lying,' he said, without moving his lips. 'I know you're lying.'

'Nope. We collected one million, one hundred fifty thousand bucks from Stephano, and it's hidden now, probably in Switzerland with the rest of it.'

'You don't know where it is?'

'She's been taking care of it. I'll find out when I see her.'

Sandy was too shocked to say anything else. Patrick decided to help. 'I knew they would grab me, and I knew they would try to make me talk. But I had no idea this would happen.' He pointed to the burn above his left ankle. 'I thought it might get ugly, but they damned near killed me, Sandy. They finally broke me, and I told them about Eva. By then, she was gone, and so was the money.'

'You could've easily been killed,' Sandy managed to say. He was driving with his right hand, scratching his head with his left.

'That's true. Very true. But two hours after I was captured, the FBI in Washington knew Stephano had me. That's what saved my life. Stephano couldn't kill me, because the feds knew about it.'

'But how –'

'Eva called Cutter in Biloxi. He called Washington.'

Sandy wanted to stop the car, get out and scream. Lean over the side of the bridge, and let flow an endless string of blue profanities. Just when he thought he had been clued in to Patrick's past, this latest twist came crashing in.

'You were a damned fool if you let them catch you.'

'Oh really. Did I not just walk out of the courtroom

a free man? Did I not just talk with a woman I love dearly, a woman who happens to be keeping a small fortune for me? The past is finally gone, Sandy. Don't you see? There's no one looking for me anymore.'

'So many things could've gone wrong.'

'Yeah, but they didn't. I had the money, the tapes, the Clovis alibi. And I had four years to plan everything.'

'The torture wasn't planned.'

'No, but the scars will heal. Don't ruin the moment, Sandy. I'm on a roll.'

Sandy dropped him off at his mother's house, his childhood home, where a cake was in the oven. Mrs Lanigan asked him to stay, but he knew they needed time alone. Plus he hadn't seen his wife and kids in four days. Sandy drove away, his brain still swirling.

FORTY-THREE

He awoke before sunrise in a bed he hadn't slept in in almost twenty years, in a room he hadn't seen in almost ten. The years were distant, another lifetime. The walls were closer together now, the ceiling lower. Over the years his things had been removed, the boyhood memorabilia, the Saints banners, the posters of blond models in tight swimsuits.

As the product of two people who rarely spoke to each other, he had made his room his sanctuary. He'd kept the door locked long before his teen years. His parents entered only when he allowed them.

His mother was cooking downstairs; the smell of bacon drifted throughout the house. They had stayed up late; now she was up early, anxious to talk. And who could blame her?

He stretched slowly and carefully. The crusted skin around his burns cracked and pulled. Too much of a stretch and the skin broke, and the bleeding started. He touched the burns on his chest, desperately wanting to dig in with his fingernails and scratch with a fury. He crossed his feet and locked his hands behind his head. He smiled at the ceiling, an arrogant smile because life on the run was now over. Patrick and Danilo were gone, and the shadows behind them had been destroyed in a crushing defeat. Stephano and Aricia and Bogan et al., and the feds and Parrish with his insipid little indictment, all had been laid to waste. There was no one left to chase him.

Sunlight eased through the window, and the walls inched together. He showered quickly and treated his wounds with a cream and fresh gauze.

He had promised his mother some new grandchildren, a fresh batch of them to take the place of Ashley Nicole, a child she still dreamed of seeing again. He told her wonderful things about Eva, and promised to bring her to New Orleans in the very near future. No definite plans to get married, but it was inevitable.

They ate waffles and bacon and drank coffee on the patio as the old streets came to life. Before the neighbors could begin stopping by to applaud the good news, they left for a long drive. Patrick wanted to at least see his city again, if only briefly.

At nine, he and his mother walked into Robilio Brothers on Canal, where he bought new khakis and shirts and a handsome leather travel bag. They ate beignets at Café du Monde on Decatur, then a late lunch at a nearby café.

They sat at his gate at the airport for an hour, holding hands and saying little. When his flight was called, Patrick hugged his mother tightly and promised to call every day. She wanted to see the new grandkids, and quickly, she said, with a sad smile.

He flew to Atlanta. Using his legitimate Patrick Lanigan passport, given to Sandy by Eva, he boarded a flight to Nice.

He had last seen Eva a month earlier, in Rio, over a long weekend in which they spent every moment together. The chase was almost over and Patrick knew it. The end was near.

They clung to each other as they walked the crowded beaches of Ipanema and Leblon, ignoring the happy voices around them. They had late, quiet

404

dinners in their favorite restaurants – Antiquarius and Antonio's – but they had little appetite for food. When they spoke, the sentences were soft and short. The long conversations ended in tears.

At one point, she had convinced him to flee again, to leave with her while he was still able, to hide in a castle in Scotland or a tiny apartment in Rome, where no one would ever find them. But the moment passed. He was simply tired of running.

Late in the afternoon, they rode a cable car to the top of Sugarloaf Mountain to watch the sunset over Rio. The view of the city at night was spectacular, but difficult to appreciate under the circumstances. He held her closely as the wind chilled them, and he promised her that some day, when it was all over, they would stand in this exact spot, and watch the sunset, and plan their future. She tried to believe him.

They said good-bye on a street corner, near her apartment. He kissed her on the forehead and walked away, into the crowd. He left her crying there because it was better than a messy scene at the crowded airport. He left the city, and flew west, changing flights as the planes and airports got smaller. He arrived in Ponta Porã after dark, found his Beetle parked where he'd left it at the airport, and drove the quiet streets to Rua Tiradentes, to his modest home, where he arranged his things, and began his wait.

He called her every day between 4 and 6 P.M., a coded call with different names.

And then his calls stopped.

They had found him.

The train from Nice arrived in Aix on time, a few minutes after noon, Sunday. He stepped onto the platform, and looked for her in the crowd. He didn't really expect to see her. He was only hoping, almost praying. Carrying his new bag with his new clothes, he found a taxi for the short ride across town to the Villa Gallici, on the edge of the city.

She had reserved a room in both names, Eva Miranda and Patrick Lanigan. How nice to be in from the cold, to travel as real people without the cloak and dagger of false names and passports. She had not checked in yet, the clerk informed him, and his spirits sank. He had dreamed of finding her in the room, adorned in soft lingerie, ready for intimacy. He could almost feel her.

'When was the reservation made?' he asked the clerk, irritated.

'Yesterday. She called from London, and said she would arrive this morning. We haven't seen her.'

He went to the room and showered. He unpacked his bag, and ordered tea and pastries. He fell asleep amid dreams of hearing her knock on the door, of pulling her into the room.

He left a message for her at the front desk, and went for a long walk through the lovely Renaissance city. The air was brisk and clear. Provence in early November was delightful. Perhaps they would live there. He looked at quaint apartments above the ancient, narrow streets and thought, yes, this would be a nice place to live. It was a university town where the arts were revered. Her French was very good and he wanted to become proficient. Yes, French would be his next language. They would stay here for a week or so, then go back to Rio awhile, but maybe Rio wouldn't be home. Flush with freedom, Patrick wanted to live everywhere, to absorb different cultures, to learn different languages.

He was set upon by a pack of young Mormon missionaries, but shook them off and walked along the Cours Mirabeau. He sipped espresso at the same sidewalk café where they had held hands and watched the students a year earlier.

He refused to panic. It was a simple matter of a late connecting flight. He forced himself to wait until dark, then strolled as casually as possible back to the hotel.

She wasn't there, nor was there a message. Nothing. He called the hotel in London, and was informed that she had left yesterday, Saturday, around mid-morning.

He went to the terrace garden next to the dining room, and found a chair in a corner which he turned so he could watch the front desk through a window. He ordered two double cognacs to fight the chill. He would see her when she arrived.

If she'd missed a flight, she would've called by now. If she'd been stopped by customs again, she would've called by now. Any problems with passports, visas, tickets, and she would've called by now.

No one was chasing her. All the bad guys had been either locked up or bought off.

More cognac on an empty stomach, and before long he was drunk. He switched to strong coffee to stay awake.

When the bar closed, Patrick went to his room. It was 8 A.M. in Rio, and he reluctantly called her father, whom he'd met twice. She had introduced him as a friend and a Canadian client. The poor man had been through enough, but Patrick had no choice.

He said he was in France, and needed to discuss a legal matter with his Brazilian lawyer. Apologies for disturbing him at home so early, but he couldn't seem to locate her. It was an important matter, even urgent. Paulo didn't want to talk, but the man on the phone seemed to know a lot about his daughter.

She was in London, Paulo said. He had talked to her on Saturday. He would say nothing more.

Patrick waited two agonizing hours, then called Sandy. 'She's missing,' he said, now very much in a panic. Sandy had not heard a word from her.

Patrick roamed the streets of Aix for two days, taking
long aimless walks, napping at odd hours, eating
nothing, drinking cognac and strong coffee, calling
Sandy and scaring poor Paulo with repeated calls. The
city lost its romance. Alone in his room, he wept from
a broken heart, and alone on the streets he cursed the
woman he still madly loved.

The hotel clerks watched him come and go. At first
he was anxious as he asked for his messages, but as the
hours and days passed, he barely nodded at them. He
didn't shave and he looked tired. He drank too much.

He checked out after the third day, said he was
going back to America. He asked his favorite clerk to
keep a sealed envelope at the desk in case Madame
Miranda appeared.

Patrick flew to Rio. Why, he wasn't sure. As much
as she loved Rio, it would be the last place she would
be seen. She was much too smart to go to Rio. She
knew where to hide, and how to disappear, and how to
change identities, and how to move money instantly,
and how to spend it without drawing attention.

She had learned from a master. Patrick had taught
her all too well the art of vanishing. No one would find
Eva, unless, of course, she wanted them to.

He had a painful meeting with Paulo, in which he
told the entire story, every detail. The poor man
crumbled before his eyes, crying and cursing him for
corrupting his precious daughter. The meeting was an
act of desperation, and utterly fruitless.

He stayed in small hotels close to her apartment,
walking the streets, once again looking at every face,
but for different reasons. No longer the prey, he was
now the hunter, and such a desperate one at that.

Her face would not be seen, because he'd taught her
how to hide it.

His money dwindled, and he was eventually

reduced to calling Sandy and asking for a five-thousand-dollar loan. Sandy quickly agreed, and even offered more.

He gave up after a month, and traveled by bus across the country to Ponta Porã.

He could sell his house there, and maybe his car. Together, both would net thirty thousand U.S. dollars. Or maybe he would keep them and get a job. He could live in a country he loved, in a pleasant little town he adored. He could work perhaps as an English tutor, live peacefully on Rua Tiradentes, where the shadows were gone now but the barefoot boys still dribbled soccer balls along the hot street.

Where else could he go? His journey was over. His past was finally closed.

Surely, some day she would find him.

Acknowledgments

As always, I relied on the knowledge of friends while writing this book, and here I'd like to thank them. Steve Holland, Gene McDade, Mark Lee, Buster Hale, and R. Warren Moak lent their experience and/or went chasing after esoteric little facts. Will Denton again read the manuscript, and again kept it legally accurate.

In Brazil, I was assisted by Paulo Rocco, my publisher and friend. He and his charming wife Angela shared with me their beloved Rio, the most beautiful city in the world.

When asked, these friends gave me the truth. As usual, the mistakes are all mine.